HOMER'S ODYSSEY: A COMPANION

HOMER'S ODYSSEY

A Companion to the English
Translation of Richmond Lattimore

Peter V. Jones

Published by Bristol Classical Press
General Editor: John H. Betts

First published in 1988 by Bristol Classical Press

Bristol Classical Press
is an imprint of
Gerald Duckworth & Co. Ltd.
The Old Piano Factory
48 Hoxton Square, London N1 6PB

Reprinted 1992

A catalogue record for this book is available
from the British Library

ISBN 1-85399-038-8

Printed in Great Britain by
Booksprint, Bristol

Contents

Preface

In this modest little commentary I try to make the text of Lattimore's translation of the *Odyssey* intelligible to those who are new to Homer. I have concentrated on the literary problems but have tried to be helpful on other issues (historical, archaeological, geographical etc.) as well. I often refer the reader to other easily obtainable works on Homer for discussion of individual points, and the short bibliography indicates some of the influences under which I have worked. It goes without saying that many of the notes are little but synopses from the excellent commentaries of Merry and Riddell, Monro, Stanford and the outstandingly fine Italian edition (Lorenzo Valla, 1981–6, six volumes, of which Books 1–8 (eds. S West and J B Hainsworth) have recently been published in a revised edition (Clarendon Press 1988), with the rest to follow). It has been a privilege to mediate such superior work to new, Greekless readers of Homer.

Everyone who knows the Department of Classics at the University of Newcastle upon Tyne will envy someone who has such impossibly argumentative and congenial colleagues to work with. I thank them all, especially David West, Trevor Saunders and John Lazenby. Malcolm Willcock (University College London) whose *Companion to Homer's Iliad* (Chicago 1976) set the standard for this sort of endeavour, gave far more time than it deserved to improving the final draft of this *nescioquid minus*.

Peter V Jones
Department of Classics
University of Newcastle upon Tyne
August 1988

Abbreviations and terms

(The key to the abbreviations of the books and articles referred to in the commentary is on p. 225)

GI General introduction (pp. ixff.)

9A, *12A*, etc., means 'section A of the introduction to Book 9'

'see on' means 'see the notes on that passage, and the passage itself'

'Dark Age' means c. 1000—c. 900

'Mycenaean age' or 'Bronze Age' means c. 1600—c. 1000

xenia: guest-friendship, or 'a bond of solidarity manifesting itself in an exchange of goods or services between individuals originating from separate social units' (*Ritualised Friendship and the Greek City*, G. Herman, CUP 1987 p. 10)

xenos (pl. *xenoi*): a guest-friend, but can also mean 'foreigner' or 'stranger'

(All dates are BC unless otherwise indicated)

A recommendation

Students will benefit greatly by having at hand a copy of Hesiod *Theogony* and *Works and Days* (see Bibliography under Hesiod *WD*), as well as a copy of Homer's *Iliad*.

List of illustrations

General introduction

A. (1) The *Odyssey*, like the *Iliad*, is an epic (Greek *epos*, 'verse'). It is the product of an oral style of composition, i.e. it was composed to be recited to a listening audience, not written to be read out to, or read by, them. It is composed in hexameters, i.e. verses of six metrical 'feet', whose syllable-length in the first five feet can be —uu (dactyl) or — — (spondee), and in the sixth — — or —u. Thus the opening line of the *Odyssey* in Greek scans:

| *āndră* | *mŏī* | *ĕnnĕpĕ* | *Mōusă* | *pŏlūtrŏpŏn* | *hōs* | *mălă* | *pōllă* |
| man | to-me | tell, | Muse, | of-many-turns | who | very | much |

Note the first five 'feet' in this line are dactyls. Compare the second line:

| *plāgkhthĕ* | *ĕpeī* | *Trōiēs* | *hĭĕrōn* | *ptŏlĭĕthrŏn* | *ĕpērše* |
| wandered | when | Troy's | holy | citadel | he sacked |

Here there is a spondee in the second foot.

(2) The most characteristic feature of oral poetry is its constant repetitions. They occur at the level of phrase and line ('formulas') and whole scene ('typical scenes' and 'themes') and are the 'building bricks' of the oral poet's trade. By assimilating and learning to adapt to context both formulas and larger structures, the poet is enabled to compose on the spot (though improvisation does not, of course, mean that the poet works without any prior consideration). Here are some examples of formulas:

a. *at the level of phrase*

(1.4)	*kătă*	*thūmŏn*
	in	spirit/heart
	cf. 1.29, 323, 4.187, etc.	

(1.294)	*kătā¹*	*phrĕnă*	*kāi*	*kătă*	*thūmŏn*
	in	heart	and	in	spirit
	cf. 4.117, 120, 813, 5.365, 424 etc.				

(5.298)	*prŏs*	*hŏn*	*mĕgălētŏră*	*thūmŏn*
	to	his-own	great-hearted	spirit
	cf. 5.355, 407, 464			

(9.299)	*kătā*	*mĕgălētŏră*	*thūmŏn*
	in [my]	great-hearted	spirit

---

1. There are metrical laws which permit naturally 'short' syllables to be regarded as 'long' for the purpose of scansion.

Observe the degree of flexibility with the system. When the poets wants to express the idea 'in/to heart/spirit', he has a range of metrical options, but they all clearly relate to, or build on, one another, and when formula 'systems' of the sort described above are examined in detail, it is clear that fixity + flexibility is their hallmark. The same applies to:

b. *whole-line formulas*

(1.213) *tēn* ⎱
         tōn ⎰   *d'āū*   *Tēlĕmăkhōs*   *pēpnūmĕnŏs*   *āntĭŏn*   *ēūdā*

         to-him/her then   Telemachos   thoughtful   in-answer said
         cf. 1.230, 306, 345, 388, 412 etc.

Compare:

(1.399) *tōn)*   *d'āūt'*   *Eŭrўmăkhōs,*   *Pŏlŭbōū*   *păĭs,*   *āntĭŏn*   *ēūdā*
         tēn)
         to-him/her then   Eurymachos, Polybos'   son,   in-answer said
         cf. 2.177, 16.434, 21.320

(4.155   *tōn*   *d'āū*   *Nēstŏrĭdēs*   *Pēĭsĭstrătŏs*   *āntĭŏn*   *ēūdā*
=15.48) to-him   then   Nestor's-son Peisistratos   in-answer said

These whole line formulas make an important point very clearly. When Telemachos, for example, appears in the whole-line formula quoted above, he is always—without exception—*pepnumenos* 'thoughtful'. It does not matter how he has been acting or what he has said or is about to say—he is 'thoughtful' come what may. For the same reason, Odysseus is frequently 'resourceful', 'godlike', 'much-enduring', Athene 'gray-eyed' and so on. This does not mean that *whenever* Telemachos speaks, he has to be 'thoughtful': the poet could choose another formula of speaking, occupying less than the whole line, e.g. 2.348 'Now Telemachos called her to the room and spoke to her.' But in certain commonly repeated metrical situations, it will frequently be the case that the poet has only one way of describing a person or action. This has made some scholars unreasonably doubt the aesthetic value of the descriptive epithet.

There is also another important consequence. Sometimes the poet uses a formula which is not appropriate to the exact circumstances in which it is being used (see e.g. the note on 9.483). Poetic reflex or association of ideas (see *4.625—847B*) accounts for this sort of 'mistake'.

Ancient commentators on Homer, not understanding oral poetic technique and offended by the frequency of Homeric repetition at the level of phrase, sentence and scene, often used to condemn such repetitions as non-Homeric.

c. *at the level of scene*

See the analysis of the *xenia* sequence at 1.102.

B. The *Odyssey* was composed by a Greek living in Ionia (i.e. on or off the coast of modern W. Turkey), probably some time during the late 8thC BC. We do not know how or when it came to be written down (but see on 3.36), who 'Homer' was, and whether he was also the poet of the *Iliad*.

C. The oral tradition of which the *Odyssey* is a product stretches back through the so-called 'Dark Age' of Greece (10–9thC) to the 'Mycenaean age' (1600–1100). During this latter period, Greece was dominated by the great palace-cultures of Mycenae, Pylos etc. Their economies and organisation—most unlike anything in Homer—are described to us in the records (the clay tablets inscribed with writing called 'Linear B') which survive from the end of the period, when many of the palaces were sacked and burned. The Mycenaean Greeks also over-ran Crete, and Linear B tablets survive from Knossos.

D. The Mycenaean age is a suitable setting for an age of great Iliadic heroes, but more important, it was a *bronze* age. Here is evidence of the length of the oral tradition. From 1000 onwards, the predominant metal of the Greek world became iron, but the arms and armour of the Greek heroes in the epics are always made of bronze. That suggests that the tradition of oral recitation was alive during Mycenaean times.

E. Because of the length of the oral tradition and our ignorance of most 'Dark Age' history (writing in Greece disappeared with the collapse of Mycenaean culture and did not reappear in Greece again till the late 8thC), it is virtually impossible to say for certain whether or in what sense the *Odyssey* reflects a historical society or accurate geographical knowledge. The poem comes at the end of hundreds of years of oral story-telling, and everything that we know of such tradition from all over the world tells us that stories were constantly being 'up-dated' for contemporary consumption. But it is almost impossible even to define, let alone to separate out, the various stages of cultural manipulation left by the re-telling and up-dating down the ages. Consequently, it is best to be very sceptical indeed about identifications of places and events in Homer with 'real' geographical and historical locations.

We assume the Homeric poems were composed in the 8thC because there seem to be very few obviously post-8thC customs, practices or artefacts referred to in the poems (writing, for example, is never mentioned in the *Odyssey*).

F. Our *Odyssey* is 12,110 lines long and would have taken about 20–25 hours to recite. We know nothing of the circumstances under which it was produced, let alone of any audience at whom it may have been aimed. Since most oral epic poetry from other comparable cultures is designed to be recited in an hour or two, we have to posit 'special circumstances' for Homeric epic. One possibility is that the poems were composed for 'serial' recitation over many weeks to leisured aristocrats (see on 1.153–5). Our

Odyssey is also divided up into 24 books, one for each letter of the alphabet, but since Homer probably did not write, let alone with an alphabet containing 24 letters, we may assume this division was made much later. Our *Odyssey* as it stands falls neatly into six 4-book groups. May this give a clue to its recitation-units?

G. Certainly by the 6thC there was a written text of our *Odyssey*. From the 3rdC onwards, under the patronage of the Greek kings of Egypt (the Ptolemies, named after the first king Ptolemaios), Greek scholars working in Alexandria produced definitive editions of all Greek literature. All our manuscripts of Homer descend ultimately from these Alexandrian editions. The three great scholars who had the most influence on the texts of Homer were Zenodotos (from Ephesos), Aristophanes (from Byzantium), and Aristarchos (from Samothrace).

The earliest complete manuscript of Homer we have is of the *Iliad* and dates from the early 10thC AD. (Venetus Marcianus A, i.e. found in the Marcian library in Venice, and known as A.) The earliest of the *Odyssey* dates from the 10th or 11thC AD. Since, generally, quotations from Homer in papyri and the works of pre-3rdC authors (e.g Plato), differ only trivially from our manuscripts, we can be fairly confident that what we have is a close enough approximation to what Classical Greeks had, but what relation that bore to any Homeric performance is impossible to say. We are very fortunate indeed that the commentaries on Homer which the great ancient editors made have *in part* survived. Quotations from them have been transmitted both in the commentary on Homer made by the 12thC AD Bishop of Thessalonica Eustathius, which has come down to us in full, and in 'scholia', i.e. comments written by 'scholiasts' on and around the texts which have come down to us. Thus, in places, we know exactly what, for example, Aristarchos thought the meaning and validity of the text in front of him were (see, famously, on 23.296).

H. The background to the *Odyssey* is the Trojan War, from which the *Iliad* relates a small incident. The main protagonists mentioned in the *Odyssey* are:

Greeks: Agamemnon, king of Mycenae, leader of the Greek expedition against Troy. His brother was Menelaos, king of Sparta. Menelaos's wife, Helen, was stolen by the Trojan Paris, who took her back to Troy. The Trojan War was fought to recover her. Also on the Greek side were Achilleus, the leading fighter; his son Neoptolemos; Nestor, the wise old counsellor and King of Pylos; his son Antilochos; the two Ajaxes (Aias in Greek); Patroklos, Achilleus' close friend, who was killed by the Trojan Hektor; Idomeneus, king of Crete and, of course, Odysseus, the hero of the *Odyssey*.

Trojans: Priam, king of Troy; his son Hektor, foremost of the Trojan fighters, killed by Achilleus.

I. Comparison with other oral traditions suggests that Homer sang many different versions of the *Odyssey* before it reached the shape in which we know it. It probably owes its *size* and *concentration on a single theme* (the return and revenge of Odysseus) to Homer, but otherwise it is impossible to say with certainty how it developed. But we can make some good guesses. Here an analogy may be useful. An oral poet, setting out to sing a song, may be likened to a motorist setting out on a journey (it may be significant that Homer calls a poet's song *oimē*, a path, or 'song-way' at 22.347 and 8.481). The motorist knows where he starts from and where he is going to: but, because he has travelled this journey frequently, he is aware that at certain stages of the journey he has to make critical decisions about where to go next. He may turn left at *this* junction, which would take him via A and B, or he may turn right, when he would go through C and across D, and these decisions will have a critical bearing on later 'route' decisions and on the eventual shape of the whole journey. Selecting the route must have been one of the oral poet's most important tasks, especially when he was developing a poem of the size of the *Odyssey*.

During the course of the commentary I shall be pointing out places where alternative 'routes' may be causing inconsistencies or awkwardness in our text. The manuscript tradition itself sometimes points to possible 'routes'. For example, after 1.93 a few manuscripts offer 'and from there to Crete, to Lord Idomeneus, who came back last of the bronze-clad Achaians'. These lines are ejected in our version, because Telemachos does *not* go to Crete (see 7E). But since the *Iliad* testifies to the closeness of Menelaos, whom Telemachos does visit, and Idomeneus (Idomeneus was always visiting Menelaos in Sparta, 3.230−3), it would have been easy for the poet to have Menelaos suggest a visit to Idomeneus in Crete; and there are some references to Idomeneus in the *Odyssey* which seem rather forced but may have been more purposeful had Telemachos actually visited him (see on 14.237).

J. We cannot be certain that the poet of the *Odyssey* knew the *Iliad*, though I incline to believe that he did. Even if he did not, Odysseus in the *Iliad* shares enough similarities with Odysseus in Homer's *Odyssey* to make it likely that there was, at the very least, some sort of received tradition about him. Thus, in the *Iliad*, Odysseus is strongly supported by Athene and known to be her favourite (11.438, 23.765−84); he is respected by the army and regarded as a vital part of it (2.272−7, 11.470−1); he is a great warrior (11.401−88, 7.168−9), unbeatable even by Aias in the wrestling (23.707−39), and a brilliant orator (3.216−24). He is determined to take Troy (2.331−5, 14.80−105), though understands why the army should wish to return home after so long (2.291−7). He insists that the army eats before fighting again (19.155−237), and is interested (like all heroes) in material gain (2.297−8). On the other side, he is acknowledged to be crafty (3.200−2) and is accused of greed and treachery by Agamemnon, though Odysseus rebuts him (4.338−63). At 8.92−8, it is possible to accuse him of cowardice, but 'gave no attention' (97) could merely mean 'did not hear' rather than the more

xiii

damaging 'did not listen'. At 9.308–13, it is arguable that Achilleus is calling him a liar to his face. The seeds of Odysseus' later reputation (intelligent, brave, and a good judge of men on the one hand, grasping, self-serving and devious on the other) are already sown in the *Iliad*. The *Odyssey* does nothing to decrease this ambivalence. See further Stanford *UT*, especially 66–80.

K. I have chosen the translation of Richmond Lattimore on which to base this commentary because Lattimore does a better technical job than anyone else. He writes in a verse with a loose six-beat rhythm; he translates line-by-line with the Greek as far as he can; and he tries to remain true to the repetitions. Lattimore's translation is carefully stylised and generally accurate. It is possible to comment on it without feeling the need to enlarge upon or re-write the translation at every turn. But I have not hesitated to correct Lattimore where I believe he has seriously misunderstood the Greek. This is, in fact, a sign of my respect of his achievement, and in no way invalidates it. Had I been using any other translation, prior correction of the English would have been the predominant activity.

There is no reason why this commentary should not be used with another translation. Lattimore's line-numbers keep close to the Greek, and the introductory *lemma* should give enough of a clue to the precise identification of the passage commented upon.

Book one

1.1–21: Introduction

A. The 'proem' (proemium, introduction) to the *Odyssey* technically ends at 10 (see note). Page *HO* 168 note 2 criticises it on the grounds that it contains no reference to the story of Telemachos (Books 1–4) or to the return of Odysseus to Ithaka and the slaughter of the suitors (Books 13–24). But it may not be the purpose of proems to foreshadow the action in full (*Iliad* 1.1–7, which bears a number of interesting structural similarities, is equally 'at fault' in this respect). The function of the *Odyssey*'s proem is primarily moral: it relieves Odysseus of responsibility for his companions' death (6–9) and stresses that it was their own 'wild recklessness' (7) which killed them (cf. 12.419 and the accusation of Eupeithes, father of the dead suitor Antinoos, at 24.427–8).

B. In fact, it is more profitable to regard the proem as including 11–21. In these lines, it is made clear that all the heroes have already got home from Troy, with the sole exception of Odysseus (11–15); that the gods are now about to ensure his release from Kalypso and return to Ithaka (16–19); and that his only enemy is Poseidon (19–21). Since the *Odyssey* is temporally quite a complex tale, with a large number of flashbacks (e.g. Odysseus's tales of his travels from Troy to Kalypso in Books 9–12 and Nestor's and Menelaos' tales of return in Books 3 and 4), it is important for the poet to clarify the time-sequences: we now know that all the action described up to 21 is 'past', and that the *Odyssey* will open with Odysseus on the point of return.

C. By announcing his design in the way he does, Homer suggests that other solutions to the problem of telling of Odysseus's return are possible. An obvious one would be to tell it in temporally linear sequence, i.e. beginning with Odysseus leaving Troy. See Book I Appendix for the advantages the poet gains from adopting the time-sequence he has.

1. **Tell**: the *Iliad* begins with orders to the Muse to 'sing' (*aeide*). In fact the poet probably chanted, using the lyre (*phorminx* or *kitharis*) to sustain rhythm and metre (Lord *SoT* 21). The oral poet (*aoidos*, from *aeidō* 'I sing') must be distinguished from the later *rhapsōidos* who merely recited the (by then) fixed text of Homer at festivals (see on 3.36), without instrumental accompaniment. See further on 21.406–8.

Muse: the Muse, daughter of Zeus by *Mnēmosunē*, 'Memory' (Hesiod, *Theogony* 912–4), is the classical goddess of culture (cf. 'music'). She is summoned at the start of the poem, and at other points where necessary, because she alone can impart the *truth about past events* to the poet, and guarantee that Homer gets his facts right (cf. 8.479–81, 11.363–9, 22.346–8, *Iliad* 2.484–92). The Muse's authority is important in two respects. First it ensures that Homer 'knows' which god was acting on any given occasion (Homer here carefully distinguishes between his, the narrator's, and his character's knowledge. See e.g. on 5.356 and cf. on 2.23). Second, the poem takes on the status of history—as, for example, Plato and Thucydides were later to take for granted. Cf. *8E*.

man: in the Greek this is the first word of the poem. The poet announces that this is to be an epic of the individual. Observe that the poet keeps Athene, Odysseus' patron goddess, out of the proemium. The emphasis is to be on *human* will and action.

of many ways: i.e. 'who travelled far' and 'of wide experience'. Both aspects are stressed in the opening lines. Odysseus is not named till 21. He is frequently nameless or otherwise concealed in the *Odyssey* (most famously, during the Cyclops episode. Cf. on 1.14).

2.   **sacked**: Odysseus thought up the trick of the Wooden Horse and led the contingent inside it (8.494–5, 11.524–5). At the beginning of a poem full of deception, the poet reminds the audience of Odysseus' greatest deception —so far.

Troy's: see *GI H*. For Troy and 'history', see e.g. Blegen in *CH* 385–6, Finley *WO* 46–7, 174–7. Strabo (64BC–21AD), in his *Geography*, distinguishes between Troy (the territory) and Ilion (the town) at 13.1.17ff. and expresses doubts over the site at 13.1.25ff.

sacred: this presumably refers to Troy's founder gods Poseidon and Apollo (*Iliad* 21.441ff., where Poseidon claims the credit for building its walls). In the *Iliad* (*op. cit.* and cf. 15.205–17), Poseidon is hostile to Troy because its king Laomedon never paid him for building the walls. Consequently, whatever reason Poseidon adduces for being angry with Odysseus, it is unlikely to be that Odysseus was the chief architect of Troy's destruction. The reason lies elsewhere—the blinding of the Cyclops (68–9).

3.   **Many were . . . learned of**: these lines presumably refer to Odysseus' wanderings related in Books 5–6 and 9–12, but in fact Odysseus only saw four cities (of the Kikones, Aiolos, the Laistrygones and the Phaiakians), and only the Kikones could be said to be ordinary men. The poet may be seeking to make some quasi-metaphysical generalisation of Odysseus' travels, of the sort that, for example, Tennyson responded to (see on 5.114, 11.136). It must be remembered that, for half of the epic, Odysseus is in fact in Ithaka (see on 5.114).

4–5.   **pains . . . struggling**: Odysseus is marked out above all other heroes for his capacity to *endure* (cf. his common epithet 'much-enduring'). These lines hint at a tragic dimension to the tale. Cf. 10.460–5.

7.   **wild recklessness**: a key word. It indicates a blatant transgression of the

limits of human behaviour. It refers to the episode of the cattle of the Sun God (8). Odysseus had been told of the consequences if his men ate those cattle (11.104–13); he informed his men (12.271–6, 298–303). But they disobeyed him. See on 1.34. Cf. Clarke *AO* 7–8.

9. **he took away**: some of Odysseus' companions had been killed earlier (by e.g. the Kikones, Cyclops, Laistrygones and Skylla).

9–10. **From some point/here**: the poet has indicated his general theme. He now calls on the Muse to indicate where he should pick up *this* version of the song. Cf. the song of Demodokos at 8.500, 'beginning from where . . .', and *GI I*.

10. **goddess, daughter of Zeus, speak**: these words repeat the opening words of 1 ('Tell me, Muse'). This device, known as 'ring-composition', is frequently used by Homer to mark off a discrete part of the narrative (especially digressions and descriptions). It can be very intricate (see on 21.9–42). Compare the whole proem with *Iliad* 1.1–7, Virgil's *Aeneid* 1.1–11, Milton's *Paradise Lost* 1.1–26 and Pope's *Rape of the Lock* 1.1–12 (a delightful parody).

11. **all the others**: we shall hear of the returns of e.g. Nestor, Menelaos and Agamemnon and the non-returns of the lesser Aias and Achilleus. They illustrate the wide variety of possibilities: a safe, almost immediate return (Nestor); a safe but late return (Menelaos); a return to death at the hands of his wife Klytaimestra and her lover Aigisthos (Agamemnon); the death of Achilleus at Troy; and the death of the lesser Aias *en route* for home (see Fenik *SO* 26–7).

13. **alone**: Athene deploys the argument based on Odysseus' unique fate at 1.49 (cf. 4.182).

homecoming: the Greek word is *nostos* (cf. 'nostalgia'). The household—which, it must not be forgotten, was for Odysseus also a *kingdom*—was the centre of a Greek's life (cf. 1.57–9). Outside the field of battle, there was no more important arena in which to perform or compete (Finley *WO* 57–8). It gave a Greek his social standing: the wealthier it was, the more powerful he was (see 1.113–7, 14.229–34; cf. *Iliad* 15.494–9). Consequently, Odysseus' desire to return home does not require justification (cf. 9.34–6): it was taken for granted (cf. 7.224–5). The *Odyssey*, virtually all of which is set in the domestic world, asks two questions of Odysseus: will he return home at all? And if he does, will he re-master his kingdom? Cf. on 11.176–7.

14. **Kalypso**: daughter of Atlas (52–4), lives on the island of Ogygia (85). She appears in Book 5. Her name means 'concealer'. She has kept Odysseus out of men's sight for seven years (7.259).

18–19. **not even then . . . people**: the meaning of these lines is disputed. They could mean 'not even *there*, i.e. even in Ithaka, was he free from trials, *even though* he was among friends' or 'not even then, i.e. when the gods made the decision to release him, was he free from trials or among friends'. The former interpretation makes a welcome reference to the otherwise entirely unmentioned situation with the suitors in Ithaka; but since the poet goes on to talk of Poseidon's anger (20–1), the lines more likely refer to

Book 5, when Odysseus, having been freed at Zeus's command, is harried across the sea by Poseidon till he reaches the Phaiakians.

21.   **godlike**: this epithet is commonly applied to heroes and others (e.g. the suitors (14.17) and even Cyclops (1.70)). It implies no moral superiority.

1.22–95: Introduction

A. The plot is set in motion by a meeting of the gods who, though not called for the purpose (26–7), are brought round to a discussion of Odysseus' plight by Athene (48ff.). The story of the return of Agamemnon to death at the hands of his wife Klytaimestra and her lover Aigisthos, and of the revenge exacted on them by Agememnon's son Orestes, has an important part to play in the *Odyssey*. First, it acts as an example to Telemachos. Orestes returned to kill his father's usurper Aigisthos: so should Telemachos kill the suitors. The Orestes example offers Telemachos a direct line into the world of heroic action (1.298–302, 3.193–200). Second, the story is used to warn Odysseus: will Penelope remain faithful to him, or will she turn into a Klytaimestra (Penelope and Klytaimestra were cousins: see on 1.276) (11.385–456)? Third, Aigisthos died because of his own recklessness (34), not because of any divine intervention. Like Odysseus' men (see on 7), he took what he had no right to take: indeed, what he had been specifically warned *not* to take (37–9) (Clarke *AO* 10–12). The fate of Aigisthos and Odysseus' men, in other words, foreshadows that of the suitors, who despite divine warnings (see 20C) take what they have no right to in Odysseus' palace, and will be punished for their recklessness (22.413–7). Cf. on 11.415, 419, 24.194.

B. This paradigm of right and wrong establishes at the start of the *Odyssey* that Zeus does not predispose people to do wrong (as he appears to do in the *Illiad*)—indeed, he actually warns humans against intended crimes,—and is much concerned about proper human conduct (cf. 4.805–7, 13.213–4, 14.83–4, 20.214–5, *22C*). Though Zeus in the *Iliad* is as concerned about the rights of the *xenos* as he is in the *Odyssey* (see e.g. *Iliad* 3.351–4), the theodicy (organisation of divine justice) in the *Odyssey* seems very different from that of the *Iliad* (see e.g. *CH* 449–50, Lloyd-Jones *JZ* 28-32, Griffin *HLD* 164–5). By contrast with the suitors, Odysseus is held up as a model of intelligent behaviour among men (66) and of respect to the gods (60–2, 65–7, cf. 19.365–8, 22.335–6). Hesiod depicts a picture of social collapse which bears some similarities to the *Odyssey* at *WD* 180–201.

C. At 80–95, Athene foreshadows the temporally rather complex plot. Typically of Homer, her first plan, that Hermes will go to Kalypso (84–7), is carried out second (in Book 5), her second plan that she should visit Telemachos and instruct him to travel to Sparta and Pylos (88–95) is carried out first (see on 3.464–7 for this typical 'reverse'). Observe that Homer was not compelled to begin the *Odyssey* in this way. For example, it is very common for gods to impel humans to action by appearing to them in dreams (see e.g. 6.20ff.). But Homer eschews this 'route', choosing another common motif for setting the plot under way, the arrival of a stranger (Bowra *HP* 86ff.). He probably chose this latter option for two reasons. First, if Athene arrives in the palace in person, the poet presents Telemachos with a natural excuse for describing to her (and us) the up-to-date situation in the palace. Second, Athene can act as a friend and guide to the despairing young man, helping him win the 'good reputation' she promised at 95 and demonstrating that he is worthy to receive divine help from his father's patron goddess. When all this has been done for him, the poet decides that a dream is sufficient to impel him to return home (15.1 ff.).

22. **Aithiopians**: Homer identifies eastern and western Aithiopians (24). Since Poseidon returns to Olympos over the mountains of the Solymoi (5.283), which Strabo (1.2.10) locates in Turkey, he must be out east.

24. **Hyperion**: = the sun.

25. **hecatomb**: strictly, a sacrifice of 100 (Greek *hekaton*) bulls (Greek *bous*). In practice, as few as 12 could make up a hecatomb (*Iliad* 6.93, 115).

26. **sat at the feast**: the gods mingle freely with the Phaiakians (7.203); Thetis and her nymphs were present at Achilleus' funeral (24.46–7, 60). But in general, gods in the *Odyssey* do not mingle with humans nearly as freely as they do in the *Iliad*; nor do they squabble among themselves as much (cf. Finley *WO* 133–4); nor is human and divine action mirrored in such a complex way. Zeus maintains an aloof dignity (see on 8.267). Cf e.g. *Iliad* 1.536–70! On the other hand, the Odysseus—Athene relationship in the *Odyssey* is unparalleled for warmth and intensity by anything in the *Iliad*, excepting perhaps Achilleus and his mother Thetis.

29. **stately**: unless this epithet should be translated 'handsome', as has been argued, it seems an odd description of the unholy murderer Aigisthos, but the oral poet's system of formulas does sometimes show signs of strain (Trypanis *HE* 41–5, Camps *IH* 44–6).

Aigisthos: an attention-catching device: is not this epic supposed to be about *Odysseus*? It is clear that Homer wishes to impress the audience with the importance of the paradigm he is about to propose.

32. **Oh for shame**: about a third of Homer consists of speeches. This feature adds greatly to the drama and characterisation of the epic, and may well be a unique contribution of Homer to Greek oral art. See further Bowra *HP* 31–6.

put the blame upon us: e.g. 348.

34. **beyond what is given**: (cf. 35). I.e., Aigisthos did not have to marry Klytaimestra: it was not fated. He did it of his own free will, though warned by Zeus, and so went beyond what was laid down for him. His fate parallels that of Odysseus' companions and the suitors (see *12D*, *1.22–95 A*). But even the gods are powerless to prevent some things (3.236–8).

36. **Atreus' son**: Agamemnon.

38. **Hermes . . . Argeiphontes**: the messenger god in Homer's *Odyssey* (Iris fulfils that function in the *Iliad*. 'Argeiphontes' probably means 'slayer

of Argos', a many-eyed monster which Hera (wife of Zeus) sent to guard Io, one of Zeus's mistresses. Zeus ordered Hermes to kill it, which he did by first sending it to sleep. Hermes is able to maze people's eyes with his wand (5.47–8, 24.3–4).

41.   **whenever he came of age**: Orestes kills Aigisthos eight years after Agamemnon was killed (3.306). The 'coming of age' of Telemachos is an important theme of the *Odyssey*.

44.   **Athene**: goddess of war (*Iliad* 5.426–30), intelligence, and female skills (2.116–8, 7.110–11), and the great patroness of Odysseus.

52–4.   **Atlas . . . together**: Atlas is envisaged as a giant with his feet in the sea, holding up the sky with his hands. He was put in this position by Zeus for leading a revolt against heaven. The idea of a god holding up the earth from the sea seems to be of near Eastern origin. The contribution of near Eastern thought and beliefs to the development of Greek culture from the 8thC onwards has been generally under-rated (see e.g. M.L. West *Early Greek Philosophy and the Orient*, Oxford 1970 and his commentaries on the poet Hesiod).

57.   **to forget Ithaka**: a temptation visited upon Odysseus and his men in other adventures, e.g. The Lotus Eaters (9.82–104) and the Sirens (12.165–200).

58.   **smoke uprising**: it is a common technique of Homer to summarise a total experience by identifying a single aspect of it (cf. 9.167, 10.99).

61.   **do you grace . . . making sacrifice**: the word translated 'grace' here means 'reciprocating', 'giving tit-for-tat'. Reciprocation is the central principle of Greek religion, as Zeus acknowledges at 65–7 (see on 4.762). (Plato (*Euthyphro* 14E) calls piety 'a skill in trading'.) Probably the main motivation for sacrifice was to allay anxiety about future success or happiness, or to ensure it continued (3.273–5). See on 3.430–63 for details of sacrifice.

Argives = Greeks, also called 'Achaians' and 'Danaans' by Homer.

62.   **harsh**: the word in Greek is *ōdusao*, and is probably intended as a pun on the name of Odysseus (see on 19.409). 'Odious' may get the pun in English. The actual derivation of the name Odysseus (commonly found in some dialects as 'Olysseus', whence Latin 'Ulixes', and so 'Ulysses') is uncertain.

63.   **who gathers the clouds**: one of many of Zeus's epithets which refer to the weather. Zeus is a god especially connected with the sky and the weather (Burkert *GR* 125–6).

64.   **what sort . . . barrier?**: a formulaic line like 44–5 (=80–1), 63 etc.

68.   **Earth Encircler**: rather 'Earth Carrier, Supporter'. Poseidon's epithets never refer specifically to his activities as a sea-god but as an earth-god (he was god of earthquake). See Burkert *GR* 136–9, who suggests he may be god of violent energy. Linear B tablets found *in situ* indicate Poseidon was especially worshipped at Pylos (3.4–6).

69.   **whose eye he blinded**: one of the few places in Homer's *Odyssey* where it is strongly implied that Cyclops had one eye. The Cyclops, called Polyphemos (70), must be distinguished from the Cyclopes who forged

Zeus's thunderbolts under Mt. Etna in Sicily. The Polyphemos episode (see *9H*) is constantly mentioned throughout the *Odyssey*. It represents Odysseus' greatest triumph and encapsulates many of the *Odyssey*'s themes—Odysseus' intelligence, his self-concealment, namelessness, and Polyphemos' corruption of the rituals of *xenia* (cf. the suitors). Poseidon, more than any other god, seems especially prone to fathering evil and violent monsters (see Grimal *DCM*).

72. **Phorkys**: see on 13.96.

75. **drives him back**: the Greek is awkward. Since Odysseus has been a prisoner of Kalypso for the last seven years, Poseidon can hardly be said to be driving him back from his homeland.

79. **can accomplish nothing**: wrong translation. Read 'will not be able to wrangle'.

90. **Achaians**: see on 61 above. The Greeks as a whole are not called Hellenes in Homer (in Homer, Hellas is an area of Greece probably around Thessaly in the north. Cf.11.496 and *Iliad* 2.681–5). The term 'Hellenes', meaning 'Greeks', is a post-Homeric development. Our term for them, Greeks, derives from the Latin *Graeci*, 'men of Graia' (but no-one knows where that was located). On the Turkish coast Greeks were called 'Ionians' ('Yavan' in the Old Testament). See Finley *WO* 17–19.

91. **the suitors**: the first somewhat casual mention of the suitors in the *Odyssey*. This is their fourth year in the palace (2.89, 13.377). There are 108 of them from Ithaka and elsewhere (see on 16.247–53), and they are aristocrats (1.245, 2.51, 23.121–2). They should be wooing Penelope by offering gifts, not consuming her inheritance (18.275–80). Their unlawful consumption of what is not theirs to consume (91–2) is immediately emphasised.

93. **Pylos**:see *GI I* for a suggestion that in other versions Telemachos may have gone to Crete too.

95. **good reputation**: the Greek for 'reputation' is *kleos*, and means 'what people say of you'. It is the account of you which will live down the ages after death and is therefore of the highest importance. A noble *kleos* is the hero's consolation for dying (cf. 11.478–91. Achilleus may reject that consolation, but see 11.538–40 for his pride in his living son's achievements). Telemachos is to find out what the great heroes of the Trojan War, and others, will say of him, and will therefore achieve a true account of himself. This will enable him to grow into the true son of his father, a man worthy of Odysseus' name (cf. 11.449, *Iliad* 6.476–81, 8.281–5). At the moment, it is clear that he is utterly despondent about the situation in Ithaka and feels himself completely incapable of taking it in hand (113–7); he cannot bring himself to believe he is the son of Odysseus and even wishes he had been the son of a different, prosperous father (215–20) or at least of one who had died gloriously in battle (234–43, cf. 4.164–7). Athene's task is to set about healing this 'identity-crisis' and she does so by likening him to Odysseus (207–12), urging him to abandon childhood (296–7) and reminding him of the example of Orestes (298–302). See *18C* for importance of Telemachos' maturity to the whole story of the *Odyssey*. The Greek value-system puts far greater

emphasis upon successful performance in the eyes of others than in inner consciousness of right and wrong (whence Greeks' concern with what people said of them), and insists on the importance of visible, material rewards for success: see on 5.38, 21.323, Finley *WO* 113–23, *WoA* Chapter 3, and Clarke *AO* Chapter 2. The hero's search for immortal *kleos* is probably one of the oldest themes of Greek epic and is commonplace in all oral epic poetry (Bowra *HP* Chapter 1).

1.96–324: Introduction

A. The theme of *xenia*, (see definition on p.vii), runs through the *Odyssey* (it is sanctioned by Zeus: 6.207–8). Here, Telemachos shows that he knows how to entertain Athene-Mentes properly, unlike the suitors who completely ignore her. The elaboration of Athene's journey and Telemachos' reception indicates the importance of the episode.

B. Though despondent (215–6, 231–43) and given to rhetorical exaggeration (1.160 ff.) Telemachos knows how to treat a *xenos* (guest) and does have his father's blood in him (207–9): he is young, but growing up (296–7). Homer's *Odyssey* maintains a tension throughout between Telemachos' youth and potential. Before the suitors came, we are encouraged to believe he behaved like any responsible young man in charge of his father's home (11.184–7 and note on 11.185), though Penelope did consider him too young to look after the maids (22.426–7). Telemachos (and Penelope) are both well-drawn characters. See Camps *IH* 21–39 for character in Homer.

C. From the very start, the suitors are playing games (106–7), causing uproar (133), feasting, singing and dancing (144–52) and behaving in such a way as to disgust any decent person (227–9). Moreover, they virtually *never* acknowledge the gods at their feasting (see on 18.418, 20.276–83 for the two possible exceptions). Athene happily counsels Telemachos to slaughter them if all else fails (295–6). In these ways, Homer prepares us to accept the justice of the death meted out to them by Odysseus at the end of the poem (Book 22). Cf. *1.22–95A*.

D. Although absent, Odysseus dominates the thoughts and feelings of everyone in the palace. His memory is constantly alluded to (e.g. 128–9, 115, 160ff, 253ff.). We are given a powerful sense of his greatness and of the desperate need for his return: only when Odysseus is master of his house again can Telemachos be a proper son, Penelope a proper wife, the suitors be expelled and the servants serve their rightful lord (cf. Philoitios at 20.217–25).

E. Irony—i.e. characters not understanding the *true* significance of what they are saying—and disbelief are common elements in the *Odyssey*, where disguise, despair, deception and ignorance are such prominent features. Athene-Mentes' conversation with the despairing and ignorant Telemachos sets the tone for much of the rest of Homer's *Odyssey*. See Fenik *SO* 157.

F. There has been much debate about Athene's instructions to Telemachos at 271–296. Page (*HO* 56ff.) argues that they are self-contradictory, and in strictly logical terms, he is right. Athene knows the suitors will not leave, nor Penelope wish to remarry, so why urge those proposals on Telemachos (271–78)? Why, next, does Athene tell Telemachos not (after all) to wait to see what happens, but to sail off to the Peloponnese *at once* (280–6)? Why, then, does she tell Telemachos to marry off Penelope when he returns (293) but *only then* to consider killing the suitors (295)—who would, naturally, all have departed once Penelope was married? But it is possible to argue that Athene's instructions are not a set of logical alternatives but a foreshadowing of what is likely to happen, and a warning and example to Telemachos. Of course, he should try to face up to the suitors *in public* (272–4) and try to clarify Penelope's feelings (275–8), but the case seems lost before it is even opened (cf. 2.144). If Odysseus is dead, it makes sense for him to marry off Penelope (292), but he had better find out first (280–92). Finally, if there still are suitors in the palace even when she has been married, it is a sign that they are all in a conspiracy together to get their hands on Odysseus' wealth, power and position (cf. 20.213–7, 22.49–53). The hand of Penelope is merely a means to it (cf. 16.383–92). This is not a tale of princes wooing a queen, but rather of a gang trying to destroy a family's inherited power. Cf. on 2.335–6. Compare the explanations in *CH* 57–8; Camps *IH* 89 note 29; Clarke *HR* 186–88.

Page's criticisms of this passage are typical of scholars known as 'analysts'. See *11B* for a simple definition and *11E−F* for the weaknesses of their approach. Analytical scholars do not all speak with one voice on any issue. When I refer to analysts, I *usually* mean Page.

99–101.   **Then she . . . angered**: many argue that it seems inappropriate for Athene to be armed as a war-goddess, but all she is doing is carrying a spear, which (disguised as Mentes 105) she will give to Telemachos when she enters the house (127–9). She will not retrieve it when she leaves (319–20).

102.   **descended**: the first typical scene of welcoming a guest, *xenia*, now ensues. Observe the repeated sequence: Athene 1. *leaves* (102), 2. *arrives* (103), 3. *finds* a situation (106), 4. Telemachos *sees* her (113), 5. Telemachos *goes to meet* her (119), 6. he is *angry* at her treatment (119), 7. he *takes her hand* (121), 8. he *offers* food and greetings (123), 9. Athene is *led in* and her *spear taken* (125), 10. she is *seated* (130), 11. *food* is prepared and consumed (136), 12. *questions* begin (170). This sequence will occur again, with variations, at 3.1ff., 4.1ff., 5.50ff. and in many other places (cf. departures, on 1.303–19). It will illustrate another aspect of Homeric route-finding: the poet always keeps to the same *order* of events though he may choose to *omit* some, if it suits his purpose (see on 5.91). For a compressed

version see 10.13–18. On variety in themes of this sort, see Lord *SoT* 88–92.

104.   **at the threshold of the court**: various efforts are made to describe accurately Odysseus' house on the basis of Homer's evidence, to find archaeological parallels for it in the Greek world, and to locate a suitably impressive palace in Ithaka where Odysseus can be said to have lived. All three efforts fail, the last completely. For what it is worth, I append here a ground-plan of Odysseus' palace as if it were modelled on a Mycenaean one (itself a dubious hypothesis, since archaeology and common sense both suggest Homer probably envisages a rather grand 8thC dwelling. For example, Homer's palace has 'high thresholds' (22.1–2). These are not features of Mycenaean palaces, but are found on models of 8thC dwellings. No Mycenaean palace survived except in ruins to the 8thC). The illustration depicts a palace consisting of a courtyard fronting a large hall, which has various rooms off and some upstairs quarters. Athene is standing at forecourt 3. The suitors are playing around the forecourts 1 and 2(?) in front of the doors (107). Telemachos brings Athene into the hall (125ff.). At 144, the suitors enter the hall for their meal.

105.   **disguised**: while gods in the *Iliad* usually appear to their favourites as themselves (e.g. *Iliad* 1.197-200) gods only come to earth once without disguise in Homer's *Odyssey* (15.9). The *Odyssey* seems more down-to-earth and realistic in this sense (cf. e.g. *Iliad* 17.333-4, 13.68-72). Athene must appear as a man to Telemachos: only thus could she explain her relationship with Odysseus (187–95).

Taphians: traders and pirates (1.182ff., cf. 14.452, 15.426, 16.426. See *CH* 308). The Taphian islands are not firmly identified. Trade is for the most part a Phoenician privilege in Homer but Greeks were trading in the Levant by the 8thC. See Finley *WO* 68–9 for the dubious ethics of trading in a world of heroes, and on 8.163. The fact that Athene *chooses* this disguise suggests that other criteria could outweigh the apparent contemptibility of trading.

108.   **cattle**: in Homer, cattle are the main form of wealth and subsistence (see on 14.96) but non-heroic Greeks lived on a grain-based diet, and arable farming predominated, as the 7thC poet-farmer Hesiod makes clear in his *WD*. Cf. on 3.86 and 14.96.

109.   **heralds . . . and henchmen**: these were free men, retained through some network of obligation by the palace. See Finley *WO* 58, 103–4. For heralds, see on 8.8.

110.   **mixing bowls**: wine was always diluted with water in the ancient world. Cf. on 9.297.

113–18.   **far the first to see . . . he saw Athene**: note the ring-composition (1.10) (see . . . sat . . . imagining/thoughts . . . sitting . . . saw). This device encircles a description of Telemachos. It emphasises his helplessness, isolation and total dependence on his father (he imagines Odysseus in the same way as Penelope does at 20.81—see note). If Telemachos is to be a support to Odysseus when he returns, Athene has no alternative to stirring him to action now.

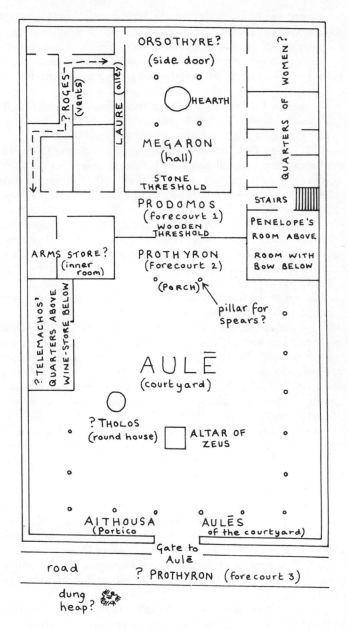

The palace of Odysseus

(after J. Lazenby)

122.   **winged words**: a famous formula. Words are winged because they fly either like birds or like arrows (also called 'winged' or 'feathered' in Homer; words are commonly likened to arrows in later Greek literature).

125.   **Pallas**: possibly derived from the Semitic *ba-alat*, 'mistress', 'lady'.

127.   **a tall column**: spears are normally left outside the hall (cf. 17. 28–30).

130–50.   **and he led her . . . drinking**: this leisurely scene, with its well-observed details (cf. 109–12) will be repeated frequently in the *Odyssey*. In particular, 136–42 is repeated almost verbatim at 4.52, 7.172, 10.368, 15.135, 17.91. Note that heroes feast sitting, not reclining (145). Homer's concern with domestic detail and with humble people is to the fore in the *Odyssey*. In the *Iliad* it emerges only in the similes (but with great force, e.g. *Iliad* 12.430–6). The aristocratic suitors in particular come out very badly indeed when set against the standards of faithful if humble servants like Eurykleia and Eumaios, though in scenes like this even they submit briefly to the formal courtesies of the rituals (but see 365–70). Homeric heroes never eat without some degree of attendant ceremony. This elevates and adds grandeur to what in other circumstances is merely the satisfaction of material needs. See Clarke *AO* 14–18, *14C*.

152.   **the end of the feasting**: as Odysseus reminds the suitors, with grim irony, immediately before their death (22.428–30).

153–55.   **A herald . . . song**: the *Odyssey* is full of details of court-singers. If Homer were one such, it would give him the continuity of audience and employment in which to develop poems of such unique size and intricacy. Homer protects Phemios' reputation by saying the poet was *forced* to sing for the suitors (cf. 3.265–72, 22.350–3). Though the phrase 'put the lyre in the hands' may suggest Phemios is blind (cf. Demodokos at 8.261–2 and Homer's reputation), he is not (22.530–43).

157.   **so that none . . . might hear**: Telemachos uses Phemios' song to cover his conversation with Athene. The implication is that everyone would be listening with the most rapt concentration to the bard—as indeed they are at 325, when the conversation ends.

160–68.   **the substance . . . perished**: observe that Telemachos cannot bring himself even to mention the name of Odysseus, such is his exaggerated and rhetorical pessimism and despair. This is psychologically sound: to believe in the worst is to give oneself some protection if it happens. See Eumaios' speech at 14.37–190 and cf. the rhetoric of 16.34–5.

170–73.   **What man . . . country**: typical questions, ending with a standard Homeric 'joke'. Cf. 14.187–90. For the importance of names in *xenia*, see 9.16–18. 355–6.

176–77.   **many other men too . . . people**: cf. 19.239–40. The *Odyssey* is full of references to the life of Odysseus before ever he left Ithaka to go to Troy. See on 17.293–4.

184.   **Temese**: not identified, though it would make sense were it the same as Tamasos, an inland town in copper-rich Cyprus (copper and tin make bronze). Since we may assume from this passage that bronze is the more

valuable of the two metals mentioned, we have here an iron-age reference. See on 9.392, 393.

187.   **guest-friends by heredity**: it is very common for *xenia* relationships to have been forged in the far distant past. They lose nothing of their hold over the *xenoi* because of this. 1.257–64 exemplifies the connection. Cf. *Iliad* 6.212–36, where two enemies agree a truce because they find they are *xenoi* from way back; and *Odyssey* 15.196–8.

188–93.   **hero . . . vineyard**: one assumes that in normal circumstances Laertes would have re-assumed the kingship on the departure of his son to Troy. But Odysseus handed the house over to Mentor (2.224–7), and he, in fact, plays no effective role at all. Homer's purpose is clearly literary. Wishing to spotlight the young Telemachos and his problems, he edges Laertes and Mentor to the side (cf. Finley's over-political explanation, *WO* 86–7). Homer might have chosen to kill off Laertes (as he did Odysseus' mother Antikleia, see 11.152ff., cf. 15.353–60). But it is typical in oral epic for the returning son to have an emotional re-union with his father at the end (24.213ff., cf. 11.187–96. See Lord *SoT* 177ff.). At 4.734–41, Penelope tries to involve Laertes when she hears of Telemachos' absence in Pylos and Sparta but nothing comes of it.

191.   **an old woman**: see 24.210–12.

193.   **making his toilsome way**: the Greek says 'crawling', 'creeping'. Laertes works a *terraced* hill-slope (see on 24.224). For the communal merriment which should accompany the vintage, see *Iliad* 18.561–72.

194.   **I have come**: ring-composition with 182.

196.   **Odysseus**: see on 1.160–8.

198.   **on a sea-washed island**: it looks as if Athene is going to describe Odysseus' sojourn with Kalypso (50 starts the same way), but instead she gives a quite different, and false, explanation of his detention. Economies with the truth of this sort are common in the *Odyssey*. Presumably it would be too depressing for Telemachos at this juncture to know that Odysseus was in the clutches of a semi-divine being. (The sexual implications are not important. See *5B*, and observe that at 17.138–46 Telemachos is in no way embarrassed to tell Penelope the truth about Kalypso).

203.   **He will not long be absent**: the first of a number of assertions that Odysseus is about to return. See on 2.146–54.

207–43.   **Are you . . . to me**: see on 1.95 for Telemachos' 'identity crisis'. Note how important the *father* is to the son (239–40: 'fame' is *kleos*, here seen as mysteriously transmittable from a dead father to the son but only under certain conditions). The loss of Odysseus without memory or memorial leaves the son lacking any authority, any sense of who he really is and what he may achieve: he can neither claim Odysseus' name, nor make a name for himself. Cf. on Laertes, 24.289. Cf. 215–6 with Athene's encouragement at 2.270–80, especially 274–5. See on 3.98–101.

246–7.   **Doulichion . . . Ithaka**: for the controversy over the location of these islands, see on 9.25.

249–51.   **And she . . . pieces**: the tension between Telemachos and Penelope is an important theme of the *Odyssey*. As Telemachos hints here, their attitudes towards Penelope's re-marriage, the destruction of the household, and their rights within the household constantly fluctuate. By keeping Laertes in the background and highlighting Telemachos' position in the house as potential overlord, the poet gives himself room to create a fascinatingly ambiguous Penelope, torn by internal conflicts and tensions, isolated and thwarted at every turn, and only reluctantly reliant upon the young Telemachos.

255–6.   **I wish . . . spears**: Odysseus will indeed reveal himself among the suitors at a feast with similar swiftness (22.1–16), but initially with a bow. War-gear will follow (22.119–25).

259.   **Ephyre**: there are places of this name in Thesprotia (the best bet?) and Elis. Scholiasts say it is an alternative name for Corinth.

264.   **my father**: Anchialos (180–1). Nowhere else does Homer mention the poisoning of arrow-tips. Presumably it was regarded as impious (263).

271.   **do as I tell you**: see *1.96–324F* for the problems with this passage. Athene prepares the audience for Telemachos' activities till he returns to Ithaka in Book 15. 272–4 is fulfilled briefly at 1.327–8 and fully at 2.40ff.; 280–89 is fulfilled in Books 3 and 4.

276.   **her . . . father**: Penelope's father is the Spartan Ikarios, brother of Tyndareos. Tyndareos was the husband of Leda and father of Klytaimestra and (in theory) of Helen (though Zeus, disguised as a swan, was said to be the real father). See 11.298–304. It is not clear whether Telemachos in fact has the power to marry off his mother. This passage and 20.341–4 suggest he has, but 15.16–18 suggest he has not (but see note there).

277.   **wedding presents**: see on 2.53.

286.   **bronze-armoured**: see on 21.434.

295–302.   **kill . . . you**: for the Orestes parallel, see *1.22–95A*.

303–19.   **But now . . . departed**: note the typical departure sequence after a scene of *xenia* (cf. on 1.102, from where I pick up the sequence numbers) (13) the guest gives a reason for leaving (303–5), (14) the host urges the guest to stay, with promises of gifts and a send-off (307–13), (15) the guest makes further excuses (315–8), (16) the departure (319).

307–8.   **My guest . . . them**: Telemachos yearns for a father-figure and has clearly found one in Athene-Mentes. He does not know that his guest is Athene yet, but he will be given evidence that it may have been a divinity (319–23), and will guess it was Athene (420–1). Since gods only support 'winners', never 'losers' (which is why heroes are enhanced, not diminished, by divine aid), Athene's encouragement of Telemachos considerably improves his self-image (see especially 320–2: note the emphasis on Telemachos' renewed commitment to his *father*).

309–18.   **But come now . . . befall you**: for the importance of material gifts, the prestige they bestowed on receiver and giver, and their place in *xenia* relationships (sealing and ratifying them), see on 1.95, 4. 589–92. See 24.284–6 for Laertes' testimony to Odysseus' past generosity in this respect. Failure to exchange gifts could be seen as an insult (see 15.193–214).

320.   **like a bird soaring high**: this must refer to the *manner* of Athene's departure, as Eurymachos confirms at 410–11. Cf. 3.371–2.

1.325–444: Introduction

A. Penelope's entry establishes a common pattern—she appears veiled and accompanied by servants (328–35), she makes a complaint (336–44), is rebuked by someone (usually Telemachos) (345–59) and retires (360–64), creating a stir (365–6). From her first appearance, we sense the tension between herself and Telemachos (see on 249–51), who seems to go out of his way to slap her down (e.g. Telemachos conveniently forgets his previous feelings about Odysseus in his rebuke at 353–5). (See Lord *SoT* 172–3). Penelope is continually trying to intervene in Telemachos and the suitors' world, but is always frustrated. Like the suitors she remains in ignorance of the true meaning of what is happening in the palace till Book 23, and it is only then that she replies to Telemachos' attacks (see on 23.99). There is some significance in Penelope's use of the veil (334), which was normally discarded in the security of the home, and in her attendance by servants (331), a sign of her modesty/chastity (see on 6.100 and cf. 18.182–4). On Penelope and Telemachos, see Camps *IH* 97 note 44. For typical features of Penelope and Telemachos' character, see *16G*.

B. The suitors are represented by their two leaders (4.269), the hostile and vicious Antinoos (who always speaks first, and is the first to be killed at 22.8ff.) and the oily, hypocritical Eurymachos (see 402–4). Cf. Camps *IH* 96 notes 41a and b. The *Odyssey* is full of such doublets (see Fenik *SO* 133ff., *17B*), which give the poet the chance to compare and contrast different types of character. Repeated scenes (of e.g. *xenia*) give a similar scope.

C. Telemachos presents a quite new face in this scene, full of the fresh confidence Athene has given him (see on 307–8). At 353–5 he is able to 'forget' about Odysseus; at 358–9 he asserts mastery over the household (but see note there); and cf. 397–8, where he states unambiguously that he will fill Odysseus' shoes. Most important of all, his reply to Eurymachos at 412–19 is full of Odyssean guile. Here is a young man asserting his identity (see on 1.95, 1.207–43). At the same time, there are signs of youthful haste in his challenge to the suitors at 368–80, one which should have been saved for, and will be repeated on, the next day (2.138–45); and one may feel his niggling at Penelope (353–5, 414–6) seems an over-reaction.

D. Eurykleia is a fine example of the humble, loving and loyal character who will have an important part to play later on. Note the thumbnail sketch of her at 429–33 (ring-composition 428–34), and the loving detail in which Telemachos' bed-time routine is described at 436–44 is typical of the *Odyssey*'s celebration of the ordinary and everyday. As 434–5 hint, she has a closer relationship with Telemachos at this stage than Penelope does, and it is to her that he will turn when he confides the details of his journey (2.348ff., especially 373). Cf. on *14C*, 17.302. 20.120–1, 20.204–25, etc.

325.   **singer**: Phemios, who began his song at 155.

326.   **bitter homecoming**: this was caused, according to myth, because Aias (Ajax) son of Oileus raped Cassandra at the shrine of the temple of Athene in Troy. For this, Athene ensured the Greeks had a stormy return (see on 3.135). The suitors enjoy hearing this song from Phemios because they hope the same fate has befallen Odysseus. (Phemios naturally cannot sing of that yet because it has not happened). The suitors also know it will remind Penelope of her plight, and perhaps hasten her decision to re-marry (340–44).

329.   **upper chamber**: somewhere above the hall (see diagram p. 11).

331.   **two handmaidens**: Penelope had fifty in all (22.421), responsible for cleaning and water-carrying (20.147–59) and spinning (22.422–3).

338.   **charm**: a common attribute of song in Homer. Cf. 17.513–20.

340.   **leave off singing this**: but Phemios only does so temporarily, taking the song up again at 421–2 after Telemachos' insistence at 370–1.

343–4.   **so dear a head**: the expression here refers to the person and personality of Odysseus, but significantly is often used in Homer in association with the *dead*. It is telling that Penelope's first words in the *Odyssey* should (i) recollect Odysseus, (ii) not name him directly (cf. on 161–8), and (iii) hint that he is dead. Observe how she judges Odysseus by the extent of his national *kleos* (see on 1.95).

344.   **Hellas and . . . Argos**: 'Hellas' probably means N. Greece, 'Argos' the Peloponnese.

356–9.   **Go . . . household**: these verses almost = *Iliad* 6.490–3 (for 'discussion' read 'war' in the *Iliad* passage). Telemachos asserts his authority over the household, and claims that he possesses one of the hero's most important characteristics—mastery over words (2.270–2). See on 21.350–8.

357.   **distaff**: better 'spindle'. See on 4.122.

360.   **house**: read 'room'. See on 16.34–5.

373–80.   **statement . . . given**: since these words are repeated at 2.139–45, and Telemachos was specifically told by Athene to address the suitors on the *next* day (272, 372), some, for example Page, suspect interference with the text (*HO* 74 note 5). We may prefer to read youthful haste into the words. The control that Telemachos attempts to exert over the suitors here (see their reaction at 381–2) foreshadows the true mastery he will show from Book 17 onwards when Odysseus has returned and the two of them work in concert together (see *16C*).

384.   **the very gods**: Antinoos' analysis is, ironically, true.

386.   **son of Kronos**: i.e. Zeus.

king: the word in Greek is *basileus*, and means here 'hereditary, or rightful, ruler'. Antinoos suggests Telemachos has not earned that title yet (cf. 400–1), and 11.184–7 backs him up: Telemachos rules the household, but does not yet claim Odysseus' 'fine inheritance' (for land as the basis of power, see Finley *WO* 95). At 1.394–6, Telemachos agrees that any local *basileis* ('princes') *could*, in theory, hold the position—but argues that he will at all events control his own household (397–8 cf. 402–4). *Basileus* is clearly a flexible term (at 8.41, Alkinoos uses it of his council of advisers). Presumably, local *basileis* ruled their own households and exerted local influence (like the suitors), but in time a 'top' *basileus* would emerge who came to be regarded as 'king' over them all. But he was not an absolute, hereditary monarch, (though birth clearly helped—1.387, 7.149–50), and as 2.26–7 and 2.230–4 imply, he had some sort of duty even to consult the 'people' on occasions (or at least Odysseus did) and the people have influence in *some* sense at 16.95–6, 375. The position is further confused by the role and function of Penelope. Would marriage to her confirm the new husband as 'king'? Not automatically, but it would give the husband such an advantage in status and material power that his emergence as top *basileus* would probably ensue fairly quickly. On the ambiguity of Telemachos' position, see Finley *WO* 87–9, but Finley is (again) too eager to see historical forces at play. The fluid constitutional position of the *basileus* may reflect a contemporary historical reality (cf. *GI E*) (the shift from rule by a single monarch to an oligarchic aristocracy?) but it may equally be a poetic choice, governed by literary considerations.

402–4. **But I hope . . . lived in**: typical hypocrisy from Eurymachos. The disjunction between what the suitors say and what they mean is very evident throughout the *Odyssey*. Odysseus, Telemachos and Penelope also play their deceptive games. The *Odyssey* is in this respect different from the *Iliad* where there tends to be no distinction between what a hero really thinks and what he says. See on 4.712–3, *17A*. For the suitors' determination to stay on in the palace whatever happens, see on 20.336–7.

411. **no mean man, by the look of him**: nobility of features usually went inseparably with nobility of birth, intelligence and the right to rule among the ancient Greeks. Cf. 8.18–23, 24.251–5, and the counter-examples at 8.166–77, *Iliad* 3.45, and cf. Thersites at *Iliad* 2.211–20. See generally *17A*.

414–6. **I believe . . . questions**: cf. Penelope's gullibility at 14.122–30. Telemachos' answer is clearly devious (420–1). His evasiveness is justified by the situation he is in and is fully worthy of Odysseus.

424. **each to his own house**: the suitors do not stay overnight in the palace, but return to their homes every evening. Cf. 18.427–8.

426. **bedchamber**: see plan of palace , on p. 11.

428–35. **Eurykleia . . . little**: new characters always receive a brief description on their first appearance (note how ring-composition—'torches' 429/34—defines the digression). It is typical to mention family (429) and then to give a brief anecdote (430–3), cf. Aigyptios at 2.15–24. Eurykleia was expensive: twenty oxen (431) were the compensation Eurymachos suggested each suitor should pay Odysseus (22.57): at *Iliad* 23.703–5 a female slave was valued at four. Most slaves were female. They were war-booty (3.154), and the men would either be killed or ransomed back to their parents at a price (*Iliad* 4.238–9, 21.100–5). Their duties would be to work in the house (Eurykleia keeps Penelope's storeroom, 2.345–7) and serve their master's beds (cf. *Iliad* 1.29–31)—even bearing heirs (4.1–14): Laertes' behaviour here (433) is worth mentioning because it was so unusual. (Cf. *Iliad* 19.175–7).

440.   **corded**: bedding was supported on cords threaded through holes in the bed-frame. See 23.198–201.

441–2.   **pulled the door . . . bolt**: Eurykleia leaves the room and pulls the door shut with the 'silver hook' (= doorknob). She now draws the bolt across with a strap. This bolt can hardly be on the *outside* of the door: for how could Telemachos then get out of the room? It must therefore be on the inside. Consequently, the strap (or thong) attached to the bolt (or door-bar) must come through a slit in the door so that it hangs *outside* the door. Eurykleia can thus draw the bolt across from the outside, as she does here. Her purpose is not to *lock* the room, but merely to close the door to prevent it banging, and leave the room accessible to those going in and coming out. (Telemachos does not need protection inside his own house). The bolt probably slid into a socket in the door-post. See further on 21.46–50 for the full locking procedure.

BOOK I APPENDIX: why does Homer start where he does? (see 1.1–21 C)

By starting at the place he does (Ithaka) and at the time he does (twenty years after Odysseus left home at the point when Odysseus is about to return), Homer creates the following advantages:

1. He can show how desperate the situation in Ithaka is and how great is the need for Odysseus' return.

2. He can set the scene fully in Ithaka (Penelope, the suitors, Telemachos etc.) so that the readers know what Odysseus is returning to and what challenges he will face. This increases our anticipation of Odysseus' return.

3. He must put Odysseus' travels from Troy to Kalypso's cave (where we will meet Odysseus in Book 5) into Odysseus' own mouth, as an autobiographical flashback. This will have the effect of deepening Odysseus' characterisation, and of bringing the past directly into the present. As a result, Odysseus' adventures take on a more immediate relevance, since they will be mediated through Odysseus, in the narrative 'present', rather than in the third person as something to be 'got out of the way' before Odysseus returns to Ithaka (see on 9.54–5). Homer's decision forces him to create a context in which Odysseus can tell his story. The Phaiakian episode solves this problem. There is a further advantage. Athene wrecked the Greek fleet on its return from Troy (see on 3.135). But it would be absurd for her to wreck *Odysseus*'s fleet. Since humans are ignorant of the gods' plans (see on 1.1 'Muse'), Odysseus himself would not be in a position to know who was causing the trouble at sea. So by putting the story of his return in Odysseus' mouth, Homer, the omniscient narrator, is absolved from telling the 'truth' about what happened. Athene can disappear entirely from the story (as indeed she virtually does). Clay *WA* 40–53 argues that Homer begins the

Odyssey where he does specifically in order to avoid the whole issue of Athene's anger against the fleet. But since Homer himself *raises* the issue, the argument does not quite work.

4. The young Telemachos, who is mentioned as the son of Odysseus in the *Iliad* (2.260, 4.354) and so is not an invention for this story, is now almost grown up and at an age when he ought to take control of Odysseus' house. The tensions and conflicts within himself and with Penelope and the suitors make the situation in Ithaka far richer and more complex than it would be otherwise (see on 1.249–51). If Telemachos were still too young to take over (see on 4.112), Penelope would have to be much more domineering, and the chance lost of suggestive interaction between the two of them. See also on 1.188–93.

5. Homer has a problem with Telemachos. The young man must not rival Odysseus, but at the same time he must be seen to be a son worthy of his father. Given that Homer must depict a situation in Ithaka in which only the return of Odysseus can solve the problems, Telemachos must be unequal to the task of handling the suitors. Consequently, if Homer decides to make the maturation of Telemachos a major theme of the *Odyssey* that maturation can only take place *outside* Ithaka. Hence the need for Telemachos' journey. But in what should this maturation consists? Telemachos is too young for a series of heroic exploits; besides, if he successfully completed them, his need for Odysseus would be less. Hence Homer's choice of a series of meetings with great heroes of the past, through whom Telemachos can be brought face-to-face with his own *potential*. It is this potential which Odysseus can exploit on his return. See *7E* for a possible alternative scenario to the one in our *Odyssey*. Cf *13F*. Andromache envisages what *can* happen to fatherless sons at *Iliad* 22.482–507. On the chronology of the *Odyssey*, see Camps *IH* 78–9, Trypanis *HE* 31–40, and *9A*.

Book two

A. The assembly which Telemachos calls fulfils the instruction of Athene given to him in 1.269–92. In the sense that the purpose of the assembly is to move the dispute from the private to the public sphere and involve all Ithakans (cf. 211, 239–41), it is a failure. But the assembly does allow the suitors to show their true colours *in public*, so that there can be no doubt about their evil intentions; and to clarify in Telemachos' mind what action he should take over his father (should he try to ascertain whether he is alive or dead?) and his mother (should he marry her off *now* or not?). In particular, the suitors' three contributions are notable for their increasing violence (cf. 123–8, 198–207, 244–51 and Mentor at 235–8). There can be no doubt that they are wholly ruthless, and will deserve the death they finally get (cf. *1.22–95A, B*). The omen signifying Odysseus' imminent return (155–207) is one of a number that increases as the suitors end draws nearer (see on 146–54).

B. The poet continues to make Telemachos a centre of attention. He is glorified by Athene (12–13) and begins his first public address confidently, but increasingly admits weakness (60–79) and ends in tears (80–1). He fights back at 130–45, and receives a good omen from Halitherses (161–76), but abandons the debate at 209–11 and says nothing more even when the suitors abruptly break up assembly (257–9). This is not the sort of 'grip' one expects from a son of Odysseus. See on 1.95.

C. Two important facts emerge about Penelope: first, her high intelligence (greater than that of the most famous heroines of the past) (115–122), and her Odyssean cunning (the shroud trick, 93–109). These newly-revealed qualities increase our expectations of Penelope and prepare the ground for richer exchanges between her, Telemachos, the suitors, and Odysseus (when he returns).

1–14. **Now when . . . him**: note the authority with which Telemachos is invested here: he is 'like a god' (5), is beautified by Athene (12) (as Odysseus is at e.g. 6.229ff.) and assumes his father's place (14). The people admire him (13) and the elders yield to him (14).

17–22. **His own . . . fathers**: Antiphos is not mentioned in Book 9, where the Cyclops' tale is related. Eurynomos appears again at 22.243, but his death is not described. Presumably the purpose of this brief description is to show why Aigyptios rather than anyone else should begin the questions: his family is deeply involved with Ithaka past and present.

23.   **He grieved**: Aigyptios does not know *how* his son was killed. The information given at 17–20 is privileged poetic knowledge (see on 'Muse', 1.1).

28.   **Who has gathered us . . .**: Aigyptios asks because an assembly would normally be called by the king—in this case, the absent Odysseus. See on 1.386 'king'.

35–6.   **dear son . . . speaking**: Telemachos' youthful enthusiasm to speak will, by the end, have turned to youthful rage, tears and frustrations (80–1): a nice character touch.

35.   **omen**: Aigyptios' words are not exactly an omen, but a significantly coincidental utterance could be taken as one cf. 18.117, 20.100–5.

51.   **hereabouts**: the suitors at this assembly are the pick of *local* Ithakan nobles, not the young bloods from neighbouring islands mentioned at 1.245–8 (who went home at 1.424, and presumably returned in time to eat 2.299).

53.   **bride-gifts**: Homer talks of three different types of marriage-gift. The usual practice is, as here, that the groom gives gifts to the family of the bride (a sort of bride-price, whose purpose is largely to impress the family with his status and wealth, cf. 16.390–2). But Homer also mentions the custom of the dowry, a gift given by relatives of the bride to the bride to ensure that her household starts off on a sound financial footing (Telemachos suggests he will dower Penelope in this way at 20.341–4, cf. 2.195–7). Third, Homer hints at a gift-contest, as if the bride will go to the largest bidder (18.275–80). As Murray points out (*EG* 68, cf. Finley *WO* 89 (footnote)), such institutions frequently exist side-by-side in the same society. Why does Telemachos claim the suitors do not wish to apply to Ikarios for Penelope's hand in marriage (Antinoos insists they welcome the prospect at 2.111–4, cf. 2.195–7)? Because Telemachos senses the suitors are after more than marriage (see *1.96–324F.*).

64–78.   **even you . . . regiven**: the people being addressed in this passage are primarily the twelve *Ithakan* suitors (16.251). The people addressed change at 73, where 'you' = the fathers of the Ithakan suitors (see 51). They, Telemachos suggests, might have refused to restrain their sons ('these', 74) because of some hypothetical wrong Odysseus did them in the past. Presumably the 'you' of 75, 76 and 79 are still the fathers, since no change of subject is indicated in the Greek. Telemachos is arguing that the suitors' fathers are basically decent: they have just been lax in reining in their sons. If the fathers were eating him out of house and home, Telemachos feels confident he would stand a chance of compensation. This is all very emotional. Telemachos' denunciation has turned into an admission of weakness. Cf. Telemachos' caution at 3.22–4.

64–5.   **scandalised . . . ashamed**: the Greek 'root' words are *nemesis* and *aidōs*. These are two important terms in the Greek value system. *Aidōs* means the internal sense of shame which makes one fear *nemesis*, public disapproval (*CH* 450). Cf. Eurymachos at 21.249–255, when he cannot string the bow. See on 1.95 for Homeric values.

66–7.   **fear . . . you**: the idea that the gods would punish human crimes was stated clearly in Book 1 (see *1.22–95B*. Cf. 2.143–5).

68.   **Themis**: when personified as a goddess (see on 14.130), a wife of Zeus, mother of the Fates and goddess of Order. She was one of the few Titans who, after they had been overthrown by Zeus and the Olympian gods, was received into Olympos. She summons an assembly at *Iliad* 20.4–6.

80.   **dashed to the ground the scepter**: at *Iliad* 1.245–6, Achilles exploits the same gesture, in a towering rage. Though heroes often break down in tears at moments of high emotion (e.g. 16.213–9), the combination of Telemachos' tears (81) together with the gesture and the people's reaction (pity, 81) suggests a frustrated and immature young man. See Griffin *HLD* 12, Camps *IH* 19–21.

94–110.   **She set up . . . finish it**: Penelope is not simply the loyal, stay-at-home cipher. She has an Odyssean cunning about her, proposing one course of action but intending something quite different on a small scale (91–2) and on the large scale (the loom-trick here described esp. 106–7). For hiding intentions, see on 1.402–4.

100–2.   **lest any . . . wind him**: for fear of public disapproval, see on 2.64–5. Andromache (*Iliad* 22.508–15) laments the fact that she will never lay Hektor to rest in the shroud that awaits him.

108.   **one of her women**: see 19.154–5 for the tension between Penelope and some of her maids.

117.   **beautiful work**: for the honorific value of women's work, see 24.276–9 (note the abundance of woven goods said to have been given by Odysseus as gifts) and cf. 19.232–5 (and note), 3.346–51, 13.10, 5.38–9.

120.   **Tyro . . . Alkmene**: Tyro was ancestor of Nestor (by Poseidon) and of Jason (Argonaut saga) by Kretheus (see 11.235ff.). Alkmene was mother (by Zeus) of Herakles. Mykene, daughter of the river-god Inachos, gave her name to Mycenae. Antinoos' argument is awkward. If these women were not renowned for their intelligence, why compare them to Penelope? He must be making a point about fame: Penelope is, or will be, as famous as these great heroines (125–6) but for her *intellectual* capacity. Yet she is misusing it (122). For the value of such as Penelope, cf. *Iliad* 13.427–33.

135.   **furies**: the furies are goddesses whose especial concern is the punishment of family crimes. Such mysterious chthonic deities, who punish crime automatically, are a rare feature of Homeric epic, in which the more straightforward, no-nonsense Olympian gods play the major parts. Cf. on 15.234.

139–45.   **go away . . . given**: cf. 1.274, 374–80.

145.   **with no payment given**: i.e. unavenged.

146–154.   **So spoke . . . city**: the first of a number of omens presaging the death of the suitors. While there are very few complex omens in the *Iliad*, there is a number in Homer's *Odyssey*, often featuring predatory birds attacking more vulnerable ones. See e.g. 15.160ff., 19.535ff., 20.242ff. The simile at 22.302ff. recalls these omens. Zeus' intervention (146) shows the seriousness of the suitors' behaviour. See on 15.172, and A. Podlecki 'Omens in the *Odyssey*', *GR* 14, 1967.

157. **Halitherses**: he appears again briefly at 17.68 and 24.451ff.

162–7. **but what I . . . Ithaka**: assertions that Odysseus will return, and return soon, increase as Homer's *Odyssey* progresses. They are, naturally, never believed (2.181–4). See on 14.120, cf. 20.358–62. Odysseus is not actually near at the moment (165), but he soon will be if Zeus (who sent the omen, 146) is to be believed (1.76–9).

171–6. **Concerning him . . . accomplished**: another flashback to the time just before Odysseus departed for Troy. See on 17.293–4.

181–2. **many . . . anything**: the sentiment is not necessarily irreligious. Cf. *Iliad* 12.237–43, 24.218–24.

209–23. **Eurymachos . . . husband**: Telemachos, having ascertained the suitors' attitude to his house and his mother's hand, now fulfils the second part of Athene's instructions (cf. 1.280–92). Note his change of attitude at 223, compared with e.g. 130–7, where he says he will on no account ask his mother to leave the house: the difference is that, here, Telemachos is proposing a course of action on the assumption that Odysseus is dead.

225–7. **Mentor . . . him**: the only place where Mentor appears in his own person: elsewhere is he always Athene in disguise. The 'old man' of 227 should, one would have thought, have been Laertes (Odysseus' father): but, from the context, it looks as if he is Mentor, and Laertes plays little part in Homer's *Odyssey*, for reasons discussed at 1.188–93; 1.249–51. Against this interpretation, Mentor is not an 'old man' (227), but the same age as Odysseus (22.209, note).

239–41. **but now . . . many**: an important issue, which is never taken up seriously in the *Odyssey*, i.e. why the people as a whole do not take a stand on the destruction of their master's royal house. (Cf. Antinoos' fears at 16.376 ff., but these are not realised.) Mentor here picks up the case T. argued at 64–9.

244–51. **It would . . . many**: Leokritos is supremely confident of the suitors' military quality: even Odysseus would be at risk, should he return. Little does Leokritos know . . . (irony).

255. **messages**: i.e. about his father. Sarcastic.

2.260–434: Introduction

A. The second half of Book 2 gives further evidence that the suitors aim at more than merely a marriage for one of them to Penelope (335–6, cf. 367–8).

B. Telemachos himself rebuffs Antinoos' oily offer of reconciliation (310–20) with a threat (316) and takes control of preparations for the expedition, though Athene's help is always at hand (see notes on 382–434). Athene's call to him to become like his father (270–86) and the suitors' acknowledgement that he is capable of behaving like Odysseus (325–33) recall the *kleos* theme (see on 1.95), and at 373–5 Telemachos plans a deception of Penelope in a manner worthy of Odysseus himself. By the end of the book, we have a sense that Telemachos may, after all, be able to live up to the model provided by his father. But observe how cleverly Homer keeps the balance throughout the book between callow inexperience and adult potential (see *2.1–259B*). In this way Homer gives Telemachos his own particular interest in comparison with the real hero, Odysseus. He makes Telemachos' youth and inexperience, like Penelope's ambivalence, a central *issue* of the epic. Odysseus will return to a complex human situation, which cannot be automatically resolved merely by his presence or even the death of the suitors. Cf. *1.325–444C*.

C. Two questions arise here. If the suitors were so ruthless why did they simply not kill Telemachos, seize the property, and have done with it? Second, why does Athene encourage Telemachos on a journey when she knows all along that Odysseus is alive, and on the point of returning (cf. 3.15–16, 13.417–9)?

261.   **washed**: see on 3.460–3.

261–2.   **Athene . . . a god**: note how carefully Homer distinguishes between what he knows (Telemachos in *fact* is praying to Athene) and what the characters know (see on 1.1 'Muse'). Telemachos guessed at the identity of Athene the previous day (1.421–2), but had not *ascertained* it for certain. So Telemachos is careful not to mention any specific god by name here.

265–6.   **all this is delayed**: in what sense are the suitors delaying him? Presumably in that, though Telemachos had asked them to give him a ship (212), they had suggested others (presumably less powerful) should help him out (253). Leokritos himself had been very sarcastic about the chance of his success (255–6). So Telemachos has good reason to believe that they are all against his enterprise.

270–80.   **Telemachos . . . fulfilment**: Athene makes the success of Telemachos' journey conditional on him behaving like his father (271, 274 (cf. 1.215–6), 279). Odysseus is the model he must imitate if he is to gain *kleos* (cf. on 1.95, 1.207–43). Note especially 272: 'words and deeds' are the key to heroic stature. See 4.204–11, 818, 11.511–6, and cf. *Iliad* 2.342 and 9.443, where Phoinix says Achilleus was trained to be a speaker of words and doer of deeds. Note the ring-composition of 270–2/278–80.

282.   **just**: wrong translation. It means 'who act correctly', i.e. who observe common usage and custom. See on 14.84.

285–95.   **And . . . sea**: Athene's instructions plot the route of the narrative from here till the end of the book.

299–300.   **He . . . courtyard**: Homer consistently impresses upon us how wickedly the suitors destroy the house (see 281–4). So people often come upon them playing, drinking or eating. Cf. 1.106–112, 2.396, 4.625, *1.96–234C*.

301.   **with a smile**: does Antinoos mean his smile? Or his promise that the Achaians will produce a ship for Telemachos (306–8, cf. on 265–6)? Clearly not in Telemachos' view (to judge by 318–20) nor in Antinoos' (4.664). Here is another example of people saying one thing and meaning another.

305.   **with me**: wrong translation. read 'I beg you', 'please'.

306.   **Achaians**: see 253.

316–7.   **I will . . . district**: an important sub-plot. The suitors treat Telemachos' threat flippantly here (cf. 323 and see on 334). But when they learn of his secret departure at 4.634ff., Antinoos proposes to ambush him before things get out of hand (4.667–72; 776–86). Eurykleia foresees the danger at 2.367–8.

321.   **drew away**: a significant gesture. See on 2.80.

326–33.   **Either . . . Odysseus**: the suitors, like Athene, see something of Odysseus in Telemachos: an interest in poisons (cf. 1.255–64) and the possibility of his death at sea. Cf. 2.363–70.

334.   **he would lighten . . . us**: the translation is wrong. Read 'so he would all the more increase the labour for us' (sarcastic).

335–6.   **Then . . . her**: the threat confirms that the suitors want control of Odysseus' possessions, and Penelope is merely a means to that end. When Odysseus returns home, he will not be able to reclaim what is his: he will have to fight for it.

337–47.   **he went down . . . Peisenor**: Telemachos surveys part of the remaining wealth of his home, immediately after the suitors have threatened it (see on Penelope's store-room, 21.9). This wealth is Telemachos' personal inheritance.

339.   **olive oil**: an expensive item, used in Homer not for consumption but to anoint oneself after bathing. In Classical Greece, it was a staple of the economy used for food, lighting, heating and cooking.

340.   **jars**: if Homer means storage jars of the sort found in excavated Mycenaean palaces, these would be anything up to seven feet tall.

349–76.   **Dear nurse . . . weeping**: further evidence of the close relationship between Telemachos and his old nurse (cf. *1.325–444D*). But Eurykleia is also a slave, and so under Telemachos' authority. His mother would be able to exert considerable emotional pressure to prevent his departure (373–6). The intelligence of Eurykleia (346) is born out by her accurate prophecy at 367–8 (see 4.669–72).

354.   **barley**: by far the most important cereal in Ancient Greece (wheat production, to judge by the temple-contribution records, was about one eighth that of barley in Attica). Barley requires less rainfall to be viable.

382–434.   **Now . . . journey**: there is a clever contrast in this passage between the apparent authority of Telemachos (e.g. 409, 415, 422) and the hidden, guiding hand of Athene (382, 392–3, 399, 420). In particular, note how the goddess leads, and Telemachos follows (405–6, 416–8). Divine help, as usual enhances the hero, it does not diminish him. Telemachos is worthy of Athene's support (cf. on 1.307–8). In this respect also, Telemachos resembles his father. Cf. 3.218–24; Lord *SoT* 164.

397. **they went to sleep in the city**: wrong translation. Read 'they got up (to return) through the city (home) to sleep'. See on 1.424.

419. **oarlocks**: the Homeric ship was equipped to be rowed as well as to take advantage of any wind there might be (they hoist the sail when Athene sends the westerly Zephyros at 420). See diagram for details of 423–6. Cf. on 12.7.

432. **poured to the gods**: an outpouring of liquids to a god is a libation (usually wine, but honey, oil and water are also used). Libations are often accompanied by invocation to the god and prayers, especially at meal-times when the cup is passed round for this purpose (see e.g. 3.45–8). They are also common before journeys (13.54, 15.149, 15.258), last thing at night (7.136–8, 18.418–28) and to greet suppliants (7.179).

The Homeric Ship

A mast; B-B yard-arm; C-C sail; D, D straps, braces; E, E sheets; F, F forestays; G, G-G halyard (running parallel to the mast and fixed at its base); H-H backstay; I oar-blades; J rudder-oar; K stem, cutwater; L, L deck, deckboards, foredeck.

Book three

Introduction

A. For the first time Telemachos comes into contact with a world quite unlike that of Ithaka. It is a world of heroes who have returned from the Trojan War (Nestor in Book 3, Menelaos in 4); it is a world where the gods are fully honoured (5, 43–53, 337–341, 380–394, and most grandly of all 430–472) and their designs understood (147, 166, 173–4, 375–9); a world where the rights of *xenoi* are acknowledged (34ff.; 346–55). In these three respects it is a very different world from the one he has just left. This world presents Telemachos with a challenge, as he confesses to Athene (22–4), but he rises successfully to it, convincing Nestor that (i) he is the true son of Odysseus both in looks and speech (120–5; 199–200), and (ii) he is beloved of Athene (375–7), despite his (Telemachos') doubts on the matter (208–9, 226–8). If a great hero like Nestor can affirm that the youthful Telemachos is a true son of Odysseus, one of the purposes of Athene's intervention—that Telemachos should achieve *kleos* (see on 1.95, 207–43)—is already being achieved.

B. Nestor himself is characterised as a kindly, generous and pious ruler who continues to be as garrulous as he was in the *Iliad* (see on 184–5). This raises interesting questions about the relationship between the *Iliad* and the *Odyssey* (see on 106–17). No less interesting are the stories of the returns of the various Iliadic heroes, whom we now see in a different light from that cast on them by the martial *Iliad* (see on 1.11). Inevitably, Nestor brings up the Orestes parallel for Telemachos to ponder, and gives one version of Agamemnon's return (254–322). The one positive thing Telemachos does learn about Odysseus is that, after setting out for Ithaka, he elected to return to Agamemnon (162–4). This must have increased Telemachos' apprehension about Odysseus' fate.

C. The travels of Telemachos and Odysseus were compared by Eurykleia at 2.365–70. There is a basic difference, in that Telemachos *leaves* Ithaka in order to establish his identity, Odysseus must *return* there to do so (see on 1.13). The rituals of *xenia* ensure that there are a number of points of comparison between their adventures abroad, but the challenges which confront Odysseus are far more complex than those which Telemachos faces in what are friendly and welcoming settings.

1. **Helios**: i.e. the sun.
4. **Pylos**: we know of three towns called Pylos in the Peloponnese, and

27

ancient writers were not certain which one was the palace of Nestor, son of Neleus. The epithet 'sandy' (1.93 cf. 3.38) would best suit the Pylos on the coast in Messenia where a large Mycenaean palace has been excavated (15.209–10 imply the palace and beach are nearby). But it is extremely difficult to assign names to places on the testimony of oral epic, let alone to decide what the relationship between 'history' (which = 'archaeological sites' in this case) and epic actually is. It is quite possible that Homer had no idea where Pylos was. Cf. Finley *WO* 172–7 on 'Troy': *CH* 422–9. On Neleus, see 11.235–57.

6.   **Earthshaker**: i.e. Poseidon. Black victims were usually offered to gods of the earth cf. *Iliad* 3.103–4. (See on 1.68). The piety of the Pylians, especially of their king Nestor, stands in strong contrast to the wickedness of the suitors.

7–8.   **There were . . . holdings**: wrong translation. The Greek says 'there were nine seats/places/stations and five hundred people sat in each'. According to the *Iliad* (2.591–601), Nestor ruled nine cities. The sacrifice of 81 bulls (called a hecatomb, 59) is the largest mentioned in Homer (see on 1.25).

9.   **tasted**: for the details, see on 3.430–63.

12–13.   **Telemachos . . . to him**: note Athene's guiding role. Cf. 3.29–30, and on 2.382–434.

14–28.   **Telemachos . . . will**: it was a hero's job to speak as well as to perform well, and in *public* (cf. on 2.270–80 and on 1.95). Telemachos senses that the task he is being set of engaging publicly with Nestor, wisest and oldest of Greek champions from Troy (see 243–6), is beyond him ('embarrassment' = *aidōs*, cf. on 2.64–5). It seems clear we should read Telemachos' encounter with Nestor as a kind of 'test', which may bring him *kleos*. Cf. 3.75–8.

31–74.   **They came . . . people?**: a typical scene of *xenia* (see on 1.102 for the various stages). Note the warmth of the greeting (especially 34–9 where the stages become very confused), and cf. the suitors' disregard of Athene at 1.105–12. The libation element (40–64) is typical enough (see on 2.432). Here the poet inserts this element to develop a new 'route' within the *xenia* sequence. Note ring-composition: 4–9, 31–3. 19.414–27 exemplify a highly abbreviated *xenia* sequence.

36.   **Peisistratos**: he, the sixth of Nestor's sons (415), occurs in no other tradition as a son of Nestor. He *may* therefore be an invention of Homer, a youthful companion and counterpart to Telemachos (cf. 3.48–50) (see *CH* 206–11 for the secularisation of epic. For the pro-Corinthian propaganda Eumelos dispensed in his epics (late 8thC), see *CHCL* I, 108). Some have thought Peisistratos may have been inserted into the epic by the Athenian tyrant Peisistratos in the 6thC. There is evidence to suggest that Peisistratos took over the two Homeric epics (both composed on the Ionian coast) and made them Attic 'property' by standardising the text for recitation at Panhellenic (i.e. national, all-Greek) festivals in the 550's. Was Peisistratos manipulating *Homer* for political effect when he returned to power in Athens in a chariot accompanied by a female dressed up as Athene (Herodotus

1.60)? But Athene in the *Odyssey* travelled with Telemachos not Peisistratos. See Finley *WO* 36–40, *CH* 215–33 and on 1.1.

    38. **seashore**: they do not move to the palace till 386–7.

    42. **aegis**: see on 22.297.

    43. **Poseidon**: this god is the enemy of Odysseus (see 1.20–1), and Telemachos has been making his journey by sea. This gives added point to Athene and Telemachos' prayers at 60–4.

    52. **just**: wrong translation. The Greek means 'who acted properly', 'upright', 'correct'. Cf. on 2.282.

    68. **Gerenian**: 'from the town of Gerenia' (evidently in Messenia)? But no other Homeric hero was named after a town, let alone one where he did nothing glorious. 'Descendant of Gerenos'? Perhaps merely 'old'? Cf. *Iliad* 1.247–52.

    72–4. **recklessly . . . people**: it is important to note that Nestor does not directly accuse Telemachos and Athene of being pirates: he merely wonders if they are roving the seas without any particular destination in view, *in the way that* pirates do. Piracy was not discreditable in the Homeric world (see on 4.81–91).

    78. **good reputation**: = *kleos* (see on 1.95). 78, which does not appear in the best manuscripts, may be an interpolation, but the interpolator's instinct is surely right. For the first time, Telemachos speaks in public, outside his own territory, and before the fabled hero Nestor (cf. on 14–28).

    88. **son of Kronos**: i.e. Zeus.

    91. **Amphitrite**: in later Greek, the name of a sea-goddess, but in the *Odyssey*, it is used to = the sea.

    92. **to your knees**: this suggests that Telemachos may be supplicating Nestor, but the phrase *need* not have its full ritual implications. On this important institution, see 6.142.

    98–101. **if ever . . . truth**: (= 4.328–31). Telemachos asks for help not because of what he (Telemachos) has done, but because of what *his father* has done. For the first time, he lays personal claim to Odysseus' past. Cf. *Iliad* 5.115–7.

    106–12. **plunder . . . fighter**: for background, see *GI H*. Achilleus led the Greeks in many raids for plunder around Troy (*Iliad* 1.163–8). Aias (son of Telamon) committed suicide when the arms of the dead Achilleus, destined to be given to the best warrior, were voted to Odysseus (in the *Little Iliad*) (cf. 11.543–64). Antilochos, who registers the first 'kill' in the *Iliad* (4.457–62), died defending his father Nestor who was being attacked by Memnon (the story is told in the *Aithiopis*). It is interesting that, of all these deaths, the only one to occur in the *Iliad* is Patroklos', and its actual circumstances are not even hinted at here (the others occur in parts of the 'Epic Cycle': see *24D*). Page concluded from this that the *Odyssey* poet did not know the *Iliad*; others, more reasonably, that he intentionally avoids it— though he certainly nods to it.

    121–2. **cunning**: (Greek *mētis*). This characteristic of Odysseus is a major theme of Homer's *Odyssey*, since it is by cunning rather than by, for example, brute force that Odysseus survives. See *9H*.

124–5.   **For . . . him**: Nestor ratifies the *kleos* of Telemachos—he has passed his first test, showing himself in speech to be the true son of his father. Cf. on 3.14–28, 78, Neoptolemos at 11.509–11.

128–9.   **one . . . Argives**: cf. 11.511–2.

135.   **ruinous anger**: later writers say that the Gray-Eyed One (Athene) was angry because Aias from Lokris, son of Oileus, remained unpunished for raping Cassandra (daughter of Priam) at Athene's shrine in Troy. Homer may be referring obliquely to some religious crime at 133, and cf. 145. Menelaos tells the story of Aias son of Oileus at 4.499–511. But Homer is not especially forthcoming about the story. Since Odysseus was a favourite of Athene, it was in Homer's interest to suppress stories about Athene harassing the Greeks on the way back from Troy (Homer's villain of the piece is, of course, Poseidon). See Book I Appendix.

167.   **the son of Tydeus**: Diomedes, a great Greek warrior who enjoyed a tremendous feat of arms in *Iliad* 5, wounding both Aphrodite and Ares (with Athene's help).

171.   **Psyros**: read 'Psyra', or 'Psyria'.

174.   **middle main sea**: Greek sailors hugged the coast in as far as they could: crossings over open sea would be made as short as possible. Cf. 320–2.

184.   **without news**: after all that, no news! Typical, perhaps, of the vague but genial Nestor. But his speech is full of problems. (i) The Athene-Aias problem (see on 135), (ii) if Athene was the angry goddess (135, 145) why does Zeus take such an important part (132, 152, 160)? (iii) If Zeus was planning an evil homecoming (see (ii) and 166), why do all the Greeks that Nestor mentions get home? (iv) What has the quarrel at 136 to do with the anger of Athene? (v) What was the quarrel at 161? (vi) Why did Odysseus return (163)? If the answer to (iii) is that Agamemnon was murdered at home, why does Nestor suggest so frequently that the danger was at *sea* (e.g. 165–6)? All this is very opaque. It may be there are stories lying behind Nestor's well-known to the Greeks, but not to us; or Homer may be characterising Nestor as effusive but unclear. The general purpose of Nestor's words is clear—*some* heroes got home, but not without difficulties and dangers. See Huxley, *GE* 162ff. on other return-stories.

190.   **Philoktetes**: his invincible bow, a gift from Herakles, helped to take Troy. He is mentioned but once in the *Iliad* (2.716–28).

191.   **Idomeneus**: king of Crete. Though of great bravery (*Iliad* 13.206ff.) he does not play a major role in the *Iliad*. See on 14.237, *GI I*.

193–8.   **Atreides . . . father**: for the importance of the Aigisthos story, see *1.22–95A*.

199–200.   **I see . . . of you**: more *kleos* for Telemachos. He *looks* the part of a hero, a young man who could be an *alter*-Orestes. This is high praise from a man of the wide experience of Nestor.

205–9.   **If only . . . it**: Telemachos' pessimism, repeated (225–8, 241–2) and criticised by Athene at 230–1, is partly a hangover from Books 1–2; but Nestor has given him no cause for confidence, especially because he mentioned that O. went back to rejoin Agamemnon (162–4), about whose homecoming there were such dire predictions (145–6).

218–24. If only . . . marrying: cf. on 2.382–434. The irony is that Athene's unknown presence demonstrates her care. Athene does not noticeably favour Odysseus above e.g. Diomedes in the *Iliad*: Homer may be relying on other traditions, or giving Nestor a sentiment fitted to the particular occasion.

243–6. But now . . . upon: compare Telemachos' confidence here with his initial modesty at the thought of addressing Nestor at 22–4.

244. the righteousness: wrong translation. Read 'his ability to settle issues'.

265–72. Now in time . . . he was: Homer has problems with Klytaimestra. If Aigisthos–Orestes is to act as a paradigm for suitors-Telemachos, where can Klytaimestra fit in? She can hardly = Penelope! Furthermore, everyone knew that Orestes, having killed Aigisthos, slew his mother too (see the evasive 309–10). Homer redevelops the myth to suit his theme. See on 11.409, and Willcock *CQ* 1964. Observe how Homer protects the singer commanded to guard Klytaimestra (see on 1.153–5). Penelope needed no such chaperon when Odysseus left.

279–80. there . . . arrows: see on 15.411.

288. Maleia: storms typically occur here. See on 9.80.

301. gathering: see 4.81–91.

307. Athens: according to classical writers, Orestes was exiled in Phokis, not Athens. Homer may be offering us an alternative here; or the right reading may be 'from Athene', who, according to Aeschylus' *Eumenides*, turned out to be Orestes' protectress.

309. grave mound: wrong translation. Read 'funeral feast'; cf. *Iliad* 23.29.

321. an open sea: the journey from S. Greece (288) via Crete (291) to Egypt (300) is full of danger, according to Nestor. For Odysseus, in a false tale, it was very easy (14.252–8).

323. with your ship: this would have been the natural way to travel. See on 3.488.

332. cut out the tongues: the final offering cut from the victim to be burnt.

340. after they . . . goblets: wrong translation. Read 'after they had poured a few drops (for the libation) into the cups'.

356–70. Then . . . runners: an important moment. From now on, Telemachos is on his own.

371–2. in the likeness of a vulture: the Greek could mean that Athene changed into a vulture, or that she departed in the way that a vulture would (i.e. swiftly, cf. 1.320). The first interpretation seems better to account for the amazed reaction of 372–3 and Nestor's exclamation at 375–84. But it is odd that Athene, having invented a natural reason why she should not spend the night with Nestor (357–70), should then change herself into a vulture and flap off.

375–7. Dear . . . thus: cf. 223–4. Nestor now has proof that Telemachos' pessimism (208–9, 226–8) is wholly unfounded. It is clear to him that Athene is honouring Telemachos as much as she did Odysseus. This means *kleos* for Telemachos; and Nestor goes on to pray that his sacrifice may result in *kleos* for him too (380).

378.   **Tritogeneia**: 'Triton-born', an epithet applied only to Athene. Its significance is not clear.

399.   **corded**: see on 1.440.

413–5.   **Echephron . . . Peisistratos**: each son has a special function to perform during the sacrifice (see 439–54).

430–63.   **The cow . . . pieces**: the most detailed sacrificial offering in Homer (cf. *Iliad* 1.458–71). The poet is not compelled to extend this typical scene of sacrifice to such length. The fact that he chooses so to do suggests he is underlining the piety and generosity of Nestor (cf. 12.336, 355–96 (and notes); 14.418–38 (and notes)). The following note partly summarises Burkert *GR* 56–7. Piety is defined by sacrifice, libation (see on 2.432) and first-fruit offerings (see on 14.423). No priest is needed for such acts to be duly performed. Since ill words may not accompany a sacrifice, a holy silence is maintained by those who play no other part in the ceremony. First the animal is prepared (437–8). There is a procession to the *temenos* (a sacred area, laid aside for this use) and the altar (gods are not worshipped in temples in ancient Greece, but at altars outside them. The gods *live* in the temples) (439–40). Lustral water is carried around to purify participants (*Iliad* 6.266–8) and mark out the area of sacrifice (440–1). Barley is brought in baskets and ritually thrown at the animal prior to its death (441–2, 447). Hair is then cut off it and burnt (446); the beast is slaughtered (449–54), and the outcry is raised by the women (452—the climax of the ritual). The blood is collected (444, 455), and the beast is then cut up. First, the entrails, thigh bones and inedible parts are cooked and offered to the gods (the entrails are tasted) (455–61); then the good meat is 'kebab-ed' and eaten (462–3, 470–2). Since the most common animals in Greece are sheep and goats (which provide milk, butter, cheese and wool) a sacrifice would be a rare chance to eat beef. Sacrifice brings man and gods together. The gods are pleased to have humans lay aside food for their use (cf. on 1.61), though gods are free to reject offerings (*Iliad* 8.545–52). Note that man gets the edible parts. This useful practice was justified with reference to the myth of Prometheus, who tricked Zeus into accepting from man at the first sacrificial offering the larger bag, full of bones and fat, rather than the smaller, full of prime beef.

Features which appear in Classical Greek religion, e.g. fertility rites, orgiastic cults and cults of the dead, are entirely absent from Homer.

432.   **the smith**: on metal-working, see on 9.392, 393.

463.   **and . . . pieces**: wrong translation. Read 'and roasted them, holding sharp-pointed spits in their hands'.

464–7.   **Polykaste . . . about him**: it is commonplace in Homer for men to be bathed by women, cf. 4.49, 8.454, 17.88 etc., and baths often precede meals. Being anointed with olive oil *after* a bath rather resembles putting hair cream on newly washed hair. At 467, Polykaste must have put the tunic on first and then the mantle, but Homer often puts second things first (*husteron* ('later') *proteron* ('earlier'), as this characteristic feature is called). Observe that Telemachos is anointed and dressed *before* he leaves the bath. It must have had a 'plug'.

479. **put bread and wine in**: it is normal at the end of *xenia* to give gifts to the parting guest. But Nestor expects Telemachos and his son Peisistratos to return after their visit to Menelaos. In the event, Telemachos will avoid Nestor on his return home (15.193–219).

488. **Pherai . . . Diokles**: Pherai, perhaps modern Calamata in Messenia, must be a one-day run from Pylos (486–7). See on 21.15. The Pherai-Sparta run also lasts one day (495–7), but geographical inconsistencies stand out. First, the vehicle is scarcely designed for long-distance travel. Second, Homer says nothing of the mighty Taygetos range which would have to be crossed on the Pherai-Sparta run. Third, the terrain is so rough it could hardly bear wheat (495). On top of this, it seems strange that this journey should be undertaken by land, when there was the option of going by sea (323, 368–70). The reason may be that, in some tellings of the story, Homer made more of the visit to Diokles (*xenia*, questions, etc.) than he does here. See *Iliad* 5.541–9.

489. **Alpheios**: the river (here personified as a river god) which rises 60kms north-east of Pherai.

Book four

4.1–624: Introduction

A. First, Telemachos travels without his divine helper Athene, though with Nestor's son Peisistratos (cf. 3.368–70), who introduces and prompts Telemachos at 4.156–7 cf. Athene at 3.76–7. But Telemachos is able to stand on his own two feet and find ratification of the *kleos* which Nestor has bestowed on him (see e.g. 140–54, 611). See further on 13.422, *16C, 24A*. It is doubtful whether Telemachos 'learns' about *xenia* rituals in this book. He has already shown (in Book 1) that he is well acquainted with them.

B. Second, we are introduced to another hero who, like Nestor, has returned from the Trojan War, but who has himself experienced the grief of loss (of his brother Agamemnon as well as of Odysseus (90–112)). This makes Menelaos especially sympathetic to Telemachos' cause.

C. Menelaos himself is characterised by his quasi-divine wealth (e.g. 71–5, 79–91) and by his wide-ranging travels around the Mediterranean after Troy, especially to Egypt (e.g. 81ff., 351ff., cf. Helen at 226–32). The story of his fabulous encounter with Proteus makes the fabulous adventures of Odysseus in e.g. Books 9–12 less out of the ordinary. Cf. Nestor's more prosaic account. In the course of the Proteus story, Telemachos does eventually get firm news of his father (555–60): the reason why it should be so disappointingly thin is discussed *ad loc*. Menelaos' adventures have borne in strongly upon Menelaos the need to care for *xenoi* (31–6), an important theme of the *Odyssey* (cf. his generosity at 587–619).

D. Third, we meet Helen, Menelaos' wife, whose elopement with Paris caused the Trojan War. She is as self-critical here as she is in the *Iliad* (e.g. 4.145, 261), but some have seen signs of latent tension between her and Menelaos at e.g. 274–89 and others have wondered if her use of 'drugs' at 220ff. is supposed to be sinister (but see 228 and see on 15.126).

E. Finally, we hear from Menelaos and Helen the first of a number of tales we shall hear about Odysseus' exploits in the Trojan War: they give firsthand testimony to two of his most important qualities—his capacity to disguise himself (244ff.) and to control himself and others (271–89) (see Austin *ADM* 188–90).

F. The constant references to Egypt and to travel around known parts of the Mediterranean raise questions about Homer's geographical knowledge—

which seems confused (see on 125–33, 355–7)—and the origins of such tales. Contact between Greeks and Egypt virtually ceased after the Mycenaean age and was not restored till Ionians and Carians, on a raid into Egypt, were hired by King Psammetichus to bring him to power (c.650: see Herodotus 2.152ff.). Egyptian tales may reflect a Mycenaean tradition, but it is surely more likely that they are contemporary (see *GI E*).

G. The poet does not exploit one possible 'route' open to him—a visit by Telemachos to Ikarios, the Spartan father of Penelope (see 2.50–4, 132–3).

1–14.   **They came . . . golden**: Menelaos is apparently giving a feast (3–4) both for his daughter Hermione (12–14), (whom he is sending off to marry Neoptolemos, son of Achilleus (4–10)), and for his son, Megapenthes, whom he is marrying to the daughter of Alektor (10–12). Observe the absolute control over marriage exerted by the father of the family; and the production of heirs through female slaves (11–12) when one's wife became infertile (12–14) cf. 14.203–4, 1.428–35. This rich social and family occasion is entirely forgotten when Telemachos arrives, (which has made some doubt its authenticity), but it offers a vision of community life quite alien to Telemachos, who struggles alone against the suitors, sons of local Ithakan gentry (see e.g. 2.62–79).

9.   **Myrmidons**: Achilleus led a contingent of Myrmidons from his home in Phthia (Thessaly) to Troy (*Iliad* 2.681–5).

15–16.   **neighbours . . . house**: ring-composition with 3–4.

17–19.   **singer . . . them**: note that the singer seems to be accompanied by dancers and acrobats. Did they 'act out' the story the singer was telling? Cf. on 8.263. For music and dance at a wedding, see *Iliad* 18.491–6, cf. *Iliad* 18.593–605.

27.   **like the breed of . . . Zeus**: cf. 62–4. More unprompted *kleos* for Telemachos (with Peisistratos)—he *looks* to be of noble family.

31–4.   **Eteoneus . . . here**: the laws of *xenia* are as important to Menelaos as they were to Nestor. Even in the middle of a wedding feast, Menelaos remembers his duty to strangers. For the structure of welcoming scenes, see on 1.102. This 'anger' element is typical (1.119), but developed differently here than in Book 1.

34–5.   **May Zeus . . . hereafter**: this hardly makes sense. The Greek translates literally 'if ever in the future Zeus should stop misery', and possibly (?) acts as a 'crossed fingers' hope, i.e. 'we have got back home after all our travels, and let us hope that our miseries are finally at an end'.

39–58.   **They set . . . goblets**: Homer has some purpose in choosing to describe in such typical detail horses and their diet, humans and theirs, the divine city of the palace (whose shining is explained at 71–3), hot baths and hand-washing routines. This is the tone and quality of life in the home of a hero like Menelaos.

41.   **millet**: 'barley' is the more usual translation.

66.   **choice portion**: see on 14.437.

71–5.   **look at . . . on it**: Homer indicated the unique nature of Menelaos' palace at 43, where he called it 'divine', a description applied to no other human dwelling. For the new 'wonder' element in arrival scenes (44, 75), see e.g. 5.75, 7.43, 133—and most movingly, 17.263–71, where Odysseus finally arrives back at his own palace in Ithaka.

73.   **amber**: the Greek word is *ēlektron*, which can mean 'gold-silver alloy', but 'amber', a fossil resin, is better, giving a contrasting balance to the palace (gold-silver, ivory-amber) which complements the sun-moon contrast at 45. Our 'electricity' derives from the properties of attraction which amber possesses (Thales, the 7thC Greek 'natural scientist' observed this characteristic). Beads of amber (bought from the Baltic?) were found in the 16thC 'Shaft graves' in Mycenae (*CH* 503). Amber has not been found widely in 10–9thC Greece, but became common in the 8thC. So this is probably another contemporary reference (*GI E*). Cf. 15.454–60.

ivory: ivory plaques and statuettes are known from the Bronze Age. Phoenicians traded in ivory, getting it from Syrian elephants.

78–81.   **there is . . . none**: Menelaos is quite prepared to believe he is the richest of *men*, but no sensible Greek challenged the gods, whose wrathful envy would at once be incurred. Cf. *Iliad* 5.440–2, *Odyssey* 13.143–4.

81–91.   **Much did I . . . property**: travelling and collecting wealth by *xenia* or raiding (not trade: see on 8.163) were respectable aristocratic pastimes in the Homeric world (though it is not surprising that non-aristocrats like Eumaios should condemn it, 14.85–7). Cf. 15.79–85, 19.282–6; *Iliad* 11.669–83, 18.509–40. For Menelaos' journey from Troy and late arrival home, see 3.276–312.

84.   **Aithiopians . . . Sidonians**: for Aithiopians, see on 1.22. The Eremboi cannot be firmly identified (Strabo 1.1.3 puts them by the Red Sea). Sidonians came from Sidon. See *CH* 307–8 for the 'geography' of Menelaos' adventures.

85–9.   **Three times . . . sucklings**: traveller's tales of this sort abound in the *Odyssey*. The fantasy of a land flowing with milk, cheese and meat must have been especially appealing to Greeks, whose soil generally offered thin pasturing to animals. Cf. on 7.84. The average gestation period for a sheep is about 5 months.

91–2.   **another man . . . treachery**: this refers to Aigisthos' murder of Agamemnon with the help of Klytaimestra. See 4.512–537.

95.   **destroyed a household**: whose household? Since Menelaos' tone here is resolutely gloomy, it seems unlikely that he is referring to the triumphant sack of Troy. Presumably he refers to the way in which his own household became run down during his 18-year absence from it (though we have no other evidence for this in myth and he has clearly made up for it handsomely through his extensive travels).

106–7.   **no-one . . . Odysseus**: the *Odyssey* is full of such ironical 'throwaway' remarks, whose significance is lost on the speaker but not on the listener—or the audience. Cf. 112 and *1.96–324E*.

112. **a young child**: an important point. If Telemachos was newly born when Odysseus left for Troy (11.447–9), he will now be twenty (i.e. on the threshold of manhood) and he will *never have known his father*. As a result, their eventual meeting will be that much more full of pathos (16.213–21): but it means that Odysseus has to be away for ten more years after the ten-year Trojan War in order to 'allow' Telemachos to grow up and play the part he does in the *Odyssey*.

114. **tears**: heroes in Homer are not usually ashamed to weep. Cf. e.g. 183–88, 539–41, 8.83–92 (where Odysseus' gesture is the same as Telemachos' here), and most famously *Iliad* 24.507ff.

116. **it**: wrong translation. Read 'him'. Menelaos has now recognised Telemachos (118, 148–54).

121. **Helen**: the woman who started the Trojan War by abandoning her husband Menelaos and running off with Paris to Troy. It is arguable whether any tensions remain between Helen and Menelaos from those traumatic (cf. 97–112) years (on the opacity of character in the *Odyssey*, see Griffin *HLD* 76–80). Observe that Helen is likened to Artemis, goddess of *chastity* (as is Penelope 17.37). In the *Iliad*, Menelaos' fidelity is emphasised by the fact that he is never protrayed sleeping with slave-girls. Helen is engaged in the traditional wifely activity of spinning (131–5). Note also her (sincere? complacent?) self-castigation at 145 and 259–64.

122. **distaff**: the word used (*ēlakatē*) can mean 'distaff' or 'spindle'. The unworked wool was fixed onto a distaff and drawn into a thread through the fingers and even teeth (to pick out knots and lumps). A spindle was attached onto the end of the thread. It was round this that the thread was wound. Since Homer talks of the *ēlakatē* being twisted, it seems more likely that it means 'spindle' rather than distaff here (see e.g. 6.53, 7.105).

125–33. **Phylo . . . beside her**: a small digression (note ring-composition 125/132–7) on the gifts given to Helen and Menelaos by the Egyptians Polybos and Alkandre (both perfectly good Greek names), in Egyptian Thebes, fabled for its wealth (*Iliad* 9.382–4). (The Egyptians called it Wise; it is modern Luxor and is nearly 400 miles inland on the Nile. One wonders what Menelaos was doing there.) The only authentic Egyptian name in Book 4 is Thon (228). Such references are often used in combination with archaeological evidence to try to date the *Odyssey* or to cast light on Greek movements about the Mediterranean (e.g. 8thC colonisation), but the results have to be extremely hypothetical. See *GI E*, and Kirk *SoH* 110–11.

141–45. **I never saw . . . that man**: more *kleos* for Telemachos, which will be ratified by Menelaos further at 147–54. One wonders *how* Helen knew what Telemachos looked like, but presumably Homer has compressed her reasoning, missing out the step 'since this man looks like Odysseus, he must be the son of Odysseus'.

158–60. **modest . . . of you**: cf. 3.13–28 for the theme of Telemachos' modesty and care in speaking before the great heroes of Troy who knew his father.

171. **he**: i.e. Odysseus.

174–7.   I would have . . . lordship: this seems a somewhat drastic way of expressing a friendship, but there is no reason to believe Odysseus would have agreed, or even that it was in any way considered practicable. Menelaos is here simply expressing his love of Odysseus in the most exaggerated terms that he can. Given such friendship, it may seem strange that Menelaos does not volunteer to return to Ithaka with Telemachos and kill the suitors (cf. 4.345–6). But the poet cannot afford to take that route in a tale in which Odysseus is to be the returning, avenging hero.

187.   Antilochos: 3.111–12, 11.467–9, and cf. 24.78–9.

194–5.   There will always . . . tomorrow: i.e. for lamentation. Peisistratos is making the point that dinner is a time to be happy (cf. 9.10–13).

194.   after dinnertime: but it is clear from 218 that the meal is not over. The Greek could mean 'during dinner'. If we accept that meaning, we must see 68 (cf. 61) as a natural stopping point for questions in the course of the meal.

204–11.   Dear . . . work: cf. on 2.270–80.

226–32.   Such were . . . Paieon: more stories about Egypt. Since there is evidence that Egyptians may have imported opium from Cyprus, it is possible that the 'drug' referred to is that. But Egyptians had a reputation for adding foreign substances to their drinks, and there is no need to assume it is opium, let alone that the party relapses into a drug-induced stupor (the text offers no evidence of that at all). The association between Helen and Egypt reminds us that Herodotus (2.113ff.) and others argued that Helen did not in fact go to Troy. Her 'image' went there, but she herself was removed to Egypt. Menelaos came back with the 'image', which disappeared when he found the real Helen on his travels back home (see Euripides' *Helen*).

231–2.   doctor: for Egyptian doctors, see Herodotus 2.77, 84. Paieon means 'healer', and is used of the gods' doctor (*Iliad* 5.410). Only in post-Homeric literature does the term become attached specifically to the healer-god Apollo.

244–64.   He flagellated . . . beauty: a story of Odysseus at Troy which appears nowhere in the *Iliad* (cf. on 3.106–12). Since it is a story of disguise (247), recognition (250) and craft (251), it fits Odysseus perfectly (cf. e.g. Odysseus' disguise as a beggar in Books 14–22, and his recognition by Eurykleia at 19.386ff., which happens during a footwash, cf. 252). For Odysseus' intelligent mistrust of Helen, cf. 5.171–9; 10.336–47; 13.250–5.

261–2.   madness . . . bestowed: early Greeks commonly describe the passions and emotions as external forces which descend on man to leave him powerless in their grip cf. 23.222–4. Aphrodite is goddess of sexual activity.

270.   enduring: while Helen's story witnessed to Odysseus' crafty deceptiveness, Menelaos concentrates on his capacity to *endure* ('much-enduring' is a common epithet for Odysseus). The two qualities work well in harness. The man of craft will often need to play a waiting game, as here, if he is to succeed. Odysseus thought up the deception of the Wooden Horse in the first place (8.492–5). See on *mētis*, 9H.

274–5.   you . . . spirit: is Menelaos accusing Helen here? Or is he taking the blame off her by saying some divine spirit must have moved her? Surely the latter.

276. **Deiphobos**: see on 8.518.

279. **made . . . Argives**: very odd. Why should the Greeks in the horse imagine their wives were in Troy? One wonders how Helen learnt this skill and how she knew which voices to imitate. But Helen's purpose is to ascertain if there are any Greeks inside the horse. How can she do that *from the outside*? Shock tactics are required—and hers certainly come within an ace of success (282).

280. **son of Tydeus**: Diomedes (282).

292–3. **none . . . him**: this praise of Odysseus' *past* greatness stirs the pessimism in Telemachos again (cf. 3.208–228).

293. **iron**: see on 9.392, 393.

296–310. **So he spoke . . . presence**: typical scenes of going to bed and getting up. Cf. 1.434–9; 3.397–403; 20.124–6; 23.288–94.

307. **War-cry**: formulaic. See on 22.81.

318–21. **eaten away . . . rapacity**: observe that Telemachos wants rid of the suitors not because they are wooing Penelope but because they are destroying his substance.

323. **destruction**: Telemachos' pessimism continues—he assumes that Odysseus is dead. Cf. on 292–3 and 3.96–101.

335–40. **As when . . . men**: the first developed simile in the *Odyssey*. Odysseus = the lion, the suitors = the fawns, but who is their mother? As often in similes, Homer has other purposes than creating exact correspondences (contrast Virgil, who goes to great pains to ensure that correspondences are exact).

339. **both mother and children**: the Greek says 'both'. Read 'both fawns'. There was a tradition that does produce twins. Mother is not killed (she is away grazing (337–8)).

343. **Philomeleides**: a king of Lesbos, who challenged all-comers. Odysseus' prowess at fighting/boxing will be demonstrated when he defeats the beggar Iros (18.95–107).

351. **Egypt**: Menelaos continues his story at the point where Nestor left it (3.300). Homer's *Odyssey* is full of such stories within the story (e.g. 491–537), cf. Nestor's tales in Book 3, Helen's in 4, Odysseus' story in Books 9–12. Since the action of the *Odyssey* takes place ten years after Troy's fall (see 9A), personal reminiscences are the only way in which Homer can present the stories of the heroes' past failures and triumphs. Frequently past suffering is directly contrasted with present happiness (cf. 15.398–401 and implicitly at 9.1–15). But what lies in the past for heroes like Menelaos lies in the future for Odysseus, if he can win through. Others' successes whet our anticipation of Odysseus' even more gloriously triumphant return, which will be no reminiscence, but will happen 'before our very eyes'.

Menelaos' story here is important because it provides evidence that fabulous adventures in exotic places involving strange monsters are not out-of-the-ordinary for returning heroes. Menelaos' story to that extent prepares us for Odysseus'.

There are interesting comparisons between Menelaos' tale of Proteus and Odysseus' visit to Teiresias in the Underworld in Book 11. Both Menelaos and Odysseus are on an island; both are advised by supernatural women to seek help from seers; both have to go through a ritual; the seers give them the help required and prophesy their deaths. See Lord *SoT* 165–9; W.F. Hansen, *The Conference Sequence*, University of California Publications in Classical Philology 8, 1972. Both attempt to explain some of the oddities in the stories of Teiresias with reference to the difficulty the poet faces in fitting a typical 'conference' sequence into a context for which it was not precisely suited.

355–7.   **Pharos . . . onward**: Homer's ignorance of, or lack of concern for, geography is shown here: Pharos, the island where Ptolemy II built the famous lighthouse, is less than a mile off the coast (cf. on 4.125–33).

368.   **fishing**: the food of heroes in epic is traditionally roast meat, not fish. But there is plenty of archaeological evidence that fish were consumed in large quantities in e.g. Mycenae. Homer's disdainful references to fish reflect the values of a supposed heroic society, not of the real world. See on 1.108, 19.109, cf. 12.327–32. See *CH* 523–30.

386.   **underthegn**: = under-thane (Anglo-Saxon spelling, for some reason). The Greek means 'servant, underling'.

404.   **The sea's lovely lady**: this term is applied to Thetis in the *Iliad* (20.207), but it could refer to Amphitrite (see on 3.91).

439–47.   **Thereupon . . . spirit**: humorous lines. This is indeed a different world from that of the *Iliad* (see on 351).

445.   **ambrosia**: see on 5.93.

472.   **sacrifices**: the ones Nestor refers to at 3.141–6?

478.   **sky-fallen**: very disputed. 'Sent from Zeus'? 'Flowing at Zeus's command'? Perhaps 'divine' is the safest translation. The river is, of course, the Nile.

496–7.   **two . . . home**: these lines refer to Lokrian Aias and Agamemnon, while 498–9 refer to Odysseus.

499.   **Aias**: i.e. son of Oileus (Lokrian Aias), who caused Athene's anger (502) by raping Cassandra at her shrine in Troy. See on 3.135 for the problems this causes Homer. See *Iliad* 23.473–89 for Aias' (son of Oileus) stubborn abusiveness.

501.   **Gyrai**: ancient writers identified Gyrai variously with Mykonos, Tenos and the s.e. Euboean promontory Cape Caphereios.

515.   **Maleia**: more very strange geography. If Agamemnon lives in Mycenae, what on earth is he doing sailing around Maleia, on the s.e. tip of the Peloponnese? But (as the line-numbering shows) this passage is as confused as the winds which randomly blow Agamemnon here and there. But the outcome is that Agamemnon arrives not in his palace but on the estate of Aigisthos—and is there despatched (535). In his version at 11.405–26, Agamemnon emphasises Klytaimestra's role, so that he can draw the comparison with Penelope. Homer, like all Greek writers, uses and adapts myths to his own purposes. There is no such thing as a fixed, 'received' version. For Aigisthos, see *1.22–95 A*.

520. **made the homeland**: i.e. reached home.

527–8. **and mindful/of his furious valour**: the Greek says 'and be mindful
. . .', i.e. so that Agamemnon would not get into the palace unnoticed and,
discovering Aigisthos's liaison with Klytaimestra, summon up his fighting
spirit to take revenge.

537. **nor one of Aigisthos' men**: the poet is indicating that a tremendous
struggle took place between the two opposing forces.

555–60. **That was . . . ridges**: News of Odysseus for Telemachos (cf.
1.195–99) — if not for the reader, of course (see 1.13–15). Proteus does not
indicate that Odysseus will actually return, but this has its purpose — it will
make the meeting of Odysseus and Telemachos in Book 16 that much more
exciting (16.156–219).

561–70. **But for you . . . Zeus**: Menelaos is to be rewarded with an after-
life in Elysium (the Greek 'paradise') not for any exceptional goodness
or piety, but because he is married to the Zeus-born Helen (569–70).
Achilleus, Agamemnon, Aias and others end up in Hades (see Book 11). Cf.
Odysseus' death foretold by Teiresias at 11.119–37. Compare the description of Elysium with that of Olympos at 6.43–5, and cf. Hesiod *WD* 167ff. In
the absence of firm doctrine on the subject of the after-life there are almost as
many different accounts as there are authors.

564. **Rhadamanthys**: son of Zeus and Europa. In later literature he is the
wise judge of the dead (e.g. Plato *Apology* 41a).

567. **Ocean**: see on 23.244.

582. **stranded**: i.e. brought to the strand, beached.

589–92. **give you . . . do so**: gift-giving is an essential part of *xenia*. The
value of the gifts reflects the greatness of the giver just as much as the respect
he has for his guest (613–4). The gifts act as a bond of obligation between the
two, and remind the guest of his duty to reciprocate should the host ever
require his help. The bond of obligation passes on down the generations. Cf.
the famous incident in *Iliad* 6.119ff., where the Greek Diomedes and the
Trojan Glaukos stop fighting and exchange their armour because they find
they have a link of *xenia* in their past family histories. See references at
1.309–18. For a typical departure sequence, see on 1.303–19.

590. **three horses**: two to pull the chariot and one to act as a trace-horse
(the 'spare'). Cf. *Iliad* 16.145–54, 562–75.

600. **stored up**: gifts (see above) are not 'used': they are put away, stored,
until they can be given again (617–9), or displayed.

605–8. **Ithaka . . . others**: see 13.241–9, and notes.

611. **true blood**: *kleos* again for Telemachos.

617. **Hephaistos**: god of metal work (8.272–5). He constructed the
magnificent shield of Achilleus (*Iliad* 18.477ff.). Menelaos visited the
Sidonians on his travels (84).

4.625–847: Introduction

A. The transition back to Ithaka may be abrupt (Page *HO* 69), but it is absolutely essential that, before turning to Odysseus, the poet brings us up to date with the situation in Ithaka. For this is the reason why Odysseus' return is so desperately required, and this is what he will be returning to. Three themes dominate this section: the murderous intentions of the suitors (e.g. 672, 771, 843), the isolation and helplessness of Penelope, and the importance of Telemachos to her now that he is gone on a mission for which she does not consider him prepared (818). But at least she (and we) are reassured by Athene's promise to her at 825–9.

B. As we have seen, Penelope's appearances follow a pattern: an entry, often with servants, a series of complaints, rejection, departure in grief, and a reaction from the suitors (see *1.325–444A*). This structure cannot but stress the negative aspect of Penelope's character, her weakness and dependence. Homer counterbalances this through the assertions of others, especially the suitors, about her worth: she is desirable (1.365–6), beautiful, faithful and intelligent (2.87–128). The scene in Book 4 brings to the fore another important feature of Penelope's characterisation: the world of sleep and dreams to which she constantly resorts (793–841). Penelope is a woman under pressure, from both her son Telemachos and the suitors, and her dream-world is her only escape. In her dreams she envisages her husband as a legendary, hero-figure but irrevocably of the past (814–6). Her real concern is now for her son Telemachos, the only person left to her (817–29). The outlines of the typical Penelope-pattern are faintly discernible. In particular, Penelope's unmotivated attack on Medon (see on 686–95) may be generated by association with the moment when Penelope launches a series of complaints; the suitors' odd response to her prayers (see on 768–77) may also be associated with the moment in the typical pattern when the suitors 'react'. For further 'associative' slips, see on 16.108–9, 21.132–3.

625.   **but meanwhile**: a sudden change of scene, back to the suitors in Ithaka. We shall pick up Telemachos again at Book 15, and Menelaos will give him the Sidonian mixing bowl at 15.115–9. By this means the poet creates the impression that Odysseus' adventures are happening at the time Telemachos' adventures in the Peloponnese are taking place. The poet's normal rule is to depict all events *as if they are happening successively*. Since Telemachos wants to get back at once (4.594), but Odysseus' adventures in Books 5–14 will take about a month, the poet uses this means to create the illusion that the adventures are taking place simultaneously. See Page *HO* 78–9.

628–9.   **godlike . . . best**: 'godlike' means merely 'handsome', whilst 'best' indicates here 'leading, chief'.

630.   **Noëmon**: see 2.386.

637. **mules**: these may seem unromantic animals but (with oxen) they are the main draught-animals of the ancient world. Horses could only pull light weights, since efficient halters had not been invented for them. For keeping animals on the mainland, cf. 14.100–2. Ithaka was unsuitable for such breeding (605).

640. **the swineherd**: this is Eumaios, who will play quite an important part from Books 14 onwards. The fact that he is not named here suggests his part in the epic was well-known.

648. **son of Noëmon**: wrong translation. Read 'Noëmon, son of Phronios'.

656. **before**: i.e. four days ago when Mentor/Athene had gone off to Pylos with Telemachos (653).

659. **stopped their contests**: since one gets the impression that nothing could stop the suitors having their fun, Noëmon's news must have struck them as especially sinister. Telemachos must, after all, be taken seriously (cf. 2.323–36).

671. **Samos**: = Same = Kephallenia (see on 9.25).

677. **the herald**: in Homeric epic the herald has a number of functions — among them serving at table (see on 8.8). Medon seems to have been a sort of major domo, to judge from 17.172–6, and was certainly a valued member of Odysseus' household since Telemachos was a child (22.357–74).

684–5. **Could this . . . reason?**: the syntax of this line in Greek is very awkward, but Lattimore's translation is not satisfactory: the meaning is literally 'May this be the last and final time they dine here, not wooing (me) or consorting again' (cf. the prayer of the grinding woman at 20.116–9).

686–95. **You . . . done you**: these harsh words seem directed at Medon. But he is only keeping Penelope in the picture (see on 677). Perhaps they are supposed to indicate how overwrought Penelope is, being unable to distinguish friend from foe; perhaps they are the result of association with the typical Penelope pattern (see *4.625–827B*). Medon is careful to distance himself from the suitors in his reply at 698–9.

708. **horses**: since Homeric heroes hardly ever ride horses, 'chariots' would be a better translation (cf. for the image, 13.81–5).

712–3. **I do not . . . Pylos**: action could be prompted by a god, some inexplicable external force (like desire, or blind recklessness, see 4.261) or one's own rational (or irrational) decision. (Greeks have a shadowy concept of 'will', i.e. apparently unmotivated volition or impulse to act, though *menos*, 'determination', (1.321) comes near it. Greeks usually act as they do for *explicit* reasons.) Whatever the cause of an action is — and Greeks often ascribe it to a man *and* a god at the same time (see on 22.347) — a constant feature of Homeric psychology is that the plan and the deed are virtually inseparable: once a deed is planned, it is done (the Greek 'plan' (*mēdomai*) also means 'achieve'). This gives an uncomplicated and natural liveliness to the characters, and turns conscious deception into an unheroic trait (cf. on 1.402–4). See 17A, and *Iliad* 9.308–13 for Achilleus' hatred of deception.

716–7. **she had no strength left/to sit down in a chair**: wrong translation. Read 'She could no longer bear to . . .'. To sit on the ground was a traditional position in which to grieve.

727-41.   **stormwinds . . . Odysseus**: Penelope's helplessness is well caught by her exaggerated reference to 'stormwinds' and suicide (734); by her feeling (740) that the whole people are against her family (delete 'of those' in Lattimore; cf. Telemachos at 2.62–79); and her hopes that old Laertes (see on 1.188–93) might be able to intervene. However strained her relationship with Telemachos, she realises now how dependent she is upon him. We can applaud Telemachos' judgement in keeping his departure secret (cf. 732–4). Cf. *4A*.

735.   **Dolios**: here, a faithful servant of Penelope. He may also be the father of the treacherous Melanthios and Melantho (17.212, 18.322), and the servant who works on the estate near Laertes (24.222, cf. 24.386ff., 24.498). But they may be two or three different people.

746.   **a great oath**: see 2.373–6.

754.   **embitter the bitterness**: rather 'Do not distress the old man: he is distressed enough'. Laertes received the news somehow (16.142–5).

755.   **Arkeisios**: father of Laertes (see 16.117–21).

761.   **barley-grains**: even though this particular style of vegetable sacrifice is unusual, the principle is normal: something is removed from human use and made over to the divinity. Cf. on 3.430–63 for animal sacrifice.

762.   **Atrytone**: a title of Athene, but its meaning is unexplained. Observe the typical prayer-form: (i) the divinity is identified (762), (ii) past favours to the divinity are rehearsed (763–4—note the dependence on Odysseus' good offices cf. 3.98–101; 1.65–7), (iii) help is demanded on the strength of the favours (765–6). The implication of the prayer-form is that there exists a contract between men and gods, which rests on the principle of 'tit-for-tat'. See on 1.61.

767.   **outcry**: cf. 3.450–2. The ritual outcry, usually raised by women, indicates the climax of a sacrifice or offering and serves to release the tension which the act has generated.

768-777.   **But . . . all of us**: the treachery, murderousness and hypocrisy of the suitors are well brought out in this exchange (but it is hard to see why the suitors draw the conclusion that Penelope's ritual cry foreshadows her marriage. See *4.625–847B* for an explanation by 'association').

782-4.   **oars . . . for them**: see on 8.52–4, and the diagram on p. 26.

791.   **as a lion**: it may seem strange to liken Penelope to a lion and the suitors to hunters tracking her. But she is a heroic woman—warriors in the *Iliad* are likened to lions more than to any other animal cf. 814—and the suitors threaten her way of life even more urgently now that they are planning to kill Telemachos. The image of a lion at bay is entirely appropriate. For the sequence sleep-simile-hopeful sign, cf. 19.510–35.

798.   **Pherai**: in Thessaly (see Map 2).

801.   **The dream figure**: Athene communicates with Nausikaa through a dream at 6.20ff.. Observe that the dream does not arise naturally from the sleeper's thoughts: it is imposed on them by the goddess.

802.   **thong of the door bar**: see on 1.441–2.

807.   **done no wrong**: for the moral emphasis of the *Odyssey*, see *1.22–45B*.

818.   **an innocent**: Penelope does not think Telemachos is of an age or maturity to be a true hero yet. Cf. on 2.270–80, 3.14–28.

846.   **Asteris**: there is a very small island indeed lying between Ithaka and Kephallenia (= Samos?), but Asteris is probably a Homeric invention. See on 9.25.

Book five

Introduction

A. Whatever the problems with the second proem (see note on 3), the opening scene on Olympos signals the change of location forcibly enough: from the 'real' world of contemporary Ithaka to the more fabulous world of Odysseus' travels. Since Homer effortlessly blends the human and the divine (see e.g. notes on 62, 192–200), the change is not as awkward as it might be: and the tale of Menelaos at 4.351ff., featuring the Old Man of the Sea and his helpful daughter, has already shown us that such fabulous adventures entirely befit a legendary hero.

B. We left Penelope isolated but soothed at the end of Book 4. It is something of a shock to find that Proteus' words of 4.556 are true. Our first sight of the man on whom all hopes have been pinned is of a helpless hero in tears (82ff.): trapped, resentful and mistrusting (e.g. 219–20, 171–9). True, Odysseus has had his pleasure with Kalypso in the past (153–4) in her ideal world (cf. Hermes' reaction at 73–5) and makes love to her still (226–7), but unwillingly (154–5). His goal is still Ithaka and his home (see on 11.176–7), whatever the cost (219–24), and it is with joy that he leaves Ogygia (see note on 269). Ancient Greeks placed an absolute value on a man's loyalty to his own household. A man who had an affair with an alien or a slave (as opposed to a married woman from another household) was not thought to compromise that primary bond (cf. on 1.13).

C. Kalypso derives from the Greek word *kaluptō*, meaning 'I cover' or 'conceal'. She has kept Odysseus hidden for the last seven years. Her primary function is to keep Odysseus in Ogygia for long enough to allow Telemachos to grow up (7 years: see 7.259 and 4.112) and it is likely Homer invented her for this purpose. But it is only out in the open, performing glorious deeds in the eyes of his peers, that a Homeric hero can prove his status. Odysseus himself admits that death at sea is an ignominious end—because none will know of it or be able to celebrate it—and at the height of the storm wishes he had died at Troy and received full measure of glory (*kleos* 311) there (306–12, cf. 1.236–43, 24.30–3, 24.83). Even when Odysseus does reach land, he is frequently forced to hide his identity (from e.g. Nausikaa in Book 6, Cyclops in Book 9 and, of course, in Ithaka in Books 13–22). How can a great hero achieve the recognition due to him in such circumstances? If Telemachos is seeking to find his real identity for the first time (see on 1.95, 207–43), Odysseus is constantly aware that he must prove his all over again, in circumstances very different from those of the Trojan War. Here is a different sort of heroism at work. For Odysseus-Telemachos comparison, see *2.260–434A* and on 1.414–6, 2.382–434.

D. Book 5 is one of the most richly characterised in the *Odyssey*. Two characteristics of Odysseus stand out: first, his capacity to endure (e.g. 151–8, 219–24), and second his ability to think for himself under pressure—to weigh, balance, consider and come up with an intelligent solution (e.g. during the storm at 324ff., 360ff., 408ff., 465ff.). If we argue that Odysseus, for all his trouble, is being helped by various divinities against the wrath of Poseidon (e.g. Athene at 382ff., 427ff., 437ff. and 491ff., Kalypso at 262ff. and Ino at 333ff.) Odysseus is quite unaware of this (cf. 6.324ff.) and gives the impression of a man who has learned to rely on himself. Indeed, he is even mistrustful of goddesses he recognises (177ff., 356ff.) but can be eminently tactful when he has to be (215ff.)

E. Kalypso is daughter of Atlas (1.52), but not an Olympian (cf. her anger at 118). She *seems* warmly affectionate to Odysseus (135, 182ff, cf. 1.14–15, 9.29–30) and obviously resents divine interference (118ff.). She does not give up easily (203–13). She readjusts the truth with exquisite delicacy in the face of divine will (160–1). She justifies her past behaviour with elegant half-truths (130), puts the blame firmly on the gods (118–9, 169), and affects complete goodwill (161), though there is a question about whether she *intentionally* omits any references to Hermes' instructions (characters who receive orders *direct* from gods do not usually mention this when they carry those orders out, e.g. Achilleus at *Iliad* 1.188–244. The difference may be that Kalypso is herself a goddess). She makes one last appeal to Odysseus, offering him immortality and reminding him of Penelope's human frailty and of the hardships that face him (203ff., cf. on 23.211). This delicate cat-and-mouse between Kalypso and her human lover is foreshadowed by that between Kalypso and Hermes. Kalypso half-senses the reason why he has come before he speaks (see on 91). Hermes implies she must know already (97–8) and engages in circumlocutions and excuses at 99–111 before coming out with the truth at 112 and offering a stern threat at 146–7. There is much in this sort of scene that prefigures comedy of manners in Menander (and late Euripides, for that matter).

F. It is often pointed out that the ancient critic 'Longinus' called the *Odyssey* a *kōmōidia ēthologoumenē*—a comedy of how people behave (*de subl.* 9.15 (183)). This was a criticism. It applied to the sketches of life in Odysseus' household, which depended on 'character' for their effect, and deprived the epic of true pathos. There is some truth in this, but we may choose to argue it is a strength, not a weakness. Respect, devotion, loyalty, hospitality, retribution—personal relations between people of all types and social status—remain the basic subject-matter of the *Odyssey* and reinforce our sense of the values of the social world.

G. Note Homer's use of doublets in this book to expand the tale—Odysseus is wrecked by Poseidon twice, has two monologues, two helpers and climbs back on his boat twice. See on *1.325–444B*, and *17B*.

1.   **haughty Tithonos**: mortal husband of immortal Dawn. 'Haughty' (*agauos*) is connected with the Greek word *agamai* 'I admire'. Perhaps 'fine', or 'admirable', would be a better translation. Many formulae seems to have lost anything other than the most generalised meaning.

3.   **in session**: Homer's practice is to recount events happening simultaneously as if they were happening one after the other (Page *HO* 64ff.). At 1.84, 88 Athene suggested that Hermes got to Kalypso, while she goes to Telemachos. Presumably the two events happen concurrently: but true to form, Homer here in Book 5 sends off Hermes *after* Athene has left Telemachos (see 18.27) The problem is that there is no need to reconvene a meeting of the gods for this purpose (it has already met in Book 1); and that Athene's words to the session at 7–20 are extremely feeble re-hashes (7 = 8.306; 8–12 = 2.230–4; 13 = *Iliad* 2.721; 14–17 = 4.557–60; 19–20 = 4.701–2). Page (*HO* 70ff.) argues that this prologue may have been used to introduce a version of the story which did without the Telemachos episodes of Books 1–4. Given the flexibility of the oral poet's art, it is indeed likely that an *Odyssey* was sung without a Telemachy. But the question is—is our version such an *Odyssey*, and the Telemachy a later addition to it? No, surely. See on 1.95 and Book I Appendix which argue that Books 1–4 are central to this *Odyssey*. On top of that, 18–27 make no sense without Books 1–4. Again, an oral poet often summarises past events (e.g. 7.241–97). Possibly Homer felt the sea-change in the story at this point was so violent that he needed to adopt special tactics to keep his listeners up to date (especially if Book 5 starts a new recitation unit (*GI F*))—and by repeating the divine council he re-emphasises the extent of divine concern for Odysseus and his family and reinforces our sense that Odysseus' and Telemachos' fates are linked.

18–27.   **And now there are those**: these lines clearly show that Athene has already taken Telemachos on his journey (cf. on 3). For the suitors' plots, see 4.625–72; 842–47.

23.   **as you have counseled it**: cf. 1.48ff.

25–42.   **Then bring Telemachos . . . of his fathers**: Athene will set about this task at 15.1ff. Observe how Homer in this passage prepares his listeners for what is to come—note especially the raft (33), hardships (33), Scheria-Phaiakians (34–5). Such a summary could not usefully serve as a mnemonic for the oral poet because of what it leaves out—Ino, Nausikaa, Arete, the games, Odysseus' tale. It serves for a general plot outline within which he can manoeuvre. Cf. 23.310–41; *GI I*.

32.   **by the convoy . . . people**: an odd sentiment, given that the gods are planning Odysseus' return, and that the Phaiakians will return him home (36–7, cf. 13.113ff.). We should read these words as instructions for

Kalypso, however, (see 140–4), and as a strong hint to Odysseus that self-dependence is the order of the day (as it will be, especially in Book 5. Cf. 6.324–31).

38. **bestowing bronze and gold**: Greek heroes were judged by their standing in others' eyes (see on 1.95) and wealth was an important index of standing, especially wealth won in war, largely because it ensured one's *independence* (cf. the quarrel between Achilleus and Agamemnon in *Iliad* 1—which began purely as a dispute about compensation for loss. Cf. 10.38–42, 13.261–3). Fine clothes were as conspicuous a mark of status then as now. See on 2.117. Cf. 13.134–8, where Poseidon makes clear his resentment of Odysseus' gifts.

35. **near the gods**: cf. 6.1–8, 7.201–6. Note that the Phaiakians are closely connected with the Cyclopes and Poseidon (6.5–7)—both enemies to Odysseus.

43. **Argeïphontes**: see on 1.38.

45. **golden**: winged sandals are strictly post-Homeric.

47. **the staff**: Hermes carries this as the insignia of his office (see 87). He herds the dead along with it (24.1–5), and it has the power to put people to sleep (as it did Argos: see on 1.38). In general, Hermes is the god of boundaries of every sort (*herma* = boundary marker), of transitions from one place to another and of exchanges and transfers (so, god of herdsmen, thieves, and later, traders). See Burkert *GR* 156, and on 19.396. For a typical boundary dispute, see *Iliad* 12.421–3.

50. **Pieria**: a mountain north of Olympos. Later, in Hesiod, it is associated with the Muses.

51. **shearwater**: i.e. a tern or seagull.

55. **the far-lying island**: Ogygia (1.85).

58–73. **There was . . . violets**: one of a number of semi-lyrical descriptions of places (e.g. 7.81ff., 9.116ff., 10.210ff., cf. 4.601ff.). Austin (*ADM* 149) makes much of the organisation of Kalypso's cave—not nature run wild, but intelligently organised around the cave, with neatly balanced trees (cf. 5.238–40), birds, vines, fountains, meadows. Lyric poets like Ibykos and Sappho exploited the erotic symbolism implicit in such scenes (especially of grapes and vines, 69). Greeks probably enjoyed such descriptions of magical far-away places, with their natural abundance of food, water and shade for which they had to struggle so hard. Such descriptions of a *locus amoenus* (delightful spot) became typical of Roman and European pastoral literature.

62. **the loom**: goddess Kalypso may have been, but she was still a woman, and had a woman's work to do. Cf. Circe 10.220ff.

83. **in tears**: for heroic weeping, see on 4.114.

91. **Come in with me**: wrong translation. Read 'follow me forward'. Some manuscripts omit this line, because Kalypso has already seated Hermes (86). But Homer is here deliberately manipulating a typical *xenia* scene for effect. Normally, one welcomes in a guest, sits him down, offers food and then asks questions (see on 1.102). But here, Kalypso sits Hermes down and questions him at once (86–90), a clear breach of etiquette, which she quickly corrects

(91–3). Why? Is it that, in her heart of hearts, she has guessed the reason for Hermes' mission and cannot hide her anxiety (cf. 88)?

93.   **ambrosia, and . . . nectar**: food of the gods. Nectar perhaps = wine, but ambrosia (traditionally the food) appears to be liquid at 9.359 and is used at 18.193 as a face-cleanser and at 4.445–6 as a primitive air-freshener! Cf. *Iliad* 5.339–42.

97–112.   **You, a goddess . . . speed**: note that it takes 15 lines for Hermes to get to the point (which he does at 112), and note how he gives responsibility to Zeus for the decision (99, 112). There is much to enjoy in Hermes' self-exculpation and efforts to delay giving the reason for his mission.

108.   **they offended Athene**: on the Trojan War and Athene's wrath, see Book I Appendix and on 3.135. This is the only passage where Homer specifically says that the return of Odysseus was hampered by the wrath of his divine supporter, Athene. In fact, Odysseus' men (110) were not killed through Athene's intervention at all, as Books 9–12 will make clear.

114.   **he shall see his people**: Dante and Tennyson, for example, make Odysseus a roamer, who must see and experience the world before he returns (cf. on 1.3). This is not Homer's idea: for Homer, Odysseus is a man with a specific goal—Ithaka.

120.   **true husband** (*philon akoitēn*): misleading. Read 'own bedfellow'. The *akoit*- stem means 'husband/wife' more often than not in Homer, but the literal meaning is 'bedfellow' and it can be used of a long-term partner (which Odysseus was) as well as of a married one (it is used of Helen in relation to Paris in the *Iliad*). Demeter and Iasion seem to have been uncomfortably short-term partners (125–6). Cf. 135–7.

121.   **Orion**: the hunter (11.572–5), whose name in Homer is identical with the constellation (5.274). There are many versions of the Orion story. This one is unique to Homer. See on 3.265–72.

123–4.   **Ortygia . . . painless**: for Ortygia, see on 15.403–4; for 'painless', on 15.411.

125.   **Demeter**: the goddess of fertility. The offspring of this union was Ploutos (Wealth), sent to those favoured by Demeter (Hesiod *Theogony* 969ff.). There seems to be no connection between this myth, that of Orion, and Kalypso/Odysseus other than that the gods kill the human consorts of divinities. Is Odysseus, then, in danger, now that the gods have found out about the relationship? Or does Kalypso exaggerate?

127.   **thrice-turned**: rather, triple-furrowed, a style of ploughing connected with ancient fertility ritual.

129–30.   **you resent it**: ring-composition with 118–120.

130.   **the one I saved**: see 12.447–50.

139.   **he himself**: refers to Zeus.

154–5.   **of necessity . . . against his will**: these lines save Odysseus from the accusation that he wanted to stay seven years with Kalypso (cf. 227). See also 14–15, 4.557–8, 9.29–30.

163–4.   **that will be on the upper / side**: i.e. raised above the base of the boat? See on 247–57.

184–6. Earth . . . immortals: the cosmos was divided into three regions, of which Zeus ruled the heavens, Poseidon the sea, and Hades the underworld. The earth and Olympos were shared by all gods (*Iliad* 15.187–93). Kalypso's solemn oath invokes the whole cosmos to be witness (the Styx was an underworld river), increasing its grandeur and inviolability. This oath signals the end of Odysseus' imprisonment and the start of his return: the real action of the *Odyssey*. Cf. Zeus's solemn oath to Thetis at *Iliad* 1.524–30, which is to direct the action of the *Iliad*.

192–200. and led the way . . . before them: the same formula as that used for Telemachos following in Athene's footsteps (see on 2.382–434). Note how the human and divine world subtly mingle and part in this passage—mingling at 194, 195, parting at 195–6, 199.

209. and be an immortal: as 192–200 have reminded us (see note), there are ways in which humans and mortals can co-exist—but also ways in which they *cannot*. Besides, it is hard to believe that immortality was in Kalypso's gift. See on 23.211.

215. do not be angry with me: but is Kalypso angry? Surely her tone has been beguiling and seductive. But the Greek says 'do not be angry with me *at this*'—where the Greek word for 'this' (*tode*) means 'what is to come, what I am about to say'. Observe the *husteron-proteron* principle (see note on 3.464–7) of Odysseus's reply (215–24)—Kalypso's points about suffering, desire for return, (im)mortality and beauty are answered in reverse order by Odysseus.

221–4. And if some god . . . follow: Odysseus is renowned for his flexibility under stress, but all heroes have a stubborn streak in them and here Odysseus enunciates the principle that will guide him through his adventures —absolute refusal to give in, whatever happens *en route* for home. There is a touch of the Achilleus in Odysseus here (cf. his common epithet 'much-enduring'). But see e.g. 10.49–55.

232. wimple: the Greek says 'covering (sc. for the head)'.

233. She set about planning: there is something amusing about Kalypso's single-minded determination that Odysseus should have to do it all himself (cf. 140–44). She may provide the tools (234–7, 246–7, 258–9), but the sweat is Odysseus'. Only at the end does she relent, giving Odysseus a bath and clothes (264), provisions (265–7), a wind (268) and, evidently, nautical advice (276–7). The passage reminds us of Odysseus' capacities—boat-builder (cf. 250), sailmaker, and sailor (270), as well as everything else.

239. alder . . . fir: fir was a timber recommended for building triremes because of its lightness (240). See Morrison and Coates, *AT* 180–1. Alder is very durable under water.

247–57. bored . . . upon this: is Odysseus building a raft or a boat here? In the best traditions of the boat-builder, he uses dowels (248) and mortice-and-tenon joints (248: 'cords' is a wrong translation). The reference to 'deck-boards' (252) and 'gunwales' (253)—'upper-deck' (254) should be 'yard-arm', cf. 318—both suggest a boat. Finally, the word 'fashions' (249) should be translated 'rounds out'. Much as we should expect Odysseus to be building a raft, the language strongly suggests he is building a boat with hull and decks. So for 'raft', read 'boat' throughout. See Morrison and Coates, *AT* 184–5, and cf. the boat depicted on p. 26.

265–6.   **two skins**: Greeks always drank wine diluted with water.

269.   **happy with the wind**: literally, the line read 'Rejoicing in/to the wind he spread his sails, did god-like Odysseus'. Note the emphatic word— rejoicing. He is going home at last (he thinks). Lattimore's 'glorious' is overstated for the common epithet 'god-like'.

272–5.   **Pleiades . . . ocean**: a star-cluster and three constellations are mentioned—Pleiades (the cluster); Bootes (the Ploughman, who is 'driving' the Wagon), of which the brightest star is Arcturus; Ursa Major, the Great Bear (also called the Wagon by Greeks, the Plough by us); and Orion the hunter (with its accompanying constellations Canis Major whose brightest star is Sirius (the Dog star), and Canis Minor). The Bear (273) watches Orion, the hunter (274)—a pleasing conceit. It has been argued that the date must be between September 1st and October 21st (if that can mean anything in the context of the *Odyssey*, but see on 467). If the Great Bear is on Odysseus's left (277), he is travelling east.

278.   **Seventeen days**: Odysseus sails east from a richly fertile island, under a gentle breeze, and on the eighteenth day, sees a land with mountains, which looks like a shield in the water (281). It is on the strength of such 'evidence' that confident guesses are made about the geography of Odysseus's travels.

282.   **the Aithiopians**: see 1.22 (and note). 'The Strong Earthshaker' is Poseidon. On his hatred of Odysseus, see 1.68–79 and notes.

297.   **The knees of Odysseus gave way**: there is nothing unheroic about being afraid, but only in yielding to fear. Odysseus remains as cool as ever (324–6).

300–2.   **the goddess . . . accomplished**: see 205–7.

303.   **Zeus**: as usual, Homer clearly distinguishes what we know (the storm is Poseidon's doing) and what his heroes know. Cf. on 2.261–2. But see 6.326 for Odysseus' calmer second thoughts, and cf. 7.271.

306–11.   **Three times . . . glory**: on the importance of this passage for Odysseus' sense of what it is to be hero, see *5C*. Cf. Agamemnon's misery at 11.405–34 and Achilleus' wish that he had died earlier when threatened with ignominious death in a river (*Iliad* 21.279–83).

309.   **on the day when**: the battle over the corpse of Achilleus is described at 24.36–42.

328.   **as the North Wind**: the first of a series of similes in this book. Cf. 368 (another wind simile), 394 (sickness simile), 432 (octopus simile), 488 (fire simile). Note here the Iliadic technique, rare in the *Odyssey*, of clustering similes around an exciting scene, developing one on the back of another (e.g. this simile, and see on 369). In general, similes are deployed at dramatically or emotionally charged moments. Homer's *Odyssey* has only about one-third of the number of similes of the *Iliad*, most far shorter in length. This may reflect the *Odyssey*'s less charged atmosphere. The *Iliad*, with its battles,

death-scenes, and to-and-fro across the plain of Troy, lends itself more readily to similes. See Camps *IH* 55–60, Bowra *HP* 269–79.

328.   **thistledown**: not 'down', evidently, but rather dried thistle *stalks*, which bunch together (329) in this way. Possibly the wattle fencing down the side of the boat (256–7) suggested to the poet the image of a large thistle.

333.   **Ino**: the daughter of Kadmos, founder of Thebes, married to Athamas (son of Aiolos, king of the winds. See 10.1–79). Ino and Athamas were driven mad by Hera. When Athamas, having killed their first son, threatened to kill their second, Ino leapt into the sea with him. Both were transformed into divinities. Leukothea, meaning 'white goddess', was a generic name for sea-gods. Homer is using myth creatively here, selecting to help Odysseus a goddess who could be expected to be sympathetic to mortals (334) in trouble at sea. It is interesting to note that in the Ino episode, as in the Aiolos episode in Book 10, the help given is regarded with suspicion (356ff., 10.34ff. and cf. 171–91). But Ino's help does seem to have been efficacious and Odysseus remembers to return the veil (348–50) at 459–62 (cf. Aiolos at 10.62ff.). Divine helpers offering useful gifts or advice occur also at 4.363ff. and 10.275ff.

337.   **likening herself to a winged gannet**: since Ino speaks and hands over the veil, she can hardly look like a gannet here: she emerges out of the water *in the manner of* a gannet. So Athene at 1.320. Cf. on 3.371–2.

343.   **Take off these clothes**: presumably because they were sodden, cf. 321–2. Odysseus is being asked to trust entirely to the divine veil—an offer he refuses temporarily (356ff.).

350.   **turn your face away**: usually chthonic deities (i.e. ones under the earth) or generally hostile forces demanded this condition. Cf. the Orpheus and Eurydice story, and Odysseus' sacrifices to the dead at 10.528.

354.   **pondered two courses**: the first of a number of scenes in which Odysseus is shown weighing up alternatives (see 408ff., and 465ff.). See *5D* for the importance of such scenes for Odysseus' character. See on 17.235 for the structure of such scenes.

356.   **which of the immortals**: on authorial omniscience, see on 1.1 'Muse'.

369.   **and scatters it abroad**: the wind which held thistle-stalks (= the boat) together at 329, here scatters chaff (= the timbers of the boat) in different directions.

380.   **laid the lash**: for Poseidon driving a chariot across the seas, see the superb description at *Iliad* 13.10–38.

382.   **But now Athene**: the presence of Athene helping her favourite (cf. 427, 437, 491, 6.13, 139, 229, 7.14, 19, but cf. 6.321–31) reminds us not only of the divine plan for Odysseus (though again cf. 29–32) but also of Athene's support for Telemachos in Books 1–3. See, e.g. notes on 1.271, 307–8, 2.1–14, 382–434, 3.12–13.

394.   **the show of life**: a simile which has parallels with 23.233–9, where Odysseus is as welcome to Penelope as a man who has escaped shipwreck (see note *ad loc.*). Both similes have their oddities. In this simile, one expects Odysseus seeing the land to = a father seeing the end of an illness, but the

intrusion of the children (395) rather dislocates the comparison. But it is typical of Odyssean similes that the subject matter of the simile should reflect that of the *Odyssey* (here a father returns to his children from the dead).

432.   **As when an octopus**: the point of contact between Odysseus and the octopus is the *tenacity* with which they both hold on. The consequences of this tenacity are different for both: for the octopus, it means it takes some pebbles *off* the rock, for Odysseus that he leaves his skin *on* the rock.

445.   **Hear me, my lord**: on prayer-forms, see 4.762: note that Odysseus does not know the name of the god here (445), so he cannot remind him/her of past services. All he can do is claim the protection due to a wanderer (448)—see 6.206–8—and supplicate (450). There may be something rather amusing to us about a suppliant claiming to come to the 'knees' of an unseen river-god (449), but this is traditional. See on 6.142.

456.   **with a terrible weariness**: a moment of tension—will Odysseus remember about Ino's veil? Even at such a moment of complete exhaustion, the ever-vigilant Odysseus does.

463.   **grain-giving soil**: the epithet 'grain-giving' is traditional, but that does not prevent its use here being especially apposite and striking.

467.   **female dew**: the translation is literally correct, but sounds odd. Alternative suggested meanings include 'gentle', 'fruitful' and 'damp'. References to early morning dew, the cold, frost and long nights are common throughout the poem and suggest the time of year is autumn. See e.g. 7.7, 11.373, 14.457, 529, 15.392, 17.23–5, 572–3, 18.328–9, 19.74.

488.   **As when a man**: another most homely simile—the great sea-tossed traveller and hero of Troy likened to a man living on his own, in the country. When Odysseus finally leaves Scheria, he is likened to a ploughman going home for dinner after a hard day in the fields (13.28–35). Similes often close scenes, e.g. 22.468–74.

491.   **buried himself**: the Greek world is *kalupsato*, cf. *5C*. The great hero conceals himself, as he will so often in the *Odyssey*.

Book six

Introduction

A. In this book, Odysseus, having reached the land of Scheria, where the Phaiakians live, faces yet another challenge: how, as a destitute, naked outcast, he is going to win acceptance by Nausikaa, the daughter of the king who encounters him on the beach, and gain an introduction into the royal palace. Face to face with Nausikaa, he summons up all his reserves of tact and intelligence (see notes on 100, 137, 139, 142, 149, 149–61, 216, 258), and succeeds in winning her confidence.

B. At first glance, it looks as if Odysseus' troubles are over. Poseidon has affirmed that he will find rest here, at least from his marine tribulations (5.288–9). The Phaiakians seem respectful of strangers (207–8, cf. 119–21); the divinity of the place is constantly stressed (e.g. 12, 16, 18, 203, 309); far away from civilisation it may be (4, 8, 204–5, 279) but the Phaiakians are enthusiastic sailors (22, 270–2); and they claim to be an unwarlike nation (202–3, 270). But are there signs that danger could lurk under the peaceful surface? Homer teases us with Nausikaa's apparent attraction to Odysseus (e.g. 239–45, 275–84) and stresses that she is of marriageable age (25–35, 282–4); there are unpleasant gossips about the place (274); and the people have connections with Poseidon and the Cyclopes (5, 267), Odysseus' great enemies. Nevertheless, Athene is making her presence felt (e.g. 13–14, 328–31, 139–40) and she has a sacred grove there (291–2). If this is to be read as a balance of tensions, Homer will maintain it cleverly in subsequent books. See Clarke *AO* 52–6; Austin *ADM* 153–62.

C. The book is famous for the encounter between Nausikaa and Odysseus— the naked, begrimed hero of the Trojan War having nothing but his wits to rely on if he is to win the confidence of the exposed and vulnerable king's daughter (see on 100, 139). Odysseus' developing relationship with Nausikaa stands in elegant and amusing contrast to his relationship with Kalypso from Book 5 (see note on 209). The 'social' world of the *Odyssey* may seem less threatening than the battle-scenes of the *Iliad*, but if Odysseus' return to Ithaka does not depend on his ability to wield a spear in these books, he is still in danger of frustration, even loss of return, if he does not show qualities no less vital for the *Odyssey*'s world than skill in battle was in the *Iliad*—tact, courtesy, self-awareness, and sensitivity to others' needs and fears. The problem for Odysseus is, of course, that he is still a Homeric hero, and concealment and reserve must at some stage be cast off—the question is, when?

D. Nausikaa is delightfully portrayed: practical (81–3, 252–3, 316–20), wheedling (56–65), courageous (139–40, 199–204), fun-loving (99–109), cautious (209–10), flattering (276–284), commanding (255–315), quite able to rise to the challenge posed by Odysseus with only one moment of slight hesitation (see on 187–90). Marriage is on her mind (239–45), and she is not afraid to state her preferences (276–84). But the conditions too are firmly implied (285–9).

4. **Hypereia**: the word means 'Beyond-land'—the land far away. The Phaiakians are constantly depicted as living far from other men (e.g. 6.8).

5. **Cyclopes**: cf. 5.35. Nausithoos (7) is a son of Poseidon (7.56–7). The Cyclopes are at one pole—utter barbarity—the Phaiakians at the other—wonderful refinement. See further on 269.

7. **migration**: there were large migrations of Greeks from the mainland in the 10th and 8thC. The mention of temples at 10 is a good example of cultural amalgamation (see *GI E*), since such buildings do not appear before 800 and in Homer gods are worshipped at altars, groves and precincts in the open (e.g. 267). The picture Nausikaa paints of the city at 262–9 with its walls, temple, *agora* and harbours is that of a typical 8thC colony (see *WoA* 1.2). Whether it also reflects a *polis* (city-state) is a difficult question. See Finley *WO* 155–7 on the danger of confusing objects with institutions.

8. **Scheria**: it is assumed that Scheria is an island (Thucydides thought it was Corcyra (modern Corfu)—see *Histories* 1.25). But the poet never actually says as much (6.204–5 is the closest he gets): indeed, the description at 263–4, describing harbours on either side of a narrow causeway, suggests the town is a peninsula. Observe that the Phaiakians, though great sailors, have no interest in *trading* by sea (cf. on 8.163).

13. **It was to his house**: ring-composition with 2–3. Cf. 21 and 24, 41–2 and 47.

21. **stood above her head**: a typical stance for a dream. Cf. 4.803 (and note), 20.32.

26.· **shining clothes**: the typical epithet 'shining' applies to the clothes whether they are dirty or not—that is their true nature. Homeric epithets constantly remind us of the unchanging quality and tangibility of the objects with which heroes are surrounded, and add a sense of the unchanging grandeur and tangibility of the world they describe.

26–7. **your/marriage is not far off**: Cf. 34–5. The possibility that Odysseus may marry Nausikaa is one with which Homer constantly teases us.

29. **a good reputation**: observe the importance of what people *say* about you. See on 1.95 and 5.38. Cf. Nausikaa's fears at 273–4, 285.

31. **washing**: observe the economy of Athene's plan. If Odysseus is stranded naked on a beach, he will need clothes. 28 ensures that men's clothes will be among those washed. Cf. 60–5.

42. **Olympos**: Homer here describes the dwelling of the gods as resembling an ideal world in the *heavens* rather than on an actual mountain. Perhaps

the purpose of this description, whose authenticity is disputed, is to emphasise the gods' distance and grandeur.

53.   **distaff**: see on 4.122 ('spindle' better). The queen is Arete (see on 310).

55.   **barons**: for Alkinoos' advisory council, see 7.136, 7.189 and 8.390. Presumably Echeneos at 7.155 is such an adviser. See on 1.386 for the 'constitutional' problem.

56.   **very close**: before ever Nausikaa speaks, it is clear she is up to something.

57.   **Daddy dear**: the speech is a masterpiece of wheedling—she starts with a 'coaxing blend of wish and question' (Stanford) and appeals entirely to her father's and brother's needs, not mentioning the dream of her impending hopes of marriage (66–7), on which Athene had played (26–8). But Alkinoos knows what she is up to (67). The closeness of the relationship between the young girl and her father is beautifully depicted in this exchange without it ever being openly stated—a fine example of character-portrayal by suggestion.

62.   **five . . . sons**: three (the bachelors?) are mentioned at 8.119 — Laodamas, Halios and Klytoneos. The first two dance at 8.370–80.

78.   **put that in**: wrong translation. Read 'climbed up onto'. There is a delightful clarity, vividness and immediacy about the description of the girls' journey and washing.

84.   **walked on**: see 319–20.

92.   **stamped on it**: in the absence of detergents, clothes were beaten clean in the ancient world.

96.   **bathing and anointing**: see on 3.464–7.

100.   **threw off their veils**: when Penelope comes among the suitors, she is invariably veiled and flanked by maidservants (e.g. 1.328–35, *1.325–444A*). These protect her person and her reputation (18.184). Nausikaa needs such protection if she is to go out into the open. But now she is unveiled; and when the servants flee from her at Odysseus' approach (138), she will be even less protected. See 15.420 for a woman seduced while washing.

101.   **dancing**: the Greek word *molpē* means 'singing' rather than 'dancing', though it can include the element of dancing too. Perhaps 'began the measure'? The girls are singing and moving as they throw the ball (100, 115) amongst themselves.

102.   **as Artemis**: goddess of virginity (cf. 109), childbirth and of the hunt (cf. 104, 106). Leto (106) is her mother. Taÿgetos (103) and Erymanthos (104) are mountain ranges in the Peloponnese.

112.   **what to do next**: it is very common for the oral poet to anticipate, and so prepare the listener for, what will happen shortly. Cf. e.g. Athene's instructions at 25–40; and the council of the gods at the start of Books 1 and 5. This device must have helped the listener to keep a grip on the plot development, Cf. on 5.25–42.

118.   **pondering**: for this particular characteristic, cf. 141 and *5D*. For the structure of the whole scene, see on 13.200.

121.   **with a godly mind**: this attribute is set in specific contrast with those

who are 'without justice' (120 but see on 3.52). For divine concern with 'justice', an important Odyssean theme, see *1.22–95B*.

130.   **like some hill-kept lion**: this simile is used of the warrior advancing to battle at *Iliad* 12.299ff.—the warrior world of the *Iliad* intruding amusingly in the very different world of Homer's *Odyssey*? The translation misses the neatness of Homer's observation—Homer says the lion goes *with/among* the (slow) cattle and sheep, but *after* the (speedy) deer.

135.   **face**: the Greek says 'mingle, mix it with'—a word used also of sexual intercourse. There are erotic undertones in this whole incident.

137.   **terrifying**: clearly Odysseus did not *want* to look like a lion—but that was the effect he had on the servants.

139.   **stood fast**: for the dangerous exposure of Nausikaa, without veil or servants, see on 100. In normal circumstances, she would certainly have fled—hence Athene's intervention (139–40).

142.   **supplicate**: to supplicate, a Greek disarmed (14.276–7) and threw himself on the mercy of another, human or divine (see 22.334–6 for seizing an altar, 5.445–50 for supplicating an unseen god). The position, stooped before the supplicatee (14.279), was humiliating; the purpose, to show one was at their mercy, and posed no threat. No Greek would willingly put himself in such a position before someone unless their plight was desperate. The moral (and religious cf. 207–8) pressure on the supplicatee to grant the suppliant's requests was very high, as long as the supplication was properly carried out (14.279–84). A supplication was not complete if the suppliant was not touching the supplicatee (normally, the knees and/or chin, see *Iliad* 1.500–2): an incomplete supplication, unlike a complete one, could be ignored (see on 22.329). Hence Odysseus' problem. He is only too aware of his own nakedness and of Nausikaa's vulnerability (exposed, abandoned, out in the open, young, beautiful, of marriageable age). To seize her knees in such circumstances could easily be misconstrued (147): but if he cannot make contact, the supplication is not complete. This is a real test of Odysseus' vaunted intelligence. On supplication, see J. Gould *Hiketeia JHS* (93) 1973.

149.   **at your knees**: the Greek literally means 'I take you by the knees'! Odysseus decided *not* to do this—but he must indicate to Nausikaa that he is in fact supplicating her, and he hopes that his crafty words (148) will do enough to prevent her rejecting him. See 168–9.

149–161.   **But are you . . . look on you**: the opening words are designed to calm Nausikaa's fear that she is about to be raped. Odysseus likens her to Artemis, goddess of virginity (cf. 102–9), while at the same time complimenting her beauty (152. Cf. 20.71 for 'stature' of Artemis); praises her in the name of her family; most of all blesses her future husband; and identifies his feelings for her, not as desire, but as 'wonder' (161) (the Greek has overtones of 'respect'). Here are the words of a man who values chastity, the family and marriage—hardly the sentiments of a potential rapist. It is a brilliantly tactful and intelligent beginning, as Nausikaa acknowledges at 187. That Odysseus did not really think she was a goddess (121–5) is suggested by

143–4 and 16.181–5: he would have offered her gifts and sacrifices when his fortunes were restored. Cf. 8.467.

162. **Delos**: an island sacred to Apollo and Artemis (151). Leto gave birth to them both there, clinging onto a palm-tree—to which the 'young palm' of 163 may be a reference. See on 102.

163. **stalk of a young palm**: Thetis likens her son Achilleus to a young shoot at *Iliad* 18.436–8.

164. **with a following**: Odysseus hints at his previous importance, and at 170–4 indicates how he has come to be in his present plight, telling Nausikaa just as much as is needed to win her sympathy. Ogygia (172) is Kalypso's island (see 5.262ff.).

175–85. **Then have pity . . . reputation**: Odysseus closes his speech with a plea for help and (180ff.) a tactful wish for Nausikaa's married happiness. Note that 'love' is not an ingredient of happiness, but rather agreement and harmony (181, 183); and observe the importance of public reputation (185, cf. on 29. See Finley *WO* 126–9). If 184–5 seems an odd sentiment, we should remember that a standard feature of Greek values was that one should do good to one's friends and harm to one's enemies (*Iliad* 9.613–5). These sentiments of Odysseus, whilst appropriate enough addressed to Nausikaa, are equally relevant to his own long-term aim—return to his wife in Ithaka.

187–90. **My friend . . . endure it**: the translation catches well the wandering, rather insecure syntax of Nausikaa's reply. Nervousness? An effort to sound suitably sententious in an adult way (cf. Odysseus at 18.125–42)? Certainly there is humour in Nausikaa telling 'much-suffering' Odysseus that he must endure (190)!

208. **the gift is a light and a dear one**: i.e. helping strangers (= 'the gift') does not cost much ('light') and is much appreciated ('dear').

209. **give some food**: there is a clever contrast between Nausikaa and Kalypso's treatment of Odysseus. Kalypso feeds him (5.196), bathes him (5.264) and sleeps with him (5.226–7): Nausikaa orders the servants to bathe (210) and feed him (246), and merely admires him from afar (237).

210. **bathe him**: bathing is a typical element in a *xenia* sequence (4.47–8), but there is something amusing about the way Nausikaa formally offers Odysseus a bath on the *beach*, as if she were receiving him into her father's palace (see on 8.459).

216. **he could bathe himself**: this does not necessarily mean that the servants are refusing to bathe Odysseus (and so ignoring Nausikaa's instructions). But if it *does* mean that the servants are telling him to bathe himself, Odysseus' reply at 217ff. must be meant to make it look as if it is *his own* decision. In this way, he cleverly protects Nausikaa from appearing to be unable to exert authority over her servants. Certainly, Odysseus' excuses seem feeble (especially 221–2—he has been naked ever since he first appeared, cf. 136); and it was common practice for males to be bathed by females in Homer (see e.g. 3.464–5, 4.48ff., 252).

233. **Hephaistos and Pallas Athene**: for their functions as divinities of

craftmanship and the arts, see 8.273ff., 2.115–8. The whole simile is repeated at 23.159–62, when Odysseus is unsuccessfully trying to persuade Penelope that it really is he who has returned at last. Odysseus' physical transformation affects Nausikaa (237), but not his wife (23.166–72). She fears deception (23.215–30).

237.   **admired him**: note that Nausikaa's feelings are not 'love' (cf. 8.459). Homer continues to tease us with the possibility that Nausikaa may become involved with Odysseus (244–5). Cf. on 26–7. But whatever we may wish to read into Nausikaa's feelings, she remains practical, bustling off, folding the clothes and yoking the mules (252–3) while the slaves feed Odysseus (247–8).

258.   **thoughtless**: observe the effect that Odysseus has upon those he meets. Cf. 187.

262.   **city**: see notes on 7 and 8.

269.   **fine down their oar-blades**: i.e. they make their oars by gradually planing down a block of wood to the right thickness (as is still done in the Mediterranean today).

273.   **graceless speech**: cf. on 29.

276.   **large and handsome stranger**: observe the Odyssean cleverness of the speech. Nausikaa reveals her name (276), flatters Odysseus (276, 280), indicates she is marriageable (284), but only to the very best (284)—all in the words of a hypothetical Phaiakian whom they may meet (275). Odysseus will need to supplant far more dangerous suitors when he arrives back in Ithaka.

288.   **making friends**: note that it is the *girl* who should not make friends with a man, not 'her dear father and mother'.

291.   **sacred to Athene**: it must have been some relief to Odysseus to hear that Scheria was a place where Athene was held dear. Cf. *6B*.

303.   **the house**: for Homeric houses, see on 1.140. Homer prepares us for the splendid description at 7.81–132.

310.   **embrace our mother's knees**: the queen Arete (cf. 52–3) is, evidently, to play a crucial part (313) in helping Odysseus to return home. But, when it comes to it in Book 7, she seems to play little or no part at all. On this famous problem, see *7B, D*.

324.   **Atrytone**: see on 4.762.

326.   **battered me**: see 5.282ff. Odysseus does not know that Athene was in fact helping him (e.g. 5.382, 427, 437, 491, 6.13, 139).

329.   **did not yet show herself**: when Athene helps Odysseus in Books 7 and 8, she does so in disguise, e.g. 7.19, 8.193. For her commitment to Odysseus, see 13.330–2, 20.47–8.

330.   **nursed a sore anger**: because Odysseus blinded his son the Cyclops (to be related in Book 9). See 1.68–79.

Book seven

Introduction

A. The book continues a number of themes begun earlier in Book 6 (see *6B*)
e.g. the divinity of Phaiakia (11–12, 49, 56, 92–4, 132, 199–206, 323–4); its
hostility (17, 32–3, 59, 206); the Phaiakian love of ships (34, 43, 108–9,
325–8); their knowledge of right and wrong (164–6, 190–2, 315–8); and
Athene's continuing care for Odysseus (14–15, 40–2). There is a further
generalised description of the site (43–5), and a fine detailed portrait of the
palace (81–132), which emphasises its utopian qualities. Odysseus, meanwhile, continues to conceal his identity, acting like a helpless stranger (22–6)
and as a needy beggar (215–21), though the compliments which the
Phaiakians, and especially Alkinoos, pour on him (e.g. 199, 226–7, 311–5)
encourage him to suggest something of his status (see note on 332). By the
end of the book, Odysseus has won acceptance into the palace. But he has
not yet been able to reveal himself.

B. The famous problems of Book 7 concern Arete. (i) Nausikaa suggests that
Odysseus' safe homecoming depends crucially on her (6.310 5); Athene too
makes much of her importance (7.47–77). Why then does she do so little?
(ii) After Odysseus has supplicated her (146–52), it is Alkinoos, prompted
by Echeneos (155–66) who takes over: Arete, after a long delay, simply asks
Odysseus two questions (237–9). Why this delay? (iii) One of her questions
of Odysseus is—who are you? But Odysseus does not answer this question,
and neither Arete nor Alkinoos pursues it. Why? This is obviously fertile
ground for those who think the *Odyssey* to be the work not of one but
of a number of authors (see on *11B*); and they ascribe the inconsistencies of
the Arete episode to this explanation.

C. Fenik *SO* 5–130 will have none of this. In a detailed study, he shows how
the *Odyssey* (and *Iliad*) are characterised by *delays, failures to answer
questions*, and *refusals to reveal identity* (cf. *13D*). Thus, in answer to
problem (iii) Fenik compares Odysseus and Eumaios (Book 14), Odysseus
and Athene (Book 1, 3), Odysseus and Penelope (Book 19), Odysseus and
Laertes (Book 24) and shows how 'the hero's secrecy about himself is used to
build scene after scene of irony, suspense and poignant emotion' (55). In
answer to (ii), Fenik shows how *interruptions* are frequent in Homer, some of
them finely conceived, some serving no obvious purpose: '(the poet) strives
for delay, suspense, retardation' (*SO* 104). He quotes e.g. Book 23, where
from 85–116, the build up to Odysseus' recognition goes smoothly, and is
then suddenly halted for Odysseus to discuss other matters, before being

resumed at 164ff. In answer to (i), Fenik argues that Arete is of central importance because she asks the vital question which puts at risk the acceptance Odysseus seems to have won from the listening Phaiakians, and raises the spectre of Phaiakian hostility again. Unless Arete is satisfied, Odysseus' cause is lost. The brilliance of Odysseus' reply, which gives Arete as much as she needs to know (no more), compliments Nausikaa and proves Odysseus himself to be a perfect gentleman, wins the day.

D. Fenik's analysis of Homer's use of such devices gives an important insight into the poet's workshop. But such devices can be used well or badly (see *24B*) and it is part of the poet's job to create a convincing scenario in which they can be used well. Delay, interruption (etc.) must *make sense*. Thus, there is much to be said for the view that in Book 7 Odysseus must delay self-revelation because he is as yet in no position to declare the truth. There are two reasons: (a) have the Phaiakians, who live so far away from human society, even *heard* of Odysseus? He can hardly risk announcing himself to cries of 'who?' (cf. 3.193–5). (b) Even if they have heard of the great Odysseus, what evidence have they that he is telling the truth? He can only announce himself when he is confident that the Phaiakians will believe him. Second, Arete's questions may be delayed, but it is a characeristic of *xenia* scenes that questions come after food (see 1.122–4): the delay or interruption may be due to nothing more than that. As for the importance of Arete (69–77), Athene offers adequate reasons why Odysseus should supplicate her. He will meet her first (53), and Alkinoos himself places some importance on the person first encountered (299–301). Second, the Phaiakians have a reputation for hostility to strangers (*6B*, *7A*), but Arete is renowned for her ability to dissolve quarrels among men she favours (74). Third, she is very highly respected (69–72). The special respect Odysseus shows her by supplicating her first will redound to his credit. (Odysseus also addresses his parting words to her, 13.59–62). See further on 147.

E. Given Homer's choice of structure for this version of the *Odyssey*, some location somewhere is needed in which Odysseus can tell his story in flashback (Book I Appendix). Homer might have chosen to land him among friends. Had that friend been Idomeneus, and had Telemachos gone to Crete as well as, or rather than, Pylos or Sparta to seek news of his father (see *GI I*), the second half of the *Odyssey* would be very different from the one we have now. The advantage for Homer in choosing to land him among strangers, who may turn out to be hostile or friendly, is that Homer can develop more fully the theme of Odysseus' mastery of every kind of situation.

F. The exchanges between Odysseus, Alkinoos, Arete and the court, are as subtle and delicate as those between Odysseus and Nausikaa in Book 6. On Alkinoos, see *8D*.

4. **her brothers around her**: it is almost as if they have been waiting for her to return. This is a close, warm and protective family. Cf. 6.62–5; 6.153–7, 6.285–9.

7. **and old woman**: for typical descriptions of humble characters, see on 1.428–35.

8. **Apeire, Eurymedousa**: those who want to make Scheria = Corfu, see Apeire = Epirus. But this is philologically impossible. Eurymedousa means 'wide-ruling': was she of royal origin? Is this why she was given to Alkinoos, who rules all of the Phaiakians (11)? Cf. the fate of Eurykleia (1.428–34).

14. **Then Odysseus rose**: observe how Homer fills the time of the narrative sequence. Since Odysseus has to wait till Nausikaa reaches home (6.295–6), the time of his waiting is filled in with Nausikaa's arrival home. But Fenik *SO* 65–6 argues that Homer does not consistently 'fill time' in this way and only the person 'in view' is important. See on 18.206.

17. **in a sneering way**: for the danger posed by the Phaiakians, see *6B*.

19–20. **in the likeness/of a young girl**: it is typical of oral poetry that heroes in need are met and helped by divinities in disguise. Cf. e.g. Odysseus and Hermes at 10.277ff.; Odysseus and Athene at 13.187ff. (especially 221ff.), where Athene uses the mist-trick (42) for another purpose.

25. **I know nobody**: not true, after his encounter with Nausikaa in Book 6, but the claim is both tactful and calculated to win sympathy.

28. **my friend and father**: the Greek says 'o *xenos* father', i.e. Athene addresses Odysseus as a paternal figure (since Odysseus, at 22, calls Athene 'child') and he is also, obviously, a *xenos*. Cf. 48.

32–3. **do not have very much patience**: see on 17, and Nausikaa's fears at 6.273ff.

34. **ships**: for this important Phaiakian interest, see *6B*.

35. **gift of the Earthshaker**: i.e. of Poseidon, Odysseus' great enemy. The Phaiakians will pay for this connection when, having returned Odysseus back to Ithaka, Poseidon turns their ship into stone (13.125–64).

42. **a magical mist about him**: ring-composition with 15. Cf. 46–7 with 78–82. This useful device (see on 1.10), as well as helping the poet keep a grip on the narrative, may also indicate to us how the poet builds up his narrative, since such passages can often be removed with minimum disruption.

45. **joined with palisades**: better, 'with palisades along the top'.

50. **you go on in**: normally, a *xenos* would wait outside the palace to be welcomed in (e.g. 1.119–20, 4.20–2). This explains why Athene says Odysseus needs to be bold (50–2) in his approach. It is interesing that all Odysseus' dealings so far have been with women (Kalypso, Ino, Nausikaa, Athene and now Arete). Women hold the key to his salvation in these early books—an unusually challenging situation for an Iliadic hero to find himself in.

54. **Arete**: the name means 'prayed to *or* for', 'invoked' (Ārētē, no connection with the Greek *aretē* 'excellence, virtue'). Athene enlarges upon Nausikaa's instructions (6.303ff.), though she does not order Odysseus explicitly to supplicate Arete, as Nausikaa had (6.310–1).

56.   **Poseidon . . .**: this genealogy fleshes out the picture given at 6.3–12. A lengthy introduction usually indicates importance. The whole genealogy of Arete, which countenances unepic marriage between niece (Arete) and her uncle (unless they are claiming divine privilege cf. 10.5–7), and uses common mythic names (there were at least twelve Periboia's), is an obvious invention.

59.   **Giants**: for Phaiakian closeness to Cyclopes and Giants, see on 206. The reference in 60 to Eurymedon losing his people and perishing may be an obscure reference to the mythological battle between the gods and Giants (Hesiod *Theogony* 617–885), which the Giants lost. The battle is not referred to anywhere else in Homer.

64.   **Apollo**: god of disease, as well as of health (Burkert *GR* 146).

81.   **Erechtheus**: mythical king of Athens, after whom the Erechtheum, a temple built on the Acropolis of Athens in the 5thC, was named. In the Mycenaean period there was a palace building on the site.

84.   **as from the sun**: cf. Menelaos' palace at 4.45–6, 71–5. For the whole description of Alkinoos' palace (84–102), workers (103–111) and gardens (112–131)—with its memories of a golden age (e.g. 88–94), of its effortless fruitfulness (e.g. 114–121, 123–6, 128) and constant water-supplies (129–31)—see on 5.58–73. Note the emphasis on olives (107, 116–7 but see on 2.339) and vines (121–26), staples of the Greeks; and on the value placed on women's work in the home—weaving (96–7, 105–111). The tribute paid to Phaiakian women is paid equally to Penelope at 2.116–7. Cf. on 5.38.

105.   **distaffs**: see on 4.122.

106.   **restless as leaves**: Lattimore refers this simile to the way the women are sitting. But the simile simply says 'like the leaves of the tall poplar'. One can hardly *sit* like that. The simile is more likely to apply to the movement of the shuttle through the warp and the vibration of the suspended threads (cf. 105).

107.   **the cloths . . . oil**: lit. 'and from the closely-woven wool the moist oil drops'. This refers to the ancient practice of bleaching wool in a bath of olive oil and other substances.

128.   **rows of greens**: greens are very rarely mentioned in Homer (see on 1.108).

137.   **Argeiphontes**: Hermes, among other things a sender of dreams and of sleep (see on 5.47).

142.   **knees**: on supplication, see 6.142. For the whole scene, cf. the parallel (with variations) in 6.141–250 and its amusing variants.

144.   **all fell silent**: in amazement at such a daring act (see note on 50).

147.   **to your knees**: note that Odysseus is careful to include Arete's husband and the feasters in the supplication, though Nausikaa did not include them (6.310-11, cf. on 54). In fact, Odysseus mentions her husband *first* (lit. 'to your husband and to your knees I come, having suffered much')! Does he have his doubts about Nausikaa's advice (cf. his doubts with Ino's advice at 5.356ff.), and so wish to hedge his bets on queen *and* king? Does he wish to avoid a charge of impropriety by seizing the woman's knees, so

appeals to her in her husband's name first (cf. with Nausikaa 6.145-9)?

149–50. **grant to . . . him**: this wish is especially appropriate in the mouth of Odysseus, who (as we know from Books 1–4) will return to a situation in Ithaka where the suitors are trying to wrest power from Telemachos.

159. **Alkinoos**: if we were expecting Arete to play any other part than being supplicated by Odysseus, our expectations are not fulfilled (see *7B*). Alkinoos now takes over till 232. For hesitation in accepting a stranger, see 4.22–36.

170. **Laodamas**: he will invite Odysseus to try his hand at the athletic contests in 8.132ff.

172–184. **A maidservant . . . wanted**: for this typical combination of eating and libating, see 3.40–66 and on 1.130–50. For libation see on 2.432. The scene does not end till 229.

186. **leaders of the Phaiakians**: since one does not question strangers till after they have eaten (see e.g. 1.122–4 and on 5.91), Alkinoos here does not address Odysseus specifically (although Odysseus offers an answer at 207ff.). Arete starts the questions (233) after food (232).

188–9. **tomorrow/at dawn**: the poet here outlines the future direction of events. These will be dramatically interrupted from Books 9–12 by Odysseus' tales (see on 11.328–84).

195. **suffer no pain nor evil**: some have seen in these lines the idea that Odysseus in Scheria is in a state of transition, suspended between the dangers of the divine world of Kalypso and of the real world of Ithaka, where he can re-sharpen in safety the human skills he will need to defeat the suitors in Ithaka. It is true that a number of his experiences in Ithaka bear a striking resemblance to experiences in Scheria. See e.g. on 215–21.

197. **the heavy Spinners**: one's destiny is spun at the moment of birth (198) in Homer, and is no way different from that dispensed by 'fate' (see e.g. 5.41 and cf. *Iliad* 24.209–10). Hesiod introduced the concept of three fates (Lachesis, Klotho, and Atropos, *Theogony* 218, 905) and Plato produced the celebrated image of these forces spinning individual fates in *Republic* 10.616b–d.

199. **one of the immortals**: a pleasing variation on the idea. At 6.149 Odysseus used it to calm Nausikaa's fears of rape; at 6.242–3, 280 Nausikaa used it for the purposes of gentle flattery; here Alkinoos uses it to boast about Phaiakian closeness to the gods.

203. **they sit beside us**: cf. 1.22–6.

206. **as are the Cyclopes**: an almost throw-away remark that must send a shiver through Odysseus—and us.

211–4. **greatest . . . suffered**: Homer now begins to prepare us for Odysseus' tales in Books 9–12.

215–21. **to eat . . . fill her**: this concern with food may seem uncouth to us (it did to the scholiasts) but it will be a standard concern of Odysseus' when he is acting the part of the beggar in Ithaka (see e.g. 15.343–5, 17.286–89, cf. *GI H*). The gift of food to suppliant or beggar is a typical feature of *xenia* (cf. 6.206–10 and Eumaios' constant generosity to Odysseus in this respect in e.g. Book 14). The Phaiakians clearly do not object (226–7).

238.   **What man are you, and whence?**: on the problem of this question, see *7B (iii)*. Some scholars argue that 'originally' Odysseus told the tales now told in Books 9–12 at this point. But as *7D* and *8A* argue, given Odysseus' state, this is thematically impossible.

244–96.   **Ogygia . . . clothing**: this version of Odysseus' travels takes the story from Book 5 to the present moment (with vague references to the storm which took him to Ogygia—249–53 cf. 12.403–449). Note revisions: no Ino (5.333ff.), no mention of the girls' cry which woke him (6.117) and, most important of all, Odysseus' claim that Nausikaa bathed him (296—see note—cf. 6.209–10). The last revision is clearly intentional: the others may have no particular point. The whole passage shows what an oral poet could do if he needed to compress a series of incidents. Much compression of this sort (and expansion) must have been observable in the different versions of the *Odyssey* which the poet sang to different audiences. See Lord *SoT* 94–8. For comparison: 253–4: 5.134; 256–7: 5.209; 259–60: 5.151; 262: 5.138; 264–5: 5.262–7; 266: 5.268; 267–9: 5.278–81; 271ff.: 5.291ff.; 275: 5.370; 276: 5.375; 278–9: 5.408ff.; 280–82: 5.438ff.; 283ff.: 5.475ff.; 290ff.: 6.117ff.; 294ff.: 6.211ff.

284.   **sky-fallen**: see on 4.478.

292–307   **nor did . . . judgment**: observe the way Odysseus compliments Nausikaa in these lines even though he lies to do so (cf. 297). 295–6 are not strictly true (especially the fact that she bathed him), and 304–6 put the responsibility on Odysseus' shoulders for what was in fact Nausikaa's decision (6.255ff.). See Griffin *HLD* 61–2

313.   **be called my son-in-law**: this offer of marriage, legitimised since it has come from Nausikaa's father (cf. 6.286–9), is the culmination of the prospect hinted at in Book 6. Observe that Alkinoos immediately withdraws it (315–6). He does not threaten Odysseus, in the way that e.g. Kalypso did (1.15). The offer shows clearly the powerful impression that Odysseus has made already on the Phaiakians.

321.   **further away than Euboia**: since Euboia could not have seemed at the ends of the earth to any 8thC Greek, we probably have here a joke: if the Phaiakians think Euboia, of all places, is that far off, they must live a very long way away *indeed*.

323–4.   **Rhadamanthys/on his way to visit . . .**: son of Zeus and Europa, brother of Minos (king of Crete (11.568)), inhabitant of Elysium (4.564), a judge of the dead and renowned for his wisdom. Tityos was punished for trying to rape Leto (11.576–81). Gaia is the goddess Earth. The incident is not referred to elsewhere in myth.

332.   **imperishable glory**: Odysseus prays that Alkinoos will gain imperishable *kleos* (see on 1.95) if he oversees the safe return of Odysseus. Imperishable *kleos* is the highest glory that a hero can achieve. If Alkinoos can get it by returning Odysseus, Odysseus is implying something about his

(Odysseus') heroic eminence and importance. Odysseus here takes the first steps in asserting his own identity—emboldened, perhaps, by Alkinoos' implied trust and respect for him (311–5).

336.   **to make up a bed**: for this typical scene of going to bed, see on 4.296–310.

Book eight

Introduction

A. Book 8 ends with Alkinoos' question to Odysseus—who are you? Where do you come from? What is your story? (548–86). This question, which Odysseus had carefully avoided in Book 7 (see *7D*), can now be answered, because in the course of the book Odysseus will have demonstrated clearly the sort of man he is, and received a response from Alkinoos which suggests that the Phaiakians realise he is a hero of no little importance. Both Odysseus and Telemachos in 1–4 have had to establish their identity—Telemachos by being assured he really is the son of his father (see *3A, C; 5C*), Odysseus by performing in such a way that no-one will be surprised when he announces (as he will at 9.19–20) who he is. For this important theme running through Book 8, see notes on 2–3, 21–3, 75, 147, 170, 207, 220, 237, 389, 491, 523, 553.

B. The book is carefully structured, and illustrates well how the oral poet expands and repeats episodes to create the required emphasis. After the meeting in the agora (1–45), the scene moves to the palace where there is a feast, a song from Demodokos, and Odysseus weeps (46–103); the scene then moves to the open air, where there are various games, broken up by another song of Demodokos (Ares and Aphrodite) in the middle (104–420); and we then move back to the palace, where after gift-giving, bathing and feasting, there is a third song and Odysseus weeps again (421–534)—compare 46–103, an identical pattern—and Alkinoos finally asks who Odysseus is (535–86). In other words, there are three blocks of entertainment, each broken up with a song, with Odysseus weeping during the first and third sessions, tears which finally prompt Alkinoos' question. This is careful organisation on the poet's part. Note the typical repetition of the weeping theme and of the numerous games; and the typical expansion of the final gift-giving scene to show its importance (see on 389).

C. Homer continues to reinforce the picture of Scheria which he established in Books 6 and 7. Note Athene's continuing help (7–15, 18, 193–200); the hostility of Euryalos (159–64), handsomely made up for by Alkinoos and Euryalos (235–40, 396–415); Phaiakian love of ships (34–7, 48–55, 111–5, 247, 253, 556–63—they even guide themselves); Phaiakian friendliness and generosity (32–3, 39–45, 59, 392ff.); and their unceasing love of joy and pleasure (248–9, 368–9, 429, 543). It is tempting to label Phaiakian values 'unheroic'. They are, to the extent that Phaiakians do not feel compelled to seek immortal glory in battle (see Sarpedon's speech, *Iliad* 12.310–28). But even Sarpedon agrees that, under different conditions, he would not fight at all (*Iliad* 12.322–5). Note the Phaiakians' luxurious way of life brings no rebuke from Odysseus' lips. Their way of life may not be Odysseus', but Homeric heroes were not puritans. Cf. *Iliad* 3.111–2, 13.636–9.

D. If Book 8 concentrates our attention on Odysseus' increasing status in Phaiakian eyes, Alkinoos' promptings and reactions help us to gauge the extent to which Odysseus is succeeding in his aims. Alkinoos is a delightfully drawn character. In Book 7, after a somewhat indecisive start (159–61), he was soon showing his generous heart (188–192), garrulous tongue (192ff.!), and pleasure in the achievements of his people (317–28). In Book 8, he continues to show these qualities in full measure (generosity 38–43, 388–432, 543–5, garrulousness (550–86, where usually 'Who are you? Where do you come from?' suffices, e.g. 1.170–7), boasting about his people (100–3, 244–5, 252–3, cf. 383–4), and concomitant love of praise (381–8!)). But to these qualities he adds a tact in the face of Odysseus' unexplained outbursts of weeping (93–103) and a willingness to admit wrong (396–7).

E. Book 8 is important for the picture it gives us of the oral poet at work. Many have thought that Homer may have modelled Demodokos on himself: certainly, Demodokos is heaped with praise and assurances of the Muses' love (44–5, 367–9, 470–98, but cf. Alkinoos' tactful 537–8). For observations about the oral poet's art, see notes on 44, 45, 67, 263, 492, 500, 523. It is important to understand that it is the poet's art that gives lasting glory, because it ensures the memory of the past is saved (579–80): without the poet, there would be no heroic glory because no-one would know what the heroes had achieved (cf. 5.306–12). So Demodokos' function in Book 8 is vital. His songs are not merely entertainment (though they are obviously that): they are the objective ratification of the heroic stature of Odysseus.

2–3.   **the hallowed prince . . . descendant of Zeus . . . sacker of cities**: these are formulaic epithets, but 'sacker of cities', used only of Odysseus in the *Odyssey*, probably signifies 'sacker of Troy' (1.2). The story of the sack will be sung by Demodokos at 500ff. It will be a critical moment (see note on 491).
   4.   **them**: who are 'they?' The Greek of 4 reads 'and them did the holy might of Alkinoos guide'. It is a formulaic line (it re-occurs at 421), here sitting slightly awkwardly in the context.
   6.   **by the ships**: cf. the description at 6.262–9.
   8.   **herald**: i.e. Pontonoos (65). Heralds in Homer keep order at meetings (*Iliad* 2.96–100, 23.567–9), make public proclamations (2.6–8), escort important people (62–70), carry messages (as here), run errands (399, 477) and serve their lords at feasts (1.143) and libations (7.179). Cf. on 15.323–4. The sceptre the heralds hold is a mark of authority—as it is with kings (cf.

41)—and a guarantor of orderly procedure. Cf. the incident with Thersites which so pleased the Greeks at *Iliad* 2.212–277. Heralds are not slaves but noble born. They seem to be in public service (19.135).

19.   **drifted a magical grace**: cf. Athene's beautification of Odysseus before Nausikaa at 6.229–235 (see note on 6.235).

21–3.   **loved . . . wonderful . . . respected . . . tested**: cf. 134–6. Odysseus now 'looks the part'. Looks and authority go together in the Homeric world. The tests he will have to pass (e.g. 184–198, cf. 213) further increase his reputation (cf. 236–7). By the end of Book 8, Odysseus will be ready to reveal who he is.

36.   **fifty-two**: a penteconter would hold fifty rowers, 25 each side. Since all 52 Phaiakians appear to be expert oarsmen (36–7) (and Phaiakian ships did not need steersmen (557)), this is a good example of Alkinoos' boasting. Odysseus' ships have 60 men (see on 10.208).

43.   **inspired**: the Greek says 'divine'—not exactly the same thing.

44.   **Demodokos**: the name means 'welcomed by the people' (cf. 472).

45.   **in power to please**: poetry is the province of the Muse, goddess of memory (480–1), who by supplying the singer with the facts, can prompt pleasure or anguish (cf. 83–92, 521–31) in listeners. The Muse incites the singer to sing (73). Cf. on 1.1, 'Muse'.

52.   **set sails**: the Greek says 'placed sails', i.e. in the ship. If the sails were actually *set*, the ship would move off under way at the first breeze. The 'leather slings' of 53 are the 'oarloops', leather straps which bind the oar to an upright peg (the thole-pin) and, like rowlocks, hold the oar in place.

54.   **set them**: see on 52. All the Greek says is 'they spread out the white sails', i.e. left them hanging free from the yard. One would not normally leave a ship at anchor with oars in position and sails spread unless a quick getaway was envisaged—as it has been (31). Cf. 4.778–786.

63.   **both good and evil**: the good being the gift of sweet singing, the evil being blindness (64–5). Physical blindness could suggest mental or spiritual insight to a Greek.

67.   **the clear lyre**: see on 1.1, 'tell'.

75.   **the quarrel**: nowhere else in Greek literature is there a story of a quarrel between Achilleus and Odysseus. The ancient commentators' opinion is that the quarrel refers to a dispute between Achilleus and Odysseus after the death of Hektor, whether force or cunning would capture Troy. Was this the subject of an epic? Or, as has been suggested, do we have here a reference to an *early* version of the *Iliad* (75–82 look suspiciously like *Iliad* 1.1–7!)? Or is it simply a Homeric invention? Whatever our conclusion about that issue, Demodokos' song is very appropriate: Achilleus is dead, but Odysseus, the man of cunning *par excellence*, has survived (cf. 11.471ff.); and the story of the taking of Troy, by cunning, will be sung later on (499–520). Odysseus, his achievements and greatness, are known to the Phaiakians. For the irony of all this, cf. *1.96–324 E*.

79.   **Phoibos Apollo had spoken**: the commentators speculate that Apollo

said Troy would fall when the best of the Greeks came into conflict. Hence Agamemnon's pleasure (78).

80.   **Pytho**: the old name for Delphi. The Python was a dragon that guarded the city, and was killed by Apollo, the archer-god, who wished to set up a sanctuary there.

86.   **shamed for tears**: see on 4.114. Here Odysseus is concerned not to disturb the jollity of the occasion (90–2).

111–5.   **Akroneos . . . Naubolos' son**: all the (probably invented) names have associations with the sea, for humorous effect e.g. Akroneos means 'top ship', Okyalos 'swift sea', etc.

121–2.   **The field . . . plain**: literally 'for (or by) them from the start (or the turning-post) the track (or the race) was stretched (or strained)'. *Iliad* 23.758 makes it likely that this means 'right from the start (or turning post) the race was run at full stretch'. Lattimore's 'yet' is not in the Greek: read 'and'.

134.   **In his build**: because of Athene's glorification at 20. Cf. 18.67–71.

137.   **youth**: but Odysseus must be at least 40 (see on 15.366), the 'prime' of life for Greeks.

147.   **no greater glory**: typical of Phaiakian peace-time values. Nevertheless, if Odysseus can succeed in any of the contests, his own *kleos* will be considerably increased.

153.   **in mockery**: *kertomeo* has overtones of cutting someone to the quick rather than mocking them. Laodamas has intentionally given Odysseus a way out (138–9), and assured Odysseus that the contests will not affect his promised departure (150–1). Euryalos thinks he has spoken fairly (141). They are clearly not *mocking* Odysseus. What they are doing is, however, making a suggestion which a man who understood natural courtesies would not make: one should not really challenge on this occasion a *xenos* with troubles enough of his own, as Odysseus himself says (154–7). Odysseus himself argues that it would be foolish for a *xenos* to challenge his host in such a context (207–11). So for 'in mockery', read 'in provocation', or 'cutting to the quick'.

161.   **many-locked**: i.e. with many oars. In classical times, warships (triremes) sailed to battle but used oars in battle, while merchants ships were sail-driven. Homeric ships used both methods, as need dictated.

163–4.   **a man who . . . his way**: wrong translation. Read 'a man who, mindful of his cargo out, watches carefully over his cargo back and the profits he can snatch'. See 15.415–6, 445–7, 454–7.

163.   **grasping for profits**: cf. 15.415–6. Greek aristocrats treated with disdain those who traded for a living. Heroes like Odysseus won wealth through *xenia* (389) or raiding. Both fulfil heroic desires to reciprocate with the powerful or master the weak. Cf. 5.36–40, 9.228–30, but also on 1.105.

165.   **looking . . . darkly**: this formula usually indicates that the rules which govern a relationship are being broken. Cf. 18.388, 18.14, 337; 17.459, 19.70, 22.34, 60, 320.

170.   **comeliness on his words**: the skill for which Odysseus is renowned

above all. Nausikaa at 6.239–46 has been persuaded as much by Odysseus' words as by his appearance (cf. 6.187). See 2.270–2, 11.366–9, 13.330–2. *Iliad* 3.192–224 makes a specific point of the contrast between Odysseus's looks and oratory.

174.   **appearance**: see on *17A*.

206.   **wrestling . . . foot race**: Odysseus demonstrated his ability in these sports at Patroklos' funeral (*Iliad* 23.700–97). Interestingly, Odysseus did not compete in the archery (*Iliad* 23.850–83).

207.   **except Laodamas**: Odysseus' tact and courtesy give vivid evidence of his comeliness of speech (169–70) and contrast strongly with Eurylaos' rudeness at 159–64.

219.   **Philoktetes**: the most famous archer of the Greeks at Troy. His bow, inherited from Herakles (see on 224), never missed. For the story of his abandonment by the Greeks and eventual restoration see Sophocles *Philoktetes*.

220.   **in the Trojan country**: by comparing himself to Philoktetes at Troy, Odysseus drops a broad hint about his experiences, possibly even his identity. Odysseus's confidence is such that he can now think of revealing who he is, with the prospect of being believed.

224.   **Herakles**: he of the twelve labours, who received his bow from Apollo. He was a hero, i.e. a mortal worshipped after his death, though in some traditions he is treated like a god. See 11.601–26. Odysseus will show his skill as bowman in Books 21–2. For the history of Odysseus's bow, which is connected with Herakles and Eurytos, see 21.13–41 and notes.

Eurytos of Oichalia: there are mythical Oichalia's in Euboia, Thessaly and Messenia. 21.13–23 suggests Homer means Oichalia in Messene. See on 21.15.

229.   **casts**: surely 'shoots'.

230.   **Only in a foot race**: Odysseus tactfully modifies the challenge he made at 206.

237.   **excellence**: *kleos* again. Odysseus' authority and stature are now openly acknowledged by Alkinoos.

238.   **this man**: Euryalos, at 159–64.

246.   **we are not perfect**: Alkinoos amusingly changes tack now (cf. 100–3) as Odysseus has just done (see note on 230).

248–9.   **lyre and dances/and changes of clothing . . .**: luxurious and decadent this may all seem, but the Phaiakians know the difference between right and wrong (see *6B*, *7A*), unlike the suitors back in Ithaka. For Phaiakian peace-time values, cf. on 147, *8C*.

263.   **well-trained in dancing**: it has been suggested that the youths dance to and accompany in mime Demodokos' song. This is possible (cf. 23.143–5), but at 265 Odysseus admires the dance and at 367–9, when the song is over, Odysseus admires the song. This suggests the events are separate. Cf. on 4.17–19 and see Bowra *HP* 201–4 for the importance of song and dance in epic.

267.   **Ares and sweet-garlanded Aphrodite**: this famous song caused problems for ancient commentators, especially since the gods, who uphold

morality in the *Odyssey* (see *1.22–95B*) seem here to enjoy and condone adultery (334–43). But Zeus, the great overseer of morality in the *Odyssey* (though see 11.267), is kept well out of it all, and Hermes' jest at 339–42 is in keeping with Phaiakian enjoyment of festal pleasure (this is not the real world, but a Phaiakian entertainment). Besides, adultery is punished (329–30), and by cunning, not force (331): so will Odysseus punish the suitors when he finally returns to Ithaka. This scene is the *Odyssey*'s one glance at the gods of the *Iliad* irresponsibly enjoying themselves. Ares (Mars) is god of war, Aphrodite (Venus) god of sex, Hephaistos (Vulcan) the blacksmith god. In the *Iliad*, Hephaistos is married to Charis (*Iliad* 18.382–3). If Homer composed both poems, one would have expected him to be consistent in the matter of Hephaistos' wife. This suggests he took the Ares-Aphrodite story from some other tradition of story-telling, and did not invent it himself. On the other hand, Homer is cavalier with myth when he wants to be.

280.   **like spider webs**: not because the trap looked like a spider's web, but because it was invisible like a spider's web. The trap is fixed round the bed-legs (278 — not posts), and then taken up to the ceiling (279), forming a sort of goal-net. Netted hunting traps for hares were like this.

283.   **Lemnos**: there was a cult of Hephaistos on Lemnos. Hephaistos landed in Lemnos when he was thrown out of heaven by Zeus (*Iliad* 1.586–94). Lemnos is volcanic and rich in metals, which makes it appropriate for Hephaistos.

288.   **Kythereia**: Aphrodite is so called because she came ashore briefly at Kythera after she had been born from the foam at sea (Hesiod *Theogony* 192). She also has a cult at Paphos in Cyprus (362–3), where she eventually landed.

294.   **Sintians**: a Thracian people who settled in Lemnos.

296.   **were bending**: the Greek says 'fell', 'poured'.

299.   **there was no longer a way out**: since Aphrodite is often represented as a goddess who like a huntress pursues and traps her victims into love, it is doubly amusing to see her trapped herself here, in love's pursuit.

306.   **Father Zeus**: Hephaistos calls on Zeus, but Zeus's brother Poseidon comes instead (322) (see on 267 for Zeus's absence).

307.   **ridiculous**: i.e. a sight which would make the gods laugh — as it does (326). Since Greeks hate being humiliated and laughed at, Hephaistos' revenge against Ares is very sweet. Cf. on 18.342.

318.   **gifts of courtship**: see on 2.53.

322–3.   **Poseidon . . ./Hermes . . . Apollo**: in fact other gods came too, though Homer does not say who they are (river-gods? Cf. *Iliad* 20.4–9). See e.g. 328–334, 343–4.

344.   **Poseidon**: why should Poseidon (Neptune) be so eager to see Ares freed? For reasons discussed, Zeus must be kept out of this episode (see on 267), and Poseidon, his brother, is next in greatness and authority to him (13.141–2). Besides, he is the Phaiakians' most important god (6.266–7, 7.34–6, 56–66). It is appropriate in this company that he should take the credit for the resolution of the dilemma with his statesmanlike intervention.

351.   **wretches . . . wretched**: the word used means 'weak, poor, miserable', and is more appropriate to Ares, who is completely helpless in Hephaistos' power, than it is of Hephaistos, who would be unlikely to proclaim his weakness at this, of all moments. So the line refers to Hephaistos' mistrust of Ares, not to Hephaistos' lack of confidence in his own capacity to enforce a deal.

356.   **I myself will pay for it**: Hephaistos is prepared to accept this offer, because Poseidon would certainly keep his word. In the previous deal (347), Poseidon had merely said he would ensure *Ares* would pay up. But, as Hephaistos argued, since Ares was a miserable wretch (351), it was likely he would skip the obligation whatever Poseidon did (352–3).

361.   **Thraceward**: the incident happens on Olympos, and Ares departs for Thrace (he may have originated there), while Aphrodite leaves for Cyprus—totally different directions!

370.   **Halios and Laodamas**: two sons of Alkinoos (119). For Phaiakian love of ball-play, cf. Nausikaa and her servants at 6.99–116.

383.   **as you boasted**: at 252–3.

389.   **gift of friendship**: the giving of a gift was the high point of *xenia*, and made the giver and receiver *xenoi* for life (431–2) (see on 4.589–92). That Alkinoos is prepared to seal the relationship with such an unparalleled quantity of gifts (390–4, 424–42) is a strong indication that Odysseus' worth is now fully recognised, his *kleos* publicly acknowledged. The elaborate gift-giving, followed by a bath, goes on till 457: this is an important moment. But then Odysseus has been very tactful in praising Alkinoos' *sons*! (370). Cf. 13.134–8.

397.   **having spoken out of due measure**: at 159–64.

403–4.   **bronze . . . ivory**: see on 9.392, 393, and 4.73. The sword is special. Mycenaean swords were bronze and all of a piece. No ivory scabbard has been found.

434–56.   **to set the great caldron over the fire**: a typical scene of bathing. Compare 10.357–64, 4.48–50, 3.464–7.

448.   **Circe**: the incident with Circe occupies most of Book 10 and the early part of 12, but no reference is made to knots there.

452.   **he had left the house of fair-haired Kalypso**: the bath that Nausikaa ordered the maids to give Odysseus in 6.209ff. hardly counts. If the maids had their doubts about bathing him then (see on 6.216), they have none now.

459.   **admired him**: cf. 6.237. There are many points of comparison between the scene here and the bathing scene at 6.216–49 (orders to slaves, Odysseus' filthy state, the bath, admiration from Nausikaa, food). This scene of proper *xenia* reminds us of that amusing, but life-saving (463, 468), episode earlier on. It is a very different Odysseus that Nausikaa sees before her now.

489–90.   **the Achaians'/venture**: i.e. the song at 72–82. Odysseus omits to mention the song of Ares and Aphrodite because that was sung not at the feast, but at the entertainment outside the palace (104–8: they return to the palace at 420–1).

491. **as if you had been there yourself**: this is the ultimate praise for an oral poet (see on 1.1 'Muse' and cf. 11.225–32). Odysseus here drops another strong hint about his personal involvement in the Trojan War (cf. on 220, and 496–8) and finds again that the Phaiakians know all about him and his 'true story', his *kleos*. There can now be no reason for him to hide his identity any longer.

493. **the wooden horse**: note how, almost too casually to be accidental, the *Odyssey* rounds out and completes the *Iliad*, which never tells of the sack of Troy, though it movingly prefigures it. The sack was the subject of another epic cycle, the *Iliou Persis* ('Sack of Troy'—see *24D*). Virgil treats the episode in *Aeneid* 2.

500. **beginning from where**: these words suggest Demodokos had the whole story of Troy at his disposal, and was able to select out any passage on request, and elaborate it into a song. Cf. 1.9–10.

503. **hidden**: the horse is a trick, involving hiding and deception. This is the sort of exercise at which Odysseus is especially good. For Odysseus as one who hides his identity, see on *5C*. Cf. 4.271–89.

518. **Deïphobos**: he became a leader of the Trojans when Hektor was killed by Achilleus (*Iliad* 22), cf. 4.276. He was a son of Priam, King of Troy, and his wife Hekabe (Hecuba).

520. **won it there too**: the final heroic accolades—glorious victory in battle (cf. the 'peaceful' Phaiakian challenges which Odysseus has to face—see on 147), *and* support from a goddess (which brings added lustre to the victory, because it shows the hero is worthy of divine aid. Cf. on 2.270–80).

523. **As a woman weeps**: a simile full of pathos, partly because of its astonishing change of focus: Odysseus, the great architect of Troy's destruction, weeps at the memory like a woman who has lost her husband in battle (one is reminded of Hektor's wife Andromache). But, unlike so many heroes at Troy, Odysseus will in fact return to his wife and family. The image of the wife and mother who, powerless to change her lot, endures loss and suffering, is used by Homer and the tragedians to point up the general condition of humanity, and at the same time to endow these women with powerful heroic stature. In the midst of Phaiakian jollity, 500–530 take us, briefly, right to the heart of the Iliadic vision of life. Odysseus' feelings, as one who *experienced* it, rather than merely heard of it, are not such as could be easily shared with his fun-loving hosts. One may care to ask—what is Odysseus weeping for/at? After all, his greatest triumph is being publicly rehearsed. The simile suggests he weeps at some sense of loss, as both Alkinoos (581–6) and Odysseus (9.12–15) hint.

543. **may enjoy ourselves**: Odysseus' grief is private: it cannot be shared with people like the Phaiakians. (See note on 523.) But it is not surprising that Alkinoos should wonder why his guest should weep, after all he has received (544–5).

546. **achievement**: better, 'wisdom'.

548. **So do not longer keep hiding . . .**: the translation suggests that Alkinoos has long been suspecting Odysseus of keeping something back.

This is not the case. Translate 'So do not now try guilefully to evade the questions I ask'.

553.   **nameless**: the 'identity-crisis' of Odysseus and Telemachos is in some ways similar. Cf. Telemachos' fear at 1.206–20.

565.   **Poseidon would yet be angry**: see on 7.35.

569.   **pile . . . it**: see 13.125–87 and notes.

578.   **Argives and Danaans**: since both these words mean 'Greek' (see on 1.90), we may wonder whether their use here is a formulaic anomaly, or an intentional attempt by Alkinoos to sound portentous.

586.   **than a brother**: cf. 546–7. Alkinoos is not merely in a 'mood of universal benevolence' (Stanford), but is making an important point about companionship in war.

Book nine

Introduction

A. Odysseus is away from home for twenty years in all (2.174–6). The Trojan War lasted ten and Odysseus spends 7 years with Kalypso (7.259). Consequently the adventures Odysseus recites in Books 9–12 to the listening Phaiakians last three years, of which he spends one with Circe (10.469). For the reasons why Homer starts the poem where he does, necessitating Odysseus' flashback here in Books 9–12, see Book I Appendix and on 4.112. These adventures, the origin of our word 'odyssey', are some times called in Greek 'apologoi', stories. One fifth of the *Odyssey* consists of tales told in retrospect. See on 4.351.

B. The world of these adventures is rather different from that of the Phaiakians. In particular, an element of magic and fantasy never seems to be far from the surface. Homer, in fact, usually eschews the bizarre and absurd (see Griffin *HLD* 172–8): it is the human magnificence of his heroes that he wishes to emphasise. But as Page *FHO* points out, Homer tends to keep the magic to a minimum in these tales and humanises even the most incredible monsters and adventures (see notes *ad loc.* on the homely qualities of the Cyclops, Polyphemos). Moreover, Athene herself is kept well out of Odysseus' tale (compare e.g. 9.317 with 339 and 381), for reasons given in Book I Appendix.

C. There are two intractable narrative problems associated with Books 9–12. First, we can guess the source for many of the stories. It is almost certainly the tales concerning Jason and the Argonauts, which share with the *Odyssey* the stories of Circe, the Sirens, the Sun God, (etc.). See 12.69–72, and Kirk *NGM* 167–9. The stories have been adapted to suit Homer's *Odyssey*, but they are being told by Odysseus in the first person. Is the telling supposed to inform us about the character of Odysseus? Should we take Odysseus' word for it that the stories all 'happened'? The fact that Odysseus repeats the stories to Penelope at 23.306–41 may incline us to believe they are in outline 'true' (cf. *13D*). Second, the stories are being told to the listening Phaiakians. Should we read them as tales adapted to that audience too, and be asking what influence upon the telling the Phaiakian presence has? Such problems raise questions about seeing the adventures of Odysseus as a paradigm of 'social and natural order' which Odysseus has to re-introduce into Ithaka when he finally arrives home (see e.g. Austin *ADM* 132ff.). But see on 7.14.

D. Whatever conclusions we draw, we can appreciate that Odysseus presents himself as a hero of considerable courage and versatility, but not without his weaknesses. It may, for example, seem foolish of him to have insisted on visiting the Cyclops Polyphemos against his men's wishes. He could be accused of cowardice in abandoning his men to the Laistrygones in Book 10. He seems to have trouble controlling his men (in Book 12, the men's disobedience leads to their death). Nevertheless, the world of the adventures is of a wholly different type from the real world, and Odysseus must respond flexibly if he is to survive. In the Cyclops episode, the incident which Odysseus sees as his greatest achievement (12.209–13), and to which constant reference throughout the *Odyssey* is made, we see how the man of intelligence, wielding the verbal, technical and social skills of the civilised man, can overcome the terrifying threat of primitive, brute force (Clarke *AO* 48).

E. One of the great themes running through these adventures, as through the whole Odyssey, is that of *xenia*: how stranger-guests are received and treated by their hosts (see on 1.102). Odysseus himself experiences many different types of treatment, to which he generally responds with considerable skill. Some argue that these have 'prepared' him for the encounter with the Phaiakians, where for example his tact with Nausikaa and temporary self-concealment with the Phaiakians pay their rewards (compare the hiding of his name, so dramatic a part of Odysseus'plan to escape Polyphemos). Do all these experiences foreshadow, and prepare him for, the ultimate challenge: the meeting with the suitors when Odysseus returns back to Ithaka in Book 13? It is arguable that Odysseus' adventures are the counterpart of the travels of Telemachos in Books 3–4. But to the extent that the purpose of Telemachos' adventures is to restore his sense of identity, I would argue that books 5–8 rather than 9–12 carry out that function for Odysseus. Whether we regard Books 9–12 as subjective or objective reports, they offer rather a continuing account of Odysseus' identity.

F. These adventures give us a chance to see further the oral poet at work. We can admire the skill with which the poet uses repeated lines, scenes and situations in most novel and imaginative ways to create a catalogue of quite different adventures out of very similar material.

G. As Page shows (*HO* Chapter 1 cf. Bowra *HP* 399–401), the Cyclops tale is one deeply embedded in the folk-tale tradition. It exists in many cultures, in many different forms. The most common form is as follows:
    (a) hero and companions are imprisoned in the cave of a one-eyed giant shepherd;
    (b) some/all of the companions are cooked by the giant on a spit over the fire;
    (c) the giant falls asleep after his heavy meal;
    (d) the hero takes the spit, heats it in the fire and plunges it in the giant's eye;
    (e) in the morning the giant opens the cave to let out the sheep and the

hero escapes by walking out on all fours under a sheepskin, or by clinging to the underside of a sheep;

(f) the hero is located when he puts on a magic ring which shouts 'Here I am', and escapes only by cutting off his finger.

As one would expect, Homer uses this version in such a way as to emphasise certain common themes that run through the Odyssey, especially corruption of *xenia* (Polyphemos ignores all the Greek conventions of the institution) and Odysseus' piety in contrast with Polyphemos' arrogant dismissal of the Olympian gods. But Homer also changes the story in certain important ways, i.e.

(a) the giant eats the men raw;
(b) the hero puts the giant to sleep by giving him wine;
(c) he uses a wooden stake as the weapon for blinding the giant;
(d) the hero plays a trick on the giant by calling himself 'Nobody';
(e) the hero is located when he taunts the giant.

These changes too have their purposes. They help to emphasise:

(i) Polyphemos' uncivilised brutality (a)
(ii) Odysseus' supreme intelligence and both verbal and technical mastery of Polyphemos (b) (c) and (d).
(iii) the theme of identity and revelation (and its consequences) (e).

H. The escape from Polyphemos, constantly referred to throughout the *Odyssey* and generally regarded as Odysseus' greatest triumph, emphasises one of Odysseus' most important attributes: his *mētis* ('cunning intelligence'). The man of *mētis* (one of Odysseus' epithets is *polumētis*, 'resourceful', 'of much cunning intelligence') is essentially a deceiver. He can change and adapt to circumstances, he seizes upon and exploits to his own advantage the passing moment. In areas where violence alone rules, and there are no laws or precedents (e.g. Polyphemos' cave), only the man of *mētis* can survive, because the only way to defeat overwhelming force is to *out-think* it (9.513–7). Odysseus will out-think Polyphemos, as he will the suitors. Note the comparison: both ignore *xenia*; Odysseus will defeat both with disguise and eventual violence, both consume what they ought not to. Cf. 20.18–22. But such a man can be condemned for slipperiness and cheating as much as praised for superb quick-thinking. The *polumētis* is open to the charge of being self-serving and too clever by half (9.19–20). It is no coincidence that Athene, Odysseus' patron goddess, is the daughter of Zeus and Mētis (Hesiod *Theogony* 886–929). At 13.291–2, Athene argues that even a god needs sharpness to discern Odysseus' tricks. Cf. on 4.270.

On all this, see M. Detienne and J-P. Vernant *Cunning Intelligence in Greek Culture and Society*, tr. J. Lloyd, Harvester Press 1978, and *GI H*. Odysseus' subsequent literary reputation, which swings from 'hero' to 'villain', is discussed in Stanford *UT passim*.

I. There has been much debate about the geographical reality behind Odysseus' tales. The 1stC geographer Strabo argued that Homer told part truth, part fiction (*Geography* 1.2.14–19). Eratosthenes, another geographer (3rdC), said that he would believe Odysseus' travels when someone found the cobbler who made the bag in which Aiolos placed the winds. The problem is that Homer gives us no clear directions from 9.82ff.; and even when he mentions e.g. wind-direction, he denotes sectors, not points of the compass. Add to that the origin of the stories (the Argonaut myths) and the difficulties we encounter making sense even of places that seem to *have* some historical reality (see on e.g. 9.25 and the debate over the location of Ithaka), and there is a very strong case for abandoning the search for Odysseus' 'real route' entirely.

J. On allegory, see *12F*. Two excellent articles on the Cyclops episode are: A. Podlecki, 'Guest gifts and Nobodies in *Odyssey* 9', *Phoenix* 15 1961; S. Schein, 'Odysseus and Polyphemos in the *Odyssey*', *GRBS* 11 1970.

   4.   **such as this one**: Demodokos (see e.g. 8.470ff.). Banquets and songs to the *phorminx* (see on 1.1 'tell') are typical features of all heroic worlds (cf. 17.261–71, and Bowra *HP* 201–4).
   5–11.   **I think . . . occasions**: delightful irony, when we consider what awaits Odysseus at home.
   6.   **among all the populace**: Odysseus is generalising here. In fact, Alkinoos was entertaining only the Phaiakians and the men who would sail Odysseus home (8.11, 40–2).
   12–13.   **But now . . . even more**: the tales bring grief to those who have lived through the experience related (8.537–41)—though pleasure too, because the sufferings are past (15.400–1)—but joy to the listeners (11.333–4 = 13.1–2, cf. 11.374–6). Observe that Odysseus is a story-teller, not a *singer*. He speaks his tale (9.1), and even the world 'recite' (14) has no necessary connotations of singing (cf. 37 'tell', the same word as is used at 1.1 and 1.10, but widely used of non-sung narration). A singer appeals to the Muse (1.1) and actually *sings* (see e.g. 8.266, 8.499, 1.325, 1.155). Characters *liken* Odysseus' story-telling ability to that of a singer (11.366–9, 17.515–21), but that praise only makes sense if Odysseus is *not* singing.
   16.   **my name**: it was essential to know the name of a guest if bonds of *xenia* between guest and host were to be firm. See 17.355–6.
   20.   **my fame** (= *kleos*) **goes up to the heavens**: the climactic moment we have been waiting for. Odysseus can only reveal himself when he feels he can assert his own *kleos* with authority in front of the Phaiakians. For Odysseus' self-revelation, and the problem of *kleos*, see *5C, 7D, 8A*.
   25.   **but my island lies low and away**: there is a famous controversy over the exact meaning of these lines. The word translated 'low' could also mean 'close to land'; 'away' could mean 'highest of all'. On top of this, modern Ithaka (Thiaki) is not 'low'—it is hilly and its peaks reach 2000'—nor is it '(far) away' from the mainland in relation to the other islands, all of which lie further away than Ithaka. The poet seems to know that Ithaka is an island in a group of other islands, which lie off the coast of north-western Greece—

other than that, his precise knowledge of its location is hazy. See map p. 237. For one solution, see *CH* 398, from which Ithaka = Thiaki, Same = Kefallenia, Zakynthos = Zakynthos, Doulichion = Leukas. Cf. Camps *IH* 85 note 25 and on 4.846. For other descriptions of Ithaka, see 4.605–8, 13.241–7. For characteristics of modern Thiaki, see *CH* 278.

29. **Kalypso . . . kept me**: for seven years. See 5.1–268 and 12.447–50. It was from Kalypso's cave that Odysseus was released to begin his travels that brought him to Alkinoos' palace, as told in Books 5–7. He has already told the Phaiakians about her (7.244–266).

31. **Circe . . . detained me**: for one year. See 10.203–574, 12.1–150. But exactly how unwilling was Odysseus to be detained? See 10.469–475. Whatever the truth of the matter, Odysseus wants to impress on the Phaiakians that his long detention was not his fault (33). See on 10.135 for Aiaia.

36. **far from his parents**: Odysseus has not yet mentioned Penelope to the Phaiakians (cf. 7.244–5, and Alkinoos' offer of marriage at 7.311–5). He keeps quiet about her here too. One might see purpose in this in the earlier books: is there any purpose here?

37. **I will tell you of my voyage home**: note the neat series of ring-compositional devices in this poem to Odysseus' adventures: 'occasion' (5)— 'occasions' (11): 'What then/shall I recite . . . sorrows' (13–15)—'I will tell you . . . troubles' (37–8): 'sweeter' (28)—'more sweet' (34).

38. **Troy land**: Troy is, to be exact, the name of the territory. 'Ilion' (Ilium) is the name of the city the Greeks sacked (see 39). Cf. on 1.2.

39. **the wind took me**: this first adventure with the Kikonians, and the ensuing storm (67–75), have been castigated as pointless (Kirk *SoH* 234) but they serve an important function. To the Phaiakians, the sea offers no terrors, and their ships need no wind to move (8.555–63). Odysseus emphasises that he was at the mercy of the winds. Odysseus makes no reference to incidents which occur in Nestor's version of his travels (3.162–4).

39. **Ismaros**: this is in Thrace. The Kikonians were allies of the Trojans (*Iliad* 2.846). Odysseus' adventures start in the known world.

40. **I sacked their city**: cf. Menelaos' wholly honourable collection of wealth on his travels (4.81–91), some of which must have been by raiding as well as from *xenia*. The scene is notably Iliadic in flavour: 42 cf. *Iliad* 11.705; 45–6 cf. *Iliad* 466–9; 51 cf. *Iliad* 2.468; 54–5 cf. *Iliad* 18.533–4; 56 cf. *Iliad* 9.84. But we shall soon be leaving the 'realistic'world of the *Iliad* (see note on 81). For the structure of the battle, cf. 14.258ff. = 17.427ff.

44. **they were greatly foolish**: the contrast between foolish and intelligent behaviour will play a decisive part in these adventures. The theme was announced in the proem, 1.6–8, with reference to Odysseus' loss of his last ship (12.260–end). Cf. 14.85–8 for the danger incurred by those who outstay their welcome.

45. **much wine was being drunk**: careful preparation by the poet. Wine will have an important function in the Cyclops episode. See on 164.

54–5.   both sides . . . they: these references to Odysseus' own men and the enemy in the 3rd person plural are slightly odd: we should expect 'we', not 'they'. Cf. 59 (which is not, in fact, as markedly 'third person' in the Greek). Clearly these stories existed in a tradition in which they were not told in the first person by Odysseus, but in the third person by a bard.

60.   **out of each ship six**: since Odysseus has twelve ships (159), seventy-two are killed in this encounter. There are c.60 men per ship (see on 10.208). The Phaiakians have 52 (8.36). Telemachos needed 20 for his journey (2.212).

strong-greaved: a formulaic epithet applied to soldiers, extremely frequent in the *Iliad*, comparatively rare in the *Odyssey*. Greaves protect the shin. Few have been found, so they were probably made of perishable leather (cf. 24.228–9). See *CH* 505–6.

62–3.   From there we sailed on . . .: these lines recur, singly or both together, at 105, 565–6, 10.77, 10.133–4. They help the poet give shape to and make easy transitions within an episodic narrative.

65.   **a cry had been made three times**: since Odysseus could not recover the corpses of the dead to give them proper burial, he piously remembered to have this ritual cry uttered. If Virgil *Aeneid* 6.506 offers a true parallel, such a cry was normally raised at regular burial services.

67.   **Cloud-gathering Zeus**: storms at sea often occur in epic. See e.g. at 3.286, 4.514, 5.291, 10.48, 12.313, 12.403, 14.301. Typical features are (i) Zeus's instigation (ii) raising of clouds and wind (iii) havoc wreaked by waves (iv) destruction of parts of boat (v) men lost overboard (vi) details of wreckage.

68.   **cloud scuds**: i.e. scudding clouds.

74–6.   **we lay up, . . . third day**: 10.143–4. See on 62–3.

80.   **Maleia**: the southern tip of the Peloponnese, a common place to be swept off course. See 3.288, 4.514–6, 19.186–7.

81.   **Kythera**: an island S.W. of Maleia. Maleia and Kythera are the last identifiable places mentioned in Odysseus' tale. From now on, we enter fairy-land.

84.   **Lotus-Eaters**: a ten-day north-wind-blown journey from Maleia would land one up somewhere on the coast of N. Africa, where the Lotus-Eaters are (therefore) located (cf. Herodotus *Histories* 4.176ff.). Page *FHO* 3–21 discusses folktales in which one's return home depends on *avoiding* certain types of food. When Persephone ate the pomegranate pips in Hades, she was unable to return to the world above.

85–90.   **and there we set foot . . .**: typical lines. Cf. 10.56–8, 100–2.

97.   **forget the way home**: for the pull of the home, and home as the major determinant of identity, see on 1.13. Cf. Austin *ADM* 138–9. Odysseus' determination that all will return (100–2) is impressive.

103–4.   **and the men quickly . . . gray sea**: typical line again (see on 62–3). Cf. 4.579–80, 9.179–80, 471–2, 563–4, 12.146–7.

106–7.   **lawless, outrageous/Cyclopes**: since the Phaiakians are connected with the Cyclopes (6.6–12, 7.56–62, 205–6), it is odd that Odysseus does not mitigate somewhat his remarks here, or make reference to the Phaia-kians' connection. This is further evidence that the Cyclops story existed in a version wholly unrelated to our *Odyssey*. See on 6.5, 9.131.

107. **putting all their trust in**: i.e. letting them get on with it. There is no impiety here.

110. **for them**: not in the Greek. Its addition here ruins one of the points about the Cyclops—that he is *not* a wine-drinker, and can therefore easily be made drunk. The force of the 'which' clause here is 'generalising'.

112. **no institutions**: the Cyclopes are completely uncivilised—which to an 8thC Greek, with a developing city-state system, meant no legal prece-dents, no *agorai* (gathering places, where communal decisions are taken) and no communal law-making. Cf. 114–5, but also on 6.7. The epic was not a medium for describing the ideology of a city-state, but it could reflect it (*GI E*). Note there was a Cyclopean soothsayer—Telemos (508–10).

116. **There is a wooded island**: this island, next to the Cyclopes', is where Odysseus' men first land (142) before a picked band sets out for Polyphemos' land (170ff.). References to its potential for growth (131–4), especially its harbour (135–9) and to the Cyclopes' ignorance of ships (125–7), put one strongly in mind of 8thC colonisation (especially 127–30. Cf. on 6.7, and on 6.8 for heroic lack of interest in the *trading* opportunities which shipping creates.). See *WoA* p.67 for a 5thC view of a perfect site for settlement.

125. **vermilion**: see on 12.173. Since the Cyclopes' land is so fertile, they hardly *need* ships. But Odysseus is addressing ship-loving Phaiakians. See on 6.269.

131. **it could bear all crops**: cf. Phaiakian utopia (7.112–32). Observe the contrast between Phaiakian intelligence and Cyclopean short-sightedness.

137. **anchor-stone**: see on 13.77.

142. **there was some god guiding**: it is common for Greeks to ascribe a lucky chance to the god, though Odysseus *cannot* know who it is—see on 1.1. There is no need to see here the 'hand of god' guiding Odysseus towards an encounter with Polyphemos.

150–2. **and we ourselves . . . rosy fingers**: cf. 12.6–8; 9.547.

158. **and the god granted us . . .**: cf. 142. The good luck attending the start of this adventure, and the soothing environment, contrast strongly with the nearly disastrous outcome. For hunting on landing, see 10.156ff.

164. **we all had taken away a great deal**: observe the care with which the poet prepares the story. Wine is to play a key part in Polyphemos' downfall (cf. 194–215, 345–74), as it did in the adventure with the Kikonians (43–6).

167. **sheep and goats bleating**: more careful preparation. The sheep will save Odysseus and his men (424–66); their ordure will hide the sharpened stake (329–31). It is typical of Homer to summarise a whole experience (seeing a distant island over water) with reference to one or two facets of it. For smoke, see on 1.58.

174. **and learn what they are**: there are a constant curiosity and inquisi-tiveness about Odysseus, which nearly bring disaster here (cf. 224–30).

176.   **hospitable to strangers**: Odysseus' motive is to get a guest-gift and increase his personal wealth (229) — a wholly honourable motive in principle (cf. on 8.163, 4.81–91).

181–6.   **there . . . foliage**: cf. Polyphemos' crude dwelling with Eumaios' hut (14.5–16).

182.   **close to the water**: preparation again. Odysseus will be able to make a quick escape, but will be within the range of Cyclops' throw (469ff.).

188.   **alone**: preparation. Odysseus will be able to blind the Cyclops and get away with the 'Nobody' trick because Cyclops lives alone (396–414).

189–92.   **lawless/. . . monstrous wonder . . . not/like a man . . . more like a wooded/peak**: Odysseus emphasises the primitiveness and inhumanity of Cyclops, as well as his giant size. In fact, the poet will not paint quite such a black and white picture of Cyclops when we see him in the flesh. See on 235–6.

195.   **choosing out the twelve best men**: eleven of Odysseus' ships are on the adjacent island; one is on the Cyclops' island (177–80). From that one Odysseus selects his twelve best men for the adventure.

197.   **sweet wine, given me by Maron . . .**: for the importance of the wine, see on 164. Ismaros (198) was the town Odysseus and his men sacked at 39ff. Maron is a name formed from Maroneia, the Thracian town where this famous wine was made. 'Euanthes' means 'with lovely flowers' — referring to vineyards? The elaboration of the description of the wine shows its importance. Cf. 8.389.

199.   **respecting him**: note the piety of Odysseus here. Cf. 64–6.

209.   **twenty measures of water**: wine in the ancient world was always drunk dilute. One part of wine to three water and two parts to three water were common measures. This wine, requiring one part of wine to twenty of water, was quite outstandingly intoxicating.

213.   **my proud heart had an idea**: is this Odysseus boasting *after* the event of his prescience? Or is he reporting what he thought at the time? Odysseus' version of the tale is certainly full of *post eventum* understanding, e.g. 106–30, 189–92, 228–30.

218.   **we . . . admired everything**: the first hint that there is another side to this uncivilised brute. The care with which the lambs and kids have been treated (220–2) is particularly affecting. Polyphemos is a careful farmer, at least. For the 'admiration' element in arrivals, see e.g. 4.44, 5.75, 7.133.

228.   **it would have been better their way**: a first admission of misjudgement on Odysseus' part. Contrast this careless confidence with e.g. 10.194–202.

229.   **presents**: the Greek says *xeinia*, i.e. the gifts due to a *xenos*.

234.   **a fire for his dinner**: but Polyphemos does not cook his food. The fire is to give him warmth and light (251) — and to give Odysseus the means by which he can harden the stake to drive into his eye (328, 375–9) (preparation).

235–6.   **terrible/crash**: observe that Polyphemos is never closely described, but the things he does and Odysseus' men's reaction create a terrible image of brute size and power. Cf. 239–44, 257, 288–93, 313, 371–4, 395–6, 481–6. Even the fact that Polyphemos has a single eye is only implied by the blinding (and cf. 512, 1.69. At 389 Polyphemos has 'eyebrows' (plural)). Description by suggestion and reaction is typical of Homer. Homer can hint at his monstrosity without denying him human credibility at the same time.

240. **the huge door-stop**: more essential preparation. As 302–5 make clear, this door-stop is the reason why Odysseus cannot kill Polyphemos outright while he sleeps. Odysseus must resort to means other than mere violence to engineer his escape.

244. **Next he sat down . . .**: more homely and domestic duties from this horrible brute. Cf. 308–10.

249. **to help himself to and drink from**: a vital element in the plot— Polyphemos is a *milk* drinker, though the Cyclopes know about wine (357–8). Consequently he will be particularly vulnerable to drink, especially a drink as powerful as Odysseus has (196–215) (preparation).

252. **Strangers, who are you?**: the normal rules of hospitality demand that a host welcomes a guest and offers food *before* questioning him (1.123–4). But the circumstances *are* a little unusual here: after all, Odysseus and his men have invited themselves in and eaten his food already (231–3)—and the *xenos* properly waited outside to be welcomed in (see on 7.50). So it is natural that Polyphemos should ask them who they are. What is culpable is that he offers them no food and rejects their pleas.

258. **but even so . . .**: observe the contrast between the real feelings of Odysseus and his men, and Odysseus' carefully 'normal' response, as if he were addressing a human hero rather than an inhuman monster. Odysseus does not, however, reveal his identity, but just sketches his heroic background. This gives him room for the 'Nobody' trick. The whole episode is characterised by the calculating intelligence that Odysseus shows in this tightest of spots.

270. **Zeus the guest god**: Nausikaa (6.207–8) and the Phaiakians (7.164–5) knew the rights of the *xenos*/suppliant—will Polyphemos?

275. **The Cyclopes do not concern themselves . . .**: cf. 214–5. Odysseus now knows the full magnitude of the danger he is in—if he had not guessed it already. Observe how neither the gods nor the world of heroes means anything to the barbarous Polyphemos, strongest of the Cyclopes (1.70–1). Cf. 293–5.

279–80. **where did you/put your well-made ship . . .?**: there is an animal cunning about Polyphemos. Naturally, he cannot fool the great Odysseus, who sees through the real meaning of the question at once (if Odysseus admits they have a boat, Polyphemos will destroy it and have them completely at his mercy).

297. **unmixed with water**: to drink unmixed *wine* would have been the mark of the barbarian to a Greek (see on 209). But unmixed *milk*?! This may be an example of Homeric humour; or it may be a confusion caused by a tradition in which Polyphemos was, indeed, a wine-drinker (cf. 357–8), so

that either an extra-strong potion was needed to knock him out (such as Odysseus brings with him here) or some other incapacitating device would have to be adopted.

298–9.   **Then I/took counsel with myself**: the whole Cyclops episode is marked by the number of times that Odysseus has to make a decision about the best course of action to take (cf. 258, 281–2). Here is the man of intelligence working at full stretch. In this instance, Odysseus has to repress within himself an instinct for an 'Iliadic' solution to the problem (just kill Polyphemos) because it would not in fact solve it (302–5).

313–4.   **easily . . ./lid on a quiver**: the ease with which Polyphemos removes the boulder stands in strong contrast to Odysseus' feelings about it (239–44). It is this formidable barrier that must be circumvented as well as Polyphemos.

315.   **whistling loudly**: another homely touch.

318.   **the plan that seemed best to me**: see on 298–9.

322.   **about the size for the mast**: Polyphemos knows nothing of shipbuilding (125–7): but the civilised, technically-minded Odysseus thinks naturally in such terms—cf. the boat he built at 5.244–61.

335.   **four men, and I myself was the fifth**: Odysseus took twelve men with him (195), and four have been eaten (289, 311). The purpose of the lot is to select the four men who must be *saved* from Polyphemos' jaws. The giant eats two more men—not from among the four—at 344.

338.   **did not leave any outside**: this will be an important factor in Odysseus' escape. He will need the strong rams to tie his men under (425ff.). These were normally kept outside by Polyphemos (237–9).

349.   **libation**: Odysseus flatters Polyphemos here. Libations were, of course, for gods.

355.   **tell me your name**: Odysseus kept his name hidden from the Phaiakians, until he was ready to reveal it (see *7B, 8C*). He has kept it from Polyphemos too (cf. on 258). When he does reveal it, it will be a false name, 'Nobody', and it will save Odysseus and his men.

356.   **guest present**: cf. 229, 267. Polyphemos *does* know about the duties of host to guest, but chooses to ignore them (273–9). This calculated barbarity increases his wickedness.

369–70.   **I will eat Nobody after his friends . . .**: a mockery of a guest-gift, of course. Demetrius *On Style* 3.130 comments that nothing shows up more clearly how terrible Polyphemos is than this show of 'wit'. For another ironic guest-gift, see 20.296–300. Cf. on 20.287.

372.   **over on one side**: important preparation. Odysseus and his men will be able to attack his eye at ground level.

379.   **glowed, terribly incandescent**: cf. 328. But a green olive-stake, even one on the point of catching fire, would hardly *glow all through*, 'incandescent'. Page *HO* 10ff. suggests this is a memory of an alternative version in which the iron spit on which Polyphemos roasted his food (he eats men *raw* in our version—e.g. 291–3) was used to drill out his eye. This, heated, would become incandescent.

382. **leaned on it**: the four chosen men hold the stake and guide it into Polyphemos' eye (382–3), while Odysseus, positioning himself at the end of the stake, leans on it (383) to thrust it home, while at the same time twisting it (384) into the eye with his hands. The ensuing simile (384–6) does not quite fit, since in the simile the men do the twirling, while the man above merely guides.

384. **with a brace-and-bit**: this technological simile (cf. the simile of quenching iron at 391, and the ship images throughout) reminds us of the difference between the primitive farming Polyphemos and the advanced, technically aware Odysseus.

386. **the strap**: the simplest form of powering a drill is with a strap, which is looped around it. Two men, pulling on either end alternately, spin the drill successively clockwise and anticlockwise. A more sophisticated version of the strap is the bow: the 'string' of the bow is looped around the drill, and the bow itself pulled quickly back and forth.

392. **into cold water**: Lattimore calls this 'tempering' (393). But to temper means to heat iron to at least 1100°c in carbon (carburisation turns iron into steel), cool it in water, reheat it to a lower temperature, and then cool it again. This is rare. The process is more likely to be 'quenching', where the iron is strengthened by being heated and then plunged into cold water. For the smith's implements, see 3.432–5; Hephaistos is pictured at work at *Iliad* 18.468–77.

393. **steel**: the Greek says 'iron'. This is a clear reference to an iron-age practice in Greece (i.e. post 1000). The heroes of the epic used bronze for their weapons and implements. The bronze age ended c.1100 (see Camps *IH* 65 note 1c). The difficulty with bronze is that it is made of copper and tin, and both need importing (though recent research suggests the mines at Laurion may have supplied tin as well as silver in the Bronze Age). Copper came from Cyprus. Iron is potentially stronger and more widely available. Iron and bronze formed part of Odysseus' wealth: see 2.338, 21.10.

408. **Nobody is killing me**: Polyphemos not only lacks technical skill: he has no verbal sophistication either (a capacity highly valued by Greeks). So he falls into Odysseus' trap.

414. **perfect planning**: one cannot blame the translation for missing an important verbal joke here. The Greek for 'nobody' takes two basic forms — *ou tis* and *mē tis* (the difference is due to the fact that Greek has two forms of the negative, *ou* and *mē*, used for different contexts). Odysseus called himself *ou tis* at 366, and that is the form Polyphemos uses at 408, 455, 460. But the neighbouring Cyclopes use the form *mē tis* at 405–6 ('no mortal', 'none') and 410 ('none'). The point of the joke is that the Greek word *mētis* (*mē* and *tis* run together) means 'cunning intelligence' (a common epithet for Odysseus is *polumētis* 'of much cunning intelligence'), and this is the word used here which Lattimore translates as 'perfect planning'. So the line has a double meaning: 'my cunning intelligence fooled him' and 'my "Nobody" fooled him'. English cannot duplicate this play on words. Cf. 20.20.

419. **I would be so guileless**: further signs of crude intelligence on Polyphemos' part — but again, far too inept for Odysseus. See on 279–80. Cf. 442.

420.   **I was planning**: cf. on 298–9.

425.   **rams**: prepared for at 337–9.

439.   **but the ewes were bleating**: strong pathos. Polyphemos, who has been so conscientious about milking his ewes and putting the kids to their mothers (244–6, 308–9, 341–2), can now no longer carry out even that most basic of tasks.

447.   **My dear old ram**: further pathos at Polyphemos' plight: all he can turn to is an old ram. His close relationship with the ram is beautifully suggested by 447, 448–52 (Polyphemos knows his habits). But pathetic though Polyphemos may be, he is still a danger (458–60).

479.   **so Zeus and the rest of the gods have punished you**: the *Odyssey* is characterised by the belief that Zeus and the gods oversee human behaviour. See *1.22–95B*. Odysseus will punish the suitors for exactly the same reason (22.235–41).

474.   **taunting him**: this boasting over a defeated enemy may seem foolish. It also has almost disastrous consequences (483–4, 492–99, 539–40). But see on 500.

483.   **it just failed to graze the steering oar's edge**: since this oar is at the *back* of the boat, the boulder could hardly land in front of the boat so as to sweep it back to the shore (484–6). The boat cannot be backing water (471–2). The poet is probably misusing a formula here. He gets it right at 539–42.

500.   **could not persude the great heart in me**: it seems greatly foolish of Odysseus to reveal his identity here (503–5) because (i) it gives Polyphemos another chance to heave a rock at ship, (ii) it gives Polyphemos his real name. Since curses can be efficaciously laid on someone only in their own name, Polyphemos now has the means to bring Poseidon's wrath down on Odysseus (which he does 528–35). The god's wrath dogs Odysseus' footsteps for the rest of his journey home (cf. 1.68–75). This seems a high price to pay for what seems a rather childish boasting. But Odysseus is a hero. It is out of the question that he should allow a brute like Polyphemos to imagine that a Nobody had blinded him: his sense of *kleos* could not possibly allow it. As we saw in the Phaiakian episode, identity can only be hidden for so long: identity and heroism cannot be separated. Aristotle (*Rhetoric* ii 3.16) argues that anger is personal and for Odysseus to consider himself revenged, Polyphemos must be told *who* punished him.

508.   **man**: meaning a Cyclops. Cf. 187, 495.

513–5.   **But . . . feeble**: *mētis* allows the weak to defeat the strong.

517.   **So come here, Odysseus**: Polyphemos' last feeble attempt to trick Odysseus (cf. 279–80, 419).

532.   **but if it is decided**: even a god cannot alter destiny—though he can play around with it at the edges. Cf. the various prophecies about Odysseus' return—2.174–6 (Halitherses), 5.41–2, 114–5 (Zeus), 11.100–37 (Teiresias), 12.137–41 (Circe).

551.   **I sacrificed him**: it is Odysseus' conclusion that Zeus is not moved by the offering (553–5). He has only partial knowledge of what god motivates what action, as we have already seen (see note on 5.303). Zeus only takes a

hand at 12.374ff., and then because of the wickedness of Odysseus' men.

556–66.   **so for the whole length . . . dear companions**: these lines are wholly formulaic. 556–7 = 161–2; 558–60 = 168–7; 561 ≏ 488; 562–4 = 178–80; 565–6 = 62–3. They give a sense of normality returning to the existence of Odysseus and his men after the terrifying experience of Polyphemos.

Book ten

Introduction

A. This book follows the same pattern as Book 9. Two shorter incidents (Aiolos, Laistrygones) are followed by a major encounter (Circe). We can observe again the skill with which the poet mixes typical elements to create new and exciting adventures for Odysseus and his men (see notes on e.g. 13–8, 30, 31, 87–102, 105, 113, 116, 118, 140–88, 348–72). By the same token, the poet develops certain important themes begun in Book 9. The tensions between Odysseus and his men continue to be brought out (27, 32, 419), and Odysseus himself seems vulnerable to charges of cowardice at 131 and obstinacy at 273. He also seems keener to stay with Circe than his men do (469–74), though she herself does not obstruct him in the way that Kalypso does (489).

B. As we saw in *9B*, Homer shapes common folk-tales to his own particular story and characters. In particular, he likes to diminish the magical elements. The tales of Book 10 continue to bear out his general truth. The Aiolos incident, for example, bears many parallels with real life, as Page shows in *FHO* 73–8. People of all ages and times have tried to control the weather by one means or another, and Page points out that in the Linear B tablets (records, mainly of economic activity, which survive from Mycenaean Greece—see *GI C*) there are references to a priestess of the winds. Aiolos, however, although his methods exactly duplicate those of magicians, has been put in charge of the winds by Zeus, and is an otherwise fully humanised Olympian god. He is extremely hospitable (14), enjoys tales (14–16), and is generous and helpful (19–26).

C. The Laistrygones are a different proposition. They seem to have been taken over from the Argonautic tales involving Jason and Medeia and the golden fleece (see on 108). Stories of cannibalistic giants are common (cf. Cyclops), but these are very Greek giants: they have assemblies and glorious homes etc. (see on 103). But though the build-up to the story is leisurely, the details of the men's destruction are compressed and hurried, and Odysseus' tying-up outside the harbour is apparently unmotivated (unless 97 gives the reason). Whatever the reason, the incident is functional: it gets rid of all the other ships bar Odysseus' and gives Odysseus a strong motivation for acting bravely in the Circe incident to make up for his cutting and running from the Laistrygones (see on 273).

D. Circe has many affinities with Kalypso, but the differences are important. The atmosphere about Circe's palace with its drugged animals is quite different from that of Kalypso's well-ordered gardens (5.55–75). Further, Circe dabbles in magic, foretells the future, seems the greater threat, but at the end has Odysseus' best interests at heart (see on 221–4). The delicate sexual duelling between Circe and Odysseus, however, reminds us of that between Odysseus and Kalypso. Odysseus cannot bring himself fully to trust either woman as they are. This sense of male-female rivalry is not present in the *Iliad* (though there is obviously great uneasiness in the relationship between Paris and Helen). Page (*FHO* 51–69) quotes many folk-tale parallels with Circe: in particular, the witch on the look out for a lover of whom she eventually tires and kills or turns into an animal (the reason for the oath at 297–301), e.g. Ishtar's attempt to add Gilgamesh to her list of lovers in the *Epic of Gilgamesh*. It is again noticeable how the magical elements of the Circe story are kept to a minimum (see on e.g. 213, 287–301, 305) and the social elements—bathing, feeding etc. (348–72)—stressed. Homer skilfully develops the character of Circe so that she can fit into a story about a Greek hero like Odysseus and, by her interaction with him, enlarge his character too (the comparison with Kalypso is especially cleverly suggested, being set up for us at 9.29–33). If there are awkwardnesses in the story, they probably arise from Homer's suppression of the magical. See Austin *ADM* 152–3.

1.   **Aiolos**: the name means 'changeful'. Since Aiolos is ruler of the winds (19–22), lives on a floating island (3), and will treat Odysseus differently on two occasions, the name is appropriate. Cf. on Ino, 5.333.

2.   **Hippotas**: the name means 'horseman'. Since Poseidon is god of horses and the sea, the ancestry is again suitable.

7.   **bestowed his daughters on his sons**: this is a practice of divine, not human, society (see on 7.56), though Aiolos' divinity is not stressed in this passage (21–2 do not necessarily imply it).

10–11.   **echoes/in the courtyard**: this makes no sense, but neither does the Greek text if the word *aulēi* is taken to mean 'courtyard' (which it normally does). The Greek word *aulos* means 'pipe'. That is surely what Homer means here. Tr. 'echoes/to the pipe'.

13–18.   **We came to . . . granted me passage**: these six lines offer in compressed form almost a complete *xenia* sequence. See on 1.102.

27.   **by our own folly**: this important theme, announced at 1.7, has already been suggested at 9.43–7 and 9.224–9. Cf. 68–9, 78–9. Note the tension between Odysseus and his men. The men cannot leave well alone. Both refuse to take good advice. Is Odysseus fully in charge? Does he really have his men's confidence? See on 419.

30.   **people tending fires**: cf. 9.166–7.

31.   **sweet sleep came upon me**: cf. 12.338ff.

32.   **I would not give it**: this mistrust by Odysseus of his companions is reflected in their lack of confidence in him at 41–2.

38.   **loved . . . and favored**: Odysseus is not yet reduced to the state

where he needs to conceal his identity wherever he goes. At this stage of his return he is still the great hero of the Trojan war. Cf. 14–16, and for the 'concealing' theme see *8A*. On material rewards, see on 5.38.

53.   **and I endured it and waited**: Odysseus even considers suicide (51), such is his despair (cf. 5.306–11 and note). Is there a strange lack of *mētis* (cunning intelligence—see *9H*) here? It certainly seems that Odysseus has nothing to offer in this desperate situation. On the other hand, what can he *do* about it? His decision to *endure* is another aspect of his *mētis*. Having decided that no action is possible, he waits until it *is* possible. He will need all the endurance he can muster in Ithaka against the 108 suitors. Cf. on 4.270.

63.   **we sat down**: a significant gesture. Odysseus is adopting a suppliant position here (see on 6.142). But why? He is surely a guest-friend of Aiolos, since he stayed there a month (14) and was given a gift (19–26). Odysseus must be conscious of his guilt in so foolishly wasting Aiolos' precious gift, for which he blames his men (which is why he does not bring them with him, 59) and himself for falling asleep (68–9).

70.   **of endearment**: cf. Odysseus' failure here with his success after his blandishing words at 6.148ff.

75.   **hateful to the immortals**: Aiolos' analysis is not in fact borne out by the text. The gods did not send Odysseus to sleep, nor did they prompt the men to open the bag of winds. But it is a reasonable conclusion for Aiolos to draw, given his previous benefaction.

81–2.   **Lamos,/Tēlepylos of the Laistrygones**: the Greek says '*tēlepulos* Laistrygonia' and Page argues (*FHO* 33ff.) that this means something like 'strong-gated Laistrygonia'. In one tradition, Lamos is a son of Poseidon. This may explain why the Laistrygones are monsters (see on 1.69).

85.   **double wages**: herdsmen go out in the morning and come back at night. If the one coming back greets the one going out, the nights must be extremely short: hence an unsleeping herdsmen could earn a double wage. This phenomenon is only experienced in the far north. The source is probably travellers' tales. The description at 11.14ff. of a land where night prevails over day is not couched in the same terms, (cloud and fog keep the sun out all the time), so is probably not a travellers' tale from the same source.

86.   **the courses of night and day lie close together**: Homer is obviously trying to explain the phenomenon referred to in 82–5, but it is difficult to see what he means by his explanation. Possibly he envisages night following day so closely across the sky that night's effects are nullified: and when day finally disappears over the horizon, night has not long in the sky before it too disappears and day begins again. See on 23.244.

87–102.   **There as we entered . . . as a herald**: a very typical description. Cf. 9.88–90; 9.165–7; 10.4–5; 10.148. But note 89 (which prepares us for 121) and 95 (this prepares us for 125–7).

103.   **smooth road**: there is much that is civilised about the Laistrygones. They build roads for wood-collection; they have glorious houses (111–2); they have assemblies (115) and live in communities (118–9).

105. **drawing water**: a typical element again. Cf. Athene at 7.20; and for the description of the spring at 107–8, cf. 17.205–6.

108. **Artakie**: this fountain occurs in the story of Jason and the Argonauts, where it is located near Cyzicus (S. coast of the Propontis). The Argonaut story may well be the source of the Laistrygones (cf. 12.69–72 for a direct reference to the Argonaut stories).

113. **as big as a mountain peak**: cf. 9.191–2. This comes as a surprise. Nothing we learned about this woman's daughter at 106–11 suggested that she had a giant for a mother.

116. **prepared him for dinner**: cf. Polyphemos' cannibalism at e.g. 9.289–91.

118. **The king raised the cry**: cf. the Kikonians at 9.47ff.

123–4. **they speared them/like fish**: the men have been killed with boulders (121–2). The simile here refers to the act of carrying the men off, i.e. 'they carried off their joyless feast as men do who pierce fish'.

131. **my ship, and only mine, fled out**: is Odysseus acting like a coward here? Or is he doing the intelligent thing—realising the hopelessness of the case and saving what he can of his men? At all events, only Odysseus' ship is now left from the original fleet of twelve (9.159).

135. **Aiaia**: Aia (= *gaia*, 'earth') is Kolchis, home of Aietes, brother of Circe (137), and father of Medeia (Hesiod *Theogony* 956–62). Jason went to Kolchis to fetch the golden fleece. He returned to Greece with it and with Medeia, who had helped him in his mission. There is strong Argonautic influence in this episode. Cf. on 108. Circe has been mentioned before at 8.448 and 9.31. Strabo *Geography* 1.2.10, 1.2.40 argues that Homer invents the bond between Circe and Medeia, and invents Aiaia by analogy with Aia.

138. **Helios**: the sun.

139. **Ocean**: Ocean is both a divine person and the river which epic imagined as encircling the disk of the world. See on 23.244.

140–88. **There we brought . . . all of them**: this sequence of events is highly typical. Compare 9.142ff., which goes: beach ship—disembark—wait — dawn — dawn — men explore — hunt — eat — sunset — sleep — dawn — meeting. The episode here adds the spying element (148 = 97). Note again the element of divine guidance (141–2 cf. 9.142) and the smoke (149 cf. 99, 9.167).

174. **sorry as we are**: Odysseus makes an effort to rally his troops. They are still clearly shocked after the Laistrygones incident (cf. 179, 198–202).

179. **unveiling their heads**: they had been mourning for their lost companions. See 143, and cf. 8.92, 4.113–6.

190–1. **where the darkness . . . rises**: hardly to be taken literally, especially since the sun has just risen (187)! These words are rhetorical overstatement by Odysseus.

193. **course . . . none**: 'course' is *mētis* (see on *9H*)—a terrible confession for Odysseus to have to make, if it is true. But is it? He puts a plan for exploration into action soon enough at 203ff.. At 193 Odysseus must be

throwing the situation open for discussion, since on previous occasions when they had seen smoke (i.e. the land was inhabited), disaster had ensued. The men remember these occasions clearly enough (199–200): hence their reaction (198, 201–2). Cf. on 9.228.

200.   **great-hearted . . . Cyclops**: for the incident, see 9.177ff. For the smoke element, see 9.167. 'Great-hearted' is a strange description of the cannabilistic Cyclops. It is an example of a slightly mis-used formula.

205.   **Eurylochos**: the only one of Odysseus' men who is given any characterisation.

208.   **two-and-twenty companions**: if there are two groups of twenty-two, each with a leader, we have a crew of 46. Since six were killed in the Kikonian incident (9.60) and six by Polyphemos (9.289, 311, 344), the full complement was at least 60 (cf. *Iliad* 16.168–70).

213.   **evil drugs . . . enchanted**: the magical element is stronger in the Circe episode than in any other of Odysseus' adventures in Books 9–12. Cf. 236–7, 239–40, 302–6.

217.   **something to please them**: something else the Greeks invented: the doggy-bag. The Roman poet Martial has a batch of epigrams about *apophorēta*, presents given to diners to take away, but this custom is not otherwise attested in Homer.

221–4.   **singing . . . their work**: cf. Kalypso at 5.61–2, *10D*. Circe and Kalypso have much in common: they both live alone, on a wooded island, both weave and sing, both have strange powers (e.g. 5.268), both are untrustworthy (5.173–91, 10.336–472, 378–87), both swear oaths. Kalypso is daughter of Atlas (1.52–3), Circe of the sun (138). But if Kalypso is too hospitable (keeping Odysseus for seven years against his will – 9.29–30, 7.259–60), Circe turns men to pigs (233–43), is a mistress of magic, knows all about the underworld, and can foretell the future. Circe, in other words, seems a more actively destructive threat than Kalypso.

232.   **Eurylochos waited outside**: for the one who gets away, cf. 125–32.

235.   **Pramneian wine**: this alarming mixture is offered with an onion at *Iliad* 11.629–40, where it acts as a restorative to Nestor and Machaon. There is no such place as 'Pramnos' known to us, though it is assumed the name originally indicated origin. Prehistoric man seems to have been keen on mixtures of alcohol and grain. So are the Scots: Atholl Brose is a mixture of whisky, cream, honey and oatmeal.

236.   **forgetful of their own country**: cf. the Lotus-Eaters, 9.94–7. If Circe's wand is merely for herding purposes (see on 238), the drugs must also have the effect of transforming the men. If it is the wand that transforms them, it would be surprising that Circe should have to use drugs to turn them back into men at 390–6. Cf. the Lotus-Eaters, 9.94–7.

238.   **wand**: but the Greek word *rhabdos* could just as well mean 'stick', and Circe works her will with potions (cf. 290, 327–8, 392), not with a wand. She needs a stick primarily to control the animals with (cf. 293, 319).

239.   **they took on the look of pigs**: they did not actually *become* pigs, but merely looked *like* them, and ate pig-food (242–3). Cf. 283.

259.   **vanished away together**: but at 431–4, Eurylochos seems to know that the men had undergone some transformation.

268–9.   **Let us rather make haste and . . ./. . . escape**: Eurylochos remembers past indiscretions which had such tragic consequences, especially the Cyclops episode (9.224–30, cf. 10.431–7, where Eurylochos is explicit about Odysseus' failure in that incident).

273.   **strong compulsion upon me**: is Odysseus' heroic obstinacy here a direct result of any sense of failure over the loss of his men among the Laistrygones, when he cut and ran (125–32)?

277.   **Hermes**: but how does Odysseus *know* it was Hermes (does he conclude it from 330–2)? The poet is usually very careful to distinguish between what he (the poet) knows and what his characters know about divine interventions (see on 2.261–2). Perhaps we have here further evidence that these tales were originally a third-person narrative (see on 9.54–5).

287–301.   **Here, . . . you are naked**: these instructions are rather odd, to say the least. At 287, it looks as if Hermes is handing over a medicine: but this does not come till 302ff. At 291–2, it would be logical if the medicine were put into the cup to counteract Circe's potion. But this does not happen. Finally, having been once protected against Circe by the medicine, it seems rather awkward that Odysseus should need to make her swear an oath before he gets into bed with her. We are clearly dealing with a long tradition of 'witch' tales centering on Circe, and Homer is trying to adapt them to the particular circumstances of the Odyssey. In particular, he is trying to cut out the excessively magical.

302.   **Argeiphontes**: i.e. Hermes. See on 1.38.

305.   **moly**: where divine names are given for objects the human name is also usually given in Homer (e.g. 12.61 and *Iliad* 1.403–4: the gods call the monster Briareus, but men call it Aigaios' son). Since moly is given only its divine name here, it must belong entirely to the realm of the gods. Hence the difficulty, or danger ('hard' 305 could mean both), for men in digging it up, cf. mandrake roots. The word 'moly' may be cognate with Sanskrit *mulam* 'root'. But armed with this root, what does Odysseus actually *do* with it? Nothing, is the answer. It gives some mysterious 'automatic' protection to its bearer.

321.   **sword**: some have seen phallic imagery here. But neither Hermes (294–5) nor Circe (333–5) appears to see any connection: quite the reverse in fact (Odysseus is to *put his sword away* and come to bed).

325.   **What man are you**: this question does not break the rules of *xenia* (cf. on e.g. Cyclops at 9.252). Circe is supplicating Odysseus (323–4), and asks her question in amazement at Odysseus' power to resist her drugs. Cf. Theoklymenos at 15.264.

337.   **how can you ask me to be gentle with you . . .?**: Odysseus may seem keener to get into bed with Circe than rescue his companions (which only happens at 383ff.), but he is merely following Hermes' instructions at 297–8.

348–72.   **Meanwhile . . . provisions**: this delightfully civilised picture of life in Circe's house, where the rituals of *xenia* are observed no less fully than they are in e.g. Scheria (cf. 8.416–57), or Sparta (4.39–67), emphasises the human side of Circe's existence. Even the divine water-nymphs who serve her (350–1) act like thoroughly human servants. Cf. Eurykleia's instructions at 20.147–59. The typicality of the scene reinforces its normality: 364 = 3.466; 365 = 8.455; 366–7 = 314–5; 368–72 = 1.136–40.

393.   **medicine**: see on 236.

398.   **lamentation**: for heroic propensity to tears, see on 4.114, 8.86, and 179 above.

410.   **as, in the country**: as usual, a simile points up a moment of high emotion (see on 5.328). The homeliness of the simile, and especially the reference to Ithaka (416–7)—which the men will never see—give it added pathos.

419.   **we are as happy to see you**: Odysseus is synonymous with homecoming to the men. This moment of child-like dependence does not last—cf. Eurylochos' rebellion at 431–7, the men's intervention at 438–45, their reminder to Odysseus at 469–74, 566–7, and especially 12.339–52.

433.   **transform the lot of us**: see on 259.

437.   **by this man's recklessness**: as Odysseus admitted at 9.224–30. Cf. the men's efforts to persuade Odysseus not to give their position away to the Cyclops at 9.494–9. But the poet is at pains to assure the listener from the start of the *Odyssey* that Odysseus was not to blame for his companions' deaths. See *1.1–21A*.

483–4.   **the promise you gave**: no such promise occurs in our text, but entertainment followed by a good send-off is part and parcel of the institution of *xenia* and Circe had sworn them no harm (342–7). We can assume too that Circe wanted Odysseus and his men to recover their spirits for some other reason than merely to be better company in her palace (460–5). Circe has obviously been an excellent hostess (the men only complain to Odysseus in her absence (484–6)).

490.   **another journey**: for the famous problem associated with this trip to the Underworld, see *11B–F*.

491.   **Persephone**: daughter of Demeter, and married to Hades, lord of the Underworld.

508.   **stream of the Ocean**: see on 139.

510.   **poplars . . . willows**: both trees associated with death and commonly planted around graves. The willow casts its fruit before it reaches full maturity. Circe does not mention the Kimmerians (11.14ff.).

513–4.   **Pyriphlegethon . . . Acheron**: the four rivers of the Underworld. Pyriphlegethon means 'flaming with fire', Kokytos 'lamentation', Styx 'hateful' and Acheron 'flowing with grief'. It is not at all clear how Homer envisages these rivers. There is a river Acheron in Thesprotia in N.W. Greece, and an Oracle of the Dead has been excavated there: but this river and its confluences may have been so named because of this passage, rather than being a source of it.

517.   **Dig a pit . . .**: for the details of the sacrifice, see on 11.25–50.

522.   **you will slaughter**: Odysseus does not do this in our *Odyssey*.

528.   **toward Erebos**: i.e. down towards the ground (not 'to the west'). Cf. 11.37.

539.   **he will tell you the way to go**: one of the major problems of the journey to Hades is that Teiresias does hardly anything of the sort. The instructions are in fact given by Circe at 12.39–141. See *11C (1)* and on 12.35.

542–5.   **and she put . . . wimple**: these lines = 5.229–32 (which see). There are many points of comparison between Circe and Kalypso (cf. on 221–4). Circe's genuine care for Odysseus and his men has surfaced by the end of the book. See e.g. 456–68, 489, 504ff., 570–4.

561.   **Now as my men were on their way**: the transition from the death of Elpenor is abrupt, and it is quite unprecedented that a friend known to have died (11.51–4) should be left unburied. This passage *may* have been inserted later to forge a link with Odysseus' sighting of an unburied Elpenor in Hades (see *11C (2)*).

572.   **a ram and one black female**: for the sacrifice outlined at 524–7. It is hard to see why Circe has to be so secretive about it all.

Book eleven

Introduction

A. Whatever the problems of its authenticity, Book 11 (the *nekyia*, 'calling-up of ghosts') as we have it falls into a neat structure:

1–50: journey to the entrance to Hades and blood-offerings to the ghosts

51–224: meetings with Elpenor, Ţeiresias and Antikleia (Odysseus' mother)

225–332: meetings with a Catalogue of Women

333–384: the 'Intermezzo': Alkinoos and Arete urge Odysseus to continue with his tale, and he agrees to stay over another day

385–567: meetings with heroes from Troy—Agamemnon, Achilleus and Aias (Ajax)

568–635: visions of the rewards and punishments meted out in Hades to various legendary figures, culminating in Herakles

636–40: the return journey.

B. Book 11 has been a prime target for 'analytical' scholars, i.e. those who believe that it is possible to distinguish between what Homer himself composed and what was added by *other* composers to the Homeric core. (Page *HO* Chapter 2, Camps *IH* 86, note 27). The method makes a number of assumptions:

a. Homer is always logical and consistent in character-drawing and plot construction.

b. the cultural world of Homer can be rigidly categorised.

c. it is possible to define clearly Homeric and non-Homeric linguistic usage.

C. On the strength of those assumptions, analysts point out:

1. Circe sends Odysseus to ask Teiresias about his return (10.538–40), but Teiresias' answer is barely sufficient (11.100–37), and in fact Circe is far more informative (12.37–141) (assumption (a)).

2. Elpenor's death at 10.551–60 and Odysseus' meeting with him at 11.51–80 are problematical. Homeric heroes do not leave bodies known to be dead unburied (see on 10.561); and Odysseus' question at 11.57 is pointless since he knows the answer (assumptions (a) and (b)).

3. The 'Intermezzo' pointlessly extends Odysseus' stay for another day, during which nothing happens (13.17–35, and see notes at 11.330, 340), is full of linguistic oddities, and is itself extremely feebly composed (assumptions (a), (c)).

98

4.   The Catalogue of Heroines is unobjectionable as epic (which enjoys lists of this sort e.g. the Catalogue of Ships in *Iliad* 2), but the women seem to have no connection with Odysseus, and he has nothing to say to them: they merely tell him their stories (assumption (a)). (Since the women seem to be largely Boeotian in origin, and there is a history of Boeotian catalogue poetry, that is probably the source.)

5.   The closing scene (568–635) presents a vision of life in the Underworld at total variance with that so carefully drawn by Homer in the rest of the Book (see on 568). On top of that, the transition to it wrecks the preceding meeting with Aias (see on 566–7) and there are many linguistic oddities (assumptions (a), (b), (c)).

6.   There seems to be confusion about the time-scale: no-one is quite certain how old Telemachos is at this point in Odysseus' travels, or what the suitors are doing (see on 116, 185) (assumption (a)).

7.   Finally, at 13.383–5, Odysseus *seems* to have forgotten everything he learnt from Teiresias' prophecies (assumption (a)) but see note on 13.384.

D. On the other hand, even the most hardened analyst would agree that the meetings with Antikleia, Agamemnon, Achilleus and Aias are powerful, moving and significant moments for Odysseus, fully worthy of Homer himself. Consequently, the sorts of conclusions that analysts draw tend to be as follows (there are, of course, as many conclusions as analysts): someone else, *possibly* even Homer himself, composed a poem about Odysseus' visit to the entrance to Hades, where a number of ghosts drank the blood and conversed with him. This was not included in the Homeric version of the *Odyssey*. But a later poet inserted it by giving Circe a motivating speech, fiddling with the roles of Teiresias and Elpenor and inserting the Intermezzo and references to Telemachos and the suitors. The Catalogue of Women and the final scene in Hades, taken from an entirely different tradition of poetry, were inserted by yet another poet, either before or after the initial insertion (see Page *HO* 46–7).

E. As a logical construct, that analysis is extremely powerful and superficially very persuasive. The problem is that it entirely fails to take into account how oral poetry is composed and, in particular, the rich cultural and linguistic amalgam on which it traditionally draws. Comparison with oral poetry from all over the world shows conclusively that:

1.   Oral poets constantly take incidents from other stories or traditions and fit them into the circumstances of a new tale they are singing, as a result of which occasionally logical inconsistencies occur (see e.g. on 13.397). Logical inconsistency does not indicate multiple authorship (see Bowra *HP* Chapter 8).

2.   Oral poets have the whole of an oral tradition to draw on. Stories from that tradition are bound to reflect the different cultural and linguistic circumstances under which they were composed (see e.g. on 25–50). The

poet may not be wholly successful in eliminating inconsistencies, even if he wants to. Cultural and linguistic oddities do not indicate multiple authorship (Bowra *HP* 519ff.).

3.   Oral poets constantly secularise and politicise their material (see e.g. on 3.36).

F.   In other words the analysts have proved that a great many different traditions of story-telling have gone into Book 11, but they have not proved that one oral poet could *not* have been responsible for bringing them all together. The inconsistencies the analysts have discovered are typical of an oral poet shaping new material to a new context. On the other hand, one could argue that, such are the general smoothness and consistency of the Homeric epics, a master-poet like Homer is unlikely to have been responsible for so many weak connections. We are in fairly subjective territory here, but on those grounds one can reasonably have grave doubts about the final scene from Hades, the transition to which is so disastrous for the Aias episode, and the conception of which is so alien to Homer's careful preparations in the earlier part of the book; and it is difficult too to discern significant purpose in the Catalogue of Women.

G. Nevertheless, it is surely time to ask what the positive virtues of Book 11 are. Some of the following points may be worth considering (cf. Clarke *AO* 59–64):

1.   The book emphasises the bravery and daring of Odysseus in making the descent (cf. Achilleus at 473–6): the descent elevates him above ordinary humanity (cf. Circe at 12.21–3). Many heroes make journeys to the underworld (e.g. Gilgamesh, Aeneas, Jesus). See Bowra *HP* 78–84.

2.   Odysseus' emotional responses, especially to his mother, show us a different, gentler side of him. See especially 197–203.

3.   The heroism of the *Odyssey* comes face to face with that of the *Iliad*: do we feel that Odysseus' refusal to maintain the enmities of the past shows a superior kind of heroism (contrast Aias at 563–4)?

4.   The Catalogue of Women shows how great families come into being, but equally how they can be corrupted. Does this vision of other heroic families' destinies have a lesson for Odysseus, especially in relation to the family he wishes to return to?

5.   'Justice' is one of the great themes of the *Odyssey*. The controversial scene in Hades shows justice at work among the dead, and in the Second Underworld scene (Book 24) we shall see the descent of the suitors to their destiny.

6.   The scenes in the Underworld are rather like those on the Shield of Achilles in *Iliad* 18: they depict a different world in the *Odyssey*, a world of failure and of success, of excellence and of error, of good and bad judgement, which has had unalterable consequences for the lives of the dead. There may be paradigms of behaviour there from which Odysseus can learn. Herakles in particular (617–626) has many similarities with Odysseus (see on 601, 626).

For further reading on the virtually unrestricted access that oral poetry gives to material from other times, places and cultures—we must not be purist about Homer—see R. Finnegan, *Oral Poetry*, CUP 1977; Svetozar Koljević, *The Epic in the Making*, Clarendon Press 1980.

See on 4.351 for a brief discussion of parallels between the Underworld scenes and the Proteus episode.

1–12. **Now when . . . darkened**: a run of typical lines. Cf. 2.388, 2.390, 4.577, 4.578, 8.50, 10.136, 10.570, 11.78, 12.148–52.

14. **Kimmerian people**: for possible comparison with Laistrygones, see on 10.85. Observe that the sun does rise here, but the fog and cloud prevent it breaking through. One scholar proposed Homer to be thinking here of Britain(!), but surely Homer is thinking in mythical, not geographical, terms: Elysium (4.565–8) and Olympus (6.41–7) are areas of shining brightness, but the route to the world of the dead is one of gloom and darkness. Later Greeks located the Kimmerians in the Crimea (Herodotus 4.11).

25. **cubit**: the measurement here (*pugón*) is from the knuckles to the elbow, i.e. c.20 cms. Cf. the cubit at 311.

25–50. **dug a pit . . . Teiresias**: = 10.517–37, with expansions. The Homeric epics seem to amalgamate two beliefs about the dead: most commonly in Homer, that the *psykhai* ('souls, ghosts') of the cremated dead are without substance, thought or speech, and entering the underworld stay there, powerless to intervene in human affairs ever again (216–22 is the classic statement of Homer's position; cf. 475–6). Consequently, they need no further honour, worship or cult. But occasionally, there is the memory of the Mycenaean practice of worship of the dead, who are interred (not cremated), imprisoned (as it were) under the ground, but could return. These *psykhai* needed appeasement (for such memories, cf. the funeral games of Patroklos, *Iliad* 23.161–261). The offerings made at 26–33 are straight memories of such cult of the dead. The blood-offerings at 34–7 are a poetic device to enable Teiresias, who is otherwise a normal Homeric *psykhē*, i.e. speechless etc., to communicate. For the cremation, see 12.8–15 (Elpenor), 24.65–86 (Achilleus' funeral). Cf. Burkett *GR* 194–9.

26. **drink-offerings**: the offerings soak into the ground and are thought to nourish the dead. Barley (28) is frequently used in sacrificial rituals e.g. 3.442. See on 2.432.

32–3. **all-black/ram**: black animals were sacrificed to the gods of the underworld.

46. **and burn them**: now that the blood is in the pit (35–6), the dead animals are burnt in a sacrifice to the gods of the underworld.

51. **Elpenor**: see *11C(2), D* and on 10.561. Elpenor's death is described by Odysseus at 10.551–60. Elpenor's version here is, as one would expect, slightly different (cf. e.g. 10.555 and 11.61). It is odd that Elpenor does not have to drink the blood to speak to Odysseus. Possibly the reason is that he is not yet buried. Only then will he become a speechless wraith.

68.   **Telemachos**: the only son of Odysseus, just born when Odysseus left for Troy. At the time Odysseus descends to the Underworld, he must be 13 if calculations at 9A are correct. Telemachos' troubles in Ithaka and subsequent travels are told in Books 1–4.

73.   **the gods' curse upon you**: Elpenor will, in death, have no strength to return himself from the dead to harass the living (see on 25–50). Cf. 9.65 for the measures to be taken when there is no option but to leave the dead unburied.

76.   **so that those to come will know of me**: all the dead can hope for is that their memory will live on. This can be achieved by a funeral mound (cf. 24.80–4)—but most of all, by the work of the epic poet, who ensures the lives of the great heroes will never be forgotten. See e.g. 8.579–80.

85.   **Autolykos**: for a story of the young Odysseus and his grandfather, see 19.392–466, especially on 19.396, 416.

88–9.   **I would not/let her draw near**: Antikleia is allowed to drink the blood at 152.

102.   **the Shaker of the Earth**: i.e. Poseidon. See next note.

103.   **his dear son**: i.e. the Cyclops (see 9.181–542, especially 527–36).

107.   **Thrinakia**: the incident, which ends in disaster, occurs at 12.260–419.

116.   **insolent men, who are eating away your livelihood**: i.e. the 108 suitors of Odysseus' wife Penelope, whom we have met already in Books 1–2 and 4. There is an unimportant temporal problem here. According to 2.89 and 13.377 the suitors do not lay siege to Odysseus' household till the 17th year of his departure. But (see on 68) this descent to the underworld takes place in roughly the thirteenth year of Odysseus' departure.

121.   **then you must take up your well-shaped oar**: 121–37 = 23.268–84. It is not at all clear *why* Odysseus has to travel where he does, carrying what he does. Possibly by sacrificing to Poseidon in a place where none knows of the sea (128) Odysseus will be helping to spread the cult of Poseidon and this will appease Poseidon's wrath against him for blinding the Cyclops. That done, Odysseus can return and sacrifice to the rest of the Olympian gods (132–4) for—what? This is all very obscure. But it is typical of Homer to project events beyond the end of his story into the future. In the *Iliad*, the death of Achilleus and the fall of Troy are predicted—but not actually described. Cf. Menelaos' future assumption into Elysium (4.561–70).

128.   **winnow-fan**: a long-handled, broad-faced shovel-shaped tool, not unlike an oar, used to separate the grain from the chaff (its casing). The grain is thrown up into the air. The wind blows away the lighter chaff, and the heavier, now chaff-free, grain falls back to the earth.

134.   **from the sea**: these words could mean '*far* from the sea', i.e. (presumably) in Odysseus' own palace. This seems to fit better with 135–6.

136.   **sleek old age**: Iliadic heroes did not actively seek death in battle, but if it came, they could ensure it was a glorious death, which would be remembered. But Odysseus' immortality is assured, despite his fears at 5.306–12 where he temporarily forgets Teiresias' assurances. In his poem

Ulysses, Tennyson imagines Odysseus tiring of home life and striking out with his companions yet again. See Stanford *UT* 202ff.

137. **All this is true**: maybe, but is it very informative? Circe had promised that Teiresias would tell Odysseus how to get home (10.539–40), but Teiresias' version is only a fraction of the tale Circe has to tell at 12.39–141—which includes Thrinakia! See on 12.35.

172. **Artemis**: see on 15.411.

176–7. **Tell me/about the wife I married**: Odysseus' first mention of his wife since he left Kalypso in Book 5, and even that is prompted by Antikleia's question at 162. But Odysseus is returning not, in the first place, to a wife, but to a *kingdom*, which it will be very difficult for him to recover if his wife, assuming him dead, has married someone else. See on 1.13 and on 2.335–6.

178. **and whether**: eject the word 'and'. The clause 'whether she stays . . . or . . .' describes precisely what it is about her thinking (177) that Odysseus wants to know. Odysseus thinks of his wife primarily as the guardian of his kingdom (see above note).

181–203. **All too much . . . from me**: note that Antikleia answers Odysseus' questions in the reverse order to that in which he asked them. This device, a form of *husteron proteron*, is common in Homer (see on 3.464–7).

181. **All too much**: fine human understanding from Homer. Odysseus asks about his wife as guardian of his kingdom: his mother replies with reference to the emotional pressure under which she lives, and refers the issue of stewardship to Telemachos.

185. **Telemachos administers your allotted lands**: more time-trouble for Homer. At 116 the suitors were 'eating away (Odysseus') livelihood': now Telemachos (aged 13—see on 116) is administering his lands in peace, as a man with authority to judge. This at first sight fits poorly with the picture of Telemachos drawn by the poet in Books 1 and 2: but of course at the time Antikleia is describing there were no suitors there.

187. **Your father**: Laertes. See on 1.188–93, 1.249–51 for his strangely diminished role.

197–203. **And so it was . . . from me**: wonderful rhetorical climax, which depends for its effect on Antikleia repeating, but denying, Odysseus' suggested reasons for her death at 172–3 (*husteron-proteron* again: see on 181–203) and finishing with the actual reason—her desire for Odysseus. The haunting melancholy of the Greek is profoundly moving. Cf. 15.358–60.

208. **at the heart within me**: Odysseus, the great survivor, who has witnessed the deaths of hundreds of men (416–7), is taught its true meaning at last, by his mother. The strength of Odysseus' feelings is matched by its futility. Cf. *Iliad* 23.97–107.

224. **so you may tell her**: as he does at 23.322–5.

225–332. **So we two . . . journey**: the so-called 'Catalogue of Women', which details the histories, and especially the divine couplings and offspring, of a great number of mythical heroines, cf. 36–41. See discussion at *11G(4), C(4), F*. Greek aristocrats had a passion for finding divine blood in the family: it helped sanction their power and status (Finley *WO* 131–2). The choice of families here may have something to do with local, political or social circumstances. See on 3.36, cf. *GI E*. Usually, the poet invokes the Muse before embarking on a Catalogue (cf. *Iliad* 2.484–93); but since Odysseus himself was an eye-witness of this parade of heroines he has no need of the Muses' information. Oral poets are *not* eye-witnesses of the events they describe (see on 8.491–2).

232.   **at the same time**: cf. 49–50, 150–3.

235.   **Tyro**: Stanford's family tree of Tyro is particularly useful (see also 2.115–22):

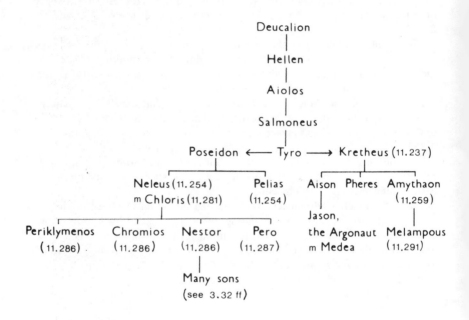

237.   **but said**: 'but' makes no sense at all. Odysseus is merely reporting what Tyro said (truthfully—see 258) to him. Read 'and'.

238.   **she was ('fell' better) in love with a river**: i.e. with the river-*god*. (So also Asopos at 261). The Enipeus is a river (a tributary of the Peneios) in Thessaly.

241.   **the god**: i.e. Poseidon.

245.   **he broke her virgin zone**: this probably refers to Tyro's maidenhead. It was only later that she married Kretheus (258–9).

257.   **Iolkos**: whence Jason set out to get the golden fleece. See family tree at 235 for Jason's connection with Pelias. 'the other king' i.e. Neleus, father of Nestor.

261.   **Asopos**: a river in Boeotia (cf. 238–40).

263–4.   **seven-gated/Thebes**: the Boeotian city, powerful and important from Mycenaean times, with a rich mythological tradition centering on the house of Kadmos and Oedipus (271–80) rather than, as here, Amphion and Zethos.

267.   **in the embraces of great Zeus**: Zeus had his way with Alkmene, a paragon of wifely virtue, by disguising himself as her husband.

270.   **son**: i.e. Herakles. Megara (269) was his first wife. Kreion (269) just means 'ruler', and has no connection with the Kreion (Creon) of the Antigone story.

271.   **Epikaste, Oidipodes' mother**: we know her as Iokaste (Jocasta) and her husband as Oedipus. Myth, as ever, is a highly flexible medium. The Greeks had no fixed body of it, handed down from early times, but details could be varied from teller to teller. See on 3.265–72, 11.409, 431. Cf. Euripides *Phoenician Women* 1–87.

275–6.   **continued/to be lord**: see above note. Homer stresses Epikaste's ignorance (272), plays down Oedipus' slaughter of his father and leaves Oedipus as king of Thebes; he also emphasises the misery of Oedipus' subsequent reign (275–7, 280). Sophocles in *Oedipus Rex* stresses Oedipus' ignorance, makes the murder of Oedipus' father Laios the main initial issue of the tragedy, has Oedipus blind himself when he finds out the truth and ends the tragedy with his return into the house (prior to exile). The only point of emphasis Sophocles shares with Homer is the hanging of Epikaste.

280.   **a mother's furies**: see 2.135 for Telemachos' fears. For Furies, see on 15.234.

281.   **Chloris**: see family tree at 235.

283.   **Amphion**: king of Orchomenos (284), not the Theban Amphion of 262.

284.   **Orchomenos of the Minyai**: Orchomenos was an important city near Thebes (see on 263–4), and may once have been chief town in Boeotia in Mycenaean times before Thebes took over. Minyas was founder of Orchomenos. Minyans lived in Orchomenos and in Iolkos (see on 257), and had connections with the Argonauts.

290.   **Iphikles**: he should be 'Iphiklos' (so also at 296). Phylake is in Thessaly.

291.   **Melampous**: see family tree at 235. For further details of Melampous, see 15.226–42 and notes. But even that passage does not clarify the opacities of this passage (e.g. 293, 296–7), which looks as if it hides a story behind it not known to us.

298.   **Leda**: she also gave birth to Helen (of Troy) (when Zeus made love to her in the guise of a swan) and Klytaimestra, wife of Agamemnon. Helen has appeared with her husband Menelaos at home in Sparta after the Trojan War in Book 4, and Klytaimestra is portrayed in the *Odyssey* as the antithesis of Penelope. See e.g. Agamemnon's words at 444–53.

300.   **Polydeukes**: known better in his Latin form as Pollux. In other traditions Castor and Pollux are known as the Dioskouroi (Dioscuri), i.e. sons of Zeus, and have astral connections (= Gemini 'twins').

306.   **but**: wholly redundant. Read 'and'.

311.   **nine cubits**: a cubit (*pēkhus*) is the measurement from the elbow to the tip of the middle finger, i.e. c.25cms. Cf. the *pugōn* at 25.

310.   **Orion**: a gigantic hunter, loved by Eos the dawn goddess (5.1), killed by Artemis in jealousy. Also a constellation. See 5.121–4; 5.272–5.

312.   **nine fathoms**: a Homeric fathom (*or(o)guia*) is about 6', the span of both arms outstretched. But the twins were not as big as the monster Tityos (577).

315.   **on Olympos**: if the purpose of the twins is to threaten the gods by reaching the sky (as it seems to be — 316), the Olympos on which they plan to pile Ossa and Pelion must be taken as the mountain, not as the home of the gods in 'heaven'. See on 6.42. Ossa, Pelion and Olympos are mountains in Thessaly.

321.   **Phaidra . . . Prokris . . . Ariadne**: Phaidra, daughter of Minos, King of Crete, wife of Theseus, was best known for committing suicide either out of shame at her love for her stepson Hippolytos, or in order to implicate him in a false charge of rape (he rejected her advances). Prokris, wife of Cephalus, was unfaithful to him. He killed her accidentally when she, suspecting him of having an affair, spied on him during a hunt. Ariadne, Phaidra's sister, helped Theseus escape from the Cretan Minotaur (see on 238), but was abandoned by him on the island of Dia. We do not know why Dionysos bore witness against her (325). In other versions, she became Dionysos' bride, after being abandoned by Theseus on Naxos. These heroines' connection with Theseus, the heroic founder of Attica, and Cephalus, another Attic hero, have suggested to some that (since Homer generally ignores Attic mythology) these women are Athenian insertions into the text.

326.   **Maira, Klymene . . . Eriphyle**: Maira, an attendant on Artemis, was killed by her for unchastity; Klymene was (probably) mother of Iphiklos (290) and queen of Phylake; Eriphyle, wife of Amphiaraos and so connected with Melampous (291) (see 15.244) was bribed by Polyneikes, son of Oedipus, to persuade her husband to join Polyneikes and do battle against Thebes — where he was fated to be killed.

327.   **own dear husband**: eject 'dear'. He was hardly that, given the way she treated him (see above note).

330–1.   **It is time now/for my sleep**: the Phaiakians had promised him transport for the coming morning (7.317–9).

331.   **my companions**: not his companions from Troy, who are all dead, but those who will take him back to Ithaka (8.34–7) and who are attending the feast at which Odysseus is telling the tale (8.55–8).

340.   **when he is in such need**: rather a forced claim, after the unparalleled generosity of the gifts already given to Odysseus (see on 8.389). The added gifts are solicited and stored aboard at 13.13–23.

342.   **Echeneos spoke forth**: as before (7.155), Echeneos tactfully intervenes to place the responsibility for a decision upon the king Alkinoos.

351.   **till tomorrow**: at 13.17 they all go to bed at last; in the morning they

store Odysseus' gifts aboard, feast (23ff.) and as the sun sets (35) Odysseus takes his farewell.

359. **with a fuller hand**: for the importance of gift-gathering in *xenia*, see on 4.81–91. Cf. Menelaos' pressing generosity at 15.68–85.

368. **as a singer**: see on 9.12–3.

382. **the sorrows of my companions**: if Odysseus means his companions left to him after the Laistrygones incident (10.130–2), then the 'vile woman' of 384 must be generalised to mean 'Helen'. They had fought at Troy, for Helen's sake, survived, but perished on the journey home. But since Odysseus now moves on to the story of Agamemnon's return, and the slaughter of him and his men at the hands of Aigisthos and Agamemnon's disloyal wife Klytaimestra (409–15, 427–34), 'companions' at 382 could mean 'other friends at Troy'—in which case, 'vile woman' of 384 would = Klytaimestra. 'On the homeward journey' (384) tips the balance in favour of the first explanation. Cf. 438–9.

385–6. **had scattered the female/souls**: Odysseus picks up the tale after the Catalogue of Women (328–30).

387. **Agamemnon, the son of Atreus**: see *1.22–95A*, and cf. 3.265–72.

399–403. **Was it with . . . and women**: cf. Menelaos' wealth-gathering on his return home (4.78–91) and the raid on the Kikones (9.39–43).

409. **Aigisthos**: for the version of the story told to Menelaos, see 4.512–37. Agamemnon, naturally, emphasises Klytaimestra's wickedness, but even so it is Aigisthos who does the main killing (Klytaimestra kills Kassandra 422 but Agamemnon does implicate her at 453). Aeschylus in his tragic trilogy (458BC) *Oresteia*, desiring to put stress on the *family* curse and its consequences, makes Klytaimestra the protagonist and gives only a minor supporting role to Aigisthos. Compare 275–6 for Sophocles' handling of the Oedipus story.

415. **for a wedding . . .**: the horror of the crime is compounded by the deceitful treachery with which it is engineered—at a time of celebration. Cf. 410, 419–20, and Agamemnon's pathetic hopes at 430–2. (The same point is made at 4.530–7.) Odysseus will slaughter the suitors at a feast to Apollo in Book 22, at a time when they will least expect it (22.12–14), but Odysseus' deceit is justifiable—it is the only means by which he can revenge himself on those who deserve their death (22.35–41).

419. **sprawled**: cf. the description of the suitors at 22.308–9, 381–9.

422. **Kassandra**: a prophetess, daughter of Priam, taken from Troy by Agamemnon to be his mistress. She rejected the advances of Apollo god of prophecy, and so was condemned by him always to tell the truth, but never to be believed. Aeschylus (see on 409) uses her memorably in *Agamemnon* 1035ff.

423–4. **with them beat on/the ground**: i.e. summoning the infernal gods to take revenge (*Iliad* 9.568–72). The meaning of the lines is disputed. If they are rightly interpreted here, why should Klytaimestra turn away from Agamemnon? To show that she does not care about his curse?

426. **press shut my eyes and mouth**: one of the traditional death rituals, often performed by the wife.

431.   **welcome to my children and thralls**: Agamemnon omits Klytaim-estra presumably because of the presence of Kassandra with him. Aeschylus fully exploits the fact that Agamemnon had sacrificed their daughter Iphigeneia in order to raise a wind for Troy in the first place, but Homer never mentions this.

436–9.   **Shame it is . . . against you**: Odysseus' mistrust of women, already evident in the Circe episode (see *10D*), is further reinforced by Agamemnon's tale here.

448.   **infant child**: i.e. Telemachos. On the importance of Homer's decision to make Telemachos a young baby when Odysseus left for Troy, see on 4.112, and Book I Appendix.

451.   **he will fold his father in his arms**: see 16.213–4. It may seem strange to us that Agamemnon does not countenance the possibility that the meeting of Odysseus and Penelope might involve embraces. But fathers and sons are generally bonded more tightly than husbands and wives in Homer. Cf. Achilleus and Neoptolemos and Peleus (489, 494).

453.   **my own son**: Orestes, on whom see *1.22–95A*. This whole exchange between Odysseus and Agamemnon, especially 427–453, reinforces the analogies between the houses of Agamemnon and Odysseus.

456.   **There is no trusting in women**: these lines seem to fit ill with 444–6, but perhaps make better sense in relation to 441–3. Agamemnon speaks embittered by his own experience. Penelope will not plot to kill Odysseus, but is still suspect merely because she is a woman.

458.   **if you happened to hear that my son was still living**: wrong emphasis. Agamemnon known Orestes is still living (460–1)—presumably because he has not seen his *psykhē*, 'soul', in Hades. The Greek means literally 'if you hear of my son still being alive anywhere'. Since Agamemnon continues by developing the 'anywhere' (459–60), he is actually asking where his son may now be living.

459.   **Orchomenos**: see on 284. Since there is a connection between Orchomenos and Nestor, ruler of Pylos, companion of Agamemnon in Troy (see 281–6 and 3.102–200), Agamemnon has good reason to think Orestes may have gone to Orchomenos or to Pylos (mentioned as the next alternative in the line).

460.   **Menelaos**: brother of Agamemnon, husband of Helen of Troy. See 4.1–619, especially 90–112.

467–9.   **Achilleus . . . Aias**: we must assume these souls drink the blood before they speak. These souls, all close friends in the *Iliad*, are among the greatest Greeks at Troy: see on 3.106–12, and on the epics of the 'Epic Cycle', *24D*. This meeting between the survivor Odysseus and the dead heroes of Troy is not merely deeply moving: different sorts of heroism are being brought face to face.

470.   **Danaans**: see on 1.61.

471.   **scion of Aiakos**: Aiakos was father of Peleus, who was father of Achilleus (see 478).

474.   **what made you think of this bigger endeavor . . .?**: wrong translation.

Read 'what still bigger endeavor will you think up in your mind?'. Achilleus seems to imply that such an endeavor was supremely characteristic of a man like Odysseus.

486.   **Do not grieve**: Odysseus is trying to console the greatest of Greek heroes (see 472, and Achilleus' reply at 488). Odysseus does so by drawing an analogy from the honour in which Achilleus was held in life.

489.   **as thrall**: the Greek word is based on *thētes*, 'unattached, propertyless labourers who worked for hire and begged what they could not steal' (Finley *WO* 57. Cf. 18.358). It is the dependency of the free *thes* on others that makes him so despicable (see on 5.38). Achilleus goes as low as he can in the social order of the free (he draws the line at slavery, of course). If a hero like Achilleus would rather have that status than be king of all the dead (491)—for the absolute centrality of status in a hero's world, see on 1.95—his hatred of death must be deep indeed. There is a terrible sadness here. Achilleus in the *Iliad* knew that he was dooming himself to an early death by avenging the death of Patroklos (*Iliad* 18.79–100). Life on any terms was not possible for him then: but it seems to be so now he is dead. Is Achilleus renouncing Iliadic heroism here? Or is he just comparing his lot (death) with Odysseus' (life) and asserting that from the perspective of the dead, life on any terms is preferable? It is touching that Achilleus at once turns to the topic of the *living*—his son and father (see on 451). Cf. Agamemnon's consolation at 24.92–4 (and role).

493.   **as a champion**: Achilleus' values are still those of a warrior-hero— but not solely. See next note.

494.   **Peleus**: it was Achilleus' memory of his father—his love for him and desire to protect him in old age—that, along with persuasion by his mother Thetis, moved him to release the body of the dead Hektor to his father Priam, King of Troy (*Iliad* 24.486–512). That passionate love and fierce protectiveness stay with Achilleus even in death (e.g. 500–3).

495.   **Myrmidon**: the people that Achilleus and his father ruled, and of which Achilleus brought a contingent to Troy.

496.   **Hellas and Phthia**: two parts of Peleus' territory in Thessaly.

509.   **from Skyros**: an island off Euboia where Neoptolemos was being brought up. Odysseus was sent to fetch him when Achilleus was killed.

511.   **in speaking**: excellence at fighting and at speaking (= persuading your colleagues to your point of view) was the quality demanded of a hero. Cf. on 2.270–80; and 3.124–9.

519.   **son of Telephos**: Telephos king of Mysia (a territory near Troy) was wounded by Achilleus at Troy. His wife Astyoche did not allow their son Eurypylos to fight there, until she was bribed by Priam, King of Troy, with a golden vine (521). 'Keteian' was an alternative name for 'Mysian'. The story was told in the *Little Iliad*.

522.   **Memnon**: king of Ethiopia, son of Eos and Tithonos (see 5.1). He killed Nestor's son Antilochos (see on 3.106–12) and was killed by Achilleus. His story was told in the *Aithiopis*.

524.   **the horse that Epeios made**: for other tales of the Wooden Horse, see 8.492–520, 4.271–89.

529.   **losing his . . . colour**: cf. *Iliad* 13.275–86 for the distinction between brave and coward.

543.   **Telamonian Aias**: he was son of Telamon, and came from Salamis. Distinguish him from Lokrian Aias, son of Oileus (see on 3.135). For the 'decision' (544), see on 3.106–12. Sophocles' tragedy *Aias* (*Ajax*) deals with Aias' madness, suicide and eventual burial with honour, thanks to the good offices of Odysseus.

552.   **conciliation**: Odysseus weeps for Agamemnon (395), tries to console Achilleus (488) and now attempts with soothing words to reconcile Aias to the loss of Achilleus' armour. Odysseus is eventually sharp with Agamemnon (463–4); unable to reconcile Achilleus, who after receiving news of his son strides proudly off (538–40); and for all his efforts (especially 556–8) is unable to reach across to Aias.

563–4.   **He gave no answer**: this magnificent silence has been admired since antiquity.

566–7.   **but the heart . . . wanted/still to see**: a disastrous two lines, which considerably weaken the profundity of Aias' silence—Odysseus has, apparently, better things to do than worry about *him*. Since the whole of what follows down to 635 may be an interpolation (see *11F*), we may assign 565–7 to the later interpolator.

568.   **Minos**: see on 7.323–4. Early Cretan civilisation is called 'Minoan' after him. He is especially close to Zeus (19.178–9). Thucydides *Histories* 1.4 discusses him as an historical figure who developed Cretan naval power. We now seem to be in Hades itself, witnessing heroes and villains being rewarded and punished, rather than with Odysseus over a pit of blood to which the dead are drawn for consultation at his request. Cf. e.g. 84–99.

570.   **argued their cases**: wrong translation. It means 'asked for settlements on issues'. The dead are seeking his opinions on knotty legal matters as eagerly as the living did. Cf. *Iliad* 18.497–508 for judges at arbitration.

572.   **Orion**: see on 310.

577.   **Two vultures**: Tityos endures the same agonies as did Prometheus, who was punished similarly by Zeus for giving fire to humans.

580.   **Leto**: mother of Apollo (see 318–9). Panopeus (581) is a city in Phokis; Pytho is an old name for Delphi, one of the major centres of Apollo, the god of prophecy. Cf. 8.80.

582.   **Tantalos**: whence 'tantalize'. He was father of Pelops. Tantalos tried to serve up Pelops to the gods at a feast, was discovered (though not till Pelops had had his shoulder eaten), and was duly punished.

593.   **Sisyphos**: son of Aiolos, king of Corinth. He had a reputation as a trickster, and in some myths is father of Odysseus! He prevented Autolykos (Odysseus' father in the *Odyssey*) from stealing his cattle by fixing lead plates to their hooves with 'stolen by Autolykos' written on them. He managed to trick the god Death twice, once by binding him, once by persuading Death to allow him to return to earth to abuse his wife for not putting the funeral dues in his mouth (Sisyphos had, of course, ordered her not to).

601.   **Herakles**: one of a very few mortals who became gods on account of

their valour. He, like Odysseus, also successfully completed a descent into the Underworld (623–6). His father was Zeus, his mother Alkmene (see 266–70). He is famous for the twelve labours he carried out at the command of Eurystheus, king of Mycenae (621–2). He is frequently depicted in art wearing a lion-skin and holding a club and bow (607). His name means 'glory of Hera' — though, as a bastard son of Zeus by Alkmene, he was hated by her (she was responsible for binding him to Eurystheus' service).

602.   **his image, that is**: a palpable absurdity. What is Herakles' image doing in Hades while his real self is enjoying life among the immortal gods?!

623.   **the dog**: known to later mythology as Cerberus.

626.   **Hermes . . . with Pallas Athene**: here is a further connection between Odysseus and Herakles. Athene is Odysseus' patron goddess (cf. *Iliad* 8.362–5 for further Athene-Herakles connections); and Hermes also helped Odysseus against Circe (10.275–308).

631.   **Perithoos and Theseus**: (it should be 'Peirithoos'). Another Athenian reference and so suspect since antiquity (cf. on 321). Theseus was the legendary founder of Athens and unifier of Attica. In later myth, Theseus and Peirithoos went down to Hades to rescue Persephone, but failed. Theseus escaped, Peirithoos remained.

633.   **green fear**: cf. 43.

635.   **some gorgonish head**: the head of a Gorgon turned those who looked on it to stone.

Book twelve

Introduction

A. The pattern of Book 12 reverts to that already observed in Books 9 and 10. Two shorter incidents—the Sirens and Skylla/Charybdis—are followed by a longer adventure, the arrival on Thrinakia, consumption of the Sun God's cattle, and loss of Odysseus' last ship and all his men. Here Odysseus ends the account of his adventures which he began in Book 9.

B. Odysseus is not one to conceal the fact that he receives a great deal of help from those he encounters: from Aiolos and Hermes in Book 10, and especially now from Circe in Book 12, who gives him detailed instructions about the dangers that await him and how to avoid them (37–150). Such help does not diminish him as a hero: it enhances his status, because he is thought worthy to receive such aid from superior powers (who only help winners). Cf. the help given him by Kalypso and Ino in Book 5, and, from time to time, by Athene, especially in Book 8. But two points should be made. If Circe judges the dangers ahead are too great even for a man of Odysseus' cunning to circumvent without advice, Odysseus on occasions uses his own judgement and ignores Circe's suggestions (see e.g. 120–4, 222–3, 226–7). Second, since the gods themselves, especially Athene, have to be kept out of the narrative, (though unspecified references to them are made—see on 169), we receive the impression that Odysseus is very much on his own and fighting his own battles.

C. We have already observed that some of Odysseus' tales are taken from the Argonautic saga (see 9C, and on 10.108, 10.135). This does land the poet with a slight problem. The antagonist of Odysseus' story is Poseidon (angry at Odysseus' blinding of his son the Cyclops in Book 9). But the antagonist of the Argonautic saga is the Sun God (see on 10.135: the golden fleece was the Sun God's property). It is rather awkward that the Sun God, not Poseidon, should be responsible for the ultimate destruction of Odysseus' remaining ship and crew. It is tempting to suggest that Homer calls the island Thrinakia (isle of the trident, Poseidon's traditional implement) to forge some connection with the real antagonist of the *Odyssey*. If we are also surprised that Homer did not take the chance to have Poseidon, rather than Zeus, send the final storm that killed Odysseus' crew (386–8), we must remember the important role that Zeus plays in this epic as overseer of human moral behaviour (see *1.22–95A, B*). Zeus is invoked here in Book 12 to punish Odysseus' men for their crime in doing what they had been warned specifically not to do.

D. The destruction of Odysseus' men at sea for eating the Sun God's catt. has been awaited ever since the proemium of the *Odyssey* where it wa. specifically highlighted (see on 1.7). The connection between Odysseus' men, the suitors and Aigisthos was also made clear there (see on 1.34). Consequently, there can be no doubt about the 'guilt' of Odysseus' men: they were warned (264–76), swore an oath (303), were aware of the risk they took in disobeying Odysseus' orders (343–51) and did not have the proper resources for a sacrifice (358). Even the ghastly semi-revivification of the slaughtered cattle on the spits (395) does not deter them (cf. on 290). Odysseus blames the gods for sending him to sleep at the critical moment (337–8; 370–3), but note that that is Odysseus' interpretation of what happened to him. It receives no authoritative ratification elsewhere (see on 2.261–2). But if the destruction of the men even so appears 'unfair' (see note on 347), their corrupt sacrifice and feasting act as a sufficiently close parallel with that of the suitors (see on 290) to suggest their guilt. They have their fate in their own hands—and pay the penalty (cf. 1.32–43).

E. Page (*FHO* 80–91) discusses the folk-tale background to the stories of the Sirens and the cattle of the Sun God. There were two Greek traditions about Sirens—the first, taken from the *Odyssey*, that they were charming but dangerous women who sang beautifully, and the second, that they were demons of the underworld, shaped like birds with human heads, who escorted the dead down to the underworld (they appear in many works of art from the 8thC onwards, especially on tombs). Since dangerous women who lured mariners to their deaths are common features of folk-tales, it looks as if Homer has combined aspects of them with some of the grislier aspects of the underworld Sirens (especially e.g. 45–6).

Herds of animals sacred to the gods were commonplace in the Greek world (e.g. Herodotus 9.93.1 for a herd of sheep in Apollonia); and Herodotus 9.120 tells the story of fried fish jumping in their pan, cf. 393–6. So the story of the Sun God's cattle was, for a Greek, perfectly comprehensible, and the details of the sacrifice (353–99) would have made it even more so. The adventure, then, is quite realistic (Page can find only one really close parallel in folk-lore). It must have suited the poet's purpose well to make the adventure which led to the death of Odysseus' men as life-like as possible; in this way the comparison with the suitor's real-life transgressions would not be submerged.

F. The adventures described in Books 9–12 have offered a field-day for moralists and allegorists, past and present (see Clarke *HR* 82–105 and Stanford *UT pass.*) e.g. Skylla and Charybdis = anger and desire; the Sirens offer irresistible temptation to those who desire knowledge—which leads to death (Adam and Eve, the apple and the serpent); the men eating the cattle of the Sun God, who is the dispenser of time (do his 350 cattle and 350 sheep = days and nights of the solar year (12.127–30)?), illustrate the perils of time-wasting, etc. Efforts have also been made to track an intellectual, moral or spiritual growth in Odysseus during his adventures, which will stand him in good stead in Scheria and Ithaka when he finally returns home. But it is difficult to identify any growth or development in Odysseus during these tales: there seems no sense of 'before-and-after' implicit in them. Moreover, only the Cyclops episode is consistently remembered by Odysseus in later books (cf. on 209), probably because that is his greatest *solo* feat. Rather, we should see these tales as a series of exemplary experiences which Odysseus has to face, and through which we can identify more clearly those capacities in Odysseus which he will need to exploit to the full if he is to defeat the suitors and win his return—intelligence (Cyclops), endurance (Aiolos), willingness to take advice (Circe), self-concealment (Cyclops), respect for the gods (Sun God), martial valour (Skylla and Charybdis), courage (Underworld). If the relationship between Odysseus and his men is characterised by tension and mistrust, Odysseus will have to be careful about his choice of helpers in Ithaka. Finally, the adventures themselves revolve mostly round the institution of *xenia*, the treatment of strangers, and thus foreshadow the major theme of Books 13–22—the suitors' treatment of the rightful lord of the palace.

1.   **the stream of the Ocean river**: cf. 10.504–12, 11.11–22.

3.   **Aiaia**: Circe's island (10.135).

4.   **where Helios . . . makes his uprising**: from this evidence, geographers try to locate Circe's palace in the east. But there is strong Argonautic influence anyway in the Circe episode (the golden fleece came from Kolchis, at the eastern end of the Black Sea—see on 10.135), and the 'geography' here as elsewhere is mythical.

7.   **there we fell asleep**: Homeric ships, whose primary purpose was not to fight sea-battles but to transport men and goods, were simple rowing-and-sailing machines. The crew ate and slept on shore. Cf. 12.170–2, 280–93, 14.346–7.

10.   **the body of Elpenor**: see 10.551–60, 11.51–80. The details of the burial are as Elpenor had requested at 11.71–8. On cremation, see on 11.25–50.

18.   **her attendants following**: Penelope's maidservants attend to protect her reputation (see on 6.100). But Circe has no such reputation to protect: her maidservants concentrate on serving the men's gastronomic needs.

21.   **Unhappy men**: hardly 'unhappy'. The word means 'reckless', 'audacious', 'hardy'.

27.   **unhappy, bad designing**: it is precisely this unthinking behaviour that has caused so many of Odysseus' problems. See on 1.7, 10.27, and 10.419.

34.   **talked with me**: wrong translation. 'Lay down beside me' is correct. There continues to be an intimate complicity between Odysseus and Circe that excludes his men (cf. 10.469–95).

35.   **I recited all**: now that Circe knows what Teiresias told Odysseus, can

we explain *her* instructions as nothing but the fleshing-out of Teiresias' rather scanty information? See *11C(1)* for the problem.

37–8.   **I will tell you/all**: Circe tells Odysseus what he must do in private, as she had done at 10.480ff. Circe leaves Odysseus, as leader, to mediate the message to his men. Odysseus is honest to acknowledge the help he gets from Circe. Even so, at 159–60 he alters what Circe told him at 49, at 222–5 he (sensibly?) suppresses all information about Skylla, and he never tells his men exactly what they can expect if they eat the cattle of the Sun God (cf. 10.561–6 with 12.154–7).

39.   **the Sirens**: at 52, Greek uses a special form of the word 'Sirens' (the 'dual') which suggests there are two of them. In other versions there are three. The origin of the word 'Siren' is in dispute. The Semitic 'sir' = 'song'; an ancient lexicon says Zeirene = Aphrodite; Greeks popularly connected the name with *seirē*, a rope, because the song of the Sirens 'binds' you to them.

46.   **of men now rotted away**: it is not at all clear exactly *how* men seduced by the Sirens were killed.

57.   **you yourself must consider**: for this important characteristic of Odysseus, see 5.354, 9.298–9.

60.   **Amphitrite**: see on 3.91.

61.   **Rovers**: these rocks seem dangerous for the storms around them (66–8, cf. 201–2), but the reference to birds flying through them at 61–5 reminds us of the Symplegades, the clashing rocks of the Argonautic legend. The Argonauts sailed through after the dove they sent on ahead also got through. (Homer mentions the Argo specifically at 69–72.) Homer has clearly conflated two different traditions here.

70.   **Aietes**: see on 10.135.

73.   **But of the two rocks**: the Greek is as awkward as the English. The words refer back to 59 and describe 'the other side', i.e. Skylla and Charybdis. But in the Greek and the English it looks as if we are about to get a further description of the Rovers (61) or of the implied Symplegades (see on 61).

81.   **Erebos**: could mean 'the underworld', or 'westwards'.

86.   **new-born puppy**: the Greek for 'puppy' used here is *skylax*, cf. Skylla.

103.   **fig-tree**: Odysseus clings onto this the second time he passes Charybdis, at 12.429–446.

104.   **Charybdis**: derivation unknown, but Homer clearly connects the name with *rhoibdō*, 'suck' 'swallow' (used by Homer cf. 104, 105, 106). 'Charhoibdis' would = 'wide-swallowing'.

107.   **Earthshaker**: i.e. Poseidon, god of the sea, and bitter enemy of Odysseus.

116–7.   **Hardy man**: Circe acknowledges the martial valour of Odysseus, an Iliadic characteristic which we do not see much of in these adventures (but see e.g. 8.517–20).

124.   **Krataiis**: the name means 'powerful woman'.

127–141.   **Then you will reach . . . your companions**: this part of the journey was also predicted by Teiresias at 11.100–15. Cf. 264–8.

132.   **Lampetia and Phaethousa**: the names mean 'Radiant' and 'Shining', appropriate enough for the daughters of Hyperion/Helios, the sun-god.

149.   **a following wind**: as Kalypso did for Odysseus at 5.268. For Circe-Kalypso comparisons, see on 10.221–4.

156.   **So I will tell you**: see on 37–8.

160.   **I, she said, was to listen to them**: see on 37–8. Odysseus further doctors Circe's account by omitting reference to the Sirens' deadly power.

169.   **some divinity**: gods are often invoked to explain natural phenomena but it is worth remembering that Homer intentionally keeps the gods out of the narrative in Books 9–12. Cf. 38, 445–6, and on 9.551. Besides, Odysseus is a narrator, not a muse-inspired bard (see on 374). He cannot know which gods helped him or not.

171.   **in the hollow hull**: see on 12.7. There were spaces in the boat for storage. Odysseus' gifts from the Phaiakians are stored under the thwarts (13.21).

173.   **a great wheel of wax**: if later ship-construction is anything to go by, wax (with pitch) was smeared into the seams between the planks of the hull. Again, ship's paint was encaustic, i.e. wax melted down with colour added to it. Homer talks of ships' prows being of various colours—dark (blue) at 12.100, vermilion at 9.125. Or the wax may serve as a general preservative for leather at sea—tackle, shields, ropes (2.426) etc. So it is no surprise to find that Odysseus has beeswax at hand. Homer does not have to prepare us for it, as he did with the vintage wine for the Cyclops (see on 9.164, 197). See Morrison and Coates, *A T* 185.

176.   **stress of the sun**: it makes more sense to read 'strength of my hands'.

184.   **honored Odysseus**: the fact that the Sirens recognise Odysseus at once (contrast Phaiakians, Cyclops) gives credence to their claim at 189–91, and makes their song that much more irresistible to a man like Odysseus, who in the Phaiakian court urged Demodokos to sing of his own exploits at Troy (8.492–5).

189.   **for we know everything**: the Sirens offer the ordinary mortal what the Muses offer the singer (cf. on 8.45)—the truth about the past. A ceaselessly curious man like Odysseus could not refuse such an offer. Cf. 9.174.

197–8.   **we could no longer/hear their voices**: it must have been clear from Odysseus' movements (192–6) that he could no longer hear the seductive Siren voice.

202.   **smoke . . . surf . . . thundering**: i.e. the Rovers (see 59–68).

209.   **Cyclops**: see 9.193–566. Note Odysseus' assessment of his achieve-ent at 211.

220.   **the sea-rock**: i.e. Skylla's rock.

222–3.   **I had not/spoken yet of Skylla**: see on 37–8. Odysseus likewise ignores Circe's instructions of 120–4 at 226–7.

224.   **for fear my companions**: further evidence of Odysseus' mistrust. Cf. on 10.27.

228. **I put on my glorious armour**: a magnificent, Iliadic gesture of defiance in the face of hopeless odds. For arming before battle with 2 spears, see Idomeneus at *Iliad* 13.241.

247. **with my other companions**: wrong translation. Read 'in search of, looking for, my companions'.

251. **as a fisherman**: as usual, a moment of high drama and pathos is accompanied by a simile.

252. **little fishes**: big fish were caught with spear or net. Cf. the simile of the dead suitors at 22.383–8.

253. **the horn of a field-ranging ox**: much disputed. The ancient commentator Aristarchos says that a hollowed horn was slipped over the fishing line above the hook so that the line could not be bitten through. Cf. *Iliad* 24.80–2.

258. **the most pitiful scene**: one wonders why Odysseus did not call upon Krataiis, as Circe suggested at 124. This scene is more pitiful than the Cyclops' consumption of his companions (e.g. 9.287–91) because the companions' death is so agonisingly drawn out, and their appeal to him so personal (257).

261. **island**: i.e. Thrinakia. *Thrinax* in Greek means a trident, the implement of Poseidon. Since Poseidon is Odysseus' great enemy, the name is clearly significant. Odyseus is on dangerous ground (see *12C* for the problem).

267–8. **Teiresias . . ./Circe**: Teiresias at 11.100–15, Circe at 127–141.

283. **greedy**: wrong translation. Read 'sweet-smelling'.

290. **in despite of the gods**: the idea that men bring destruction upon themselves—as Odysseus' men ironically do here by agreeing to an action which they think will save them—is first proposed at 1.32–4, by Zeus. The moral lessons programmed at 1.1–43 are now about to be exemplified.

300. **evil and reckless action**: the word used of the companions at 1.7.

312. **the third part of the night**: *Iliad* 21.111 divides the day into three parts. Since the stars (312) have set, we are clearly nearing the end of the night. So by analogy from the day we may conclude that the 'third part' means the 'last' part of the night.

313. **let loose on us a gale**: for storms, see 403–19, and on 9.67.

318. **the nymphs**: the nymphs, female nature-spirits, are often said to inhabit caves, mountains, springs etc. See e.g. 13.102–9, 17.204–11, 6.123.

331. **fish and birds**: the plight of the men is desperate. Heroes in Homer normally eat beef or lamb or pork. But see on 4.368–9.

344. **and sacrifice them**: see on 3.430–63.

346. **we will build a rich temple**: see on 6.7. Eurylochos is, in effect, praying to the gods and (typically) offering a condition—if they survive, Hyperion will gain a temple (cf. on 4.762). Eurylochos knows he is taking a calculated gamble (348–9) on the outcome. Homer does not make it clear that any other options are open, and Odysseus, that man of *mētis* (see *9H*), has been strangely lacking in ideas.

358. **no white barley**: cf. on 11.26. For the absence of wine (362), see

3.459–60. The impropriety of Eurylochos' suggestion (346) is reflected in an incomplete, and soon to become horrific (395–6), sacrifice.

360.   **they cut away**: for the details of sacrifice, see on 3.430–63.

374.   **Lampetia of the light robes**: see 132. But how can Odysseus know all this, being a mere mortal, and not a bard, inspired by the Muse (see on 1.1, 2.261–2)? Homer is careful to explain at 389–90.

395.   **The skins crawled**: this chillingly effective occurrence is not typical of Homer: he normally eschews the fantastic and grotesque. He is careful to explain that it is a special occurrence, though—see 394. This supernatural intervention is merited by the enormity of the men's sacrilege. Cf. on 20.347–57.

410–1.   **running gear/. . . wash**: read 'ship's tackle (ropes etc.) . . . hold'.

420–4.   **to where . . . and mast**: i.e. the seas tore the side of the boat from the keel (420–1), so that the keel floated along on its own (422) with Odysseus on it; the mast, originally fixed into the keel, had also broken loose (422). But there was still a rope attached to it (423–4), and with this rope Odysseus tied mast and keel together (424).

432.   **tall fig-tree**: see 101–7. On his previous visit, Odysseus had kept clear of Charybdis (244) and risked it with Skylla.

439.   **a man leaves the law-court, for dinner**: Odysseus emphasises the weariness and exasperation of the judge at the many young men around him. (There was no codified law in the Homeric world. Judgments were given orally by those deemed fit to deliver them. See e.g. 11.568–71, 11.185–7, *Iliad* 18.497–508). Can the reference be humorous? Odysseus is appealing to the common experience which he, as lord of Ithaka (cf. 11.185–7) and the listening Phaiakians, especially Arete (7.74), must have shared. (A moment ago, Odysseus likened himself to a bat (433)!) On the other hand, light-heartedness, even coming at the end of his tale, is hardly in place after what Odysseus has just described.

443.   **between and missing**: read 'in mid-strait (or 'plump into the sea') and alongside'.

451.   **yesterday . . . I told it**: see 7.244–97.

Book thirteen

Introduction

A. The *Odyssey* here undergoes a sea-change. After twenty years' absence, Odysseus finally returns to Ithaka and prepares to face the challenge of regaining his wife and kingdom from the 108 suitors who took over his palace three years' earlier (377). The tale of return becomes one of return and revenge (193). But there are other changes too, particularly in the nature of the world which Odysseus will now inhabit. Kalypso, who kept him for seven years, was a divinity; the Phaiakians were related to Poseidon and their world had elements of the divine about it; Odysseus' tales of his three-year journey from Troy to Kalypso were full of monsters and mythical beings. Homer, it is true, took pains to play down the fabulous elements of this now-past world and by frequent introduction of such Greek institutions as *xenia* and supplication gave it a greater air of Greek reality than it might otherwise have had. But the fairy-tale is from now on firmly banished from the world of Odysseus. Supported by Athene, he is otherwise on his own, disguised as a penniless beggar, in a world of swineherds, peasant huts, dogs and dungheaps. When he finally gets to his palace, he will be abused and attacked by the suitors within. As Athene stresses in this book, Odysseus' means to victory will be concealment/disguise and endurance (307–10). On those conditions, heroic victory through the slaughter of the suitors will be his (393–6). Ever since we met Odysseus in Book 5, we have seen that he possesses the qualities of self-control, endurance and heroism that he will now need in abundance.

B. Book 13 has three major functions. First, it re-introduces us to the Ithaka and the Telemachos we left in Book 4. The wickedness of the suitors is restated (375–8); punishment is not merely Odysseus' duty, it is the concern of Zeus (213–4). We are reminded of Penelope's despair (336–8) and her own efforts to delay marriage to a suitor (379–81). Athene makes it clear that Telemachos has gained the *kleos* ('true identity') he sought in Pylos and Sparta, and is consequently ready to prove himself true son of Odysseus (421–4).

C. Second, Book 13 re-establishes the harmony between Athene and Odysseus which had been so notable by its absence in Books 5–12, but which had been such a feature of people's memory of Odysseus in Books 1–4 (e.g. 3.218–24). There were technical reasons for Athene's absence (see Book I Appendix) but there were literary advantages too. Odysseus could be depicted as an independent hero, a man of sufficient flexibility and resource

119

and internal strength not to have to rely constantly on divine help. But for a Greek, it was a sign of greatness in a man to be helped by a god: no god ever supported a loser. Consequently, it was important for Homer to re-assert the full extent of Odysseus' greatness in Book 13 before his final test. The playful, bantering, teasing meeting between Odysseus and Athene (or are Odysseus' criticisms wholly serious?) is one of the most remarkable scenes of intimacy between a man and god in all Greek literature. In particular, it is noteworthy that Athene sees *mētis* as the quality which predominantly defines the sort of hero Odysseus is—and the sort of goddess she is (see on 293). It is a quality we have seen Odysseus use to the full, never more so than in the Cyclops' cave (see *9H*) and one he will need now.

D. Third, in Book 13 we see the first of a number of false tales that Odysseus tells to conceal his true identity and to convince people of the reality of his assumed one. The glibness and expertise with which Odysseus tells them, and especially the ease with which he appears to move in and out of his real experiences (see on 276), may raise further questions about the truth of his account to the Phaiakians in Books 9–12. However that may be, the disguise that Odysseus has to adopt during these books gives the poet plenty of chances to exploit the possibilities of despair, pathos, happy recognition and most of all irony that have been partly in evidence so far (in e.g. Athene's visit to Telemachos in Book 1, Telemachos' to Pylos and Sparta in Books 3 and 4, and Odysseus' stay in Scheria) but will now reach a crescendo (Fenik *SO* 30ff.). The meeting between Odysseus and Athene in Book 13 gives a fine example of the strengths and weakness of these devices (cf. *7C*). Clearly, there is no need for the poet in *practical* terms to drag the scene out to such lengths. It is not as if Athene could not have engineered a meeting and recognition at once. But the despair of Odysseus in not knowing whether he is really in Ithaka; the irony of his telling a false story to Athene herself (of all people!); the suspense engendered by Odysseus' suspicions of Athene's motives; and the release of pleasure at Odysseus' eventual, certain knowledge that he is finally back, all combine to make a marvellously enjoyable scene between man and goddess. Most of all, Athene is instrumental in guiding the meeting in this direction: she and Odysseus are all of a piece when it comes to disguise and deception (291–299). Book 13 gives us the first example of many such scenes of pathos and irony to come, which the poet exploits to their full capacity. The pleasure to be gained from Books 13–24 depends largely upon the reader's response to the subtlety and irony of the *human* interaction.

E. A note on the world of Odysseus' false tales. They often feature Cretans and Phoenicians. We have met Phoenician traders already (4.615–9), and will meet Cretans frequently. Bronze Age Cretans (Minoans) traded widely in the Aegean (see on 256), and the Phoenicians traded and settled (e.g. Dido in Carthage) all over the Mediterranean from the Bronze Age through the Classical period and beyond (273) (see Murray *EG* 69–74). It is probable that such references reflect the ever expanding contemporary world of 8thC Greece, though since Phoenicians and Minoans traded with Bronze Age Greeks, it is possible that such stories were traditional, handed down as typical elements of epic travel stories (*GI E*). Travel and overseas adventures, so much a feature of the *Odyssey* to date (Telemachos' travels, Odysseus' adventures after Troy) clearly had much appeal to Greek audiences—cf. Jason and the Argonauts who went to the far east of the Black Sea to get the Golden Fleece. So if Book 13 lands us firmly in Ithaka, Odysseus will ensure that our horizons are not thereby automatically restricted.

F. Homer faces an important problem: when and where to re-unite Telemachos and Odysseus? Clearly, they must *be* re-united before taking on the suitors (otherwise there was little point in Telemachos' search for *kleos* in Pylos and Sparta—see on 422). At 404–15, Athene plans the 'route' of Odysseus' first steps: he must visit the swineherd Eumaios. Since it is *tactically* advisable for Odysseus to know the precise situation in the palace before he arrives there, the invention of a friendly pig-man from whom Odysseus can learn the lie of the land is a sensible step. That decision at once opens up the possibility of re-uniting Odysseus and Telemachos there, rather than in the palace, and this is indeed what Athene sets up (15.36–40). Its advantages are that Odysseus and Telemachos can present a united front against the suitors immediately and that Telemachos comes under the control of his father before he confronts the suitors again in the palace. Telemachos, for all his *kleos*, will be kept under a firm rein: there must be no rivals to Odysseus as he prepares for his return and revenge.

4.   **bronze-founded**: cf. the description at 7.84–94.

10.   **Clothing for our guest . . .**: see 8.387–93; 417–20.

13–14.   **a great tripod/and a caldron**: these are the gifts promised by Arete at 11.339–41 and ratified by Alkinoos at 11.350–2. The bronze that went into making a tripod and the caldron which fitted into it, would make it a very valuable gift indeed (quite apart from any artistic merit the object possessed). A caldron and tripod would normally be used for cooking: but *xenia*-gifts are concerned with prestige and status (of both giver and receiver), not with practicality (Finley *WO* 61–7). Given 8.48–58, there could have been *hundreds* of these! Probably the gifts are to come from the 13 kings only (8.390–1). The constant references to gifts emphasise their importance.

18.   **But when the young Dawn showed again**: this day, which ends with Odysseus' departure at 78, is filled with very little. It is needed because Odysseus accepted Alkinoos' offer of a further day's stay at 11.350–1.

24–5.   **sacrificed an ox**: on the importance of sacrifice, see on 3.430–63, 3.375–7.

27.   **Demodokos**: the court-singer who entertained Odysseus throughout Book 8. See e.g. 8.43–5, 62–91.

31.   **as a man makes for his dinner**: there is something typically Odyssean about these homely similes. Here the great hero of Troy and traveller over the vasty deeps is likened to a ploughman wanting to go home for dinner after a hard day at the plough. The *Odyssey* constantly exalts the humble and everyday and the unheroic. Cf. on 5.488. See *Iliad* 18.541–9 for a different picture of a day's ploughing.

50.   **Pontonoos**: on his function as herald, see on 8.8 and cf. 8.65, 474.

54.   **libation**: see on 2.432. For a libation on departure, see 15.147–53.

57.   **into the hand of Arete**: why the queen? For her important, but rather baffling role, see *7B, C, D*. For the honour bestowed by giving a cup to a specific person, see Peisistratos' offer to the disguised Athene at 3.35–53.

67–9.   **mantle . . . chest**: for these gifts, see 8.438–48.

70.   **where the ship was**: this ship had been got ready at 8.34–55.

77.   **its hole in the stone post**: the stern cables are fixed to this useful stone. The bow cables are tied to anchor-stones and thrown into the sea. See 9.137.

83.   **lifting high their feet**: the Greek says 'lifting high themselves' (no mention of feet). The point of comparison is between the rise of the stern of the ship (as the oars pull through the water) and the rise of the horses. If the mention of the lash (82) is supposed to guide our mental sight, the poet is talking of the horses' hindquarters, not their feet (this would make a better comparison with the ship's stern).

88.   **so lightly did she run**: for the ease and speed of Phaiakian ships, see 8.556–63.

89–92.   **She carried . . . he had suffered**: cf. the proemium at 1.1–5. It is as if one episode is closing and another opening. It is easy to see why Odysseus, wrapped in sleep 'most like/death' (80–1), should in these lines be understood to be undergoing more than a merely physical transition from one world, the Phaiakian, to another, Ithaka.

92.   **now he slept still**: ring-composition with 79–81.

93.   **that brightest star**: probably Venus (later Lucifer). At other times of the year it heralds sunset.

96.   **Phorkys**: grandfather of the Cyclops (1.70–3)! The harbour too is uncomfortably like that on the Cyclops' neighbouring island (see 9.135–141) and for the jutting promontories cf. the island of the Laistrygones at 10.89. But this is a typical description, not intended to carry any hidden threat.

104.   **Nymphs of the Wellsprings**: see on 12.318. Cf. 17.205–6.

107.   **looms**: like the bowls and jars of 105, these must be natural features, duly given divine functions. Are they stalagmites?

111.   **has more divinity**: misleading translation. It means 'is more for the gods (in contrast with the mortal North entrance)'.

121.   **urged by great-hearted Athene**: nowhere in our text are the Phaiakians so urged by Athene. Perhaps these words reflect a version in which Athene did play a leading part in persuading the Phaiakians to give Odysseus gifts (cf. her role at 8.7–23 — which might *just* be taken to be the reference point for these lines — and at 8.193–200). At 304–5 Athene herself claims she was instrumental in Odysseus receiving so much.

125. **Earthshaker**: Poseidon. For his threats, see the Cyclops' curse at 9.526–36, and cf. 5.282–90, 11.100–4.

128. **Father Zeus**: Zeus was, in fact, Poseidon's brother (154—though 'brother' is not actually in the Greek there!). Poseidon is using the normal form of address to the King of the Gods.

130. **these are of my blood**: see 7.61–3.

131. **I had said to myself**: see 5.377–9.

137. **more than Odysseus . . . Troy**: see on 5.38 and 8.389 for the promise of these gifts and their importance. It was bad enough for Poseidon that Odysseus should get back home at all; but that he should return with even greater *kleos* than that which he would have got direct from Troy was insupportable.

143–4. **But if there is . . . punish him**: a classic statement of the power-relationship that exists between man and god in the Greek world. A god demands respect from a man, as a master from a servant. Anyone foolish enough to trust in his own mortal power and believe he can get away with insulting a god will meet retribution. Cf. on 4.78–81.

158. **But do not hide their city under a mountain**: this is the reading given by the ancient commentator Aristophanes from Byzantium (257–180, see *GI G*). The ms. give 'And hide their city under a great mountain', supported by the other great commentator Aristarchos of Samothrace (217–145), against Aristophanes! If we accept Aristophanes' reading, we may assume that the Phaiakians sacrifice at 181–3 is efficacious: if not, we do not know whether Poseidon fulfilled his threat or not.

168. **swift ship**: even though turned to stone. This is a formulaic phrase. See on 6.24.

172. **the prophecy of old**: see 8.564–9, and on 7.34, 35.

188. **his own fatherland**: Ithaka.

189. **having been long away**: this cannot be the reason why Odysseus did not recognise the land, since Homer at once gives the reason—Athene had poured a mist all over it (190). We may here be witnessing an intentional pathos-generating device (see on 191). But if it is a slip it is typical of oral poetry. Doubtless there were versions told by Homer in which Odysseus' long absence *did* account for his failure to recognise Ithaka. Cf. the problem of Odysseus' disguise at 397.

191. **unrecognisable and explain all the details**: it is hard to see why Athene needs a mist for this, especially since she lifts the mist at 352 before she had done any of it! Fenik argues that it is typical for the poet to use such 'favourite details and ironies': 'secrecy, disguise, despair, pathos, long-witheld identity and happy discovery' (*SO* 30–5) without regard for absolute consistency and practical value. Odysseus' encounter with Athene here is such an example, Fenik claims, and cf. the whole Phaiakian episode (*7B-D*).

193. **and friends**: Odysseus is revealed to his son Telemachos and the herdsmen Eumaios and Philoitios, and is unintentionally recognised by Eurykleia and the dog Argos before the show-down with the suitors.

193. **overbearing oppression**: in the proemium (see on 1.7) and the

opening scene in heaven (see *1.22–95B*). Homer laid out clearly the moral boundaries of the *Odyssey*. He repeats them here and at 213–4; and cf. 375–8, 393–6. The tale of the return is fast turning into a tale of revenge. Cf. 386–7.

200.   **Ah me, what are the . . .**: the very words with which Odysseus despairingly greeted the cries of the young girls on Scheria at 6.119–21. The two scenes have a basic structural similarity: Odysseus awakes on a shore, does not know where he is, considers his problems, meets a young stranger and receives help (see Fenik *SO* 33). For the irony of the whole scene, see *13D*.

203.   **where shall I take all these many goods?**: Odysseus' concern with his goods throughout this speech (207–8, 215–6) may seem indescribably petty to us, but see on 137 for the indissoluble bond between wealth and status in the heroic world, and observe that Athene will be just as concerned about them (304–5, 362–71). Odysseus justifies murder in the name of his booty gathered from Troy (259–84).

204.   **I wish I had stayed among the Phaiakians**: cf. 209–14! Odysseus' thoughts veer wildly in his despair and rage. The fact that he actually is in Ithaka makes his frustration all the more poignant.

210.   **righteous**: see on 2.282 (where 'just' is the translation).

213.   **Zeus of the suppliants**: for supplication, see on 6.142. A supplication scene is coming up at 226–35.

222.   **likening herself in form**: a typical ploy of Athene, cf. 7.18–21. There is much amusing thrusting and parrying on both sides as Athene and Odysseus argue about the extent to which Athene has been faithful to him. For a more serious interpretation, see Clay *WA* 186–212.

241.   **up and away toward the mist and darkness**: lit. 'behind towards the gloomy west', i.e. in the other direction, westwards.

242.   **this is a rugged country**: the description of Ithaka is typical. At 4.601–8, Telemachos repeats that it is poor for horses but good for goats; at 9.27, Odysseus says it is rough. For grain, wine and rainfall, cf. Cyclops' island at 9.110–1; for woods, see 9.118.

248–9.   **the name of Ithaka . . ./to Troy**: Athene holds back the name of Ithaka till the end to create suspense. There is flattery and 'a sly touch of humour' (Stanford) in the reference to Troy.

255.   **using to every advantage the mind that was in him**: the ensuing false story may seem pointless, but see on 191. This is the first of a number of false stories that Odysseus will tell. His purpose is two-fold: to conceal his real identity and to convince the listeners of the authenticity of his assumed one.

256.   **Crete**: the island of Crete (see map) is frequently given by Odysseus as the land of his origin (14.199, 19.172). Minoans (Cretans of the Bronze Age, so-called after King Minos) traded intensively around the Aegean during the Bronze Age and archaeology shows that they had contacts as far afield as Egypt and Syria. Minoan influence upon the Mycenaeans (Bronze Age Greeks) was very marked. Minoan culture was probably destroyed by a Mycenaean onslaught in the 14thC (*GI* C).

259. **Idomeneus**: a Cretan hero who took a contingent of 80 ships to Troy (*Iliad* 2.652). Odysseus claims to be a brother of his at 19.181, and an ally at 14.237.

262. **plunder**: on its importance, see on 203.

267. **I lay in wait for him**: Odysseus had to ambush Orsilochos because he was too fast to catch in the open (260–1).

273. **Phoenician men**: they and their main city Sidon (286) are frequently mentioned in tales. Cf. 15.415ff., 4.83–4. See on *13E*.

spoil, to stay their eagerness: the Greek says 'satisfying,/heartwarming spoil' (i.e. as payment).

276. **force of the wind**: many of Odysseus' false tales contain elements of personal experience. Cf. 9.80–1 for being beaten off course by the wind, and, of course, 13.187–97, 217–19 for awaking on an unknown shore with one's booty.

291–99. **It would be a sharp one . . . sharpness**: the *locus classicus* for the character of Odysseus—lover of tricks, deceits and tales. He will need all of these to defeat the suitors, as Athene makes clear (303–10).

293. **wretch**: hardly. 'Hardy, tough' would be better.

devious: the word is based on the *mētis* stem, and means 'with various, changeful, *mētis*'. This characteristic of Odysseus is shared with Athene who claims the same quality for herself at 299 ('wit' = *mētis*) and plans to help to devise a scheme (*mētis*) at 303–4 (cf. 386 'design'). On the importance of *mētis*, see on *9H*.

306–10. **tell you all the troubles . . . violence**: Athene announces her general programme for Odysseus: she will prepare him in advance for his return to his palace; Odysseus must endure; he must conceal the news of his return. Endurance and concealment are the keys to Odysseus' success in Ithaka, as they have been in other ventures too. Cf. e.g. on 10.53. On concealment, see e.g. *5C, 6C*.

312. **It is hard**: Odysseus briskly argues back with Athene, accusing her of unfaithfulness (318 cf. 3.218–222) and duplicity (324–5). The relationship between Athene and Odysseus as depicted in this passage has some parallels with that of Sappho and Aphrodite, as Sappho envisages it ('Prayer to Aphrodite'). See also Kalypso's reaction to Odysseus at 5.173–83.

317. **the god scattered the Achaians**: on this problem for Homer, see on 5.108.

323. **yourself in person**: but Odysseus did not know this at the time (7.14–81). This seems to break the careful convention maintained by Homer of what a character knows about divinities' actions, unless Odysseus can be drawing conclusions from 302. See on 1.1 'Muse'.

334–6. **but it is . . . wife**: almost unintelligible. If Athene's thought-processes are assumed to be highly condensed, we could interpret as follows: 'This behaviour of yours is typical (330): you are always (among other things) restrained (332). Example: any other wanderer, learning he was home, would immediately have rushed off to enquire after his family (333–4). But it is not characteristic of you to behave like this ('investigate and ask questions (sc. of your family)', 335)—not, at any rate, till you have carefully checked (on everything), even your wife (336) (who may, like Klytaimestra, be waiting for you with an axe, and against whom you have been specifically warned, 11.455–6): but she, in fact, is completely faithful'. See Clay *WA* 203 for a different approach.

341.   **I did not want to fight**: cf. 6.328–31.

343.   **his dear son**: the Cyclops. See 1.68–75 and 9.181–542, especially 526–35.

345–51.   **This is . . . forest**: see 96–112 and notes.

360.   **my dear son**: Telemachos, whose adventures we followed in Books 1–4. It is significant that he bulks so large in Odysseus' thoughts at this time. See on 422.

378.   **gifts**: on marriage customs, see on 2.53.

379–81.   **And she . . . intentions**: we have already seen that Penelope shares with Odysseus a streak of cunning. Cf. 2.94–110.

384.   **like . . . Agamemnon**: see 11.405–61 for the ghost of Agamemnon's tale of his death and warning to Odysseus. Teiresias warned Odysseus of what he would find in his palace when he returned (11.100–18). Has the poet forgotten this? Or does Odysseus not wish to appear ungrateful by saying 'I know already'? (See *11C, D* for the problems). Cf. on 15.347–8.

386.   **vengeance**: see on 193.

388.   **as when together**: Odysseus realises he will require the same help from Athene to defeat the suitors as the Trojans. The arenas of conflict may be different, but the conditions for heroic behaviour do not change: Odysseus will need might (387) and (see next note) cunning too. Odysseus' cunning and courage in taking Troy have already been celebrated in song by Demodokos in the court at Scheria at 8.499–520. Athene has to intervene dramatically in the final battle at 22.205–40 to recall Odysseus to his former bravery.

395.   **spattered by the blood and brains of the suitors**: Athene agrees that martial valour will be needed to defeat the suitors, but goes on to disguise Odysseus as an old beggar. They will destroy the suitors as they did Troy—by a mixture of courage and cunning, involving disguise and concealment (the Wooden Horse; and cf. 4.240–89).

397.   **so that no mortal can recognise you**: a man can go unrecognised because he is *made* unrecognisable or because absence has dramatically altered him. Homer looks as if he is going to use the first device; but Odysseus is unintentionally recognised by Eurykleia at 19.467–75 and is not re-embodied at 22.1ff. (he merely strips off his rags and announces himself— though the suitors do not at once believe him, 22.45). This is slightly awkward, but (i) the poet always exploits situations for their full effect, even if this does land him in trouble with the *strict* logic of the situation (see *13D*). (ii) Odysseus is only changed *externally* (hair, skin, eyes, though cf. 16.456) —the shape and stature of the man remain the same for those who can see underneath the surface. Cf. 18.66–9, 20.194, Page *HO* 88–91.

404.   **swineherd**: Eumaios. Odysseus will be with him during Book 14.

Athene will go to Sparta (412) at the start of Book 15. This neatly organises a complex plot for the listener.

414.   **Menelaos**: we left Telemachos at 4.620.

417.   **Why then did you not tell him . . .?**: a good question and one asked by analysts who see no purpose in the journey of Telemachos in Books 3–4! On the purpose of the 'Telemachy', see *3A*.

422.   **reputation**: the word is *kleos*. For the importance of the *kleos*-theme as it applies to Telemachos, see *3A*, *16C* and on 1.95. Athene here confirms that Telemachos has won the *kleos* he set out to gain: he is being treated like a hero with all material gifts beside him (424). See on 17.111, 21.128.

425.   **young men with their black ship**: the suitors at 4.842–7.

430–8.   **withered . . . to dangle it**: many of the so-called 'problems' of subsequent books—especially Odysseus' apparently interminable false tales and rather petty grubbing—arise because it is easily forgotten that Odysseus' change of appearance also involves a change of *character*. He must not merely look like a beggar: he must *act* like a beggar too.

436.   **big hide**: probably to keep off the rain. Cf. Hesiod *WD* 544–5.

Book fourteen

Introduction

A. In the course of this book, it becomes clear that Odysseus' disguise has a subtly different function from that which it has had so far. In Books 5–12, Odysseus' self-concealment was a calculated response to a difficult situation. In Scheria, for example, his purpose was, by a series of acts of self-revelation, to win acceptance as the great hero of the Trojan War (see *8A*). But in Books 13–22, his disguise has been divinely imposed upon him as the means by which the death of the suitors can be encompassed. While there is a specific, long-term end in view—recognition, revenge and the restoration of Odysseus' heroic *kleos*—the price to be paid is a long period of disguise and, in the palace, humiliation. The poet, as we have already seen aplenty (*13D*), will exploit to the full the potential irony and pathos of the situation (see e.g. on 32, 36, 396–7).

B. This part of the *Odyssey*, and Book 14 in particular, have never been the critics' favourite. 'Long-winded', 'disproportionate' are typical responses (cf. Kirk *SoH* 360–8; Clarke *AO* 73). Odysseus' unending false tales, his harping on his stomach, his exploitation of the good-hearted Eumaios and general meanness of spirit seem to drag the narrative out to little purpose and lend an air of cheap unattractiveness to the proceedings. But it is worth emphasising that through these books Odysseus is *playing a part*. He is disguised like, and so much act up to the part of, a beggar. Demands for cloaks, moans about his stomach, long tales, shameless self-serving are expected of such vagrants (as Eumaios and later the suitors make clear—see e.g. on 110, 120, 132, 466). These books are partly an elaborate essay in *ēthopoia* (character-construction) by Odysseus, and the question is whether Odysseus will succeed. There are signs here and there of cracks in his disguise. (See notes on 315, 440, 443). These are important moments. Odysseus is as much under test himself here as he is testing others. But at least in Eumaios' hut he is among friends: it is an ideal arena in which Odysseus can prepare himself for the much stiffer challenge presented by the suitors in the palace (Fenik *SO* 29–30).

C. There may be another reason for the lukewarm critical reception of these books, that is, that in them the *Odyssey* turns briefly from epic into something approaching a morality play. The warmth of Eumaios, his immaculate *xenia*, his piety towards the gods, his love for the dead Odysseus, his closeness to the family, and his unshakeable conviction that Zeus punishes wicked behaviour set the tone for much of the book, and we warm to the 'uncomplicated generosity' of a man who can least afford it treating the beggar Odysseus as he does. But there is purpose to all this. First, the climax of the work will be Odysseus' revenge against the suitors, and we must be convinced that Odysseus' enemies are justly punished. Second, as Austin points out (*ADM* 165–8), Eumaios (like the old servant Eurykleia) holds firm as a 'stalwart paradigm of order' in the face of the collapse of authority in the palace. In his ordered world (5–16), his distance from the palace (372), his closeness with the family from of old (137–47), his concern for careful husbanding of Odysseus' whole estate (100–8, 523–7), we (and Odysseus) see what the palace used to be like. It is on these loyal, secure foundations, through his faithful servants, that 'Odysseus must rebuild what once was his'. (For the elevation of the humble and lowly, see e.g. on 1.130–50, and note the homely details which so enliven the picture of life in Eumaios' hut in Book 14—the pigpen (5–16), the brushwood seat (49–50), Eumaios hitching up his tunic (72) etc. There is much here to remind us of late Euripides and the 'comedies of manners' of Menander. See *5F*; Camps *IH* 96 note 43).

D. Finally, it is worth observing how Odysseus, a nameless beggar, a stranger in his own homeland, and even attacked by dogs (29–31), slowly and imperceptibly begins to assume command over and both guide and direct the men who are going to be so vital to him as he prepares to kill the suitors. G.P. Rose ('The swineherd and the beggar' *Phoenix* 34 1980) shows how the use of address between Eumaios and Odysseus indicates the changing relationship between the two: Eumaios calls Odysseus 'Old sir' at 37, 122, 166 and 'guest/stranger' (*xenos*) at 80, while Odysseus calls him *xenos* ('host/stranger') at 53 and 'Dear friend' at 115 and 149. By 361, Odysseus has become 'sorrowful stranger' and at 402 'friend'. There follows the sacrifice of the 'best of pigs' (414) in Odysseus' honour, and the gift to Odysseus of the choice cut (437). Odysseus by now is emboldened to call the swineherd 'Eumaios' at 440 (but see note). See on 17.274–9, 525 for Odysseus' increasing dominance.

1. **left the harbour**: of Phorkys, where Odysseus had been landed by the Phaiakians (13.96–7). The stages of the *xenia* sequence (see on 1.102) are immaculately observed up to questions at 185, with delightful variation (e.g. anger, 35!)

3. **noble swineherd**: Eumaios. 'Noble' may sound strange, but he was in fact of noble birth (15.412–4). At 22 and elsewhere he is called 'leader of men' (so Philoitios, 20.185). But such formulaic epithets do not need to be squeezed for their full significance.

4. **cared for the house properties**: the loyalty of the faithful few will be set in contrast in later books with the disloyalty of those servants of Odysseus who sided with the suitors.

5–10. **lofty/enclosure . . . with a view . . ./large and handsome . . ./topped it off**: even a humble pig-pen has a grandeur about it when it is built by a man like Eumaios (there is surely no parody here). See on 49–50). For the whole description, including the details of the pigs' sleeping arrangements, cf. the Cyclops at 9.181–6, 273–9, and Odysseus' palace at 17.265–8.

9.   **far from his mistress and . . . Laertes**: i.e. Penelope and the father of Odysseus (on whom see on 1.188–93). Eumaios is very far from taking advantage of his masters' absence. Cf. 17.318–21.

17.   **godlike suitors**: see on 1.21.

28.   **sacrifice**: the word used in Greek, *hiereuō*, often means this, but it can also mean simply 'slaughter'. It is a feature of the suitors behaviour that they never remember the gods when they feast. Cf. Eumaios at 420–4.

31.   **sat down on the ground**: this is apparently a recognised method of dealing with an assault from wild dogs. That it could not be guaranted to succeed seems to be suggested by 32. Observe how well Odysseus acts the part of a beggar.

32.   **beside his own steading**: the first of many instances in which Odysseus, unrecognised, will be attacked in his own domain. Cf. Athene's warning at 13.307–10. The poet exploits to the full the possibilities for pathos and irony in these situations. Compare the use of dogs at 16.4, 162–3, 17.290–327.

36.   **to his own master**: delightful irony, to be followed with fine irony and pathos at 40–4.

38.   **you would have covered me with shame**: i.e. 'you would have hurled abuse at me'. Cf. 1.119–20.

46.   **first may be filled . . . then tell me**: Eumaios knows the proper way to treat a *xenos*. Cf. Telemachos at 1.123–4.

49–50.   **brushwood . . . hide**: Eumaios may not have the fine furniture and coverings of the palace (cf. 1.130–1), but he takes care to seat his guest as well as he can, as is right in *xenia* rituals. Some have seen parody here, surely wrongly (see on 5–10). Homer adapts the rituals of *xenia* to the circumstances of a poor man's hut: it is greatly to Eumaios' credit that he treats Odysseus as courteously as he does when he can so ill afford it (note 51 'from his own bed').

55.   **Then, O swineherd Eumaios, you said to him**: this use of the second person + vocative of address to introduce a speech is restricted in the *Odyssey* to Eumaios. (In the *Iliad*, it is restricted in the main to Menelaos and Patroklos). It seems to suggest a bond of special sympathy between poet and character, and is used to powerful emotional effect in the *Iliad* with the gentle, but doomed, Patroklos.

57–8.   **All vagabonds/and strangers are under Zeus**: see 6.206–8, and note. Cf. 402–6. Eumaios' piety stands in strong contrast to the suitors' impiety. Cf. 80–4.

59.   **for that is the way of us**: i.e. any gift from a slave, especially one under the thumb of new masters, is likely to be small.

61.   **of that one**: i.e. Odysseus. Eumaios is as chary of mentioning Odysseus' name (not till 144) as Telemachos was in Book 1 (see on 1.160–8).

62.   **who cared**: wrong translation. Read 'who would care/would have cared'. Cf. 21.212–6.

68.   **Helen's seed**: on the Trojan war, see *GI H*.

75.   **cut them into little pieces**: Eumaios is making kebabs.

84.   **justice**: the word is *dikē*, which normally means 'characteristic behaviour', 'way in which people should behave', 'judgement, principle of law' in Homer (see on 2.282). This is the only place in the *Odyssey* where *dikē* is conceptualised into the abstract idea of 'justice'. *Iliad* 16.388 gives the one other Homeric example. See Lloyd-Jones *JZ* 5–7, and notes. For comparison with *themis* see on 130.

85.   **those**: Eumaios compares pirates, who may ravage the land but do at least leave it eventually, with the suitors (89). Odysseus' men were duly punished for their folly in not leaving the land of the Kikones immediately at 9.39–61.

88–88a.   **fear, which is stronger than/on these . . . regarded**: something has gone wrong with the text here. Delete all 88a ('on these . . . regarded'), and in place of 'fear which is stronger than', read 'powerful fear of retribution'.

96.   **an endlessly abundant livelihood**: a careful master like Odyseus does not need special help from the gods to generate almost utopian excess (cf. Alkinoos at 7.103–32, Cyclops at 9.107–11). At 19.107–14, Odysseus connects natural wealth with good rule (see on 19.109, cf. 20.211–3). All this stands in strong contrast with the suitors' wickedness (90–2). For epic exaggeration of the size of this holding, see Finley *WO* 51. Cf. on 1.108.

100.   **on the mainland**: Ithaka is an island. By the mainland, Eumaios may mean Elis (4.635) or the region NW of the Corinthian gulf (Epirus? Akarnania?). Ithaka itself is poor country for cattle (cf. 4.606, 13.242).

110.   **greedily**: Stanford suggests that, since Odysseus is not hungry, he cats like this because his mind is elsewhere, 'devising evils for the suitors'. More likely, Odysseus is acting the part of a man who, if the story he tells at 339–358 is true, should be starving.

120.   **I have wandered to many places**: it turns out to be a characteristic of wanderers to seek favour with the house they are lodging in by giving 'news' of the house's loved ones (see 122–32). Odysseus plays this part to the full — releasing much irony in the process, since he is not believed. (See e.g. 165–6, 391–406; Fenik *SO* 154–8).

128.   **(She) receives him well**: fine psychology. Penelope will not be persuaded by what wanderers say (122–3), but any news is better than no news for the unhappy woman: the more desperate you are, the more you clutch at straws. Cf. 1.414–6.

130.   **the right way for a wife**: the Greek word is *themis*. This, like *dikē* (see on 84), veers between the approving (what one should do in the circumstances) and the normative (what normally happens in the circumstances). A *themis* seems to be more of a general principle of behaviour given by Zeus, from which a *dikē* can be deduced. The meaning here leans towards the normative — 'since this is what women normally do when . . .'. See on 2.68 for Themis personified.

132.   **a cloak or tunic to wear**: another characteristic of beggars is their

natural desire to get some decent clothes on their back which will keep them warm. Odysseus plays this part to the full throughout these books (see especially 149–155). Note that clothing has honorific value too (24.274–7).

133–6.   the dogs . . . deeply upon them: for such exaggerations, see on 1.161–8.

133.   dogs and flying birds: (*'flying'* is wholly redundant). Eumaios speaks here of death by land, in contrast with 134–6.

138.   me most of all: Eumaios feels so close to Odysseus as to be almost a member of his family. Cf. his care for Telemachos at 174–84; and closeness to Penelope at 372–4. Indeed, even Eumaios' parents are not as dear to him as Odysseus is (140–44). This feeling of Eumaios' for Odysseus' family will receive moving expression when Telemachos returns at 16.12–22 (note the simile).

145.   even when he is not here: fine irony.

145–6.   I feel some modesty about naming him: for the wider associations of the theme of namelessness, see *5C*. Cf. the death threat to Telemachos mentioned by Eumaios at 179–82, especially 182.

158–64.   Zeus be my witness . . . due honour: one of the first of a number of oaths and signs that Odysseus' return is imminent. See on 2.163–7.

161–2.   within this very year . . ./at the waning of the moon, or at its onset: the problem is the meaning of the Greek word *lukabas*, here translated 'within this very year'. Odysseus repeats this prophecy before Penelope (19.306–7). When Penelope says that she is planning to set up the trial of the bow and the axes, Odysseus encourages her because Odysseus will be back before the suitors can succeed at it (19.582–7). This suggests *lukabas* refers to something imminent. Some have connected *lukabas* with Apollo, worshipped under the cult-name *Lukeios*—which *can* mean 'of the light', possibly 'of the new moon'. The meaning may then be 'on Apollo's feast-day' or 'by the end of the month'. The suitors are killed on Apollo's feast-day (20.167, 276–8, 21.258–9), and Apollo was god of the bow (with which Odysseus will slaughter them).

178.   upset the balanced mind: so it must have seemed to Eumaios, but (irony again) the purpose of Telemachos' visit to Pylos (179–80) was to prove that he *was* the son of his father (see 1.95 and *3A*). On implications of high birth, see on 212.

180–1.   are lying/in wait for him: see 4.842–7.

181–2.   Arkeisios'/stock . . . nameless in Ithaka: for namelessness, see on 145–6 and ref. Arkeisios is father of Laertes, but otherwise almost completely unknown. See 4.755.

187.   What man are you and whence?: Eumaios waits till after Odysseus has eaten before he asks the question—the right procedure (see 45–7).

190.   on foot: an islander's 'joke'. Cf. 1.173.

195.   we could feast quietly: the setting is more humble, but the appurtenances—food and drink—and sentiments ('my troubles'—196–8) are the same as when Odysseus told his story to the Phaiakians (9.1–15).

199.   my origin is from Crete: Odysseus frequently claims this in his false tales (see *13E*). Odysseus' purpose here is to persuade Eumaios that he is not really a beggar: he is in fact a fighting, adventurous hero down on his luck. He appeals to Eumaios' sympathy because Eumaios himself had been tricked by Phoenicians (15.415ff.). Cf. 17.226–8.

203–4.   **I was favoured with the legitimate/sons**: if your father was the 'lord of the manor' there was no inevitable loss of status in bastardy in the Homeric world. The legitimate sons may have cut Odysseus out of a fair share of the estate (208–10), but his birth (see note on 212) and fighting skill brought him a good marriage. See Finley *WO* 59–60; cf. 4.1–14.

212.   **courage**: but the Greek term used, *aretē*, has strong overtones of 'fine birth' (which, to a Greek, would automatically imply fine looks, courage etc.—see on 1.411). Translate 'qualities'.

220.   **but far the first I would leap out**: Odysseus tells of his expertise in the ambush in his false tale at 13.259–71. Odysseus invented the Wooden Horse strategy (8.492–5).

229.   **sons of the Achaians**: see on 1.61.

231.   **against outland men**: presumably Odysseus means he won his substance through piracy. Cf. his men's actions at 261–5. See on 4.81–91.

232.   **I took out an abundance of things, but much I allotted**: wrong translation. Read 'a satisfying amount I took for myself' (i.e. leader's privilege), 'and much I was later allotted' (in the general share-out, cf. 13.138). The wrath of Achilleus in the *Iliad* hinges partly on the distinction between what the leader gets (because he is leader) and what others get (*Iliad* 1.163–71).

235–6.   **hateful/expedition**: i.e. the Trojan War (Ilion 238 = the city of the Trojans, Troy).

237.   **Idomeneus**: see on 13.259. Observe how widely disparate are the uses Odysseus makes of Idomeneus in these tales.

238–9.   **there was no remedy,/nor any refusing**: Odysseus was in *fact* a reluctant participant in the Trojan War. See Agamemnon at 24.115–9. For Odysseus' exploits at Troy, see *4F*.

242.   **and the god scattered the Achaians**: cf. Nestor's account of the return home at 3.130–83. For the problem this causes Homer, see Book I Appendix.

244.   **one month only I stayed**: humorous Homeric *para prosdokian* ('against expectation'). After being told that the Achaian ships were scattered (242) and then that Zeus was planning 'more hardships' for Odysseus (243), we naturally assume Odysseus is going to give us some of his famous high-seas adventures—but no. He got home perfectly safely.

254.   **like sailing downstream**: the word 'stream' is *rhoos*, which means basically, 'flow, current'. Since Greeks did not navigate rivers, translate 'like sailing with the current'.

257.   **stream Aigyptos**: i.e. the River Nile. Odysseus' account of the delightfully easy journey is quite different from Nestor's (see on 3.321). We could argue that we are dealing with different traditions; or that Odysseus is lying; or that Nestor was exaggerating; or that was how it was. For Egypt and

other Egyptian tales, see the tales of Menelaos at 4.81–92, 351–587 (with notes). Cf. on 4.125–32, 226–32.

261–271.   **but they . . . sharp bronze**: the story bears many resemblances to the battle with the Kikones at 9.40–61.

276.   **I put the . . . helm from my head**: an act of supplication. See on 6.142. Cf. on 22.329.

284.   **who beyond others is outraged**: Odysseus echoes the sentiments of Eumaios at 83–4; cf. Eumaios' comments on the duties of *xenia* at 402–6.

288.   **a Phoenician man**: see on 13.273.

296.   **with lying advices, that with him we could win a cargo**: wrong translation. Read 'telling me falsely that I should carry the cargo with him' (and, presumably, share the profit when it had been sold).

299–300.   **above/the middle of Crete**: there is dispute about the geography of this episode (see on 315). It is possible that this phrase means S. *or* N. of Crete. A ship from Phoenicia (= Lebanon) would travel to Libya (S. of Crete) via Crete because ancient mariners kept in sight of the coast-line, and with a north wind blowing, it was better to keep away from southerly coasts—in this instance, the North African coast.

301–15.   **But after we . . . Thesprotia**: this storm and its after-effects bear a striking resemblance to the incident after Odysseus left the Island of the Sun God at 12.403–25, 447–8.

315.   **Thesprotia**: a district on the coast of Epirus, which contained the oracle at Dodona (327). It is hard to see how Odysseus could have arrived there from somewhere near Crete (299–301) with a north wind blowing (299). But either we may allow Odysseus a little lee-way, especially in a false tale to a swineherd, or, if we allow him to be travelling *north* of Crete (see on 299–300), he may have been caught by the prevailing current which runs northwards up the Adriatic from S. of the Peloponnese (Meijer *HSCW* p. 29).

316.   **Pheidon**: the name means 'the one who spares'.

317.   **without price**: since *xenoi* were entertained free, Odysseus must be hinting here that Pheidon would, in normal circumstances, have demanded a ransom for him. But since it was his son who brought Odysseus back to the palace (317–8), Odysseus was treated as a *xenos* after all.

317–20.   **his . . . son had come on me . . . as clothing**: an incident which, in extremely compressed form, bears some resemblance to Odysseus' meeting with Nausikaa at 6.115ff.

328.   **out of the holy, deep-leaved oak tree**: Greek gods could contact humans by any number of means—through human mediums (Delphi), rushing waters, clanging pots and, as here, the rustling of leaves in an oak tree. See *WoA* 2.15–17 for classical practices.

344.   **they made their way off**: i.e. they arrived at.

351–9.   **thus swimming . . . is still my portion**: there is, again, some similarity between this incident and Odysseus' swimming ashore on Scheria and hiding himself (5.438–93).

352.   **close to where they were**: wrong translation. Read 'well away from where they were'.

357. **the gods who concealed me**: the theme of Odysseus' concealment is, of course, an important one in the *Odyssey*. See e.g. *5C*.

373–4. **Penelope . . ./asks me to go**: for Eumaios' closeness to the family, see on 138.

375. **sit beside me and question me**: wrong translation. Read 'sit beside the messenger and question him'—something Eumaios has no liking for, since he has been deceived before by an Aitolian (379) and now again, as he thinks, by Odysseus (386–8). This is the ultimate irony: Eumaios swallows Odysseus' *false* tales hook, line and sinker, except for the one *certain* fact— that Odysseus will return. (See on 120).

376–7. **whether they are . . ./or are**: these are the people doing the questioning of 375. Both those who love and those who hate Odysseus would have their reasons for listening carefully to any news.

380. **This one had killed a man**: a common theme cf. 13.259, 15.272–3.

384. **he said he would be coming back**: presumably this tale had been told some time ago and turned out, in the event, not to be true. Eumaios, so close to Penelope (374–5), must have been full of remorse at the anguish it caused her (cf. on 128). This gives excellent motivation for his absolute refusal to entertain any further hopes from travellers' tales.

396–7. **send me/on my way to Doulichion**: heavy irony.

399. **set your serving men on me**: one of Eumaios' serving-men, Mesaulios, is named at 449–53, but 434–6 suggest that there are four in all and cf. 24–7.

405. **then murdered you**: Eumaios' piety stands in strong contrast with the suitors' wickedness again. They would kill Odysseus if he returned back to his own home (2.246–51).

411. **their accustomed places**: see 13–16.

420–1. **nor did the swineherd/forget the immortal gods**: see on 28, for contrast with the suitors.

423. **as dedication**: the Greek says 'making a first-fruit offering' (for the god is owed the first of everything). Eumaios further acknowledges the gods by burning the first cuts of the animal (presumably, thigh-bones) for them all (427–9), and then singling out Hermes and the nymphs (435). See on 3.430– 63 for the full ritual.

435. **for the nymphs and Hermes**: for the nymphs, because they were worshipped in the vicinity (13.102–12, cf. Odysseus' prayer at 13.356–60), and for Hermes because he was god of herdsmen (see on 5.47).

437. **the chine's portion**: for the honour attached to receiving special cuts of meat, cf. 4.65–6, 8.474–83.

440. **Eumaios**: presumably Odysseus knows the name of the swineherd to whom Athene directed him (13.404–10) because he must have known him before he went to Troy (see on 15.366), though he would not know where he now lived (15.368–70). But Odysseus is acting the part of a wandering beggar who *should* know nothing about Ithaka. See on 443.

443. **strange man that you are**: the word for 'strange' here is *daimonios*, meaning one under the influence of *daimōn* (Eng. 'demon') or god, and so

acting oddly. Does Eumaios use this term of address to indicate that he has spotted Odysseus' 'mistake' over his name at 440?.

446.   **sacrificed**: wrong translation. Read 'burnt'.

first-offerings: presumably those referred to at 435.

447.   **sacker of cities**: a formula, referring to Odysseus' part in sacking Troy (the Wooden Horse was Odysseus' idea—cf. on 4.270, 8.503, 11.524). The epithet has not been used of Odysseus since 9.530, and is powerfully ironic here since it is being used of an Odysseus disguised as a poor old beggar, in one of his swineherd's huts.

450.   **owned himself by himself**: it is interesting that Eumaios, himself a slave, can purchase a slave to serve him. This is part of what Finley (*WO* 58–9) calls the 'patriarchal' treatment of slaves in Homer (in strong contrast with the pattern of plantation slavery).

452.   **Taphians**: see on 1.105.

457.   **the dark of the moon**: the Greek word means 'with darkened moon'. It could refer to a moon obscured by clouds because of the weather; but it could also refer to the time of the month when the moon was invisible. This would fit in well with the prophecies of Odysseus' return (see on 161–2, 19.307).

458.   **always watery**: see on 7.118 for the West Wind (Zephyr).

466.   **better unspoken**: Odysseus' purpose is to test Eumaios (459–61). To achieve his end, he remains perfectly in character as a drunken beggar (cf. 18.1–3) presuming embarrassingly upon the company (beggars were expected to be shameless, cf. 17.347, 578). The episode has seemed pointless to some but 'testing' episodes seem a standard feature of epic (cf. e.g. *Iliad* 2.73–4, which has been regarded with equal suspicion). Also, Odysseus is a great tester of men (see on 16.304–5 for other examples).

473–7.   **all about the city in marshy ground . . . rimming them**: cf. the fine description by Aeschylus (*Agamemnon* 449ff.) of the conditions endured by the Greeks at Troy.

483.   **third time of the night**: see on 12.312.

484.   **I spoke to Odysseus**: there is much self-referential humour here, as a disguised Odysseus shows how clever the real Odysseus is by telling a complimentary (470, 490–1) tale of a fictional Odysseus in order to test the reality of Eumaios' loyalty.

499.   **Thoas . . . son of Andraimon**: he led the Aitolian contingent to Troy with 40 ships (*Iliad* 2.638–44). It is interesting that Odysseus should choose an Aitolian after an Aitolian received such a bad press from Eumaios for suggesting that Odysseus would soon return (378–85).

515–7.   **When, however . . . to be sent**: genuine enough in other contexts (e.g. 15.337–9), these lines are omitted in many sound mss. at this point. They do not add much, and rather contradict the spirit of pessimism which informs Eumaios' feelings about Telemachos (183–4).

Book fifteen

Introduction

A. In this book of the *Odyssey*, the returns of Odysseus and Telemachos begin to be woven together in preparation for their meeting in Book 16. This is achieved with consummate skill by the poet (see notes on 1, 5, 301, 495). The temporal interlocking of the two returns also enables the poet to compare their differing fortunes: the ignorance and pessimism of Telemachos (see notes on 16–17, 20–3, and 519, and cf. 266–70) contrast with the patient waiting game that Odysseus is playing. Observe the intelligent tact of 307–24. Odysseus here motivates his departure from the hut to visit the palace (note specially 309, 314, 316–7), but agrees at once to delay his departure (346) in response to Eumaios' loving care for him. In the event, Telemachos will give instructions to Eumaios to bring Odysseus to the palace (17.9ff.)—but the ground has been prepared. Again, Odysseus continues to draw out and win the confidence and sympathy of Eumaios in the most convincing manner. Odysseus' question about Antikleia and Laertes (346–50) arises quite naturally from the discussion of conditions in the palace (326–39), as does his further enquiry about Eumaios' abduction to Ithaka (380–8), prompted by Eumaios' throw-away comment about his upbringing (361–70). Eumaios himself continues to come over as the soul of good-heartedness, e.g. 335–9, and on 390–401. His story has a thematic uniqueness about it (it cannot be duplicated elsewhere in the *Odyssey*) which gives it the ring of truth in comparison with Odysseus' devious tales which are frequently a *pot-pourri* of common centos (see Fenik *SO* 167–71).

B. But there is more to Telemachos than ignorance and pessimism. This is our first sight of him since we left him in Book 4. The poet has to re-establish him before he can be re-united with his father. What stands out in 1–300 is the emphasis the poet gives to gifts and *xenia*. Menelaos loads him with splendid gifts and would happily go with him around the Peloponnese to get him more (75–85); the gifts are fabulous (113–4; 125–32); and Telemachos makes clear that he is well aware of the significance of all this (155–9). Nestor too would entertain him royally again if he could (209–14). Here is a young man whose *kleos*, a large part of which is measured by other heroes' reception of you (4.589–92), is now firmly established in the heroic world in which his father was so dominant a figure (see on 13.422, cf. *13F*).

C. Analysts have long been concerned about the purpose of Theoklymenos in the *Odyssey*. As Page points out in his hilarious dissection of Theokly-menos' role (*HO* 84ff.), he is trumpeted more loudly and longer than anyone else in the *Odyssey* (225–55), but his part turns out to be 'very small, and wonderfully unimportant'. There may be some truth in this broad accusation, but Page's criticisms of Theoklymenos' individual interventions in the narrative are not convincing (see notes on 264, 519, 533–4). It may well be that we have here an example of the introduction by the poet of a new character into his version of the *Odyssey*, whose integration is not yet fully complete. But the *idea* of having a prophet in the palace is a fruitful one. His presence will increase the chances for irony and pathos so beloved by Homer in these books (see *13D*); and he can add a *religious* dimension to the narrative—a dimension that Homer begins to enlarge upon in these later books as the doom of the suitors draws nearer (especially 20.345–7).

1.   **At this time**: the poet now weaves together the adventures of Odysseus (Books 5–14) and the journey of Telemachos (Books 3–4). (Athene had promised to bring this about at 13.404–15.) There is a technical difficulty here. The poet usually presents events which are *supposed* to be taking place simultaneously *as if* they were taking place one after the other. So we might ask—what was Telemachos doing during the 29 or so days it took Odysseus to leave Kalypso and return to Ithaka? Or, why has Athene, who said she was going to bring back Telemachos in Book 13, taken a whole day (the day of Book 14) to reach Menelaos' palace? See on 5 for Homer's way of smoothing over the transition between Telemachos and Odysseus' adventures. (See further Page *HO* 66–9 and Fenik *SO* 65ff., for an attack on the whole concept of 'time-filling' in Homer.)

2.   **the shining son**: i.e. Telemachos.

4.   **son of Nestor**: i.e. Peisistratos, who had accompanied Telemachos on the journey (3.368–70, 477–85).

5.   **sleeping**: the poet's purpose in describing him now as asleep is to suggest that we have turned our attention to Telemachos on the very same night that we have left Odysseus asleep in Eumaios' hut (14.520–33). See on 4.625.

8.   **with anxious thoughts of his father**: cf. our first sight of Telemachos at 1.113–7.

9.   **Gray-eyed Athene stood close by his head**: it is unique in the *Odyssey* for a god to *appear* to a human without disguise (though typical in the *Iliad*, e.g. 1.194–200). If Telemachos does in fact see Athene here (it does not say he does) we could agree that this further increases his heroic *kleos*. Fenik *SO* 166 discusses the observation that this scene has a number of similarities to Athene's visit to the sleeping Nausikaa at 6.1–47.

10.   **it no longer becomes you**: for the reason why it 'became' Telemachos in the first place, see *15B*.

16–17.   **since now . . . Eurymachos**: there is no evidence at all for this in our *Odyssey*. But since this lie is sure to motivate Telemachos to return home at once, it is functional; and it may reflect a version of the *Odyssey* in which increasing pressure was put on Penelope by the suitors during Telemachos' absence. 16.375 suggests a version in which the *people* pressurised the suitors.

18.   **gifts . . . presents**: the 'gifts' are Eurymachos' gifts to Penelope, the 'presents' are the marriage-gifts given to the father of the bride. See on 2.53.

20–3.   **For you know . . . think of him**: nothing could be less true of Penelope who constantly remembers Odysseus and thinks of Telemachos (see e.g. 4.681–823). But again, the words serve Athene's purpose well, since Telemachos has a distinctly uneasy relationship with his mother and may well suspect her of such intentions (see e.g. 1.346–59; 16.73–7).

24.   **you should turn over everything**: stranger and stranger: why should Telemachos entrust everything to a faithful servant when *he himself* is in the palace? Telemachos at any rate ignores the instruction, and forgets Athene's equally strange orders concerning his marriage (26). Do we have recollections of alternative 'routes' here (see *GI I*)?

28.   **the suitors are lying in wait**: see 4.842–7, and note on 4.846.

33.   **away from the islands**: Telemachos' journey is described at 295–300, but there is no certainty over the identification of the landmarks (see note there). Athene's instruction to Telemachos to keep away from islands may be another way of telling him to hug the coast around Elis (298) before crossing over the gulf opposite, say, Pleuron and working round the mainland towards Ithaka from the east. It is tempting to argue that Athene's instruction to keep away from islands is connected with the dangers of sailing at night. But the mainland is as dangerous as any island in this respect.

36.   **at the first promontory**: some argue that this is the southern tip of Ithaka (= Andri), but it is better to take it to mean 'the first place you come to'. If Telemachos went straight to the city he would probably be delayed there; Athene wants him to meet Odysseus as soon as possible, and then return to the city.

38.   **that man**: i.e. Eumaios.

40.   **speed the man**: Telemachos carries out Athene's instructions at 16.130–4.

42.   **from Pylos**: Telemachos is with Menelaos in Sparta at the moment, but he has travelled there overland from Pylos (3.486–97), where his ship is still beached (3.4–6). It is to Pylos that Telemachos returns with Peisistratos (193).

45.   **with a nudge of his heel**: the Greek says 'with a kick from his foot'. Ancient critics ejected the line, feeling it to be far too uncouth. But Telemachos is a young man in a hurry. Observe how Telemachos is now in control of matters. Cf. 4.156–67, 190ff.

51.   **But wait . . .**: Peisistratos reminds Telemachos of the duties of a guest. The exchange of gifts is an essential part of the *xenos*-relationship, as Telemachos well knows (1.307–13).

60–1.   **he . . . the hero**: both refer to Telemachos.

68–85.   **Telemachos . . . goblet**: there is the same pressing, sententious garrulousness about Menelaos in this passage as there is about Alkinoos at 11.348–76: they both strain to show their generosity. For the *xenia* departure sequence, see on 3.303–19.

80. **Hellas and midmost Argos**: see on 1.344.

82. **be your guide**: see on 4.78–91.

84. **tripod or caldron**: see on 13.13–14.

90. **I must not . . .**: Telemachos repeats the reason for departure given him by Athene at 10–13.

95. **Eteoneus**: see 4.20–38; 15.140.

99. **fragrant**: aromatic wood preserved clothes (105) from moth.

100. **Megapenthes**: Menelaos' son by a slave-woman (see 4.11–12).

113–19: = 4.613–19. If these lines are Homeric, rather than a later addition, they make a further bridge between Book 15 and Book 4 (see on 15.1).

126. **for your wife to wear**: Homer frequently looks beyond the limits of his story to create a broader frame of reference. See on 11.121. The Helen who values marriage so much here is a different woman from the one who deserted Menelaos, ran off with Paris and started the Trojan War. A marriage had just taken place in her home (4.1–19).

135–43. **A maidservant . . . drinking**: these lines are typical (for 135–9, see 1.136–40; 140–1 are adaptations of 1.141–3, to give Eteoneus (= son of Boethoös) and Megapenthes a small role).

149. **a libation**: see on 2.432.

156. **I wish that even so I too, . . .**: Telemachos is rather awkwardly trying to 'equate his appreciation of Menelaos' kindness with his yearning to have his father safe at home again' (Stanford).

158. **having had all . . .**: cf. on 13.422.

160. **on the right**: the lucky quarter. Cf. 2.154. For another goose-eagle prophecy, see 19.535–58.

172. **I shall be your prophet**: the art of prophecy is not confined to a specific class of people, though some do make a living out of the skill by reason of their descent from a prophetic family, e.g. Theoklymenos 225. In Euripides' *Electra* Aigisthos the king reads the entrails and sees that they portend evil—when Orestes cuts him down. This is the first in a series of prophecies in these later books which give increasingly powerful evidence that Odysseus is about to return. Cf. 533–4, 17.152–61, 19.535–58, 20.350–7, and on 2.163–5. For others, see on 14.158–64, and on 2.163–7. Cf. on 2.146–54.

175. **that was nursed in the household**: a little too loving. The word *atitallō* is used of rearing animals (horses) at *Iliad* 5.271. Perhaps we should translate 'that was being fattened in the household', a term that would apply equally to goose and suitors.

186. **They came to Pherai**: they had stayed with Diokles in Pherai on the journey out (3.488–9). See note there.

195–8. **Son of Nestor . . .**: Telemachos' long preamble to his request shows how embarrassed he feels at what he has to say: i.e. help me to avoid your father! See also next note.

197. **because of our fathers' love**: see on 1.187.

199–201. **Then do not take me . . .**: Telemachos had promised to pass Menelaos' greetings to Nestor at 155–6—a further source of embarrassment.

199. **past my ship**: sc. 'and further along that road to your father's palace'.

201. **quickly**: in normal circumstances, Telemachos would have been only too pleased to be re-entertained by Nestor. Now we can understand why Athene's assessment of affairs back in Ithaka was so pessimistic (see on 16–17, 20–3, 24)—it was to ensure that Telemachos had powerful motives for not delaying.

214. **very angry**: see on 1.309–18.

223–4. **an outlander/from Argos**: this could suggest that Theoklymenos was Argive. But the Greek makes it clear that Argos was the place where Theoklymenos killed the man, not the place where Theoklymenos originated. 254–5 suggest strongly that Theoklymenos came from Hyperesia, i.e. Achaia (see on 254).

225. **a prophet**: Theoklymenos, as we learn at 256, whose great grand-father was Melampous (225–6), ancestor of the great prophetic family called the Melampodidae. Homer tells us one of Melampous' famous exploits (225–38) and then describes how he moved from Pylos to Argos (238–40), and what his connection was with Theoklymenos. The family tree described at 241–56 can be reconstructed as follows:

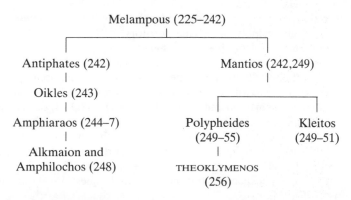

226–38. **Melampous once . . . house**: the story is complex and oblique, and is a version of a story already told at 11.281–97. Melampous had a brother (238), called Bias (he is not named in Homer). Bias fell in love with Neleus' daughter (233, called Pero 11.287). Neleus' bride-price for her was the cattle of Phylakos, father of Iphiklos (231, 235–8, called Iphikles at 11.290). Melampous undertook the task on his brother's behalf (233), but was captured by Phylakos (231–2). Melampous, however, listened to the worms in the roof of his prison telling him that it was about to fall in and prophesied its collapse to Phylakos (not in Homer, cf. 235 and 11.296–7). Phylakos, impressed, released him, Melampous drove the cattle off back to Neleus and won the lady for his brother (235–8). For the connection between

Neleus, Nestor and Melampous, see the genealogy at 11.235. for the collapse of the prison, see *Hesiod* ed. Merkelbach and West (Oxford Text) fr. 261.

228.   **to the land of other men**: i.e. to Argos, as described at 238–40.

230.   **until a year was fulfilled**: Melampous was held by Phylakos for one year (11.294–5).

kept much of his substance: presumably Neleus confiscated Melampous' goods while he was held in prison by Phylakos.

233.   **infatuation**: i.e. the influence which drove Melampous to an undertaking that nearly proved so disastrous for him.

234.   **goddess Erinys**: a 'Fury', one of a number of Erinues ('Furies') who exact vengeance for inter-family crimes, especially murder (cf. 11.271–80, 2.130–5 and Aeschylus' *Oresteia*). But in Homer they are also responsible for ensuring that oaths are not broken (*Iliad* 19.258–65). Perhaps Melampous swore an oath to capture the cattle and could not wriggle out of the obligation when things went against him.

247.   **because his wife had been bribed with presents**: Amphiaraos' wife was Eriphyle. See on 11.326.

250.   **Dawn . . . carried Kleitos away**: Dawn had a habit of doing this. Cf. Orion at 5.121.

252.   **Apollo**: Apollo was god of prophecy.

254.   **angered with his father**: no reason is known why Polypheides should have been angry with Mantios.

Hyperesia: apparently = Aigeira, on the S. coast of the bay of Corinth, (almost opposite Delphi), in Achaian territory.

256–7.   **came to Telemachos . . . vessel**: ring-composition with 222–3.

261.   **spirit**: i.e. the god to whom you are sacrificing. The word for spirit, *daimōn*, is not normally used of a specific deity, but of 'an occult power . . . the veiled countenance of divine activity' (Burkert *GR* 180). See on 14.443.

264.   **What man are you and whence? . . .**: Page (*HO* 84) objects to these lines as offensive, since a suppliant is not supposed to begin by asking the supplicatee's name. But for Theoklymenos, on the run from relatives of a man he has killed, nothing could be more important than that he ascertain the name and origin of the man he is asking for help. Cf. on 10.325. Priam asks an equally unexpected, but no less vital, question about Hermes' identity at *Iliad* 24.387–8.

273.   **a man of my tribe**: if the argument at 223–4 is accepted, this man must strictly be an Achaian, from Hyperesia. But then why should relatives in Argos be the ones who respond to his death (274)? Perhaps the dead man was one who had come from Argos to Hyperesia with Polypheides (254–5). Alternatively, **a man of my tribe** (273) could be taken to mean 'Argive', since Theoklymenos' family was Argive in origin (238–40); hence the Argive reaction.

284–92.   **Then he himself . . . stern wind**: cf. 2.416–29. But there is a problem. At 221, the men were sitting at the oarlocks; now they cast off the ropes to *sail* away (289ff.). Possibly there is a confusion here; or Athene's wind at 292–4 explains why there was a change in plan. Homer handles it more smoothly at 2.403 where the men wait at the oars, 418–9 where they row off, and then receive a favourable wind (420), as a result of which they hoist sail (423–6).

295–6. **They ran past . . . Pointed Islands**: cf. on 33, and see maps 2 and 3 for possible identifications. But there are insoluble problems with these lines. In the first place, 295 appears in no ms. of Homer at all, but is a quotation from the geographer Strabo who describes Chalkis in one place as 'with fair streams', in another as 'rocky'; second, the mss. give *Pheras* at 297, but editors prefer Strabo's reading *Pheas*; third, 295, 297–8, re-appear, but in different order, and with some variations, in *Homeric Hymn to Apollo* (425–7).

300. **whether he would escape death**: at the hands of the suitors who were lying in wait for him (4.842–7, 15.28–30).

301. **But now in the shelter**: the poet turns from Telemachos at sunset (296) to Odysseus and Eumaios after their evening meal (302). In fact, two days have passed since we last saw Odysseus (Telemachos and Peisistratos spent a night with Diokles (186–8)).

307–24. for the importance of these lines, see *15A*.

314. **with a message**: Odysseus acts the part of a needy beggar well. Eumaios has already told him how eager Penelope is to reward strangers who bring information (14.122–32).

318–24. **For I tell you this . . . betters**: further good acting by Odysseus. It is typical to accuse beggars of laziness (17.226–8, 18.362–4, 20.378–9), and typical for beggars to rebut such accusations by claiming that they are good workers (as here and 18.366–80; cf. Iros' message-running at 18.6–7). See Hesiod *WD* 298–319 for the advantages of working and the shame attached to idleness.

319. **by . . . Hermes**: Hermes as god of trade and commodities is essentially a Roman development (Burkert *GR* 159), but this function is foreshadowed here and e.g. Aristophanes *Peace* 210ff., where Hermes is left behind on Olympos to look after the pots, pans and furniture abandoned by the departed gods.

319–20. **dispenses glory/and beauty upon the endeavours**: rather 'dispenses renown and recompense upon the endeavours', i.e. ensures that men's efforts are acknowledged and rewarded.

322. **good fire**: Odysseus will guard the fires at 18.312ff.

324. **bestow on**: very awkward. Read 'perform for'. Odysseus is not claiming heralds are inferior (see on 8.8). It suits Odysseus' purpose to cast himself as inferior.

329–30. **iron/sky**: the sky is called 'iron' only here and at 17.565–6. Elsewhere it is called 'bronze'. We may see here the influence of contemporary culture (Homer lived in the iron age) upon oral poetry. See on 9.393.

332. **with neat oiled heads and handsome faces**: rather, 'with heads and handsome faces gleaming' sc. with oil, with which they anointed themselves after bathing (cf. e.g. 3.464–6). The point is that the suitors' servants live as luxuriously as their masters do on the wealth of Odysseus' house.

335.   none . . . annoyed: Antinoos (17.446ff.).

344.   for the sake of the cursed stomach: Odysseus continues to act the part. Beggars and wanderers typically need food, e.g. 7.215–21, 14.124–5, 17.286, 473, 558, 18.53.

346.   and bid me stay here: rather, 'and bid me wait here for him (i.e. Telemachos)'.

347–8.   tell me about the mother . . ./and his father: Odysseus already knows about them (11.187–203), but it adds credibility to him in his role as a stranger to enquire after them.

357.   green untimely: i.e. premature. Since Laertes was on the threshhold of old age when Odysseus left (348–9), the description seems slightly odd. It is tempting to translate *ōmós* ('green, untimely') as 'cruel, savage'. The problem is that *ōmós* everywhere else in Homer means 'untimely' or 'raw'; the meaning 'cruel, savage' appears to have developed later.

364.   Ktimene: from 16.119, it looks as if Odysseus was an only child. But not so: he has a younger sister Ktimene. She is not mentioned elsewhere in the *Odyssey* (presumably because her marriage took her to Same, 367).

366.   lovely prime: the word is the same as 'youth' at 8.137 (see note), where it refers to an Odysseus who must be at least 40. Since it looks as if Eumaios and Ktimene were roughly the same age (364–5), and when Ktimene reached her prime she was married off (366–7), 'prime' here must mean c.20. If the events Eumaios describes here took place while Odysseus was away in Troy (and since Antikleia died while he was at Troy, it looks likely), Eumaios must be less than 40. It is a mistake to think of him as an old man. 450–2 suggest he was aged between 3 and 8 when he was stolen.

371–9.   Now I go . . . people: observe how destructive of the basis of family and institutional life the suitors' presence has been. The suitors have created changes in the behaviour not merely of the lowly and humble but also of the great (Penelope, in this case). There is again a sense here of the value placed upon the humble by their masters, a feeling so characteristic of the *Odyssey* (cf. on 1.130–50).

374.   but there is no sweet occasion: Eumaios has already indicated that he no longer goes to the city as much as he used to (14.372–8). Now we understand there is another reason.

388.   this man's house: the man referred to must be Laertes, however long it has been since he was last mentioned.

390–401.   My guest . . . sorrows: for similar sentiments about the pleasures that story-telling brings, however painful the events that are recounted, cf. Odysseus at 9.1–15, 14.192–8. But when Odysseus and Penelope are re-united in bed, the re-telling is all pleasure (23.300–9). Note how thoughtful Eumaios is to his fellows, who have heard it all before (395–7).

403–4.   Syria . . ./. . . Ortygia: there is no island known to us as Syria (but n.b. Psyra, 3.171); and Ortygia was a name for both Delos and the island part of Syracuse. If Ortygia ('quail-island') = Delos, Syria is most likely to = Syros, an island roughly 35km. west of Delos. Syros could be said to lie 'above' Delos (404) for a traveller approaching from the east, and the clause 'where the sun makes his turnings' suggests the point where the sun seems to change its movement at the solstice (vaguely north, so 'above' Delos). But it is worth pointing out that 405–6 describe the *land* of Syria rather well, and the references to the Phoenicians in Eumaios' story strongly suggest an eastern setting for it. There is probably a major geographical confusion here, perhaps between the islands of Syros and Psyr(i)a, and the land of Syria (see *GI E*).

411.   **a visitation of painless arrows**: this phrase is used to indicate that death was swift and easy. Cf. 3.279–80, 5.123–4, 11.172–3, 15.477–9, *Iliad* 24.757–9.

415.   **Phoenician men**: see on 13.273, and on Menelaos' tale at 4.73.

426.   **men from Taphos**: see on 1.105.

445–6.   **homeward/cargo**: cf. 14.296. Traders would move around the Mediterranean selling and buying from port to port: an empty ship was no use to anyone. Cf. 455–7.

452.   **take him aboard**: child piracy is attested in Greek comedy, if that is reliable evidence (e.g. Plautus' *Poenulus*, a 2ndC BC Roman comedy, based on a Greek original. 'Poenulus' means 'Carthaginian'). Phoenicians colonised Carthage in the 8thC.

460.   **amber**: see on 4.73.

495.   **glorious dawn came on. Ashore . . .**: more careful linking of the narrative. We left Telemachos under sail at night (296); we picked up Odysseus and Eumaios after dinner (301–3); they have now conversed till nearly breakfast (493–5); and this is the time when Telemachos now arrives back in Ithaka, at dawn.

505–6.   **I will come back/to town**: Telemachos does not fulfil this promise. He stays the evening with Eumaios (16.480–1).

519.   **Eurymachos**: Page (*HO* 84) objects fiercely to this proposal. It is indeed absurd if Telemachos is *seriously* suggesting that Theoklymenos should stay with his bitterest enemy. But he is not. He is being heavily sarcastic. First Telemachos is replying to a questioner who asks whose house he should go to of those who rule Ithaka. Telemachos has heard from Athene that Eurymachos is the leading contender for Penelope's hand and thus most likely to 'rule' Ithaka (16–18). Since Telemachos cannot entertain Theoklymenos at home (513–7), he pessimistically suggests Eurymachos is the man to go to. But the suggestion is also sarcastic. The Greek heavily emphasises the 'could' of 518; and Telemachos implies the hope that Eurymachos will not achieve his ends (523–4). Finally, if the suggestion were seriously meant, Telemachos would have to rescind it before inviting Peiraios to entertain Theoklymenos. He does no such thing (540–3). That Telemachos is not serious about the proposal is strongly suggested by 16.85–9. For other explanations, see Stanford on 519 and 539, and Fenik *SO* 233ff.

533–4.   **No other family . . ./forever**: Page (*HO* 85) thinks Theoklymenos should at least have interpreted the omen as a sign that Odysseus would kill the suitors. But given that Telemachos has just indicated that others are trying to seize Odysseus' inherited position and may well succeed (522),

Theoklymenos' prophecy is exactly what Telemachos needs to hear: they will not succeed. In context, this is perfectly adequate. There are, of course, many 'kingly' families on Ithaka (1.394–6).

Book sixteen

Introduction

A. Homer continues to manoeuvre his pieces skilfully into position. In Book 17, the pieces will all be brought together—Odysseus, Telemachos, Penelope, and suitors, and Eumaios. Meanwhile, the logic of the story demands that Odysseus evaluate the situation from a distance, in Eumaios' hut, in 14–15; and the logic of story-telling demands that we be re-introduced to the world of Ithaka, Telemachos, the suitors and Penelope whom we have not seen since the end of Book 4, though we have heard much of them through the words of Athene in Books 13 and 15, and Eumaios in 14–15. This is done in Books 15–16. Structurally, Homer works as follows:

Book 13: Odysseus and Athene
Book 14: Odysseus and Eumaios (in the country)
Book 15: Telemachos in Sparta sets off/Odysseus and Eumaios (in the country)
Book 16: Telemachos and Odysseus reunited (in the country)/suitors and Penelope (in the palace)
Book 17: Telemachos to the palace/Odysseus to the palace

B. Note how carefully organised the movement from country to palace is. First, Odysseus is present virtually throughout—he is at the centre, the unknown guiding force of the action. Second, before all the parties meet up in Book 17, we are given a strong reminder of their individual identities. Homer achieves this by giving each leading roles in simply-constructed, self-contained scenes (it is especially important that Homer re-establishes the roles of the suitors and Penelope since we have not seen them for so long). Third, note (a) the unifying role of Telemachos, who moves from Sparta (where he has heard that Odysseus is still alive) through Eumaios' hut (where he finds him returned) and back to the palace (in Book 17), hugging the secret to his bosom; (b) the mediating role of Eumaios. He links country and palace for the first time in Book 16, when he announces to Penelope that Telemachos has arrived; and, in Book 17, he will accompany Odysseus from his hut to the palace and so to revenge. Book 16 is the book of preparation, where all the threads are finally gathered together, before starting to be woven into the tapestry of revenge from Book 17 onwards. One can easily imagine radical changes taking place in the structure and tempo of Books 14–16 as the oral poet decided how best to bring this about.

C. The reunification of Odysseus and Telemachos at 156–320 is of obvious importance. Odysseus never doubts that his son is now of an age to help him effectively (see on 4.112, though Athene will have to remind him of it at 20.34–5), and it is important to note that Odysseus' challenge to Telemachos is to perform in the way that Odysseus has had to (274–304)—i.e. to endure and keep the secret of Odysseus' identity (cf. 13.307–10). Telemachos must behave like his father (cf. 'true blood' at 300) and thus demonstrate the *kleos* he has been seeking since Book 1 (see on 2.270–80, Clarke *AO* 26). Both Odysseus and Telemachos will be sorely tested in the way that Odysseus predicts here—by the attacks made on Odysseus at 17.462, 18.394 and 20.299 (cf. Odysseus' silent endurance at 17.465 and 20.301, and Telemachos' restraint and entreaties at 17.489, 18.406, 20.304). Odysseus will be abused in other circumstances by Melanthios (17.212ff., 20.176ff.), Melantho (18.321ff., 19.65ff.) and the suitors generally (17.375ff., 21.305ff.). Cf. *17B*; and on 18.396.

D. Both the suitors and Penelope are re-introduced and remain true to type. Penelope's entry, complaints, rebuke and departure in tears (409–51) follow the patterns of her appearances in Books 1 and 4 (see *1.325–444A*). Homer quickly re-establishes the suitors in their true light—they are ruthless (370–3, 383–6), their power is based on naked force, without regard to community sanctions (361–2, 376–82) or the wishes of the woman they pursue (385–6) (Clarke *AO* 21–3).

E. The two leading suitors are characterised in the usual way—Antinoos openly aggressive and uncompromising (he clearly has no time for the deal he proposes at 386–92), Eurymachos hypocritical and oily (435–49) (see *1.325–444B*). But there is a purpose to the spotlight that Homer plays on a newly introduced and rather more sensible and humane suitor Amphinomos (394–405). Like Theoklymenos (see *15C*), he adds a warning note to the proceedings (a warning he does not take, since he too is slaughtered (22.89ff.)) and enables Homer to emphasise that the retribution hanging over the suitors is divine as well as human—if only they could recognise it.

F. Book 16 is interesting for the number of small awkwardnesses of plot or diction that it contains (see notes on 281–98, 316, 375, 422). None is serious enough, in my view, to warrant the analysts' wrath, but they may give us an insight into the possible developments of plot that were always open to Homer. There are hints that in previous Homeric versions, for example, Theoklymenos may first have approached the suitors, not Telemachos, that the people may have objected openly to the suitors about their planned murder of Telemachos, and so on. These small awkwardnesses may arise here in Book 16 because the plot is becoming more complex and able to sustain richer variety of treatment. Homer's previous treatments perhaps show briefly through here (cf. *13F*, *15C* and *GI I*).

G.   Finally, note how the oral poet has at his disposal, as well as repeatable phrases, lines and scenes, repeatable centos of sentiments which fit the personality of his characters. Thus Telemachos talks about himself, and others talk about Telemachos, as a *young man* not yet fully *grown up*, who would like to *threaten* the suitors because of their *wickedness*, but finds their *strength* and *superior numbers* hard to handle. 16.71–89 gives a good example of typical sentiments attaching to Telemachos, and may be compared with e.g. 2.312–20, 3.199–209, 4.817–23, 18.227–37, 21.370–5, 19.530–4, 20.308–14, 21.131–5 (etc.). Many of Telemachos' later remarks are made intentionally to deceive the suitors (see above on Telemachos responding to his father's challenge). A similar cento of ideas can be seen to run through Penelope's utterances. The most common sentiments in Books 1–4 are that the suitors are *destroying* her possessions, that she is overwhelmed with *grief* and that she is in *desperate need* of the *kindly* husband she has *lost* and of *Telemachos* too (see e.g. 1.337ff., 4.680ff., 4.721ff., 4.810ff.). These are the very sentiments she picks up again when we meet her in Book 16 (418–33). This cento of ideas does not account for all Penelope's utterances, of course, but it acts as a constant feature of them. The art of the oral poet depends on how skilfully he can deploy and vary them. See further on 108–9, 122–8.

2.   **at dawn**: Homer completes the intercalation of the journeys of Telemachos and Odysseus with another smooth change. We left Telemachos in Book 15 just after dawn rose (495–557); we turn to Odysseus and Eumaios in the hut stirring the fire at dawn. See on 15.1, 5, 301.

4.   **came fawning around**: a lovely contrast with the dogs' reaction to Odysseus at 14.29–36. Cf. 10.214–7.

11–12.   **beloved/son**: does Odysseus recognise Telemachos here? It seems unlikely: Telemachos was a baby when Odysseus left for Troy (4.144–6). Nevertheless, might Odysseus have recognised the family resemblance (cf. e.g. 4.138–46)? The poet's silence leaves the matter teasingly unresolvable.

17.   **And as a father**: a simile rich in pathos and irony: while Telemachos' actual father looks on in silence, Eumaios greets Telemachos as a father greets a son (Fenik's law cannot surely apply here (see on 18.206)). The simile says much for Eumaios' closeness to the family. It is typical of the *Odyssey* that the subject of the simile reflects the subject-matter of the whole *Odyssey* (in this case, the reunion of fathers and sons after long, painful absence. See on 5.328, 8.523).

24.   **when you had gone**: cf. Eumaios' pessimism at 14.174–84.

27.   **you do not come very often**: Eumaios had distanced himself from the palace because of the suitors' presence and its effect upon Penelope (14.372–3, cf. 15.374–9).

31.   **my father**: highly misleading translation. The Greek is *atta*, which in Homer is a term of intimate address to an elder. 'Uncle' (Rieu)? 'Dear Eumaios' (Shewring)? 'My dear old friend'?

32.   **to look upon you**: in fact Athene had given no indication as to why

Telemachos should go to Eumaios' hut when he arrived back at Ithaka (15.36–42).

34–5. **the bed of Odysseus/lies forlorn of sleepers**: in fact, it had so lain for some time, since Penelope no longer slept in it, but in an upstairs room (1.329, 362 etc.). Odysseus' bed, constructed around the base of a tree, must have been on the ground floor (23.188–204). But in context, Telemachos' pessimistic hyperbole is understandable. For other emotional overstatements of his, cf. 1.160, 1.215–6, his speech at 2.40–81 (especially his reaction at 80–1) etc.

41–2. **his father . . . place**: lovely irony and pathos. Odysseus exerts fierce control and continues to act the part of the beggar (cf. 16.191).

44. **another seat**: on the important courtesies of offering a seat to guests, see e.g. 1.130, 14.49. These small rituals do much to reinforce our sense of right and wrong in the *Odyssey*. Eumaios' and Telemachos' observation of them stands in strong contrast to the suitors' disregard.

50. **earlier**: the meat referred to here must be that left over from the sacrifice at 14.418–56 and, presumably, the meal at 15.301–3. Such luxurious food would not normally be available to a man like Eumaios. It is reasonable to assume it would not have been brought out for a usual breakfast (being prepared at 2, 13–14).

57. **Father**: see on 31.

61. **the whole true story**: see Odysseus' long false (!) tale at 14.199–359, especially 334–6.

69–70. **Eumaios . . ./. . . house?**: cf. Telemachos' disclaimer to Theoklymenos at 15.513–7.

73. **my mother's heart is divided**: cf. 1.249–51, 16.126–8.

79. **I will give him . . .**: as Eumaios had promised at 14.515–7, 15.337–9.

82. **keep him here**: Telemachos shows the generosity and thoughtfulness which Odysseus confidently predicted of him. See 15.488–92. Telemachos is as concerned as Odysseus is that Eumaios will not be put to inconvenience by the beggar's presence. See 15.308–9, 335–9.

85. **I will not let him go down**: for Telemachos' embarrassment at the behaviour of the suitors, see e.g. 1.132–4. Cf. Athene at 1.227–9. Lines 69–98 are a good example of the art of the oral poet in building up a convincing and apposite speech for Telemachos out of a cento of wholly typical ideas, though their modes of expression may be different. See *16G*.

95–6. **Do the people/hate you . . .?**: Nestor too wondered whether the people supported Telemachos or not (3.214–5). On the constitutional question, see on 1.386.

97. **your brothers**: an intelligent piece of intentional 'ignorance' on Odysseus' part.

100–1. **or a son . . ./. . . wandering**: fine irony.

103. **if I did not come as . . .**: for beggarly boasting, see 15.318–24.

108–9. **rudely mishandling/the serving women**: Odysseus has not heard of any such behaviour by the suitors either in Eumaios' hut or earlier. It is probably an unconscious slip on the poet's part. The suitors are commonly accused of maltreating servants (17.389, 18.416 = 20.324, 22.37, 20.318 = 16.108), and to develop that idea in the context of other accusations directed at the suitors would be an easy slip for an oral poet to make. The powers of 'association' between one idea and another may be stronger in the mind of an oral poet, composing on the spot, than they are in the mind of a literary author. See *4.625–847B*.

119.   **only one son, Odysseus**: Laertes had a daughter as well, Ktimene (15.364).

122–8.   **For all . . . pieces**: a cento of ideas exactly repeated at 1.245–51. For the problem of the location of the islands, see on 9.25.

130.   **Father Eumaios**: see on 31. Telemachos now carries out the instructions given him by Athene at 15.40–2.

132.   **You go there quickly, and give this**: wrong translation. Read 'But you return here, having given this'.

142.   **since you went away**: this is the first time we have heard of Laertes' reaction to Telemachos' departure. Laertes had been told of it on Penelope's instructions (4.735–41).

153.   **she can give the news to the old man**: these instructions are not carried out in the text of our *Odyssey*, but one can assume their fulfilment from 16.338–41.

173.   **First she made . . .**: Athene here undoes what she did to Odysseus at 13.429–38. She will re-transform him again at 454–9, but from then on, no further transformation will take place, and Odysseus becomes one who has been superficially transformed but can be recognised by intimates or by his signs and actions. See on 13.397. This is the first of the recognitions. Cf. Argos (17.301), Eurykleia (19.467), Eumaios and Philoitios (21.207ff.), the suitors (presumably: 22.45), the household (22.498), Penelope (23.205), Laertes (24.345), other servants (24.391).

175–6.   **His dark colour . . ./. . . the beard . . . turned black**: cf. 13.399, where his hair is said to be *xanthos*. This colour appears to cover the range from yellow through chestnut to auburn. But there is no contradiction. Colour relationships are very difficult to define anyway: Plato (*Lysis* 217D) uses *xanthos* and *melas* ('black') indistinguishably as the opposite of 'white'.

194.   **you are not Odysseus my father**: Telemachos could not recognise Odysseus outright, since Telemachos was a baby when Odysseus went to Troy. For recognition scenes, see on 21.188–227.

194–5.   **some divinity/beguiles me**: Telemachos, arguing that only a god could effect such a transformation (194–200), speculates why the divinity should behave in this way and concludes that it must be to make him grieve all the more (195). This is not meant to be an argument *why* Telemachos does not believe the beggar to be Odysseus, but is a natural train of thought, given that Telemachos does *not* believe him to be Odysseus (clearly stated by Homer's gloss at 192–3). If we should wish to speculate why Telemachos does not believe him to be Odysseus, the text calls constant attention to Telemachos' pessimism e.g. 1.166–8, 234–43, 2.46–7, etc. We must also bear in mind Odysseus' brilliant acting-out of the part of a beggar. See on 4.535–60.

202.   **Telemachos, it does not become you**: since Telemachos has offered no rational grounds for disbelief, Odysseus deploys non-rational methods to persuade him: he asserts paternal authority, expressing shock at Telemachos' ingratitude (202–3), and then moves into an emotional register (204–6). Only finally does he solve the problem that Telemachos raised—which god could have done this? By assuring Telemachos that it is Athene, Odysseus at once solves Telemachos' problem—Telemachos himself knows what a supporter of the house Athene is (3.373–9).

217.   **ospreys or vultures**: 'ospreys' (*phēnai*) are said to be 'bearded vultures' by D'Arcy Thompson (*Glossary of Greek Birds*, Oxford 1895, 303). If that is so, 'vultures' (*aigupioi*) are better translated 'eagles' (Stanford says they are noted by later writers for their parental affection.)

217–8.   **whose children/were stolen away**: the image is not 'inept' (Stanford). Telemachos and Odysseus do not cry *like* birds whose young have been stolen, but *more intensely than* birds whose young etc. ('even more than' 216). Reunion is to Odysseus and Telemachos a far greater cause for emotional display than loss, such is the intensity of their feelings after the years of separation and dashed expectations (cf. Aeschylus *Agamemnon* 48ff.).

226–34.   **The Phaiakians . . . enemies**: see 13.116–24, 366–71, 404–15.

239.   **others**: Odysseus gets help from Eumaios and Philoitios at 21.188–225.

242.   **you were a . . .**: the classic description of an Iliadic hero. Cf. *Iliad* 1.258, where Agamemnon and Achilleus are given the accolade, 7.228 (Aias), and *Odyssey* 11.511–6 (Neoptolemos, son of Achilleus). Telemachos is challenged to be like Odysseus in roughly the same terms at 2.270–2.

247–53.   **From Doulichion . . . carving**: the total numbers are—suitors: 52 + 24 + 20 + 12 = 108; serving men: 6 (248) + 2 (253) = 8; Medon (cf. 4.675ff.) + divine singer (Phemios, cf. 1.153–5) = 2 (both are friendly. See 22.330–77). Total: 118. The number is very large, but exaggeration in this sort of story is typical. Cf. on 14.96.

260.   **Athene with Zeus father helping**: since Zeus stands for justice in the *Odyssey*, Odysseus here asserts the justice of what he will do (see on *1.22–95B*). Cf. 24.472–548.

263–5.   **Those indeed . . . immortal**: Stanford thinks these lines are ironic. But that does not make good sense of 265, where Telemachos says the two gods have power over others, both men and gods. If Stanford is right, Telemachos cannot really believe this. But Telemachos has plenty of evidence of the gods' power and support—e.g. 3.22–8 + 371–9—and has just been assured by Odysseus that Athene is on their side (207–12, 233–4).

281–98.   **And put away . . . them**: there are problems of plot consistency here. Odysseus says (i) he will nod (283), (ii) Telemachos will remove all the weapons in the hall (284), (iii) the suitors will be fobbed off with excuses (288–94), (iv) some weapons will be left behind for Odysseus and Telemachos (295–8). The plan is carried out at 19.1–52 but in circumstances radically different from those envisaged here. (i) is irrelevant, (ii) is modified

(Odysseus helps Telemachos carry out the weapons), (iii) remains, but Telemachos uses one of the excuses to fob off Eurykleia, and (iv) is forgotten completely—a fact which Odysseus and Telemachos regret at 22.99–107 (though they make no mention of the original plan at that point). The suitors never remark on the weapons' absence (but they notice it at 22.23–5), and Melanthios draws the correct conclusion about them at 22.139–41, cf. 24.164–6. For the full analytical attack, see Page *HO* 92–5. If we delete the lines in Book 16 as non-Homeric, we solve most of the problems. But how did they get there in the first place? It is likely that Homer developed the incident of the armour differently in different versions: his decision to use the armour in one way, foreshadowed in Book 16, is revoked by the changed circumstances of Book 19. Such a change of plan would not be untypical of an oral poet (see on e.g. *11E, 15C*).

284.   **the warlike weapons**: we first saw them at 1.128–9.

294.   **iron**: on the iron-bronze issue, see on 9.393.

304–5.   **you and I . . . men**: Odysseus is an enthusiastic tester of men (13.333–6, 14.459–61, 15.304–6, 16.312–5, 24.239–40).

316.   **find out about the women**: Odysseus does not consciously test the women, though he is concerned about the behaviour of some of them (20.5–21). At 19.496–502, Eurykleia volunteers information about them and Odysseus rejects her help. But at 22.417–24, Odysseus seems to appeal to her for the same information, and she gives it. Again, there is a slight lack of 'fit' between what is proposed here and what actually happens (cf. on 281–98). One can well imagine versions of the *Odyssey* where testing of the servants in the holdings (312–4) and of the maidservants played a larger part than they do here.

323.   **now came into Ithaka**: companions left for the town of Ithaka at 15.547–9 on Telemachos' instructions at 503–4.

326.   **henchmen**: it does not seem that Telemachos' companions took any henchmen (i.e. servants) with them on the journey (at 2.413–5 the companions load the ship themselves). Either the poet has forgotten this; or we are to assume the servants have been summoned to do the job.

armour: presumably the armour (and weapons) they took to defend themselves against pirates. The suitors had weapons (474) which their servants off-loaded at 360. (It is just possible that 'armour' should be translated 'ship's gear'.)

327.   **presents to the house of Klytios**: Klytios is father of Peiraios (15.540). The presents are those given by Menelaos to Telemachos (15.101–29).

328.   **they sent a herald**: this was not part of Telemachos' orders given at 15.503–7.

333.   **the herald and noble swineherd**: Eumaios had been sent by Telemachos to tell Penelope of his arrival at 16.130–55.

350.   **our others**: i.e. those waiting for Telemachos (4.842–7).

370.   **some divinity brought him home**: true (15.28–42, cf. 15.299–300). Note that Antinoos draws no conclusion from Telemachos' escape about the

rightness or wrongness of the suitors' plans. He is blind to the possibility that the gods might *actually* intervene.

375.   **no longer show us their entire favour**: Antinoos may have drawn this conclusion from the unfavourable speeches of Halitherses and Mentor at 2.161–76, 229–41; or must we assume the people have got to hear of the plot against Telemachos' life and have made their feelings clear? This seems unlikely from 377–81. Perhaps Homer included an episode in other versions of the *Odyssey* in which the people made their feelings known.

376–92.   **But come now . . . presents**: Antinoos appears to think that the combined power of Telemachos (374) and the assembly (375–82) is such that, unless the suitors strike now, kill Telemachos and marry off Penelope to one among them (383–6), they will have to abandon their plan to wear Telemachos into submission (389–90) and resort to more traditional forms of wooing, in the hope (presumably) of mastering Odysseus' property that way (390–2). Antinoos' reaction can be read as panicky. No other suitor takes it up, and Amphinomos' proposal (400–5) is readily accepted. See on 2.53 for gifts of courtship.

402.   **we should first have to ask the gods**: this is the first time that the suitors have brought the gods seriously into their considerations.

412.   **Medon . . . overheard their planning**: cf. 252 and 4.675–7. That Medon is favourable to Penelope is suggested by 4.696–702.

416.   **her shining veil**: for the significance of the veil, see on 6.100.

422.   **take no heed of suppliants**: but who are they? They can hardly be Telemachos! 423 suggests Antinoos and Telemachos should not be harming each other, and Penelope's subsequent story gives a reason why: Odysseus once saved Antinoos' father from death at the hands of the people (428–30 cf. 4.686–95). Perhaps Penelope in her clumsy, distraught way, means that Antinoos takes no heed of (the bonds of obligation between the families of) suppliants (cf. on 432). Alternatively, one could easily envisage an *Odyssey* in which Theoklymenos came as a suppliant to Ithaka, was rejected by the suitors and accepted by Telemachos (see 15.256–81). So previous Homeric versions of the *Odyssey* may be causing slight inconsistencies here.

424.   **your father**: Eupeithes (1.383).

432.   **try to murder his son**: a perfectly possible translation, but 'try to' is not actually stated in the Greek. It is more in character for Penelope to say 'murder his son'—the exaggeration of a distraught woman.

435–49.   **Daughter . . . the murder**: the devastating hypocrisy of Eurymachos is made clear by 448–9. For Eurymachos' character, see *1.325–444B*. Cf. on 4.712–3.

452.   **the noble swineherd came back**: Eumaios left the palace without further ado at 341. Cf. 465–7.

456.   **made him once more an old man**: Athene had restored him to his former self so that he could be recognised by Telemachos at 172–6.

468.   **joined my company**: Eumaios recounts the incident at 333, where he met the herald sent by Telemachos' companions at 328.

472.   **a fast vessel coming in**: Eumaios refers to the sight also seen by Amphinomos at 351–60.

477.   **but avoided the eyes of the swineherd**: Telemachos maintains the deceit enjoined upon him by Odysseus at 300–2.

Book seventeen

Introduction

A. With the departure of Odysseus from Eumaios' hut, Homer finally unites the different strands and locations of his story established in Book 13 (Sparta, Eumaios' hut, the palace) and the action from now on takes place in Odysseus' palace. Homer takes in full the chance to exploit the richer scale of tensions and ironies that arise from a situation in which ignorance and knowledge, deception and honesty, hostility and sympathy, youth and experience, and hope and despair are now combined. In particular, Homer begins to draw an increasingly sharp contrast between appearance and reality cf. on 1.411, 1.402–4, 8.167–77. The suitors are young princes and feast and listen to the lyre like epic heroes (261–71, 604–6); but they are hypocrites (66, 403, 454–5), lack all common decency (483–7, 375–9) and have had a destructive effect upon everyone with whom they come into contact (e.g. Melanthios 212ff., Argos 296ff.). Eumaios' and Argos' loyalty stands in sharp contrast (604, 302), and the sense of distance between the suitors and Telemachos, Eumaios, the disguised Odysseus and Penelope is well brought out (166, 342–7, 589–92 and on 492). Meanwhile, Odysseus and Telemachos continue to play their duplicitous game (25, 196—Odysseus must *know* the conditions—237–8, 260–71, 366–7, 568; 12–13, 345–7, 490–2). Odysseus, the real master of the house, acts out the part of a poor beggar (cf. 7.215–21) and begs for food from suitors who do not own it yet treat it as if it were theirs, and Telemachos intelligently responds as Odysseus had instructed. All the time Odysseus, who has been tested so relentlessly on his travels abroad, is now himself testing the suitors (360–4).

B. Fenik points out well how Homer works in doublets to bring out the contrasting characters of the players, and the opposition between the two sides. Thus Eumaios and Philoitios (introduced at 20.185ff.) and Eurykleia and Eurynome stand in contrast to Melanthios and Melantho; Antinoos and Eurymachos, the one hostile, the other hypocritical, are set against Amphinomos (who has good qualities cf. 16.394–406, 18.119–57, 20.244–6) and Leodes (rather ineffectual: 21.146–7). (One can extend the list to cover more of the *Odyssey*—Phemios and Demodokos, Circe and Kalypso, (and Nausikaa?), Klytaimestra and Penelope, Mentes and Mentor, etc.). Again, Fenik sees a pattern to the assault scenes: an attack is usually combined with a moralising lecture and an appearance from Penelope (e.g. 17.415ff., 462ff., 492ff., 18.1ff., 125ff., 158ff; 18.366ff., 394ff; 20.299ff., 351ff; 21.1ff.). This broad pattern helps the poet to keep control over his material and gives him a framework within which he can flexibly explore the possibilities for irony,

character-depiction and tension—will Odysseus give himself away or not?—
created by them. Cf. *13D*.

4.   **a powerful spear**: the spear which Telemachos had taken from him at
16.40. See on 28–30.
6.   **Father**: see note on 16.31. 'I am going to the city': in accordance with
the plan of Odysseus explained at 16.270–3.
12–13.   **it is not for me to put up with/everybody**: these harsh words
ensure that Eumaios will not suspect any collusion between Telemachos and
Odysseus, but they are in fact in character anyway, cf. 16.69ff. (spoken
before Telemachos knew the beggar's true identity).
24–5.   **morning/frost**: for the autumnal weather prevalent throughout the
poem, see on 5.467.
25.   **They say . . .**: wrong translation. The Greek says 'You say'. Note
how carefully Odysseus disguises his local knowledge. Cf. 196–8.
28–30.   **he carried . . . went inside**: at 1.127–9 it is clear that there is a
rack for spears inside the palace of Odysseus.
31–5.   **Far the first . . . shoulders**: like father, like son. The returned
Odysseus will be given a similar highly emotional greeting at 22.495–501. Cf.
Eumaios at 16.12–16 with Penelope at 17.38ff.
37.   **like Artemis, or . . . Aphrodite**: Penelope combines chastity with
desirability (cf. the suitors' reaction to her at 1.366).
44.   **what sights you have been seeing**: wrong translation. Literally the
Greek means 'how you met his (= Odysseus') sight', i.e. 'what sight you got
of him', 'whether you saw him'. Penelope repeats the question in specific
terms at 104–6.
46.   **Mother, do not stir up**: the tension between Telemachos and his
mother that we observed in earlier books still exists (see on *1.325–444A* for
the typical pattern at work here).
53.   **my guest**: i.e. Theoklymenos. See 15.540–6.
57.   **She had no winged words for an answer**: the translation is possible,
but there are problems. The word *apteros*, 'no wings' could also mean 'very
winged', i.e. swift; and given the frequency of lines such as 'X spoke, and his
words pleased/annoyed/(etc.) Y', the 'words' are likely to be the speaker's,
i.e. Telemachos'. So more likely are either 'So Telemachos spoke, and his
words did not fly from Penelope' (i.e. sunk into her), or 'and his words flew
swiftly to her' i.e. she got the message immediately.
62.   **a pair of light-footed dogs**: compare 2.9–14 for the whole scene. Dogs
may not seem a grand accompaniment, but Athene's glorification (63) is
enough to make the people admire him (64).
66.   **in the deep of their hearts**: typical hypocrisy from the suitors. See
16.448–9.
68.   **Mentor . . . Antiphos . . . Halitherses**: for two of these old friends,
see 2.224ff. (Mentor) and 2.157ff. (Halitherses). Antiphos represents a
problem: at 2.15ff. he is son of Aigyptios, and was killed by the Cyclops!

72.　**the guest**: i.e. Theoklymenos. See 15.222–81.

76.　**so I can send back the gifts**: see 16.321–7.

82.　**if I can plot their death**: Telemachos is becoming a little more confident in public than he has been before.

85–99.　a typical scene of bathing and feasting. See on 10.348–72.

104.　**you had no patience**: at 44, Penelope asked a direct question about Odysseus' return and was rebuffed. Her approach now is more indirect and subtle.

108–49.　a very compressed account of Books 3–4, 15.1–300. Telemachos selects the more optimistic elements for Penelope's information.

109.　**to Pylos**: see Book 3.

111.　**as a father would**: Penelope would be impressed by the signal marks of favour that no less a man than Nestor bestowed on Telemachos by treating him like a son. See on Athene's description of Menelaos' treatment at 13.422.

114.　**But he said**: see 3.184–5.

116.　**he sent me**: see 3.473–4.619.

118.　**I saw Helen**: see 4.120ff.

124–41.　**Oh, for shame . . .**: = 4.333–50.

142–6.　**He said . . .**: see 4.555–60.

148.　**The immortals gave me**: see 15.292–300. Telemachos does not mention the ambush of the suitors—to save his mother's fears? (Telemachos is not to know that she knows about it—16.409–12).

153.　**he**: who? Surely Menelaos, not Telemachos. Menelaos was passing on to Telemachos news already two years old (4.81–2), and was quite unaware of the new developments in Ithaka. The purpose of Theoklymenos' words here is to expand upon Menelaos' partial information.

157.　**Odysseus is already here**: throughout these later books, the signs multiply that Odysseus is about to return. See on 15.172.

160–1.　**Such was the bird sign . . .**: see 15.531–4. Page (*HO* 86) makes much of the discrepancy between what is said here and in the parallel passage in Book 15.

164.　**soon you would be aware of my love**: in fact, Theoklymenos leaves the palace before his prophecy comes true (20.371–2) and is never mentioned again.

170–1.　**sheep . . . them**: see 212–4 for the special consignment of goats brought inby Melanthios, and 14.95–108.

172.　**Medon**: on Medon and heralds see on 4.677 and 8.8.

187.　**guard the steading**: Odysseus had rejected this option at 20–1.

190–1.　**most of the day is already gone**: cf. Odysseus' request at 22–5. Odysseus has stayed longer in the hut than he intended.

196.　**They say**: a wrong translation. Read 'You say'.

207.　**Ithakos . . . Neritos . . . Polyktor**: Ithakos gave his name to the island and Neritos to the mountain (13.351). Polyktor is probably another founding father. He can hardly be the father of the suitor Peisandros (18.299–300).

211.   **nymphs**: see on 14.435.

212.   **Melanthios, son of Dolios**: He is in fact called Melantheus here, but Melanthios everywhere else (including 247). For Dolios, see on 4.735.

218.   **like guides . . . god does**: the meaning of the line is in doubt, but is probably easier to understand if translated 'So ever a god brings like into company with like' i.e. 'birds of a feather . . .'.

222.   **never for swords or caldrons**: i.e. beggars are parasites. Heroes would claim a hero's gifts through the rituals of *xenia* (for swords, see 8.401ff., caldrons 13.13–15) but beggars just want handouts.

231–2.   **footstools/flung at him**: see e.g. 17.462, 18.394.

232.   **heroes**: the Greek says 'men'.

233.   **recklessly lashed out**: this is the first of five assaults by foot, chair, fist and hoof that Odysseus endures in his kingdom (see *16C*). The basic pattern seems to be (i) abuse of Odysseus (ii) an attack on him (iii) a defensive reaction against the attacker (iv) further threats. In the later examples, reactions from the suitors, sometimes sympathetic, and from Telemachos, become common (they obviously cannot happen here). See *17B*. Strings of common elements (see *16G*) appear in these assault patterns. Thus 'beggars wreck feasts' occurs at 17.220, 17.377, 446, 18.403–4; 'beggars should be made to work' at 17.223, 18.362; 'beggars are gluttons' at 17.228, 18.364; 'threats of deportation' at 17.248, 17.447, 18.83, 115; and so on.

235.   **while he pondered**: in typical scenes of pondering, a hero usually considers two possible courses of actions and chooses the second cf. 5.354–64, 464–75, 6.141–7, 18.90–4, 23.85–95. As we have seen, thought and action are very closely connected in the Homeric world (see on 4.712–3) so that it is an indication of powerful self-control that Odysseus restrains himself here.

237.   **like a jug**: the meaning of the Greek word *amphoudis* is disputed. It could mean 'by both ears' or 'round the waist', but hardly 'like a jug'.

238.   **kept it all inside him**: see Athene's instructions at 13.307–10, cf. 16.274–7.

244.   **glories**: the Greek word *aglaia* means 'pomp, show, extravagance' and is used of those who keep show-dogs at 310. Eumaios is accusing Melanthios of getting above himself: perhaps read 'put an end to all that extravagant behaviour you flaunt in your insolence'.

250.   **win me a good livelihood**: i.e. by being sold as a slave. Cf. 448–9, 18.115–6.

251.   **If only Apollo . . .**: for the Apollo theme at the death of the suitors, see on 21.406–8.

257.   **whom he was fondest of**: was it Melanthios who was fond of Eurymachos or Eurymachos of Melanthios? Probably the latter, since Eurymachos would have the power to demonstrate his fondness (*philia*) for the more humble Melanthios. But whatever the answer, the fondness probably arises from the fact that Melanthios' sister Melantho was Eurymachos' mistress (18.321–5).

261–71.   **stood close in front . . . feasting**: the moment Odysseus has been waiting for for twenty years. His self-control at such a moment is remarkable, but he manages to compliment his own palace prettily enough without giving anything away. For the 'wonder' element, see on 4.71–5. Cf. Camps *IH* 36–9.

262.   **Phemios**: the palace bard. See 1.153–4.

268.   **belittle**: the Greek could also mean 'overpower' or 'outdo'. The ancient commentator Aristarchos preferred 'overpower', a meaning that lends itself to ironical interpretation with the suitors temporarily in control inside.

271.   **of the lyre**: see on 9.4 for the connection between singing and feasting in the heroic world.

274–9.   **let us think . . . careful**: observe how Eumaios defers here to Odysseus. Even though a beggar, Odysseus has gradually asserted his intangible authority over him (see *14D* and 525).

283–9.   **I am not unfamiliar . . . enemies**: for this string of ideas commonly coming from beggars, cf. 7.216, 15.344, 17.473, 17.559, 18.53 (stomach), 16.276, 17.231ff., 18.28ff., 19.69, 20.179ff. (being attacked or ejected). For Odysseus' capacity to endure cf. 5.221–4, 7.213, 10.49–55.

293–4.   **since before that he went to sacred/Ilion**: (cf. 314–9) there is a number of references in the *Odyssey* to Odysseus' world before he went to Troy. For Odysseus as a hunter, cf. here and 19.392ff.; Odysseus as a baby, 19.355, 19.399–412, and cf. 15.364; Odysseus as a young man, 19.413ff., 24.337; Odysseus as a wise king, 2.230–4, 4.687–95. We also learn of pre-Troy days and e.g. the household, the slaves, the suitors, Odysseus' marriage, Laertes, Odysseus' friends, Odysseus' travels, Odysseus' piety etc. This pre-Troy 'world' is an important and generally ignored dimension of the epic: it puts in proper perspective the meaning of Odysseus' absence and of the suitors' invasion of his palace. Cf. 318–9, *21A*.

301.   **as he perceived**: for dogs' sensitive perception, cf. 16.162–3.

302.   **he wagged his tail**: it is the humble and loyal who recognise the master. Observe the sympathetic portrayal of Argos here. In the *Iliad*, dogs are scavengers. See on 16.173, 21.188–227.

305.   **secretly wiped a tear away**: cf. Odysseus' secrecy at 8.93–4 and Telemachos' at 4.113–6. Odysseus knows that he has been recognised. There is no danger that Argos will tell the world: the danger is that Odysseus' reaction may give him away.

322.   **takes away one half of the virtue**: Eumaios is not condemning the institution of slavery. He is pointing out that, once a man is a slave, he loses all sense of duty so that if the master is absent (318–9), nothing gets done. Eumaios himself is a shining exception to this generalisation (14.59–61). Observe that there are very few references to slaves in Homer (though many to servants). Cf. on 14.450. If Homeric heroes do not treat their servants with brutal authoritarianism, the disloyal are still savagely punished (22.461–76). Slavery was common in Classical Greece.

339.   **ashwood threshold**: presumably this is different from the stone threshold of e.g. 20.258 (see diagram p. 11, and cf. Camps *IH* 5–6 on the house). Beggars beg at the threshold (poised nicely between 'inside' and

'outside' the house, cf. 18.32, 110, 20.258). The threshold gives the suitors an escape route (22.76–7), so it is from the threshold that Odysseus attacks (22.2, 204, cf. 21.124).

341. **and drawn it true to a chalkline**: confusing. Read 'and made it straight with reference to a chalkline'. The 'chalkline' would probably be made on the wood by chalking a length of suitably tensile thread, holding it tight at either end along the appropriate line, and 'pinging' it against the wood to produce the mark. Cf. 5.245.

360. **the suitors raised their tumult**: i.e. once the singing stopped, the suitors went back to their normal riotous behaviour. Cf. 1.325–6.

363. **and so learn**: for testing, cf. 16.304–20 (and notes).

376–7. **enough other/vagabonds**: e.g. Iros (18.1ff.).

378. **men gather here**: grim sarcasm from Antinoos: he is, of course, referring to the suitors.

383. **he**: i.e. the stranger. 'one who works for the people': see Finley *WO* 36–7, 55–6 for these professionals (heralds also come into the category at 19.135). They serve those who summon them (e.g. Demodokos, 8.43–5), but note that Phemios the singer was forced into service in the palace by the suitors (22.350–3). Both he and the herald Medon are classed as Ithakans, not members of Odysseus' household, at 16.251–2.

401. **And do not have any respect for my mother**: i.e. 'do not let respect for my mother (or other servants) stop you behaving like this'. Telemachos is being heavily sarcastic in return (cf. 397–9 and see on 378).

403. **such is not the kind of intention**: for the suitors' hypocrisy, see on 16.435–49. Cf. on 407.

407. **this kind of present**: i.e. the footstool (409–10). Further double-edged sarcasm from Antinoos.

419–44. **I too once lived . . . hardships**: cf. in general Odysseus' tale to Eumaios at 14.229–72, and note in particular that 427–41 = 14.258–72 (cf. the Kikonian episode at 9.39ff.). It is important that Odysseus tells largely the same tale to Antinoos that he told to Eumaios, since Eumaios is present. The only novelty is 442–4 (in Book 14, Odysseus arrives in Ithaka via Thesprotia, not Cyprus), but it is clear from 516–7 that Eumaios understands Odysseus' tale here to be a compressed version and Eumaios himself expands on it at 524–7 (not wholly accurately—see on 522).

448–9. **in a sorry Cyprus/or Egypt**: i.e. by being sold into slavery there.

454–5. **the wits . . ./beauty**: cf. Argos at 308–10, a pointed contrast, and see on 17.403, 1.411, 8.170, *17A*.

463. **in the back**: at 453 Odysseus started to retreat from Antinoos. Odysseus either had his back to him when the stool was thrown, or turned his back as the stool came.

471–2. **for the sake of his own/possessions**: heavy irony. Odysseus is preparing to fight for his own possessions (i.e. his own house) and is willingly submitting to abuse in this cause.

487. **which men keep the laws**: on divine concern with justice in the *Odyssey*, see on *1.22–95B*.

489–92.   But Telemachos . . . evils: as instructed by Odysseus (16.274).

492.   But when . . . Penelope heard . . .: Penelope reacts here as if she witnessed the incident herself (500–2) rather than merely heard it, and she seems to know what the beggar looked like (511). Where then is she? From 505 we assume she is in her bedroom, which must be the same as her 'upper chamber' (49, 101). See on 16.34–5. It is not precisely clear how Penelope knows what she does know here. At all events Penelope is keeping herself well away from the action in the hall, wherever the poet envisages her actually to be.

495.   Eurynome: the first appearance of a servant who seems to be in many ways Eurykleia's double. On doublets, see *17B*.

508–9.   tell the stranger/to come: as Penelope could never resist the temptation of doing, often to her emotional detriment (14.126–30).

515.   Three nights I had him: day one ends at 14.457, day two runs from 15.301–494, day three from there to 16.481.

518–9.   has been given/from the gods the skill with which he: wrong translation. Read 'taught by the gods', i.e. knowing the truth of what happened because the gods have told him. For the oral poet as purveyor of truth, see on 1.1 'Muse'.

520.   and they . . . to them: forced translation. Read 'and they desire passionately to hear him, whenever he sings'.

521.   so he enchanted me: Eumaios is thinking of Odysseus' tale at 14.192–359 (cf. 14.387), but we know of Odysseus' skill resembling that of a 'bard' from his recitation through Books 9–12 (see on 9.12–13). Cf. the simile at 21.406–8 and the effect on Penelope at 19.203–9.

522.   he is a friend by family of Odysseus: Odysseus did not say this to Eumaios (he is from Crete, 14.199), though he does to Penelope (19.185).

525.   driven helpless along: a reference, presumably, to 14.301ff., as a result of which Odysseus came to Thesprotia (14.316ff., cf. 17.526). Eumaios' enthusiasm for Odysseus' tale shows that he has changed his mind about the beggar since his earlier pessimism (14.165ff., 14.386–9). Cf. *14D* and the discussion of the way in which Odysseus gradually assumes command over Eumaios.

534.   day by day visiting our house: see on 1.424.

545.   my son sneezed for everything I have spoken: anything unexpected or involuntary stood a chance of being of divine origin (how else explain it?), and hence an omen, in the ancient world. See E.R. Dodds *The Greeks and the irrational*, U. California Press 1951, (2nd edn. 1963) 13. See on chance remarks at 2.35.

568.   Telemachos could not save me: good acting from Odysseus here (Telemachos, of course, was merely obeying Odysseus' instructions given at 16.274ff.).

569.   Tell Penelope . . . to wait: why should Odysseus delay the interview? If we assume the reason he gives at 572–3 is a typical beggar's reason (cf. 23) and not to be taken seriously, the real reason must be that Odysseus wishes to have the suitors out of the way (564, repeated by Eumaios at 581, and agreed by Penelope at 586–8). Odysseus is presumably taking precautions against giving himself away (either because Penelope may recognise him, or because he may make a fatal slip—as he nearly does, 19.388ff.). As we shall see, the meeting is delicately poised (19.209–12, 379–85, 473–86).

586.   **So it shall be**: wrong translation. The Greek probably means 'however matters may turn out'.

593.   **I am going back to guard the pigs**: cf. 14.524ff. Eumaios' loyalty and the suitors' thoughtless hedonism are well contrasted at 604–6.

600.   **bring us beautiful victims**: because the next day, which will bring the suitors' death, is a feast-day of Apollo (20.276–8), when three pigs will be brought in (20.162–3), as against the usual one (14.19, 27).

Book eighteen

Introduction

A. Assaults against and abuse of the beggar Odysseus (Iros 1–157, Melantho 304–345, Eurymachos 346–428) frame an important Penelope-scene (158–303). The assaults and abuse serve two general functions. First, they give evidence of the suitors' absolute disregard for the laws of hospitality and so help to justify the revenge Odysseus will take upon them (e.g. 346–8); but second, they are a testing-ground for both Odysseus and Telemachos, who have made plans how to deal with them (16.274–80), but who still need to assert their self-discipline so as to give nothing away before the time is right to act (e.g. 90–4, 406–9). In particular, Odysseus now has to endure being laughed at, a form of abuse which no Greek took lightly (see on 18.342). But there is a sense that Odysseus' control over events in the household is growing, and that his intangible authority is gradually asserting itself (see notes on 130–46, 342).

B. The Penelope-scene (158–303) has been attacked by analysts (see Page *HO* 124–6 and notes on 161, 271, 291) and is not without its problems. The most difficult one is—does Penelope *mean* it when she says she is considering marriage? Those who argue that she is not serious point to Athene's motivation for the whole scene, and its apparent purpose, i.e. that Penelope should wheedle gifts out of the suitors as some kind of compensation for the ravages they have inflicted upon the palace (158–62, 274–80). Odysseus too seems to think she is tricking them and has other purposes in mind (281–3).

It may strike us as demeaning for a woman like Penelope to act in this way, but she is wife of Odysseus, has herself a reputation for trickery, (see on 2.94–110), and has many characteristics which she shares with her husband, whose love of material gain is well-documented (e.g. 13.215–6). Odysseus senses Penelope's interest in material possesions when he describes to her the treasures 'Odysseus' has stored up in his travels (19.277–95). Consequently, her efforts to deceive the suitors into giving her gifts would indeed make her more valued by her son and husband (18.161–2). Cf.19.528–9.

Nevertheless, there is no need to conclude that she *must* be deceiving the suitors about her intentions to get married. She may be simply using her decision to get married to her financial advantage (cf.15.20–3). Odysseus' interpretation of her action, i.e., that her mind 'had other intentions' (283) and that she was wheedling gifts merely for the sake of it is exactly what Odysseus *would* think anyway, especially in the light of 13.379–81.

C. Later developments strongly suggest that marriage *is* on Penelope's mind. In particular, at 19.571–81, Penelope will say to the beggar Odysseus that she has made up her mind to re-marry and will announce the trial of the bow and axes. The purpose of this passage in Book 18, then, is to prepare the ground for the official announcement in Book 19; and what makes it of such critical importance is that her decision to re-marry is based upon the finest of motives, i.e. loyalty to the instructions that Odysseus left her before he went to Troy, namely, that when Telemachos reached maturity (cf. the *kleos* theme, on 13.422), she should consider herself free to marry again (269–73). She is not, in other words, reneging on her obligations to her household: she is fulfilling them, in accordance with Odysseus' strict instructions. This inevitably brings her grief (272–3); in her heart she does not wish to have anything to do with the suitors (164–5). But her husband has spoken, Telemachos is now grown-up (175–6, *20B*) and the time has come. If the evidence that Odysseus is about to return is mounting e.g. 17.152–61, 522–7, 541–7, (and will contine to mount in Book 19) Penelope greets it with silence, or merely with the hope that the suitors will be killed. She does not seem able to believe that Odysseus *himself* will ever return. This is all part of the irony of the situation: unknown to her, she will not in fact re-marry, but will be re-united in marriage with her true husband.

Penelope's announcement, then, in Book 18 is of high significance for the *Odyssey*. The day which began with the return of her son from Sparta (start of Book 17) will end in Book 19 with her decision, foreshadowed here in Book 18, to marry again. It is this decision which will set in train the events that lead to the death of the suitors. Her decision to re-marry and set up the trial of the bow and axes will make possible Odysseus' final victory over his enemies. It is not surprising that Athene should have been the motivator of Penelope's crucial entrance in Book 18 (158–62): she, one assumes, knew where it would lead.

D. We have already briefly discussed Penelope's character (*4.625–847B*). She is a woman 'under pressure', for whom sleep and dreams are an important means of escape. We can now enlarge the picture. She is a woman of great beauty and chastity (17.37, 18.212), faithful and intelligent in the eyes of the suitors (2.115–122, 18.245–9) and Agamemnon (11.444, 24.192 — where Penelope is directly contrasted with Klytaimestra, cf. 16.397–8, 19.325–6). She is clever and deceitful (the shroud trick (2.89ff., 19.141ff., 24.131ff.); 18.281–3; her testing of Odysseus at 23.173–208). She is in conflict with her son Telemachos, unable to impose her will on him, but equally intent that others will not impose theirs on her (see on 1.249–51, *1.325–444A*). Her love for Odysseus is as deep as it ever was, but she despairs of him ever returning (18.203–5); yet she hangs on the words of any charlatan who claims to bring news of him (14.122–130). The despair she now feels at the prospect of re-marriage is moving (even death seems preferable 202–5) and her loyalty to the memory of Odysseus, which drives her to take this hateful decision (260–71), is truly heroic.

2.   **ravenous belly**: cf. on 17.283–9.

3–4.   **no real strength/ . . . big to look at**: for appearance vs. reality, see *17A*.

5.   **Arnaios**: the name probably means 'Getter', but the scholiast suggests a connection with *arna*, 'sheep', and a possible meaning 'smelling of sheep'.

6–7.   **Iros/because he would . . . give messages**: the messenger goddess of the greeks was Iris. Iros would be the masculine form.

8.   **had come to chase Odysseus**: the poet prepares the ground for the third assault on Odysseus. For the assault pattern, see on 17.233. For Odysseus' fighting skills, see 4.341–4.

9.   **insulting him**: compare the insults Odysseus receives from Euryalos at 8.159ff.

17.   **This doorsill is big enough for both of us**: a nice irony from the master of the house. For Odysseus' past generosity to visitors, see e.g. 1.176–7, and for his kindness as king, 2.234. For rivalry between beggars, cf. Hesiod *WD* 24–6.

26–7.   **like/an old woman at the oven**: a term of abuse, of which a modern equivalent would be 'fishwife'. There is a 'fishwife' simile at *Iliad* 20.251–5.

29–30.   **a wild pig rooting/the crops**: ancient commentators refer to a law in Cyprus that farmers who found pigs destroying their crops could have their teeth pulled.

32.   **the threshold**: see on 17.339.

51.   **with crafty thoughts**: Odysseus knows well that he has the capacity to kill Iros with a blow (91) but brilliantly seizes the opportunity to act the part of a helpless old man (52–4) who needs protection (54–7). Telemachos reponds intelligently (note the irony of 65).

56.   **lightheartedly**: wrong translation. The Greek says 'wickedly, presumptuously'.

66–71.   **But Odysseus . . . limbs**: here Athene emphasises the physical grandeur she had disguised by turning him into a beggar (13.429–33, 16.454–6). The suitors do not recognise him now any more than they do at 22.1. (see 22.27—even when Odysseus announces himself at 22.35–41, Eurymachos still has his doubts (22.45)).

79.   **I do not care . . .**: observe the treachery and disloyalty of Antinoos to one who claimed to be on terms with the suitors (11–12).

85.   **Echetos**: a person referred to again at 116 and 21.308. The name means 'Holder' (Greek *echō* 'have, hold'). We know nothing more about him. The mainland referred to at 84 is presumably the Greek mainland opposite Ithaka, though ancient commentators guess it may be Sicily (see on 20.383). The extremity of the punishment should not make us assume that Echetos is a fanciful, exaggerated invention. See next note.

86–7.   **he with . . . feed on**: a punishment visited upon Melanthios at 22.474–6 by Telemachos, Eumaios and Philoitios.

90.   **Odysseus pondered**: see on 17.235.

101.   **dragged him by the foot through the porch**: the poet foreshadows the

fate that awaits the suitors at 22.448ff. Cf. Telemachos' prayer at 235–42, where he hopes the suitors will suffer the fate of Iros.

117.   **Odysseus was pleased at the omen**: because the suitors expressed the desire that the gods should grant Odysseus whatever he wished (112–3). See on 2.35.

125.   **Amphinomos, you seem to me . . .**: for the moralising lecture associated with beggar-assaults, see *17B*. It was Amphinomos who prevented the suitors trying to murder Telemachos at 16.394–406. This is the first occasion on which any suitor has shown anything resembling kindness to a *xenos*, though cf. 17.483–7. Cf. 414, 20.240–7.

126–8.   **I have heard of . . . they say**: Odysseus is careful to ensure that the suitors have no reason to wonder how an itinerant beggar should come to know so much about one of their number—Odysseus has just *heard* of these things.

130–46.   **Of all creatures . . . friends**: the argument of this melancholy passage seems to be as follows: man is weak (130–1) because he is in the grip of a rhythm which brings him alternately good and bad fortune (132–5). This alternation affects his whole outlook on life (136–7). It is foolish to try to break this inevitable rhythm, especially by committing crimes displeasing to Zeus—because that will ensure the swing from prosperity to misery is that much more severe (138–40—I expand on the text here to show how 'doing wrong' enters the argument at this point). So do not act unrighteously (140–1), but take whatever gifts (both good *and* bad) the gods give (142) (i.e. do not upset the natural rhythm of life, because if you do, your disaster will be that much greater). Odysseus talks from his own 'experiences' here as a beggar in the grip of misfortune (cf. 123). The lesson applies to you suitors, because you seem to be having such a good time at the moment, but are in fact criminals (143–6) (and so can expect extreme punishment when it comes). The whole passage is well in line with archaic thought. Cf. Archilochos 67a, 6–7: 'Keep some measure in the joy you take in luck and the degree you give way to sorrow. All our life is up-and-down like this' (tr. Lattimore). Solon 1 63–4: 'Fate brings humanity her good; she brings him her evil; and what the gods give us for gifts no man can refuse' (tr. Lattimore). Solon's image of man's life resembling the fluctuations in the weather is telling (17–33). For a powerful statement of man's propensity to move from prosperity to misery at the whim of the gods, see Achilleus' speech to Priam in *Iliad* 24.521–51. That Odysseus can speak in this vein indicates how he is gradually extending his authority over the house (as over Eumaios earlier on — see on 17.525.).

138–40.   **For I myself . . . brothers**: Odysseus' references to his prosperity, use of violence and subsequent misery seem to refer to his false tale at 17.419–44 (especially 419–23, 430–40, 442—and note the references to Zeus' wishes at 424). But his reference to his reliance on father and brothers (140) cannot be found in that tale—or in any other.

155.   **could not escape his doom**: see 22.89–94.

161.   **so that she might seem**: in our version of the story, Penelope remains

entirely ignorant of the identity of the beggar till she is told who he is. But there may have been other versions of the story in which Penelope recognised the beggar early on (and did or did not reveal that she had so done) or in which the beggar revealed himself to Penelope (as Odysseus did to Telemachos in Book 16) to further his plans. If these alternative versions show their heads occasionally, there is no need to explain them in terms of multiple authorship (see *11B,E* on the whole issue). In this passage, analysts argue that the clause 'so that she might seem' suggests that Penelope has recognised Odysseus. We may treat this as an oral 'slip'; or argue that the motive is not Penelope's but Athene's (it is after all Athene who puts the plan in motion (158)).

163.   **She laughed**: for this whole scene, and Penelope in general, see *18B,C,D*.

184.   **I will not go alone**: see on 6.100 for this type of scene.

193.   **Kythereia**: i.e. Aphrodite (see 8.288). For ambrosia, see note on 5.93.

195.   **thicker**: Greeks connected beauty with, among a number of other things, bulk. Cf. the height of Nausikaa implied by the simile at 6.101–9, and 18.216–7 (Telemachos).

196.   **whiter than sawn ivory**: paleness was valued in the woman, darkness in the man in Homer (cf. 16.175). 'White-armed' is a common female epithet e.g. 6.101, cf. 23.240.

202.   **Artemis**: Penelope wishes for death sent by Artemis because she was believed to bring as painless a death to women as Apollo to men (see e.g. 11.172–3, 15.409–11).

206.   **and made her descent**: one of the great silences in Homer. Odysseus is about to set his eyes on his wife for the first time in twenty years—and the poet ignores him completely. It is not till 281–3 that we read Odysseus' reaction to her, and it is one of delight at her craftiness and acquisitiveness (both characteristics typical of Odysseus). Against this, Fenik *SO* 65–6 argues that a character out of the text is out of mind in Homer: a 'silent presence' is not meaningful. Cf. on 16.16.

215.   **Telemachos, your mind and thoughts . . .**: Penelope launches into a typical complaint about Telemachos' behaviour (for this theme, see on *1.325–444A*), but it is noticeable that Telemachos' response is considerably milder than it usually is (compare 227–42 with, e.g., 1.346–59). He is 'acting up' his helplessness well in front of the suitors.

221–2.   **you/permitted**: from 233–5, it is clear that Telemachos interprets Penelope's words here to refer to the fight between Odysseus and Iros which occurred earlier in the book. But her words refer more easily to the incident in which Antinoos threw a stool at Odysseus and which (somehow) she came to hear about (17.492–3).

233.   **Yet it was not by the will of the suitors that this struggle took place**: this is literally what the Greek means, but is extremely awkward since it certainly was the suitors' will that the fight happened (36–9). The problem is eased if we interpret Telemachos' words to mean 'that this struggle *turned out as it did*'.

236–8.   **if only . . . each of them**: as will in fact happen (see on 101).

246.   **Iad Argos**: 'Iad' in Greek is *Iason*. The likely meaning is 'Ionian', a term normally applied to Greeks who settled on the Turkish coast during the migrations of 1000 onwards, but which also seems to have been used to apply to some Greeks on the mainland. Cf. 'Achaians', strictly 'men from Achaia', = 'Greeks' in Homer.

251–80.   **Eurymachos, . . . without payment**: observe how typical the cento of Penelope's thoughts is. 251 (destruction of beauty) cf. 18.180–1, 19.124–5; 253 (loss of Odysseus) cf. 1.343, 4.724, 4.814, 17.103–4, 18.181–2, 19.136, 19.259–60, 23.67; 256 (her grief) cf. 1.341–2, 4.722, 4.812, 17.102, (cf. 18.173), 19.128–9, 23.15; 272 (hateful marriage) cf. 19.157, 20.82–3, 21.75–9; 275 (disgraceful wooing tactics) cf. 16.431–2, 19.133, 21.68–72; 280 (suitors' consumption) cf. 1.339–40, 4.686, 16.431 (etc. etc. – this is a very common element indeed). It is appropriate that from now on Homer begins to weave in more references to Penelope's impending (and hateful) marriage to the disgraceful wooing tactics of the suitors (since she is about to make a decision to marry again).

259.   **Dear wife . . .**: another reference to Odysseus before he left for the Trojan War (see on 17.293–4). Note his gentle realism, and the delicacy of 258.

263.   **riders with fast-footed horses**: not cavalry (they played no part in Homeric warfare) but charioteers are meant.

271.   **all this is being accomplished**: i.e. Penelope is about to marry one of the suitors. This may seem an odd way of making herself more valued in the eyes of her husband (161–2), but Odysseus knows she is playing the suitors along (281–3). On this passage, and on 283, see *18B,C*.

291.   **Each man sent his herald off . . .**: there is some awkwardness here. Homer seems to have forgotten that the suitors are not living in the palace but commuting to it every day (see 18.427–8). To be strictly accurate, Homer should have described the heralds returning with the gifts the next day.

293–4.   **twelve double pins . . . easily**: the Greek says 'twelve *peronai*, all golden, fitted with well-twisted *kleides*'. *peronai* means 'brooches'; *kleides* 'bars', 'hooks' or 'clasps'. The probable meaning is 'bar', i.e. pin, which is 'well-twisted'.

298.   **with triple drops**: Hera wears earrings like this at *Iliad* 14.183.

307.   **cressets**: a cresset is an iron basket, often hung from the wall or ceiling, in which wood is burned to give light and heat (19.64, cf. 20.122–3, 160–1).

314.   **go back into the house**: Odysseus' instructions serve two purposes – they give him a legitimate reason for remaining in the room with the suitors, and they test the maidservants' attitude towards Penelope (for whom Odysseus is clearly concerned – note 316). For testing, see 16.304–7; for Odysseus' claims to practical skills (317), see on 15.322; for weaving (315–6), see on 4.122.

324.   **her heart had no sorrow**: another example of the corrupting effect of

the suitors upon once loyal and loved members of the household. Melantho is sister of Melanthios (see 17.257). For Dolios, see on 4.735.

328.   **where the smith is at work**: the smithy is a warm place for a beggar to sleep (see Hesiod *WD* 493–5 where identical advice is given. For cold weather, see on 5.467).

338   **I will go to Telemachos**: tactful restraint on the part of Odysseus.

342.   **They thought he was speaking the truth**: the servants start by laughing at Odysseus (320)—a great humiliation for a Greek (cf. 350, on 8.307, and 18.35, 40, 100, 111); the scene ends with them in fear of him. Odysseus continues slowly to assert his authority over his own house.

344–5.   **the heart within him/was pondering other thoughts**: what thoughts? Perhaps how to take revenge for these insults? Certainly this theme begins to build from now on, e.g. 19.1–2, 20.5, 20.38–43, 20.121.

356.   **Odysseus, sacker of cities**: the formular system of composition was flexible enough to allow the poet to engineer the line so that 'sacker of cities' was the epithet to use for Odysseus here. The insult to Odysseus that the great 'sacker of cities' should act as a serf (see next note) is amply repaid.

358.   **to work for me**: the Greek means 'to be a *thes*'—the most humble worker there was. See on 11.489.

363–4.   **work hard . . . ravenous belly**: on these two common elements, see on 2, 17.233.

366–80.   **Eurymachos . . . of my belly**: some see this as an 'anti-aristocratic' statement by Odysseus, but this is to misread the scene. Odysseus is adopting a tone of calculating irony to reply to Eurymachos' insulting suggestion. He cleverly throws Eurymachos' proposal back at him, suggesting that he (Odysseus) would beat him whether Eurymachos wanted to play the part of mower (366–70), ploughman (371–5, see on 13.31) or soldier (376–80). Eurymachos understands the insult very well (389–93). Odysseus is certainly sailing close to the wind with his unprecedentedly reckless abuse at 382–6, but he clearly feels he can get away with it. See 17.19–21 where Odysseus claims he is *not* of an age for farm-work!

385.   **the gates . . . would suddenly/be too narrow**: in the event, Odysseus makes sure the suitors get no chance to try the gates (cf. 22.76–8).

396.   **and hit the cup-bearer**: the attacks on Odysseus have become less and less successful. At 17.234–5, Odysseus is kicked but stays his ground; at 17.464–5, Odysseus is hit by a stool, but stays his ground; at 18.95–100, Odysseus is punched by Iros but rides it and lays Iros flat; and here the throw misses. At 20. 300–1, Odysseus will easily avoid the hoof thrown at him by Ktesippos.

403.   **there will be no pleasure**: the whole scene is structurally similar to *Iliad* 1.531–611 in which Zeus and Hera quarrel (= 349–393), Hera retreats in fear (= 394–8), the gods complain at the ruination of their feast (= 399–404), but peace is made (= 405–28). There is no parody or pale imitation here (despite the similarity of 403–4 with *Iliad* 1.574–6). In the *Iliad*, the gods decide to sink their differences over mere mortals, and feast on, oblivious to human suffering. In the *Odyssey* the feasting is brought to a

close, and the episode underlines the increasing helplessness of the suitors, apparent masters of the house, to do anything effective about this infernal beggar, who is Odysseus, its real master.

406. **Fools, you are out of your minds**: this is the first time that Telemachos has actively intervened to calm down things when Odysseus has been attacked (cf. 17.489–92). Telemachos' intervention is in line with Odysseus' instructions at 16.278–80: but observe that Telemachos does not go too far (409).

414. **no man must be angry**: for the conciliatory role of Amphinomos, see on 125.

418. **let the cup-bearer pour wine**: possibly the only occasion when the suitors unambiguously acknowledge the gods in their feasting and drinking (see on 20.276–83, 21.267). They only do so here because the comparatively righteous Amphinomos suggests it. For the ritual, see on 2.432.

Book nineteen

Introduction

A. Book 19 is played out at night, by fire- and torch-light (34, 48, 64, 389, 506), in the palace. Both the setting and the exchanges between Penelope and the beggar Odysseus are characterised by a rich and subtle *chiaroscuro* (light-and-dark). When Odysseus arrived in Eumaios' hut in Book 14, we witnessed how cleverly Odysseus settled into his new role as beggar, maintaining his disguise, eliciting both the sympathy of Eumaios and much important information about the situation at the palace, and gradually asserting his authority over the swineherd. Since arriving at the palace (Book 17), Odysseus has been severely tested by the abuse and assaults of the suitors but, with the help of Telemachos, has maintained his dignity with his disguise, and now has a clear idea of the challenge that lies ahead. The night meeting with Penelope, prepared at 17.505–90, is an encounter of a quite different but no less demanding order. The issue at stake is not primarily what it was with Eumaios or in the palace, i.e. who the beggar is, how he became one, and what should be done about him, but rather what the beggar knows about Odysseus and whether this information will affect Penelope's decision to re-marry (see on 218–9). Moreover, the encounter for Odysseus, is not with 'friends' or 'enemies' but with his wife, whom Odysseus has valued more than a goddess (5.210–20), who has for the last twenty years been waiting in increasing despair for his return and who has now reached the point where she is facing the crucial decision to abandon all hope of her husband's return, leave the palace to her adult son, and marry someone else. If Odysseus has been tested so far to the limits of his capacity to act a role, endure abuse and withstand physical assault, it is now his emotions that are laid on the line. The delicacy, care and restraint with which Odysseus approaches his encounter with Penelope (107–22, 165–7, 336–48, 209–12) stand in strong contrast to the instant mastery he shows over Eurykleia when she recognises him (479–502).

B. Analysts and psychologists have had field-days with Book 19. The analysts argue that throughout Books 18 and 19, there are clear signs that two versions of the *Odyssey* are here being confused: one in which Odysseus is recognised by and plans action jointly with Penelope before the slaughter of the suitors, one in which he maintains his disguise successfully all the way through. We have already discussed the evidence for this from Book 18 (see *18B,C*). In Book 19, analysts point to the Eurykleia incident (what can be the point of Odysseus asking for an older servant to wash him when she will be the only one who could possibly recognise him? i.e. he wants to be recognised by her); and to Penelope's plan to set up the trial of the bow and axes (why set up the trial now, of all times, when the signs have never been stronger that Odysseus will return? 'Because Penelope knows who the beggar really is').

C. The psychological approach argues that Penelope recognises Odysseus 'intuitively' in Book 19. She senses that there is more to this beggar than meets the eye, and 'psychologists' point to passages which, they argue, indicate a warmth of feeling, a *rapprochement* between Penelope and someone who is apparently nothing but a grimy beggar, that can only be explained on those grounds (e.g. 253–4, 325–8, 340–3, 509, 535, 589–90). Some even go as far as to talk about 'sensual undercurrents' to the meeting between the two. Consequently, they argue, when Penelope decides to set up the trial of the bow and axes, she does so 'knowing' Odysseus has returned.

D. There is obviously something in what the analysts (above, B) say, but the conclusion, that these 'inconsistencies' point to 'multiple authorship', will not stand. What the analysts have pointed out is that other versions of the *Odyssey* are discernible beneath the surface of our version.

This is surely right. As the ghost Amphimedon suggests at 24.167–9, there could indeed have been a version in which Odysseus and Penelope did plot together beforehand; and if our poet occasionally exploits the potential of such a version for irony, drama and pathos in his realisation of the epic, he would be doing nothing out of the ordinary for an oral poet. What is unquestionable is that our poet does have a single and wholly consistent vision of the function of Odysseus' disguise: it is to try to ensure that he will *not* be recognised (see also on 346 for the Eurykleia episode).

E. The 'psychological' approach (above, C) raises severe methodological problems: how can we explore the psychology of fictional characters, who only exist in as far as the poet allows them to? Unless the poet chooses to make their psychological problems explicit (which he is perfectly capable of doing, e.g. 209–12, 23.85–110), or offers substantial clues in the text itself to their state of mind, we have no evidence on which we can establish the existence of such undercurrents. But the approach is also suspect because it does not take enough notice of what happens either side of Book 19, and because it fails to appreciate the irony which is so characteristic of an epic in which disguise plays a central part.

First, in Book 18, we have seen Penelope prepare to take the decision to re-marry and have discussed the importance of her reason for it—it is to remain faithful to the instructions of Odysseus. We have also seen that she is in a state of mind that makes it impossible for her even to countenance the return of Odysseus after all these years (see *18C*). It is typical of our poet to exploit to the full the possible irony and pathos of the situation by getting Penelope at this last, critical moment, to submit to questioning the one man who will (after all these years) tell, and be proved to have told, the truth about Odysseus; and masterly of the poet to get Penelope to *refuse to believe it*. The poet, *suo modo*, makes no comment on the refusal to believe (582–99). But if one felt like making a statement about the 'psychology' of a woman who has been trapped for twenty years by her loyalty to her husband and now, out of that continuing sense of loyalty, and after years of lies (14.122–30), has finally decided to re-marry despite all the apparent evidence that he is about to return, Penelope's refusal to believe, and the icy clarity of mind that accompanies it (570–81), offer one. It need hardly be said that elsewhere there is no indication at all that Penelope has recognised Odysseus 'subconsciously' or in any other way, (see e.g. 19.603, 20.80–2, 21.54–7, 314–7; 23.1–110). For the other problem with the 'psychological' approach, that it does not take the irony of the text into account, see notes at 253–4, 590, and 598–9.

On the whole issue, see the excellent discussion by C. Emlyn-Jones in *GR* 31 1984 'The Re-union of Penelope and Odysseus'.

F. The clinching argument against the belief that Penelope sets up the trial because she has, at whatever level, penetrated Odysseus' disguise, is given by the use to which the bow is put. 'Psychologists' argue that Penelope puts the bow into Odysseus' hand so that he has the means by which he can kill the suitors. But at what point in the narrative does this second use for the bow become apparent? Immediately after the meeting of Penelope and Odysseus, it is not obvious to Odysseus that the bow could serve this function (20.39–40), and Athene in her reply to his question 'How shall I kill the suitors?' does not put the thought into his head. The poet is preparing us for it, naturally (see 20.390–4, 21.1–4, 98–9, 153–6), but it is not until 21.228–41 (esp. 234–8) that Odysseus actually makes it clear that he has seen the use to which the bow can be put (though his reasoning is never made explicit). Nor is there any sign in the text that Penelope understands the implications of her decision to set up the trial, let alone that she thought the bow might be used to kill the suitors. In other words, Penelope sets up the trial for one purpose only—to produce the man whom she will marry.

G. One teasing possibility is opened up by F. Combellack (*CSCA* 6 1974, reprinted in H.W. Clarke (ed.) *20thC Interpretations of the Odyssey*, Prentice Hall 1983): that is, that Penelope knows that no-one will be able to string the bow and so offers the trial as a delaying tactic (cf. the shroud-trick). If the omens are right to claim that Odysseus is about to return, Penelope argues she will be creating time in which this can happen while the suitors struggle with the bow. But as Combellack honestly admits, the text itself does not offer much evidence that this *is* the reason why Penelope set up the trial.

2. **with the help of Athene**: see 18.344–5 for a possible first reference to this important consideration (cf. 13.393–6). Given the plan Odysseus proposes (4–13), he is already thinking of a battle *in* the palace, not outside it.

4.   **we must have the weapons**: see on 16.281–98 for the problems connected with these instructions. In the event, the suitors have only their swords with them (22.74).

13.   **iron all of itself . . . attracts him** (sc. **'to fight'**): See on 9.393 for iron.

16.   **detain the women inside the palace**: why should they be detained while Telemachos puts away the weapons? Presumably so the unfaithful would not be able to tell the suitors where the weapons were when the battle started. (Penelope knows all about disloyal maidservants—154–5 cf. 22.151–9.)

19.   **I was a child**: Telemachos embroiders convincingly upon the excuse offered him by Odysseus (cf. Eurykleia's approving reaction at 22–3) and is quick-witted enough to invent a persuasive reason why Odysseus should help him out (27–8). For beggars' traditional refusal to work, see on 17.233.

29.   **no winged words**: see on 17.57.

32.   **massive in the middle**: wrong translation. The Greek says 'knobbed' or 'studded', with reference not only to the single boss in the middle but to the concentric rings of smaller knobs with which shields were set (see *Iliad* 11.32–5).

34.   **a golden lamp**: torches, not lamps, are the usual means of illumination in the Homeric world (cf. 48). But lamps were known in the Mycenaean –Minoan world, and *may* have been associated with cult.

36.   **here is a great wonder**: it is clear that Telemachos cannot actually see Athene (cf. 16.160), and there is no indication that Odysseus can either (see on 15.9). But Odysseus knows the explanation (43). Whereas Odysseus and Telemachos are enveloped in supernatural light, the suitors are enveloped in supernatural darkness, according to the prophet Theoklymenos (20.351–2). Some see a connection between this light (and that at 18.354–5, 317–9), and the metaphorical 'light of victory' common in the *Iliad* (e.g. 6.6). This is far-fetched. Such light attends heroes either engaged in battle or in otherwise clearly marked military contexts. This is not the case in any of the *Odyssey* passages, where the meaning is clearly non-metaphorical (cf. further 19.64). The 'light of victory' metaphor is not even used during the fight with the suitors in Book 22 (against Clarke *AO* 73–5).

45–6.   **I can . . . stir up the maids, and also/your mother**: one would expect Odysseus to want to 'put to the test' the servants and Penelope (cf. 13.334–6) rather than stir them up, but Odysseus is combative and challenging, even with loved ones. Cf. his treatment of his father Laertes at 24.239–40. The effect he has on Penelope is to reduce her to tears (203–12, 249–50). This is no time for softness on Odysseus' part.

51–2.   **Odysseus still remained . . ./suitors**: ring-composition with 1–2.

56.   **inlaid**: the Greek refers to the 'spiral' design of the inlay.

57–8.   **joined on/a footstool**: the special comment on the connection between chair and footstool suggests they were normally separate. Cf. e.g. 1.131.

61.   **a great deal of food**: these lines point up again the extravagant wastefulness of the suitors.

65.   **for the second time**: see 18.321–36. The nuisance-value of a beggar (66) is a well-attested element (see on 17.233), but spying on the women (67) is a new, and in the context, appropriate one, since Odysseus is now alone in the hall with Penelope and the maidservants (Telemachos has gone to bed (47–8), the suitors home (18.428)).

75–80.   **I too . . . wished to**: = 17.419–24. Note the irony: the house Odysseus refers to, if in slightly exaggerated terms, is the palace he now begs in. For Odysseus' generosity to friends, see 1.176–7; for his kindness, 2.234, 4.686–95; for his wealth, see 14.95–9.

83.   **Beware of your mistress**: Odysseus implies a compliment to Penelope on her authority, and at 85–8, on her growing son. Odysseus is beginning to 'work on' Penelope as he has already on Eumaios (see on 17.274–9), the suitors (see on 18.130–46), and the maids (see on 18.342).

86.   **by grace of Apollo**: one of Apollo's cult-titles is 'nurturer of youth' (*kourotrophos*).

87–8.   **none of the women/will . . . escape**: Telemachos is entrusted with executing the twelve faithless maidservants at 22.435–72.

92.   **you will wipe it off on your own head**: according to Herodotus (1.155), the sacrificer of a victim would wipe the blood of his knife off onto the head of the animal in order to transfer his guilt for its death onto the animal itself. Here Penelope is saying that Melantho will *not* be able to transfer the guilt for her crimes onto someone else. For a further example of her maidservants' disloyalty, see 154–5.

93.   **you had heard it**: presumably Melantho was with Penelope at 17.505–11.

107–122.   **Lady, . . . in liquor**: for the preamble, cf. 9.2–20, and for avoiding the question, see *7B,C* (Odysseus and Arete). A very tense moment: these are Odysseus' first words to Penelope in 20 years, and they form a deeply moving compliment while still being in character for a beggar (see on 108).

108.   **your fame . . . wide heaven**: almost the identical wording to that which Odysseus uses of himself at 9.20. The compliment is well in character for a beggar, who was expected to please (14.387).

109.   **as of some king**: this famous passage, which links piety and good government (109–111) with prosperity (111–4), was much used, e.g. Hesiod *WD* 225–37, Plato *Republic* 363b. But there was no *necessary* connection betwen the two: the Cyclops' territory brought forth in abundance, but he was a paradigm of incivility (9.106–115). Doubtless a good Homeric king frequently bailed out his people during bad harvests (cf. 2.234, 14.95–104). See on 1.108, cf. Hesiod *WD* 225–37.

116.   **do not ask who I am**: Odysseus' excuse is reasonable (see on 117), but the generally complimentary and evasive tone of his reply to Penelope's question may be more than merely good acting. Odysseus suddenly seems strangely vulnerable at this critical time.

117.   **its burden of sorrow**: for the grief which accompanies tales of past adventures, cf. 9.12–15, for the pleasure of survival, 15.398–401.

122.   **drowned in liquor**: Odysseus knows the accusations typically made against beggars (18.331–2). Cf. 14.463–7.

124–9.   **Stranger . . . upon me**: = 18.251–6. These words, now spoken (though Penelope does not know it) to her actual husband, are full of pathos and irony.

130–3.   **For all . . . house out**: ≃ 16.122–5, = 1.245–8.

134–5.   **'I pay . . . service'**: Eumaios thinks Penelope pays too much attention to strangers (14.122–30), not too little. But Penelope is here pointing to the effect of her private grief (136) upon her public duties, which would include (among other things) the reception of strangers and suppliants (a divinely sanctioned responsibility—see 6.206–8) and attention to public announcements. Eumaios talks of her *private* concern about the fate of Odysseus.

137.   **my own wiles**: Penelope shares with Odysseus a love of trickery.

139–52.   **to set up . . . returning**: = 2.94–107 (see notes there).

158.   **my parents are urgent with me**: such pressure was hinted at by Athene at 15.16, but there is no evidence, either there or in this passage, that Penelope's parents were in fact urging her to re-marry. (See on 525–34). Penelope here, presumably, is trying to defend the reputation with which Odysseus has complimented her (107–11) by explaining why she is now reluctantly choosing to re-marry. It is not unusual for those under consHelp. siderable pressure to pour out their hearts before total strangers to justify decisions of which they are secretly ashamed.

159.   **my son is vexed**: see, e.g. 1.249–51.

160.   **he is a grown man now**: see *18C* for the part that Telemachos' maturity plays in forcing Penelope into re-marriage.

163.   **You were not born from . . . boulder**: i.e. you are a human and so must have human parents. There were myths which described the human race originating from e.g. stones (Deukalion and Pyrrha). There may be a humorous allusion to such myths here.

175–7.   **Achaians/. . . Pelasgians**: the earliest description of Crete we possess, but its meaning is much disputed. The Achaians are presumably Mycenaean Greeks (who controlled Crete from 14thC); according to Strabo, Eteokretans are an indigenous population, as are the Kydonians who lived by the R. Iardanos, in W. Crete (3.291–2); but the Dorians are a mystery (Greek tradition saw them entering the Peloponnese in the 12thC, and only much later spreading down to Crete); as for the Pelasgians, they appear to come from Asia Minor (*Iliad* 2.840, 10.429), and are also associated with Argos (*Iliad* 2.681)!

178.   **Knossos**: the city was excavated by Sir Arthur Evans in the early 20thC. In myth the city was associated with the legendary King Minos (178), the labyrinth, the Minotaur and the great craftsman Daedalus.

179.   **was king for nine-year periods**: or 'when nine years old', or 'for nine years' or 'after nine years'. The reference is mysterious. For Minos' close relationship with Zeus, cf. 11.568–71, where he judges the dead.

181.   **Idomeneus**: one of the Greek heroes who fought at Troy. To have

a brother such as Idomeneus is to claim association with a very royal line indeed (*Iliad* 13.449–53). In his story to Eumaios, Odysseus said that he fought alongside Idomeneus at Troy (14.235–42), though did not claim fraternity with him (Odysseus was son of a Cretan concubine in that story— 14.199–203). It is fortunate for Odysseus that Eumaios did not go into more detail about the beggar's past than he did at 17.513–27: see on 13.259.

187.   **past Maleia**: see on 9.80.

188.   **Amnisos**: the main port of Knossos. '**Eileithyia**': goddess of child-birth. Such a cave has been identified above Amnisos.

197.   **I collected from the public**: for this practice, cf. Alkinoos at 13.13–15.

197–8.   **barley . . ./wine . . . cattle**: barley for bread or cakes (see on 2.354), wine to drink and cattle for meat (a luxury for a Greek).

203.   **He knew how to say**: read 'he invented'.

204.   **her body was melted**: read 'her flesh was bathed in tears' (cf. 208).

205–8.   **as the snow . . . tears**: it is tempting to give weight in the simile to the mountain (= Penelope's majesty and unchanging grandeur) but Homer concentrates entirely on the parallel between the melting snows and her tears.

209.   **who was sitting there**: magnificent pathos and irony.

211.   **but his eyes stayed**: Odysseus' appearance again deceives. He is in fact deeply moved by his wife's tears (210, 212).

215.   **a test**: this is the first test to which Penelope subjects Odysseus (see 23.174–81 for the second). Testing is something that Odysseus knows well (16.312–20): it is a further interest which Penelope and Odysseus have in common. Cf. on 137.

218–9.   **what sort of clothing . . . what sort/of man . . . his companions'**: Odysseus answers the questions about clothing (225–43) and companions (244–8) but only obliquely the questions about what sort of man Odysseus was (239–40, 247–8). But the response satisfies Penelope (249–50). There is a poignant contrast between the luxurious clothes Odysseus wore when he left and the rags which he, the great conqueror of Troy (8.492–520), now sports on his return. It is indicative of Penelope's single-minded obsession with one question (have you news of my husband?) that she never bothers to ask the beggar, the brother of Idomeneus himself, how he came by his lowly state (I assume Penelope could not have heard Odysseus' account of himself at 17.415–444—see on 17.492).

226.   **pin**: i.e. brooch.

227.   **sheaths**: these probably refer to the clasps into which the pins fitted.

228.   **a hound held . . .**: archaeologists have tried to date the brooch with reference to the scene, but with little success. Such animal scenes are typical of Minoan gems (14thC Crete) but the brooch itself seems to be of a style not found before the 12thC.

229–30.   **preying on it . . ./preyed on**: the verb *laō* elsewhere in Greek seems to mean 'see', which is rather weak unless it can be taken to mean 'fix the gaze keenly on'; the commentator Aristarchos takes it to mean 'seize, grip, bite'.

235.   **Many of the women**: women would naturally be attracted to a superbly woven tunic, since weaving was their business (cf. Penelope's skill at 138–40). Odysseus' tunic was clearly a credit to Penelope's art—and his comment here compliments her prettily.

241–2.   **sword . . ./cloak**: such gifts are typical. Cf. 16.79–80.

247.   **Eurybates**: he is mentioned as Odysseus' herald at *Iliad* 2.184. He does not feature in Books 9–12 as one of Odysseus' companions. The description (246) suggests he is a black African, but there is no hint of this in the *Iliad*.

253–4.   **you now shall/be my friend and be respected**: since Penelope now believes that the beggar met Odysseus, it is likely that she believes his whole story (i.e. that he is brother of Idomeneus too (see 21.334–5 for confirmation)). This makes the beggar a person of some status, and the worthier to be trusted with her secrets (e.g. 509–99).

265.   **For any woman mourns**: Odysseus is likened to a woman who has lost her husband in battle at 8.521–32. See on 8.523.

271–82.   **He is near . . . harm**: for Thesprotia see on 287–99 below; for Thrinakia (273–8) see 12.260–443; for Phaiakians (279–82), see 5.451–93 (arrival) and 13.10–15 (gifts, now hidden in a cave on Ithaka, 13.366–71).

273.   **he collects**: for touring in order to collect gifts, see e.g. Menelaos at 4.78–91 and his offer to Telemachos at 15.79–85.

284.   **collecting possessions**: both Odysseus and Penelope have an interest in ensuring the material prosperity of their household (cf. 18.281–2).

287–99.   **Pheidon . . . absent**: for the whole passage, see 14.316–35 (and notes).

307.   **waning . . . onset**: see on 14.161–2.

316.   **for receiving respected strangers**: *we* know how properly Telemachos received e.g. Athene (1.113ff.), and Theoklymenos (15.256ff.).

320.   **you shall give him a bath**: the 'bath' is to be differentiated from the 'wash' (317) which Odysseus is about to get from Eurykleia (357ff.). In fact, the bath promised Odysseus here does not take place. When he is next bathed, it will be after the suitors have been slaughtered, and its purpose will be to convince Penelope that he really is her husband (23.115–6, 153–65).

326.   **good sense**: the word used is *mētis*, that cunning intelligence for which Odysseus also is so famed (see *9H* and cf. on 19.137).

340–1.   **sleepless/nights**: Odysseus tells a convincing false tale about such a night in order to test Eumaios' loyalty and maintain the part of the shameless beggar at 14.468–506.

344.   **nor shall any woman lay hold of my feet**: Eurykleia supplies the reason for Odysseus' request here—the beggar does not want to be abused again by the maidservants (371–4). Cf. for abuse, 18.321–36, 19.65–9.

346.   **some aged and virtuous woman**: analysts make much of this retraction, arguing that the only reason for Odysseus to request such a woman to wash his feet is that only thus could he be recognised (the younger

women would not know about the scar). But the beggar has a duty to be courteous (he is, after all, brother of Idomeneus): he can hardly turn down Penelope's request flat. Since beggars may have had a reputation for ogling the womenfolk (see Melantho's accusation at 66–7), there may be another reason for Odysseus' request for an old and virtuous woman to wash him: he is cleverly assuring Penelope that he is not that sort of beggar. Penelope is obviously very impressed with his tact (350–3). See further Fenik *SO* 42–6.

354.   **who was nurse to that unhappy man**: for Eurykleia's past, see 1.429–33 and 19.399–404.

357–60.   **Come then, . . . suddenly**: fine irony, in which the whole scene is especially rich, e.g. Eurykleia's address to her absent lord which seems like a direct address to the beggar (363–71), her exact description of Odysseus' plight at 371–2, and her comparison at 379–81.

359.   **such hands and feet as you do**: cf. Menelaos' perceptiveness at 4.148–50 and Eurykleia at 19.379–81.

362.   **to him**: these words are not in the Greek. Their insertion here makes it seem as if Eurykleia is addressing the beggar. She is, of course, addressing the 'absent' Odysseus.

369.   **for you alone**: an exaggeration (consider the dead whom Odysseus meets in Hades in 11.385–564), but understandable in the context. The idea is used at 1.13–14 but more successfully: Odysseus there is the only one to have had his homecoming so *delayed*.

380.   **I have never seen one as like as you are**: Page argues that this does not say much for the transformative powers of Athene (*HO* 88–91), but see on 13.397.

387.   **foot-washing**: for the whole scene, cf. 4.244–64, where Helen tells how she recognised Odysseus when she bathed him after he had entered Troy in disguise as a beggar.

393.   **which once the boar inflicted**: as we shall see at 449–51. The digression lasts till 467. The scar is one of three signs identifying Odysseus— together with the bow (Books 21–2) and the bed (Book 23). There is no need to assume they represent different versions of the *Odyssey* (*CH* 54–5).

394.   **Parnassos**: a mountain in Greece overlooking Delphi.

396.   **thievery and the art of the oath**: we have here the antecedents for Odysseus' famed 'trickery'—they descend to him through his grandfather, Autolykos. The name Autolykos means 'Self-wolf' or 'Very-wolf'. In the *Iliad* wolves are used in similes to describe warriors banding together to fight (e.g. *Iliad* 16.155–66) and are generally noble, if ferocious beasts, distinguished by their sense of communal purpose. In later Greek tradition they became symbols of deceit and treachery, but this aspect also appears in *Iliad* 10.334, where Dolon wears a wolfskin on his night expedition.

Hermes: already in Homer god of tricks (10.275–306) and thievery (*Iliad* 5.385–91). See further on 5.47.

407.   **distasteful to many**: the Greek is *odussamenos*, meaning a man who deals out and incurs hatred. Cf. on 1.62.

414–28.   **Autolykos . . . fingers**: all typical, cf. 3.35–7, 3.461–3, 9.556–9,

16.481, 17.36–40. For an extended version of the scene, see 3.4–66.

416.   **Amphithea**: so Odysseus' family tree looks like this:

```
Autolykos  =  Amphithea
           |
Antikleia  =  Laertes
        ┌─────┴─────┐
    Odysseus    Ktimene (15.364)
```

436.   **casting about for the tracks**: cf. Argos, whose special skill this was (17.315–7).

439–43.   **lair . . . profusion**: the description accords roughly with that of Xenophon *On Hunting* x 5–6. Odysseus' hideaway at 5.475–85 is described in very similar terms (440–2 = 5.478–80, 443 = 5.483).

448.   **who swept in**: there is something rather odd about this hunt. In classical times at any rate the hunters staked out with nets the area where the boar had gone to ground, then sent the hounds in to flush it out, and waited for the boar to charge into the nets, where it was despatched. But the dogs seem to have no such special function in Odysseus' hunt (444–5), and it is Odysseus who charges the boar (448) (not the other way round), eager to stab when throwing might have been wiser. The poet seems to be envisaging a sort of hand-to-hand encounter as between heroes (cf. *Iliad* 21.67–9, where Achilleus raises his spear, furious to stab Lykaon, and Lykaon avoids the initial thrust, rather like the boar). Perhaps the poet's purpose is to highlight the rash impetuosity of the youthful Odysseus, who is wounded for his pains (449–50).

451.   **tearing sidewise**: (sideways, presumably). The boar's short, curved tusks cannot inflict a wound head on. The boar hits with a glancing blow from the side, thrusting up with the tusks.

452.   **stabbed at him**: Xenophon *On Hunting* x.12–16 gives advice to the man who loses grip on his spear in a close encounter of this kind. It is a very dangerous moment, he warns. Odysseus does well to hang on to his and counter-attack, and his final thrust into the shoulder is exactly what Xenophon recommends.

452–4.   **stabbed . . . him**: a thoroughly heroic and Iliadic death, cf. *Iliad* 5.98, 11.253, 16.468–9 (cf. *Odyssey* 10.163, 19.454).

457.   **incantations**: in the *Iliad* (4.217–9, 11.843–7) herbs are used to stop the flow of blood. This is the only place in Homer where an incantation is used (Homer normally avoids 'magic' (see *9B*)), but note that the wound is skilfully bound up first (456) and there is nothing to suggest that the 'healing' of 460 is supernatural.

464–8.   **wound . . . boar . . . Parnassos . . . this scar**: an excellent example of ring-composition. At the end of the digression, Homer repeats the words with which it started (393–4 scar . . . boar . . . Parnassos), so bringing the story back to the point where it was interrupted (see on 1.10).

472. **the springing voice was held within her**: from 4.704–5 it is clear that this means 'she said nothing'.

473. **She took the beard of Odysseus**: this is traditionally the gesture of one supplicating another (cf. *Iliad* 1.500–2). Since Eurykleia makes no plea here, it is difficult to read it as a supplication unless Eurykleia is asking forgiveness in advance for an imagined offence (i.e. spilling the water, failing to recognise Odysseus). More likely, since at 475 Eurykleia argues that she only recognised Odysseus when she touched him, she may be seeking further confirmatory evidence by this gesture. See next note.

475. **touched my lord all over**: since a child's nurse saw to all the 'heavy-duty' chores (carrying, washing, suckling, etc., cf. 19.401–4, 482–3, *Iliad* 6.466–8), she would probably be in physical contact with the child more than the mother. It is as if Eurykleia, recognising the man after twenty year's absence, recalls the moment when he was a babe in her arms (cf. 'my dear child' 474 with 'my lord' 475). Eurykleia recounts this incident at 23.73–7.

479. **Athene turned aside her perception**: given the clatter of the basin (469), and the spilling of the water (470), it was necessary for the poet to invoke Athene's intervention to explain why Penelope paid no attention. Odysseus takes his own precautions at 507.

485. **you have learned . . . the god put it**: a neat example of the 'double motivation' for actions so common in Greek literature. Cf. 488, 22.346–8.

486. **let nobody else . . . know of it**: this would have been an even more dangerous moment for Odysseus had the suitors been present (which is why Odysseus took precautions about the meeting—see on 17.569). Odysseus has already had to think fast during this encounter (379–85, 388–91), and control himself (209–12); but now he must act fast.

490. **when I kill**: as he will (22.440–72), through the offices of Telemachos.

501. **I myself will properly study each**: see on 16.304–5, 316. Odysseus gets some idea of who are loyal, who disloyal at 20.1–21, to add to the information he has already gathered.

502. **Leave it . . . silence**: Lattimore has reversed the order of the sentiments. The Greek says (literally) 'But hold your word in silence, and entrust (*something not stated*) to the gods'. 'Your word' presumably means the account of the maidservants which Eurykleia had promised (497–8). If Odysseus is replying to Eurykleia in reverse order (cf. on 11.181–203), 'entrust (*something*) to the gods' may refer to Eurykleia's hopes at 496 (cf. 488), i.e. 'trust the gods to bring about my victory'. On the other hand, Odysseus may be telling Eurykleia to entrust *speaking* to ('the care of') the gods, (cf. 22.288–9), i.e. keep quiet and let the gods do the talking.

511. **for one delicious sleep takes hold of**: i.e. whomever sleep takes hold of. For Penelope's sad days and nights, cf. also 20.83–7.

518. **Pandareos' daughter**: Pandareos was king of Crete and had a daughter Aedon (= 'nightingale' 518). She married Zethos (522), and had one child Itylos (522). But one of her sisters-in-law, Niobe, had many children. In jealousy, Aedon decided to kill Niobe's eldest boy; but in the

darkness she chose the wrong child and killed Itylos (523). Zeus, taking pity on her, turned her into a nightingale so that she could pass her life lamenting her son's death (518–21). For the sequence—'no sleep-simile-helpful reply' cf. 4.787ff. Penelope recalls Pandareos' daughters again at 20.61–83.

524.   **so my mind is divided**: the point of comparison between Penelope and Aedon is Penelope's division of mind and Aedon's 'varying . . . manifold' lamentation (520–1). But there is a general comparison between Penelope's sorrow (517) and Aedon's (521), and a more remote one between Penelope's and Aedon's loss of someone infinitely precious to them.

525–34.   **Shall I stay . . . devouring**: Penelope summarises her problem: while Telemachos was young (530), she was right to stay (525–7), but now he is mature (531–2, cf. 18.269–70) he begs her to leave and the suitors press her (528–9). This cento of ideas is typical (see 11.178–9 (525), 7.225 (526), 16.75–7 (527–9), 4.371 (530), 18.270 (531), 18.217 (532), and for 533–4 cf. 16.126–8 (= 1.249–51). But it is worth pointing out that nowhere in our *Odyssey* does Telemachos openly order his mother to leave the house, though the sentiments are certainly his (16.73–7, 125–8), (cf. on 158). However, when challenged in public, he has stood up for her (2.130–7). As for the role of the people, they supported Penelope in her decision while Telemachos was young (527), and Telemachos has also acknowledged that he will not incur their resentment by ejecting Penelope (2.130–7): he certainly does not feel they hate him (16.114). Cf. Telemachos' fencing at 20.341–4. The point that emerges strongly from all this is that Penelope is on her own: only *she* can make the decision to stay or leave.

535.   **interpret it for me**: the trust Penelope is placing in the beggar here is justified (see on 253–4). If it seems odd to ask a beggar to interpret a sign, remember that Odysseus was claiming to be brother of Idomeneus, whose grandfather was Minos (11.568–71). With such a paternity, the beggar has a good claim to authority on this sort of matter.

537.   **I love to watch them**: cf. 541 'I began to weep', 543 'sorrowing'. The problem with Penelope's dream is that she seems to love her geese and grieve at their death, but the geese are the suitors. Whence then the sorrow? Many have been tempted to seek psychoanalytical explanations (Penelope's secret attractions to the suitors, etc.), but there is no need for such subtlety. The whole point about the dream is that it *is* baffling, and that is why Penelope needs help with its meaning. On bird omens, see 2.146–54. Note how often birds recur in omens and similes at important moments, e.g. 5.337, 13.86–8, 16.217, 19.518, 20.242, 22.302, 24.538, cf. 1.320, 3.372.

556.   **since Odysseus himself has told you**: clever irony.

562.   **There are two gates**: Vergil used this passage at *Aeneid* 6.893ff. when he described Aeneas emerging into the upper world from the Underworld. Cf. 24.12–13.

571.   **This dawn will be a day of evil name**: Penelope makes her fateful decision to re-marry, the conclusion to the earlier public announcement (18.251–80) and to days and nights of heart-searching (19.509–34).

572.   **for now I will set up a contest**: the famous problem of the axes: how

were they set up, and how did the archer shoot an arrow *through* them? The crucial points are: (a) 19.574–5: set up, the axes look like the trestles on which a ship's keel was placed when construction began. (b) 19.578: the arrow goes *through* the axes, cf. 586, 21.114, 21.422–3. (c) 21.118–21: the axes are set in a line, in a trench. (d) 21.420: Odysseus sits to shoot, but could stand (19.575). (e) 21.421–2: Odysseus does not miss 'any axes from the first handle on': literally, 'Odysseus did not miss the *prōtē steileiē* ('first handle' or 'handle-tip') of all the axes'. (e) is crucial. What is the *prōtē steileiē*? Some have taken it to mean a *hole* in the axe, either where the axe-handle fitted or somewhere else, but *steileiē* seems to mean 'handle', not 'hole' (cf. 5.236, *steileion*, 'handle'), *prōtē* means 'first' or 'top' or 'outermost, on the edge'. Many solutions have been proposed, but the evidence does not seem to point decisively one way or another. The Greeks illustrated (on vases) Odysseus shooting the bow and killing the suitors, but never the trial of the axes. They probably did not understand the mechanics of the situation either. We are surely in the world of folktale. For those who are interested, I supply hypothetical reconstructions of the trial taken from *LV* and Page's *FHO*, and add the following comments:

1. See on 21.62 for possible evidence that the axes must be *double*-axes.
2. The axes are never used during the battle in the hall. Are they handle-less? Or ornamental?
3. If the note at 21.62 is correct, the axes must be light enough for the maids to carry. See *CH* 518–20.

590.   **and entertain me**: there is nothing suggestive about this. Penelope is confirming that Odysseus has been as entertaining a story-teller as Eumaios had prophesied (17.513–21). But it is ironical, in that Penelope is using language that would be appropriate between husband and wife—only she does not know that the beggar is her husband. In good time she will hear his story, re-united with him in the marriage bed (23.300–43, esp. 308–9).

598–9.   **but you can sleep**: Penelope's instructions are brusque, to say the least; and when she departs, she falls asleep thinking of Odysseus (603–4). There is no suggestion of any sensual 'electricity' sparking off between her and the beggar. But there is irony: at 23.295 Odysseus and Penelope *will* share the bed from which Odysseus is strictly barred at the moment.

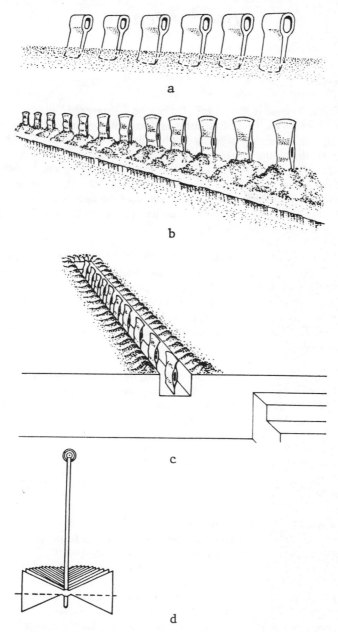

Hypothetical reconstructions of the axe trial in the Lorenzo Valla edition (a–c) and Page *FHO* (d).

Book twenty

Introduction

A. Whatever Odysseus had in mind when he encouraged Penelope in her decision to set up the trial of the bow and axes at the end of the last book (19.582–7)—and it is not exactly clear what that is (see *19F* and on 20.39)—it is natural that, with the climax now at hand, Odysseus should have a night of doubt (see on 30, 43, 100). But a combination of Athene's promises (45–53), Penelope's despair (92–4) and two omens (103–4, 120–1) reassures Odysseus, and further indications of the wickedness of the suitors and some of the servants (5–13, 176–82, 284–302) reconfirm in Odysseus and Telemachos the need for action (183–4, 384–6).

B. The omens too are building. At 19.535–53, Penelope reported a favourable dream; Odysseus receives two omens from Zeus early on in Book 20 (see above): while Theoklymenos' vision is the most powerful foreshadowing yet of what is to come (351–70). More help emerges in the shape of Philoitios (185–237) and Eumaios joins in his prayer for Odysseus' return (238–9). Meanwhile it is clear that Telemachos is now playing a more confident role in the palace than ever before (see on 266, and on 304–19, 320–37, 338–44 and 345 for contrasts with Telemachos' response to the suitors in 2.46–145). All this, combined with the suitors' absolute ignorance of the true meaning of what they are doing and its consequences (358–62, 373–80, 390–4) and further evidence vouchsafed to the reader that all will be well (88–90, 240–7, 393–4) develops in the reader a powerful sense that a triumphant climax is at hand.

In other words, Book 20 produces in Odysseus the conviction that his decision at 19.582–7 to push the matter to its conclusion was right and that he now has the human and divine backing he needs to see it through successfully.

C. But it would be repugnant if the slaughter of the suitors were not seen to be morally justified. Theoklymenos' supernatural vision (especially 367–70), Athene's and Zeus' willing support for Odysseus (45–53, 102, 393) and the witness of the lowly to the ruthlessness of the suitors' behaviour (116–9, and especially Philoitios' comment at 213–7 which describes precisely what the suitors intend and links wickedness with divine judgement as Eumaios had done at 14.83–4) all help to make up an irresistible case against them. Finally, even though their last day on earth is to be a feast-day in celebration of Apollo, the poet is careful to distance the suitors from any close involvement in the rituals due to a god at such a time (see on 276–83).

D. Book 20 is just as much the book of final decision for Penelope as it is for Odysseus. She announced her decision to re-marry at the end of Book 19. But she gave no indication of time-scale, though the beggar urged her to act at once (19.584). In Book 20, she is for the first time unambiguous about her belief in Odysseus' *death* (79–82, cf. e.g. 1.342–4, 4.722–6, 17.539–40, 18.202–5, 19.136, 19.313), and characterises as *evil* a dream which brought him strongly to mind as he was twenty years ago (87–90). At the end of the book, she has heard her son saying that he urges her to re-marry (341–2), and Theoklymenos' prophecy, not that Odysseus will return, but that the evil is coming upon the suitors (see on 388). With whatever hopes and fears (see e.g. 21.54–7), she at once moves to set up the trial of the bow and axes and settle her fate one way or another (21.1ff.).

2–3.   **hide of an ox/fleeces**: the profligacy of the suitors' destruction of Odysseus' herds and flocks was implied when the suitors were introduced for the first time (1.108–9). For the size of Odysseus' holdings, see 14.95–108, 20.211–3.

6–7.   **out of the palace issued/. . . the suitors**: the women were going to sleep with the suitors, who returned to their own homes every evening (see on 1.424).

10–30.   **much he pondered . . . suitors**: see on 17.235 for typical 'pondering' scenes. Usually such scenes result in a decision, one way or the other. Here Odysseus decides to endure the maids' faithlessness (18), but as Odysseus remembers his endurance in the Cyclops' cave (18–21), he looks back also to the intelligence which saw him through to victory over the Cyclops. This triggers off a second thought: how to kill the suitors (since he can hardly kill the maids otherwise)? So one problem is solved—his heart endures the maids' faithlessness (23)—and another arises: he twists and turns physically and mentally (28–9) wondering how to kill the suitors (29–30).

14.   **as a bitch**: this simile, like the one of the paunch-pudding (25–30), is homely and familiar, drawing its subject from the everyday life of the palace (for dogs, see Argos at 17.290–327, for puddings see 18.44–5). Odysseus' heart growls like a dog which sees its own pups (= maidservants) threatened by another man (= suitors).

19.   **Cyclops ate up**: see 9.287–98, 344, and *9H*.

20.   **intelligence**: the same word (*mētis*) as is translated 'perfect planning' at 9.414 (see note there).

23–4.   **the heart . . . endured . . ./but the man himself**: another contrast between the external look and the internal reality (see *17A* and 18.3–4).

30.   **Athene**: in the *Odyssey* this is the only occasion when a divinity helps to solve the problem raised in a scene of pondering. (The gods often intervene for this purpose in the *Iliad*, e.g. 1.188–95.) Homer increases the tension of the narrative by Odysseus' doubts about his ability to win back his home at the very moment when the climax is at hand. See further 37–43 (and notes), 100 and cf. on 10.53 for another moment of paralysis.

34–5.   Here is your . . . long for: Athene reminds Odysseus in specific terms (house . . . wife . . . son) of the reasons why he had fought so long and hard to get home, when there were so many other possibilities (e.g. Kalypso). Cf. 5.219–20, 9.33–6. Note the tribute to Telemachos (cf. *18C*).

39.   how . . . I can lay hands: see *19F* for the problem here. Athene asks Odysseus to consider this problem at 13.375–6 and Odysseus replies that he is fully confident of her ability to help him (389–91). In Book 20, Athene almost seems to be reminding him of what he said then, since she replies in similar terms (48–51). Cf. 3.218–20 and Odysseus' confidence at 16.259–61. Athene gives Odysseus her full support in the final battle, though not without some preliminary testing (22.236–8).

43.   how shall I make my escape?: Odysseus knows that the relatives and friends of the suitors will try to exact revenge for their slaughter. This theme dominates the end of the *Odyssey* from 23.362 onwards.

64.   misty: this epithet is used of the darkness of the underworld at 11.57 and 11.155.

65.   recurrent: Ocean was thought of as a stream which circled the world (see on 23.244). Perhaps the place referred to here is the same as the place where Odysseus disembarks at the entrance to Hades (11.13–21).

67–83.   Pandareos . . . husband: Penelope returns to the daughters of Pandareos (see 19.518–24). The gods killed their parents (for some unstated reason, 67) but Aphrodite, Hera, Artemis, and Athene looked after the orphans and richly blessed them (68–72); when Aphrodite sought marriage for them from Zeus (73–6), the Harpies (= stormwinds cf. 4.727–8) carried them off for the Furies (goddesses of vengeance) to 'care for', i.e. punish— presumably to atone for the crimes of their parents (for Furies as wreckers of houses, see 15.234 and cf. on 2.135). At 79–83 Penelope wishes to be destroyed in the same way, so that she can meet again her lost husband Odysseus (81) and avoid a hateful re-marriage (82–3). These lines suggest that Penelope sees some sort of connection between herself and Pandareos' family. Pandareos was killed for no reason (67)—Odysseus too is dead (81— and no-one knows anything about him): the daughters were blessed by the gods—so too is Penelope (e.g. 2.115–22, 17.37, 18.190–1): they were swept away before marriage, against their will—but Penelope *wants* to be swept away before her *re*-marriage (82–3). This brings out well the depth of Penelope's despair. Her attributes, like Pandareos' daughters', seem to her pointless now that her husband is dead, and she would prefer even destruction to re-marriage to a suitor.
The passage has been regarded as non-Homeric for a number of reasons, especially because it seems to contradict 19.518–24 (not quite true, because the passage in Book 20 does not say the Harpies carried off *all* Pandareos' daughters) and because at 71 and 80 Penelope uses the third person to refer to Artemis, when it is to Artemis that she is praying (but Homer does this elsewhere, e.g. 101, lit. 'let a portent of Zeus show outside').

81.   the Odysseus I long for: wrong translation. Read 'the Odysseus I keep in my mind'.

92–4.   **Great Odysseus . . . already**: is Odysseus awake? asleep? half-awake? Odysseus must be fully awake. First, dawn has risen (91); second, he has heard Penelope's cries of lamentation (92); third, he at once sets about clearing away the bedclothes (95–7); and finally, were he asleep, or half-awake, Homer would have told us (compare Penelope at 4.787–841, who goes through a complex pondering-sleeping-dreaming-waking sequence; note especially 793–4, 809). What is the nature of his mental vision ('pondering' 93, cf. 4.793)? There seem to be two possibilities. *Either* Odysseus, hearing Penelope crying, starts up in the half-light of dawn and actually thinks for a moment she is present with him; *or* her crying triggers off in his mind a powerful and vivid image of her, having recognised him, there beside him. The latter is preferable, perhaps, on the grounds that it would act as a stimulus to action after his night of doubt and sorrow—re-union with his wife is at hand. Whatever the interpretation, Penelope too has been having the same vivid presentiments as Odysseus (88–90), though this has brought her anguish (87). The vision does not bring anguish to Odysseus: indeed, 'in his mind' (93) could mean 'in accordance with his desires'. 'In his fancy' gets the possible connotations neatly. The juxtaposition of the two visions emphasises Odysseus' and Penelope's closeness but also their psychological distance.

95–7.   **He rolled together . . . laid it down**: Odysseus gets up and neatly tidies away the bedding provided at 1–4.

97.   **with his hands lifted**: Greeks did not kneel to pray. They stood, and raised their hands.

100.   **send me an omen**: after the doubts of the night, Odysseus seeks confirmation from Zeus that the gods are on his side. The thunder omens are unique to Odysseus.

103–4.   **he sent his thunder . . . clouds**: observe that it is thunder in a cloudless sky (113–4). 'High above the clouds' is to be taken as a conventional description of Olympos. Zeus will thunder again when Odysseus strings the bow (21.413–5). Cf. 24.539. For Zeus' role, see *1.22–95B*.

106.   **the shepherd of the host**: i.e. Odysseus.

120–1.   **Odysseus welcomed the ominous/speech**: again the poet reminds us of the value of the lowly. The feeblest slave in the palace here gives hope to her great master. Cf. *14C*.

129.   **have you treated**: the Greek is plural—'have you (*all*) treated'.

136–7.   **For he sat here . . .** **she asked him**: none of this is true. Eurykleia is obviously protecting her mistress from criticism. But what Penelope did offer Odysseus—a wash (19.317–20), to which he eventually agreed (19.343–8)—is suppressed by Eurykleia, presumably because it was during this incident that she recognised Odysseus and was sworn to silence over it (19.485–94). See on *17A* and 7.292–307 for duplicity in the *Odyssey*.

139–43.   **she did tell . . . over him**: see 19.317–8, 336–42, 20.1–4.

149–56.   **To work . . . public festival**: the day opens with the palace being specially cleaned for the feast of Apollo (= 'public festival' at 156, cf. 276–8 and on 14.161–2). Near the end of this fatal day, the palace will require re-cleansing and fumigating after the slaughter of the suitors (22.448–57; 493–4).

158.   **spring**: described at 17.204–11, when Odysseus and Eumaios walk in from Eumaios' hut to the palace.

162.   **the swineherd**: i.e. Eumaios (169), who left the palace at 17.604.

163.   **which were the best**: see 17.599–600, and cf. 20.174.

167.   **do they slight you still . . .?**: since Eumaios left the palace, Odysseus has been attacked by Iros (18.1–107), abused by Melantho (18.321–40), attacked by Eurymachos (18.346–404) and abused again by Melantho (19.65–88). As if to prove the point, Melanthios now turns on him (20.177–84).

173.   **Melanthios**: for Odysseus' encounter with him at the spring, see 17.212–255.

178–9.   **to pester/the gentlemen**: but the suitors had agreed to allow the winner of the Iros-Odysseus encounter the privilege of being the only beggar let in to their feasting (18.46–9).

182.   **other Achaians**: i.e. there are other feasts you could go and beg at, a ripe hypocrisy coming from a friend of the suitors (cf. 1.374–5).

185.   **Philoitios**: this faithful herdsman, who forms an effective 'doublet' with Eumaios (see *17B*), will play an important supporting role in Odysseus' defeat of the suitors.

185.   **leader of people**: see on 14.3.

187.   **The ferryman had brought these over**: from Kephallenia (210), where Odysseus had placed Philoitios in charge of them (209–10). See 14.100–2 for the stocks Odysseus kept elsewhere than in Ithaka.

194.   **he is like a king**: see on 13.397.

195–6.   **Yet . . . princes**: very unclear translation. The Greek itself is awkward, but seems to mean 'when the gods spin disaster for kings too, then wandering beggars are plunged into misery', i.e. since beggars are vulnerable and need all the help they can get from the powerful (cf. 6.206–8), disaster for a king spells disaster for the beggar.

204.   **It has come home to me**: wrong translation. Read 'I broke into a sweat' (a sign of being in the grip of powerful emotions in the ancient world).

204–25.   **My eyes . . . scatter**: Philoitios' feelings about his 'lost master', his reflections on the wealth of Odysseus' household, the depredations of the suitors, the gods' wrath at wrongdoing and his problem about whom to serve next, are typical of such loyal servants. Eumaios makes the same points when he meets Odysseus at 14.40–4, 61–8, 83–108, 132–47. The humble understand far more about the workings of the gods' wrath than the noble suitors.

211.   **marvellously grown**: see on 14.96.

218.   **While the son is here**: it is not just Penelope who is having to decide her future, now that Odysseus appears dead and the suitors do their worst in the palace. But Philoitios remains stubbornly hopeful (224–5).

234.   **you can watch him killing the suitors**: the tremendous confidence

of Odysseus here, so different from earlier doubts (see on 30), remains with him till the final battle (e.g. 22.106–7, 147, 224–35).

241–7. **death . . . them**: when such a plan was proposed by Antinoos, Amphinomos used an appeal to the higher authority of Zeus to stop it (16.394–405). The bird of omen at 242–3 is presumably heaven-sent for the same purpose (273—unless that refers to Book 16). Cf. on 2.146–54 where Zeus sends a bird-omen to support Telemachos.

250–1. **sacrificing . . . sacrificing**: see on 8.59.

259. **little table**: each of the diners has his own table and chair. See e.g. 17.447, 22.19–20, 74.

266. **hold back your spirit for insults**: Telemachos is considerably more hostile to the suitors here than he has been before (cf. his attack on them at 18.406–8, strongly modified at 409). The confidence of Odysseus is rubbing off on him? The suitors at any rate acknowledge his authority (271–2); and Telemachos disregards Antinoos' words (275). Cf. Telemachos' more juvenile reactions and the suitors' obvious dominance at 2.296–336.

276–83. **The heralds . . . Odysseus**: this seems to be a *public* celebration (277) of the feast of Apollo. (N.b. 'communal' 280 is not in the Greek.) If the suitors are part of it, the text does not make that clear; indeed, the suitors seem to have started their own private celebrations earlier (250–6). Homer maintains a distance between the suitors and the people of Ithaka here, and suggests that the suitors are not celebrating the *god* with quite the fervour they might. See on 18.418; cf. 1.225–9.

287. **villainy**: the Greek is *athemistia*, from *a* + *themis* 'lacking *themis*', which = understanding of the right way to behave (see on 14.130). The same accusation is made of the Cyclops (9.189), who understands as little about *xenia* as Ktesippos does here (compare his 'gift' at 296, 299 with the Cyclops' at 9.356, 369–70).

300. **threw it**: at least the other assaults on Odysseus have been provoked. Ktesippos' is motivated purely by desire to mock (see 22.285–91, especially 287).

300–1. **Odysseus avoided/this**: the assaults on Odysseus have been becoming less and less effective (see on 18.396). When Odysseus launches his assault on the suitors (Book 22), it will be his first—and last.

304–19. **Ktesippos . . . palace**: this controlled attack on the suitors contrasts well with one of Telemachos' earlier efforts to get them to mend their ways (2.46–81). In Book 2, Telemachos admits to absolute dependence upon Odysseus (58–9) and personal weakness (60–2); he asks for nothing but to be left alone (70–1); the argument ends in complete disarray (74–6); and he bursts into tears, arousing the pity of the people (80–1). In Book 20, Telemachos makes clear that he will take action if he has to (306–8); challenges the suitors to kill him if they so wish (315–6); sharply commands them to desist (308–9, 314); and asserts his manhood (309–10). He makes no references to dependence on Odysseus, or personal weakness. It is no surprise that the suitors admit the justice and force of his case (320–5). See notes on 320–37, 338–44 and 345 for further comparison with the scene in Book 2.

306.   **I would have struck you**: as Telemachos threatened at 18.63 (cf. 20.266–7).

309–10.   **I now notice all . . . an infant**: when Telemachos claimed to have grown up at 2.312–5, the suitors mocked him (2.323). At 16.69–72, Telemachos seems genuinely unable to cope. Penelope accuses him quite unfairly of immaturity (18.215–25), as perhaps a final, despairing assertion of authority over the son she admits has grown up (18.175–6, 269–70, 19.530–2). Telemachos' reply is calm and reasonable (18.227–32). Here in Book 20, Telemachos' assertion of adulthood is greeted with respect (320–3). There is clearly a clever progression here. See on *kleos* at 13.422.

320–37.   **So he spoke . . . of another**: there are again important comparisons with the scene in Book 2.85–128 (see on 304–19 above). When Antinoos replies in Book 2 to Telemachos' pleas, he is immediately hostile (85–6); blames Penelope outright (86–7); tells Telemachos what to do (111–4); and accompanies his instructions with outright threats (123–8). Agelaos' reply in Book 20 is appeasing in tone. He admits Telemachos has a case (322–5); offers gentle advice (326); argues his case reasonably; and makes no threats (334–7). 334 'sit beside your mother' is a nice touch.

321.   **Agelaos**: we have not met this suitor before. He is a reasonable man, of the same sort as Amphinomos (see on doublets, *17B*). He will lead the suitors in battle at 22.241ff. and be killed at 22.292–3.

336–7.   **So you . . . another**: a lie. The suitors have no intention of leaving the palace once Penelope is married (see *1.96–324F*). (Cf. 16.383–92, where the second alternative is not seriously proposed, and the sarcasm of 1.402–4.)

338–44.   **Then the . . . makes of it**: compare again the scene at 2.129–45. In Book 2, Telemachos adduces a battery of arguments to counter Antinoos. In Book 20, he hardly bothers to argue, but puts the responsibility for the decision firmly on Penelope's shoulders. There is a self-confident authority about Telemachos here.

342.   **them**: not in the Greek, and wrong. Read 'him' i.e. the successful suitor. See on 2.53.

345.   **In the suitors**: at 2.146, Zeus sends an omen in support of Telemachos which foretells the death of the suitors (160–7). Here Athene is involved with an omen with the same message (367–70). It is greeted with the same lack of comprehension (373–83, cf. 2.177–86).

346.   **uncontrollable laughter**: the suitors are used to laughing among themselves at other people's expense (358, 374 and see on 18.342). The laugh is now very much on them (347, 353–4).

347–57.   **Now they laughed . . . come over**: presumably only Theoklymenos can *see* the horrible vision he describes in this passage. 347–9 describe the effect that Athene's intervention has in the eyes of him who can observe it. Supernatural forces combine to reveal the true meaning of the suitors' incursion into Odysseus' household. The suitors think Theoklymenos has lost his senses (360, 380), but it is they who have lost theirs (on appearance vs. reality, see *17A* and cf. 390–5). By such means the poet reinforces our sense of their wickedness, and so justifies Odysseus' revenge on them (cf. 367–70). For the other supernatural condemnation of human behaviour (Odysseus' men eating the cattle of the sun-god) see 12.393–6. See Stanford *ad loc.* for references in folk literature and epic to supernatural interventions involving night and blood which foreshadow death. See on 348, 354, 355, 356 (and cf. 367–8) for the fulfilment of Theoklymenos' prophecy.

348.   **mess of blood**: the food is mixed with blood and dust at 22.17–21.

350.   **Theoklymenos**: the prophet encountered by Telemachos at 15.222–81 and welcomed into the palace at 17.71–85. He prophesies to Penelope at 17.150–65, but since then has not been mentioned. His 'big moment' is now at hand (see *15C* for analysts' problem with Theoklymenos).

354.   **the walls bleed**: for the cleansing of the palace after the slaughter, see 22.493–4.

355.   **the forecourt . . . the yard**: *prothuron . . . aulē* in Greek. This prophecy is fulfilled at 22.448–50 (*aulē*), 457–60 (*aulē*), 473 (*prothuron . . . aulē*).

356.   **down to the underworld**: the prophecy will come true at 24.1ff.

372.   **Peiraios**: see 15.539–46, 17.71–85.

377.   **this vagabond**: i.e. Odysseus.

383.   **Sicilians**: *Sikeloi* in the text, the Classical Greek term for the inhabitants of E. Sicily (Thucydides 6.2–3)—and possibly the Homeric term too. But at 24.307, Homer uses the term *Sikaniē* which Herodotus (7.170) says is the *ancient* term for Sicily. So *Sikeloi* may indicate not the original inhabitants of Sicily, but a later immigrant (?) people. Archaeology shows strong trade links between Sicily and the Mycenaeans, and Syracuse was colonised by Corinthians in 733. We are in no position to judge whether this reference to the *Sikeloi* derives from the Mycenaean period or from the 8thC., but the implication is that the Sikels were slave-traders. Cf. 24.211 and on 18.85.

385.   **always waiting**: see *19F* for the implications of this line.

388.   **just outside the door**: the meaning of the Greek is disputed, but since Penelope went to bed at 19.600–4, 'near the door of her upper-storey room' would give good sense. (21.5 does not *necessarily* mean that she is on the ground floor.) But Penelope does not seem to be listening secretively (cf. on 17.492). She will have heard Telemachos asserting his authority over the house at 304–19 and over her at 341; and Theoklymenos' prophecy, especially 367–70. These events may have confirmed her decision, revealed in 19.570–81, to set up the trial of the bow and the axes. She moves to get them at 21.1ff.

391.   **they had made a very big sacrifice**: again, the Greek could simply mean 'they had slaughtered many beasts'. See on 276–83, and cf. on 250–1. This feast will in fact be 'unpleasant' (392)—see on *17A*.

Book twenty-one

Introduction

A. This is the book of the bow. The bow has a rich and important history (9–41; see especially on 14) and though it is now but a memory of Odysseus, it attaches Odysseus to a heroic past and recalls what he was like as a young man in the palace (21, cf. on 17. 293–4 and the story of the scar in Book 19). No wonder that Penelope weeps when she takes it out (54–7). In handing over the bow, Penelope seems to be giving her final farewell to Odysseus himself.

Rather like Sophocles' *Philoctetes*, Book 21 is shaped around the bow: who has it? How are they treating it? What are they doing with it? First, it moves through the hands of the faithful and loyal—from Penelope, its rightful guardian in Odysseus' absence, to Eumaios (80–4) and on to Telemachos (124). The 'young pretender' would have strung it, had not Odysseus stopped him (128–30). From its rightful owners it then moves to the other side (135–9 are the important verses of transition). Almost as if it has a life of its own, it proves intractable in the suitors' hands. After their efforts have failed (184–5, 245–7), Antinoos proposes to put the bow aside till tomorrow (259–68).

B. Odysseus, who has been a silent onlooker while the suitors have struggled to string his bow, now intervenes and a tense debate ensues over the bow's destination (273–377). After the usual bullying and hypocrisy from the suitors, (305–10, 320–9, 359–65) and a moment of dramatic hesitation (366–8), Telemachos, whether intentionally or not (see on 376), defuses the situation and after twenty years the bow finally rests in the hands of its rightful owner (379). The simple but rich simile describing the ease with which Odysseus strings this familiar object places the bow at the very centre of the epic (see on 406–8). The bow has gone full circle—from its guardian, through its next master, over to the enemy and finally back to its present master.

The tense and absorbing struggle for the bow inside the hall is counterpointed by Odysseus' secret preparations outside the hall for the suitors' slaughter (188–244, 380–92). The suitors are as ignorant of those preparations as they are of the real significance of the struggle for the bow which is taking place before their eyes. It is wholly in keeping with their nature that they yield the bow to Odysseus with a laugh (376–7). It will be their last laugh on earth.

1.   **Athene put it in the mind**: there is no contradiction with 19.571–81. Penelope is waiting for the right moment to set up the trial (20.387–9), and Athene now intervenes to indicate this is it.

3.   **gray iron**: i.e. the axes.

4.   **the beginning of the slaughter**: it is unlikely that these words are part of Penelope's thought processes. They are either part of Athene's or a poetic aside (see *19F*).

9–42.   **of the chamber . . . chamber**: note the intricate ring-composition (see on 1.10) of the whole digression:

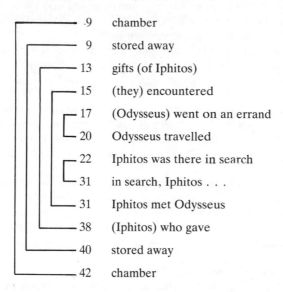

.9	chamber
9	stored away
13	gifts (of Iphitos)
15	(they) encountered
17	(Odysseus) went on an errand
20	Odysseus travelled
22	Iphitos was there in search
31	in search, Iphitos . . .
31	Iphitos met Odysseus
38	(Iphitos) who gave
40	stored away
42	chamber

The bow is the subject of a long digression of the sort that Homer typically grants to objects of high significance.

9.   **chamber**: presumably not the same chamber or store-room as that overseen by Eurykleia at 2.337–47. If it is, it cannot be from long disuse (as Stanford suggests) that the doors roar as they do on being opened (48–50).

10.   **difficulty**: read 'difficultly'.

11.   **backstrung**: the Greek word *palintonos* means either 'springing back' (= 'elastic'), or 'bent back'. For horn in a bow, see *Iliad* 4.105–11.

14.   **Eurytos**: Eurytos is the great archer mentioned by Odysseus at 8.222–8, who was killed by Apollo for challenging him to an archery contest (8.227–8). Eurytos, according to some traditions, had been trained by Apollo, and used a bow which Apollo had given him (he even taught Herakles how to shoot). It was this bow which Iphitos inherited (32–3) and gave as a gift to Odysseus (13–14, 31–2). It is no ordinary bow that Odysseus will wield to kill the suitors, but one originating from the archer-god himself.

15.   **Messene**: according to Homer, this is a town in Lakedaimon (13), whose chief city is Sparta (4.1–2, with 11.460). We know of no such town so named in Lakedaimon (classical Messene was founded in 369, in the area to the west of Lakedaimon, Messenia). Homer may mean Messenia. If the Ortilochos of 21.16 is the same man as Ortilochos at 3.488–9 (see note), the equation of Messene with Messenia looks likely. In that case, Homer may be referring to an undocumented time when Messenia was regarded as part of Lakedaimon (in the Bronze Age?). Messenia means 'middle-land', and the Pherai of 3.488–9 lay in between the powerful kingdoms of Nestor in Pylos to the west and of Menelaos in Sparta to the east, and may have been the subject of dispute between them. More likely than all of this, Homer's understanding of the geography of the region was hazy.

17–21.   **went there . . . elders**: (17: for 'on an errand', read 'to recover a debt'). Athene excuses herself at 3.365–8 by claiming to be recovering a debt owed her by the Kaukones. For raids, cf. 15.425–9, 16.424–7 and on 4.81–91.

22–3.   **twelve mares/he had lost**: according to some ancient commentators, Autolykos (Odysseus' grandfather— 19.394–8) had stolen the mares and sold them to Herakles. If this is the version Homer had in mind, Iphitos goes to Herakles to recover the mares (25–9) but Herakles kills him and keeps them (29–30).

26.   **Herakles**: it is strange that Herakles should appear as a contemporary of Odysseus since in most traditions Herakles pre-dates the Trojan War (he is aptly placed in the Underworld at 11.601–26, cf. on 8.224. Kirk *NGM* 167–9 suggests that, since Odysseus and his family have so few connections with pre-Trojan mythical figures, Odysseus is a comparatively 'young' hero of myth).

guilty of monstrous actions: i.e. stealing the mares and killing Iphitos who was his *xenos* (27–9). This passage and those in Books 8 and 11 suggest that Homer is seeking to establish some (rather vague) comparisons and contrasts between Herakles and Odysseus, all complimentary to Odysseus. See Clay *WA* 89–96.

28.   **without shame for the watchful gods**: cf. Herakles' disgraceful behaviour here with e.g. Philoitios' remarks at 20.214–5 about the suitors' disregard for *xenia*.

44.   **and drawn it**: see on 17.341.

46–50.   **first she . . . spread open**: controversial. At 1.441–2, Eurykleia left Telemachos' bedroom and closed the door in such a way that it would not bang about. She did this by pulling to a bar *inside* the door by means of a 'strap' attached to it which passed through the door to the outside. She did not *lock* the door. People outside could still enter (see notes *ad loc.*). The door to the treasure chamber may have a simple device of this sort. The 'strap' of Book 1 could be the 'fastening' (46). It has been wound round the 'hook' or 'door-handle' as a small security measure. Equally, the 'fastening' round the 'hook' could be simply some form of external lashing unrelated to any bolting device (21.240–1 does not help either way). But whichever it is, it is clearly not enough to keep secure a treasure chamber. The door to this one has a *lock*, which can only be opened by a 'key' (47). The key must be inserted 'straight' (48) and the 'bolt' (plural in Greek) must be knocked 'upward' (or 'back') (47). We do not know how it worked, but it was obviously rather noisy (48–50).

51.   **high platform**: to keep perishable items (like clothes) off the ground.

55–6.   **laid the bow . . . weeping**: Penelope's simple gestures and tears are profoundly moving. Cf. on 2.80.

62.   **iron and bronze**: 'iron' = the axes. They are called 'iron' by Homer (e.g. 81, 97). They are 'prizes' won by Odysseus, and at *Iliad* 23.850–2 axes are indeed the prize for archery (note that the winner's axes are double-headed—*Iliad* 23.855–6, 882–3, a fact which may be relevant to the problem of the axes (see on 19.572)). 'Bronze' may conceivably refer to other sorts of axes (a bronze war-axe is wielded by Peisandros at *Iliad* 13.612). But since the arrows are bronze-tipped (21.422) and the word for 'box', *ogkion*, (61) may be connected with 'arrow-barb' (*ogkos*), the 'bronze' may refer to more arrows or to the bronze *tip* of the arrows (see AM Snodgrass, *Arms and Armour of the Greeks*, Thames and Hudson 1967, 23). There is perhaps an element of the ceremonial in this display of Odysseus' past prizes.

63–6.   **When she . . . of her**: = 18.208–11 (see on 6.100).

71.   **saying**: 'pretext' is better.

75–9.   **And the one . . . forget it**: = 19.577–81.

83.   **the oxherd**: Philoitios (introduced at 20.185ff.).

91–2.   **a terrible one . . . easily**: the meaning of the word used here— *aaatos*—is uncertain. It is claimed to mean either 'destructive', 'terrible' or 'harmless', 'easy'. Cf. 96–9, and on 22.5.

94.   **I myself have seen him**: Eurymachos too had direct experience of Odysseus before he left for Troy (see 16.442–4).

96.   **So he spoke, but the spirit**: see on 16.435–49.

98.   **he was to be the first**: the poet whets our appetite for the contest to come (22.8–21) and gives the first unambiguous indication that the bow will be the means by which the suitors are slaughtered.

99.   **to whom . . . paid no attention**: far too mild a translation. The Greek says 'whom he was then in the process of dishonouring', i.e. depriving of the *timē* (valuation, status, worth, honour) which was the due of every hero. See on 323, 1.95.

100.   **and encouraged**: see Telemachos' testimony at 17.393–5, and cf. 17.406–8, 478–80.

105.   **I laugh and enjoy it**: Telemachos cannot be laughing because he knows that the climax is approaching (hardly a laughing matter), or that Odysseus will win (he cannot tell). He laughs because Antinoos has unwittingly uttered words of omen: he has acknowledged that the contest will be terrible (91—irony), the bow difficult to string (91–2) and that Odysseus has no equal (93–5). Cf. 20.105–21. See on 2.35.

110.   **You . . . know this**: cf. Antinoos' praise of Penelope at 2.115–22.

111.   **delays**: the word appears nowhere else in Greek literature. The

ancient commentators suggest that it means 'excuses, pretexts' rather than 'delays'.

115–6.   and leave me/sorrowing here in the house: Lattimore catches the ambiguity of the Greek well here. Does Telemachos mean 'if I can do what my father did, Penelope will stay here because I have proved myself worthy of Odysseus', or 'If I can do what my father did, it will be no grief for me if Penelope leaves because I will have proved worthy of Odysseus'? Probably the latter: Telemachos continues to act the part of a young man resigned to losing his mother yet still naturally keen to emulate his father.

117.   take up his father's glorious prizes: The Greek idiom means '*win the prizes*'. Telemachos must be referring to winning the axes of his father, which his father won at archery contests before him (see on 62). He would do this by successfully completing the trial.

119.   took off the sharp sword: see 20.125.

120.   setting up the axes: see on 19.572 for some possible visualisations.

124.   tried the bow: see on 11 and 409 for stringing the bow.

128.   he would have strung it: Telemachos effectively passes another 'test' on his way to demonstrating that he can stand in his father's place (see on *kleos* at 13.422).

132–3.   my hands . . . quarrel: = 16.71–2. The lines fit well in Book 16, where Telemachos argues his inability to defend a *xenos* in his own house, but less well here. See on *16G* for typical ideas attached to Telemachos.

138.   handle: so far we have met doors with handles on the outside (see on 1.442, and on 46–50), but that does not preclude the possibility of there being handles on the inside also—as possibly here. But 'handle' can also mean 'bow-tip' in Greek. So Telemachos may be propping the arrow up not against the door, but against the bow itself. 136–9 = 163–6.

144.   Leodes . . . son of Oinops: possibly significant names. Leodes probably comes from a Greek word meaning 'smooth, soft' (cf. 150), while Oinops means 'Wineface, Winelike', an appropriate father for a son who lurked near the drink (145–6).

147.   he disapproved of . . . the suitors: Fenik makes Leodes a 'double' of Amphinomos (*SO* 192–7) (see 16.397–8) but Agelaos is equally conciliatory (20.321–37).

153–4.   it will sunder . . . soul: Leodes, who is a diviner (145), probably means no more than that the bow will break the suitors' hearts (see 159–62), but his words will come true in a very different sense, for himself no less than others (22.310–29).

177.   a great chair with fleeces upon it: 'broad stool, bench' better. Presumably Antinoos wants to be comfortable while he works. Cf. 19.97–101.

188–227.   Two men . . . to them: an 'intentional recognition' scene. Its closest counterpart is the scene between Laertes and Odysseus at 24.226–348. Note the following common elements: testing comment (193–8/24.309–14); supportive response (200–4/24.315–7); 'I am he' (207/24.321); proof (217–20/24.331–44); examination (222/24.345–6); embrace and tears (223/

24.347–9). The two other major such scenes are with Telemachos (16.178–221) and Penelope (23.1–242). Both show similarities and differences. Note the 'doubt' element (16.194, 23.88–110) which is also a feature of the Laertes scene (24.327–9), and the formulaic 'the sun would have sunk/dawn arose' element at 16.220, 21.226, 23.241. Odysseus proposed the need for more helpers at 16.235–9.

189.   **went out**: as Antinoos had suggested at 89–90.

214.   **I shall get wives . . .**: see 14.61–7 (and note on 14.62).

219.   **that scar**: see 19.388–466. For the problem of Odysseus' disguise, see on 13.397.

236.   **doors that close the hall**: these must be doors leading off the great hall to the women's quarters (238–9, cf. 381–5). They must be closed so that the suitors have no hiding places; and so that traitors among the women cannot intervene (22.158) or communicate with the outside world (cf. 19.151–5, 22.75–8).

240–1.   **Noble Philoitios . . . upon it**: Philoitios carries out these instructions at 388–92 (see note on 380–92).

255.   **A shame . . . to be told of**: cf. 325–9 (see note) and on 2.64–5.

259.   **for the god**: i.e. Apollo (see on 20.149–56).

267.   **dedicating the thighs**: this is probably the first time that the suitors have seriously acknowledged Apollo on his feast-day (see on 20.276–83), and almost the first time they have acknowledged a god at all (see on 18.418). But they will be dead before the sacrifice can be made.

270–3.   **The heralds . . . wanted**: a scene of libation, as if the suitors are retiring (see on 2.432). But see 428–30.

274.   **in crafty intention**: note how Odysseus selects exactly the *right* moment to ask to use the bow (when the suitors have abandoned their efforts). This is typical of the man of *mētis*, who bides his time before moving (see *9H*).

289–3.   **Is it not enough . . . talk**: see 18.46–9, where this promise was made to the winner of the Iros vs. Odysseus contest.

293.   **The honeyed wine has hurt you**: for this typical idea attached to beggars, see 19.121–2, 18.391–2 (= 18.331–2), 18.1–3, 14.463–6. For other descriptions of beggars, see on 17.233.

295.   **the Centaur, famous Eurytion**: the Centaurs, described in Homer as 'mountain-dwelling beast-men' (*Iliad* 1.268)—i.e. not necessarily the half-man, half-horse of later tradition—were invited to the Wedding of the Lapith king Peirithoos (296). But the drink-sodden Eurytion (297, 304) tried to rape Hippodameia, the bride ('did much harm'—298) and was punished for it (299–301). Both the Parthenon and the Temple of Zeus at Olympia carried scenes from battles between Centaurs and Lapiths, which were symbolised as the clash between civilisation and barbarism.

299.   **heroes**: i.e. Lapiths. Observe the irony of Antinoos' comparison. He clearly thinks that the suitors = heroic Lapiths, enjoying a peaceful celebration in the palace (296–7) of a marriage (implied by 298, Hippodameia = Penelope) but disturbed by a drunkard (Eurytion = Odysseus)

who receives a terrible punishment (300–1). In fact, it is the suitors who are behaving barbarically and who will be duly punished (and Melanthios will receive almost exactly the same punishment at Eurytion; see 22.473–6).

308.   **Echetos**: see on 18.85.

323.   **We are ashamed to face the talk . . .**: Eurymachos justifies the suitors' concern that the beggar should string the bow by reference to the traditional values of the heroic world, i.e. that 'worth' (*timē*) (and so respect from others and so future *kleos*) depends upon public assessment (what men say about you), and any diminution of your worth results in shameful diminution of status and prospect of *kleos*. Penelope coolly replies that people who behave as the suitors have done can lay no claim to glory (*eukleia* 'good repute', a word based on *kleos*) (331–3). Iliadic *kleos* was won on the battlefield, but there is a *kleos* of the social world of the *Odyssey* too. See on 1.95.

333.   **Why be concerned over reproaches?**: wrong translation. It means 'why do you consider this (i.e. your inability to string the bow) a disgrace (same word as 'disgrace' at 329)?' Penelope is pointing out that the suitors' behaviour in Odysseus' house (331–3) is so disgraceful anyway that it makes little difference to their 'honour' whether they can string the bow or not.

335.   **son of a noble father**: of no less a hero than Deukalion, in fact, with Idomeneus for a brother. See 19.180–3. But there is fine unintentional irony here too.

347.   **off horse-pasturing Elis**: i.e. Doulichion, etc. (see 1.245–8).

350–8.   **Go therefore . . . eyelids**: almost = 1.356–64. The difference is significant. At 1.358 Telemachos asserts his right to control *muthos* ('words, speech, discussion'), at 21.352, the bow. Words and deeds are the key to heroic success (see 2.272 and on 2.270–80). Telemachos has proved his way with words (see 3.120–5, 20.274, and on 20.304–19): now is the time for the bow (action). Cf. Hektor at *Iliad* 6.490–3. If Penelope's dismissal seems somewhat abrupt, it is necessary for the plot because it removes her from the hall and prepares the ground for the dramatic and moving recognition scene in Book 23.

354.   **house**: the word must mean 'room' here. Penelope will sleep through the slaughter in her familiar world of dreams (23.4, 15–19).

364–5.   **if only Apollo . . . toward us**: i.e. if one of the suitors completes the contest and wins Penelope. In that case, the suitors will control the palace and will have their revenge on Eumaios for disobedience—his body will be left unburied when he dies (363–4, cf. 22.30).

376.   **the suitors laughed happily**: why? The suitors are always game to tease Telemachos, (2.296–336, 20.373–4) and his efforts to demonstrate his authority over Eumaios are amusing. He does not address Eumaios as a master would a slave, but demands obedience because of his greater strength and youth (370, 371). Yet the only punishment for disobedience he can think of is to throw stones at him (370–1). Contrast the suitors' threats at 363–5. In these circumstances it is not surprising that Telemachos confesses himself no match for the suitors (372–5). Is this intentional 'acting-up' by Tele-

machos (20.257)? (Compare his cover-up at 105 and mock admission of weakness at 131 with the stricter line he took with Penelope at 344–53 and the suitors at 20.304–20, 20.262–74). On the other hand, one could argue that Telemachos is reacting immaturely to the tension.

380–92. **Then he called . . . had risen:** see 235–41 and notes. Philoitios here is closing the main gates of the palace (389), lashing them tight shut with a ship's cable (390–1). No-one can now enter the palace from outside; and even if the suitors break out of the main hall (22.75–8), leaving the palace from inside will take that much longer. At 392 'went in' means Philoitios returns to the main hall from the courtyard.

386. **no winged words:** see on 17.57.

395. **to see if worms had eaten the horn:** the flea-ridden dog Argos (17.300) was a symbol of the suitors' maltreatment. But the bow, kept in Penelope's store-room (42–62), bears no signs of decay. For 'horn', see on 11.

406–8. **as when a man . . . peg:** a rich simile because of the associations between Odysseus, Apollo, the bow and the *phorminx* (see on 1.1). Apollo is god of bow and lyre (*Iliad* 1.35–52, 603: note that both hang on pegs (*Iliad* 5.209, *Odyssey* 8.67) and may need new strings (*Iliad* 15.469)); the bow is Apollo's (see on 14); it is Apollo's feast-day (see on 14.161–2); the *phorminx* follows the feast (430). Odysseus is a great archer and often likened to a singer (see on 9.12–13). Finally, the *phorminx* is the means by which the glory of heroes' achievements is immortalised (3.203–5), and the bow the means by which Odysseus will achieve one of his greatest feats for subsequent immortalisation. See Camps *IH* 61–3.

407. **on either side:** rather, 'at either end'.

408. **peg:** pegs were a later invention. The meaning of *kollops* here is disputed. It may mean 'bridge' (they do collapse under the strain); it may mean 'leather strap', to which the string was attached at the bar end of the *phorminx* and by twisting or moving of which the string tension was increased. See A Barker *Greek Musical Writings: 1*, (CUP 1984) 4, 30.

411. **like the voice of a swallow:** (*voice?*). Homer may have chosen to liken the sound of the bow to the song of a swallow because swallows *return* in season to their former nests. Athene appears as a swallow at 22.239.

413. **Zeus . . . thundered:** for Zeus as god of right and wrong behaviour, see on *1.22–95B*. Cf. *22C*.

419. **head grooves:** probably the notch cut into the end of the arrow into which the string fitted.

420–1. **bending the bow/before him:** wrong translation. Read 'aiming straight'.

422. **from the first handle on:** see on 19.572 for the problems of this passage.

428–30. **Now is the time . . . end of the feasting:** heavy with double meaning. The 'feast in the daylight' refers to the ensuing slaughter. There will be the dance and the lyre after it, to maintain the pretence that nothing out of the ordinary has happened (23.133–40). See on 1.152.

432.   **put his sharp sword about him**: Telemachos had taken it off at 119.

434.   **all armed in bright bronze**: i.e., presumably, Telemachos' sword and spear (20.127, 306). Odysseus' men get full defensive armour at 22.113. The 'Dendra' armour, found near Argos in 1960, and dateable to c.1400BC, is full bronze body-armour of a sort that could have given rise to the epithet 'bronze-clad' so common in the *Iliad*, cf. *Odyssey* 1.286. This a heroic, martial scene.

Book twenty-two

Introduction

A. A number of incidents occur in this book which are characteristic of the *aristeia*, one man's heroic feat of arms against a series of powerful enemies. Typical elements in an Iliadic *aristeia*, for example, are: divine exhortation and inspiration of a hero, arming, enthusiasm for battle, the advance of the hero through the ranks, a number of single combats, various counter-attacks, a moment of danger or weakness (often a wounding), a grand duel, and finally victory, with ritual boasting over the dead man. The whole episode is frequently enlivened with similes (often multiple similes) and divine interventions at critical points. See, for example, Diomedes' *aristeia* beginning at the start of *Iliad* 5 and Agamemnon's at the start of *Iliad* 11.

B. It is obvious that the conditions which apply to battle in the hall in the *Odyssey* 22 are radically different from those that apply to the battlefield. First, the arena for conflict is the palace, not an open field, and battle is joined by subterfuge, before the opposition realises that a battle is going to take place at all. Second, until his arrows run out (119), Odysseus is fighting exclusively with a bow, a weapon which scarcely encourages Iliadic hand-to-hand conflict, and it is with this instrument that he despatches his two deadliest rivals Antinoos (14–21) and Eurymachos (81–8) at the very start of the contest. Third, the odds are so numerically stacked against Odysseus that before ever the contest starts he has organised some help, in the shape of Telemachos, Eumaios and Philoitios. These have a part to play—indeed, one of the functions of Book 22 is to show how those loyal to the household, under Odysseus' leadership, finally bring to an end the rule of the suitors in the palace—and so must, to some extent, detract from the mighty achievements of one man.

In these ways, the battle in the hall in the *Odyssey* cannot be said to fit the *aristeia*-structure typical of the *Iliad*. Yet there are distinctive *aristeia* elements present. For example, divine inspiration has spurred Odysseus on ever since Book 13, and cf. 20.32–53, 22.233–5. There is an arming scene (108–25). Enthusiasm for battle is shown at 203–4. At 233–5, Athene urges Odysseus to follow her forward into the attack, after which a number of mass and individual combats is joined, with counter-attacks from the suitors (241–96). Moments of weakness and slight wounding occur at 147–8, 208–9, 277–81, and while there is no single, climactic grand duel (the two main suitors have been killed with the bow at the start of the contest), there is the scene of triumph at the end (381–417), but *without* any ritual cries of triumph (see note on 412). The whole is enlivened with runs of similes

(299–309, 381–9, 401–6) and divine interventions (205–40, 256, 273, 297–8—see on 205), typical of the *Iliad*. So there is much in Book 22 to remind us of a hero's triumphant feat of arms (see on 384), suitably modified to the special circumstances of this battle in the palace.

C. In one important respect, however, the battle is very unIliadic, that is, in the moral judgements that are made about its outcome. The death of the suitors is seen as the triumph of good dealing over evil (374, cf. 35–41, 63–4, 287–9, 317) and is firmly ascribed to the gods (413–7). The poet here reminds us of the moral programme which he laid out at the start of the epic (1.26–43). The suitors have been destroyed not by fate but by their own recklessness, just like Aigisthos (1.32–6) and Odysseus' companions on his travels (1.7–9). They were not forced to behave in the way they did. They chose to, and paid the price. The hideous deaths visited upon the maid-servants (465–72) and Melanthios (473–6), and the mercy accorded Phemios and Medon (330–80), are parts of the same pattern of justified revenge.

D. When the battle is done, the house is purified (493–4) and the household gathers to greet and re-acknowledge its rightful lord (495–501). But the house is not quite fully restored to right order (440): the reunion of Odysseus and Penelope, intentionally delayed by Homer (428–32, and see on 487), is yet to be completed.

1.   **stripped his rags**: but not entirely (see 488–9, cf. 23.113ff.). Odysseus is not recognised at this point. He announces himself (35–41) and even then Eurymachos has his doubts (45). See on 13.397.

2.   **the great threshold**: where Telemachos placed Odysseus' chair and table (20.257–9). Odysseus shot the arrow from his chair (21.420). See on 17.339.

5.   **without any deception**: doubtful translation. Odysseus here uses the same word (*aaatos*) as Antinoos had used of the contest at 21.91 (see on 21.91–2). If the word does have two different meanings, its use here is richly ironical.

7.   **Apollo**: for his significance, see on 21.406–8.

10.   **goblet of gold**: the ancient grammarian Dionysios from Thrace claims that the saying we know as 'there's many a slip 'twixt cup and lip' derives from this moment.

11.   **so as to drink**: continuing after the libation poured at 21.263–73.

13.   **many men at their feasting**: it is appropriate that the suitors who have acted throughout the *Odyssey* contrary to every principle of correct behaviour—forcing their way into Odysseus' palace, misappropriating his goods, abusing his family and denying the courtesies of *xenia* to others (cf. 35–81)—should be slain during what would be, in any other context, a time for fellowship and conviviality. Cf. on *1.96–324C*, 1.130–50, *9E*, *14C*. See also 2.244–51 and compare Agamemnon's death at 11.415 (see note there).

18–21.   **thick jet . . . together**: the bloodiness of Antinoos' death recalls the way in which the Cyclops treated Odysseus' men (e.g. 9.287–98). See *9H*. (Cf. Theoklymenos' vision at 20.345–70, especially 348.)

20.   **the table**: see on 20.259.

25.   **never a shield there nor . . . spear**: they had been removed by Odysseus and Telemachos at 19.1–52. All the suitors have is swords (74). Eurymachos suggests they use their individual tables for shields (74).

30.   **the vultures shall eat you**: because Odysseus will be left unburied. But it is the suitors who will, in the event, be left unburied until 24.412–9.

34.   **darkly**: see on 8.165.

37.   **forcibly**: we have seen no example of this in the *Odyssey* (quite the reverse—e.g. 20.6–8—but cf. 16.108–9 (with note), 20.318–9). But it is a legitimate accusation for Odysseus to make in the circumstances.

38–40.   **fearing . . . future**: see on 1.7, 34, *1.22–95A,B* for the morality that lies at the heart of the *Odyssey*.

47.   **much in the country**: through the depredation of flocks (14.90–108).

52–3.   **kill him . . . and then be king**: see 4.660–72, 16.376–86. There is no reference in the *Odyssey* to Antinoos' plans to usurp the throne without marrying Penelope, but there are many places where it is clear the suitors simply regard Penelope as a means to an end (see *1.96–234F*). It is a natural accusation for the hypocritical Eurymachos to make at this juncture. Odysseus learnt of the suitors' plot to kill Telemachos at 13.425–8.

54–67.   **Then spare . . . destruction**: compare the climax of the *Iliad* where Achilles threatens Hektor (*Iliad* 22.268–72) and where he refuses to return Hektor's body for compensation (338–54).

55.   **we will make public reparation**: misleading. The Greek says 'making good among the people'. It seems hard on the 'people' that they should have to pay for the suitors' extravagance. But the practice is acknowledged: at 13.14–15, Alkinoos says he will pay for Odysseus' gifts through a public collection.

57.   **twenty oxen**: see on 1.428–35 for comparative values.

76.   **from the doors and the threshold**: see on 21.380–92.

81.   **crying his terrible cry**: a typical element in a battle between charging warriors, e.g. *Iliad* 5.302.

91.   **but now Telemachos**: as predicted at 18.155–6. For Amphinomos, see *16E, 17B*.

92.   **spear**: see on 21.434. This is the first martial encounter in which Telemachos has ever engaged. He is not the weakling he pretended to be or feared he was (21.131–3).

96.   **for fear**: Telemachos is reacting intelligently to a situation which he is not experienced to handle. Retreat in such circumstances is not regarded as cowardly. (Cf. *Iliad* 15.585–91.) For a successful recovery of spears, see 270–1.

109.   **inner room**: see p. 11. See on 16.281–98 for the problems with this passage (especially that, although Odysseus had planned for armour to be

made available for them at this crisis—16.295–8—in the event it never is). Cf. 1.255–6.

126–8.   **side door . . . way through the alley**: for side door (*orthosurē*) and alley (*laurē*), see p. 11.

131.   **Agelaos**: see 20.321–44.

143.   **vents**: Greek *rhōges*. There is no agreement what these are. On p. 11 *rhōges* are taken to be a winding side-alley leading off the main hall to the arms chamber.

155–6.   **I left . . . angle**: clumsy. Literally 'Opening the well-fitted door of the chamber, I left it (open)'. Presumably it could be fastened somehow (157). It is closed at 201.

174.   **fasten boards behind him**: if this is the right meaning, Melanthios' legs and arms are to be racked round a plank fixed to his back before being tied. He is then hoisted up to the ceiling (173, 175–6, 189–90, 192–3). That his hands and legs should be bound before the plank is put in position (173–4) is probably nothing more than Homeric *husteron-proteron* (see on 3.464–7); but it is odd that no mention is made of the plank when Eumaios and Philoitios are said to be carrying out Odysseus' instructions (188–93). But is 'soft bed' (196) an ironical reference to it? (See 17.244–6 for Melanthios' soft life and cf. 15.330–4). Herodotus 9.120 and Aristophanes *Thesmo.* 931, 940 describe such a punishment.

185.   **of the hero Laertes**: another flash-back to a past apparently long gone, when Laertes, Odysseus' father, (see on 1.188–93) was a young man. If 184 suggests that Laertes' heroic days are over, the return of Odysseus will rejuvenate him (24.365–82, 513–25).

199.   **goats to the palace**: as at e.g. 20.172–5.

205.   **Athene**: the contest of the bow is Apollo's domain. But Apollo is not the patron god of the *Odyssey*. That role is reserved for Athene, Odysseus' protectress. Now that the bow has done its work, she can take control—testing her favourite (237–8), foiling the enemy (256 = 273) and finally routing them (297–309). See on 1.44. There is no doubt whose the glory is for the final victory of Odysseus.

206.   **likening herself . . . to Mentor**: as she had done at 2.401, a disguise maintained while she accompanied Telemachos to Pylos (e.g. 3.22). Mentor himself had been entrusted with looking after Odysseus' palace while he was gone (2.224–7; cf. 17.68). See on 1.188–93.

209.   **done you much good**: since Odysseus has recognised that Mentor is Athene in disguise (210 cf. 24.445–9), it is likely that the vocabulary of sacrifice in the phrase 'done you much good' (also = 'sacrificed many things to you') is intentional wordplay.

'**We . . . together**: the Greek says 'you are of the same age as me'. See on 2.225–7 for the problem.

226–35.   **No longer . . . kindness**: note how Athene recalls Odysseus to the heroism of his Trojan days. She makes no reference to intervening years of travel over the high seas. These are irrelevant now that Odysseus has thrown off his disguise and is in open conflict against a numerically superior enemy. Athene here fulfils the promises of e.g. 13.393–6, 20.45–53. Such challenges from a god to her favourite are typical, cf. *Iliad* 5.799–834.

230. **by your counsel**: i.e. the Wooden horse (cf. 1.2, 8.492–5).

232. **you complain, instead of standing up to the suitors**: wrong translation. The Greek says (literally) 'you lament to be brave', i.e. 'you lament (saying that you want) to be brave (but cannot be)'. Cf. *Iliad* 2.290, *Odyssey* 5.153. Odysseus is hardly lamenting (Athene overstates her case, to taunt and inspire Odysseus) but he does ask for help at 208, which suggests to Athene that he does not feel ready for the task in hand (cf. Odysseus' doubts at 20.37–43, which Athene must have thought she resolved at 20.45–53). Athene taunts Odysseus because, while he was brave at Troy (226–230), he lacks courage now.

239. **in their sight**: i.e. of Odysseus' men, but certainly not of the suitors (249–50).

shot up: a strange thing to do when she had urged Odysseus to stand beside her at 233.

242–3. **Demoptolemos . . . Polybos**: of these, we have met before or will meet again outside the context of this battle Amphimedon (24.103), Peisandros (18.299), and Eurynomos (2.21–2).

267. **Euryades . . . Elatos**: otherwise unmentioned by Homer.

287. **Polytherses**: significant name, 'of much brashness'.

288–9. **recklessness . . . gods**: Philoitios makes the connection between human folly and divine punishment which is so important a feature of this book.

290. **that hoof**: see 20.287–319. It is appropriate that Ktesippos, who threw an ox-hoof at Odysseus, should be killed by the oxherd Philoitios (285).

294. **Leokritos**: here he receives the retribution awaiting him since 2.242–56.

297. **aegis**: in later Greek art the aegis is a short cloak worn by Athene over the shoulders or the left arm, with a border of snakes and Gorgon-head in the middle. In Homer, it seems to be some sort of weapon or armour, which can be used for attack and defence, by Zeus and others (cf. *Iliad* 15.307–11, 17.593–6, 21.400–1). Athene puts it on as if it were a breastplate at *Iliad* 5.738–42, and inspires battle-lust with it at *Iliad* 2.446–54.

299–309. **like a herd of cattle . . . broken**: there are two similes here. 299–301 describe the suitors in flight like cattle stung by a gadfly; 302–9 describe Odysseus' men (= 'the other men' 302, 'these men' 307) pursuing the suitors like vultures hunting birds. Combination similes are used frequently in the *Iliad* at moments of high importance, e.g. 2.455–83. See on 2.146–54.

302. **men, who**: read simply 'men'.

304. **on the plain**: Homer means 'low to the ground' here.

306. **and men are glad for the hunting**: the intrusion of these men would make more sense if they were witnessing an organised spectacle like falconry. But falconry was unknown to ancient Greeks, who caught birds only by

trapping them. The sudden intrusion of human perspective on a natural event is better handled at e.g. *Iliad* 8.559.

310.   **Leodes**: see 21.144–74.

311.   **supplication**: see on 6.142.

314.   **wrong to . . . the women**: cf. 21.146–7, 22.37. But Odysseus has the answer—he must have wished to marry Penelope (321–5).

326.   **a sword**: Odysseus and his men fight with spears, fetched for them by Telemachos (101–15), the suitors with the swords they wear (see on 25).

329.   **while he was still speaking**: i.e. Leodes, who must have continued pleading. It would be unparalleled in Homer for a man to be killed while engaged in a full supplication (i.e. clinging on to the knees, etc.: see on 6.142). Even during Achilleus' rampage in the *Iliad*, supplications are technically broken before he despatches his enemies (20.463–71, 21.115–6, cf. 6.45–65, 10.454–7). Leodes' despair may have been such that he broke it himself anyway (319); or we may assume that, in reaching for Agelaos' sword (326–8), Odysseus automatically broke the contact. But it may be that supplication by an enemy, in the heat of battle, did not have the same force as a peace-time supplication by a complete stranger. But see e.g. 14.276–84. At all events, it is out of the question that Odysseus should be seen to act sacrilegiously here.

330.   **Phemios**: the court singer who was compelled by the suitors to sing for them (350–3), a claim confirmed by 1.153–5.

330.   **Terpias**: significant name—'Delight'.

333.   **pondering**: for such scenes, see on 17.235. It is not surprising that Phemios should ponder which course of action to take after seeing how Odysseus has treated Leodes. Since Telemachos intervenes on Phemios' behalf and asks pity for Medon too (356–60), it is not surprising that Medon should supplicate Telemachos (365), not Odysseus. Odysseus confirms that only Telemachos' word has saved them (372–4).

335–6.   **where once Odysseus/and Laertes . . . burned . . . thighs**: but not, note, the suitors. See on 18.418, 20.276–83. For Odysseus' piety, cf. 1.65–7, 19.365–6.

347.   **taught by myself, but the god has inspired**: it is very common for Greeks to assign the explanation for events to human and divine causation simultaneously, e.g. 19.485–6. See on 1.1 for the relation between poet and Muse.

349.   **as to a god**: cf. e.g. 4.160–1, where Peisistratos flatters Menelaos in identical terms, and 13.230–1 where Odysseus in supplication addresses the disguised Athene as if she were a god.

357.   **Medon**: see on 4.677, 686–95.

363.   **the hide of an ox**: this amusing incident recalls Menelaos' tale of the sealskins at 4.435–56. Skins lie about the palace at e.g. 1.108, 20.96–7.

383.   **lying fallen**: for comparison with the death of Agamemnon, see on 11.415, 419 and cf. on 1.34.

384.   **like fish**: the death of the suitors is a climactic moment in the *Odyssey* and Homer, typically, dwells on it with a simile. See also 402–6,

where Odysseus triumphant is pictured as a lion which has killed and fed on an ox. Lion similes are the commonest of all similes used in the *Iliad* to depict triumphant warriors. Odysseus is the epitome of the Iliadic warrior at this point.

399.   **she opened the doors**: which she had been instructed to close in order to keep the maidservants in (see on 21.236, cf. 21.380–7).

408.   **monstrous**: the Greek, *mega*, means 'large, great, mighty'.

412.   **It is not piety to glory so**: since it is commonplace for heroes to boast over dead enemies (e.g. 22.286, cf. *Iliad* 13.373, 413, 445, 619), this sentiment has been taken as a considerable departure from (and advance on) normal Homeric ethics. But it is worth noting that Odysseus restrains Eurykleia because the death of the suitors is the *gods'* doing, not humans' (413–7). Since it is a major theme of the *Odyssey* that Odysseus is the instrument by which the *gods* punish the suitors (see *1.22–95B*), Odysseus' injunction to Eurykleia is merely prudent: do not claim a human triumph when it is really a divine one. See on 23.59 for another example. Menelaos advises against imprudent boasting at *Iliad* 17.19–32.

426.   **Telemachos . . . lately come of age**: see on *18C* for the importance of this event. Cf. on 19.525–34.

431–2.   **Do not . . . presence**: Odysseus takes up the offer from Eurykleia he had rejected at 19.500–2, cf. 16.304.

440.   **in good order**: surely symbolical of the restoration of the old, correct order in Odysseus' household. Cf. on 20.149–56.

443.   **hew them**: Odysseus invests Telemachos with the authority fore-shadowed at 19.85–8. Odysseus had witnessed the maids' disloyalty at 20.5–12.

448.   **carried away the bodies**: see on 18.101.

459.   **round-house**: the description of the hanging is rather abbreviated and the location of the 'round-house' a matter of guesswork. See p. 11.

466.   **about the round-house**: the translation is missing a line of the Greek here, which may be translated 'making it fast high up, so that their feet might not reach the ground'.

468.   **snare**: if the snare is envisaged as a number of open nooses, in which the birds entangle themselves and, struggling to get free, only draw tighter around them, the connection with the hanging of the maids is more pointed.

473–6.   **They . . . anger**: Melanthios had been left hanging from the roof-beams at 192–200. The punishment is parallel to Antinoos' description of the way Echetos treated people (see 18.85–7 and notes).

480.   **brimstone**: Achilleus cleans a cup with brimstone at *Iliad* 16.228, but here Odysseus is fumigating the palace (493–4). There may be an element of ritual purification here, since Odysseus calls brimstone 'cure of evils'. Pliny (*Natural History* 35.50) mentions the use of sulphur in ritual cleansing of houses.

487.   **let me bring you out a mantle and tunic**: Odysseus refuses this offer—there are other priorities—and Homer will take advantage of his grimi-ness to delay yet further the recognition by Penelope at 23.115–6, 153–72.

500–1. **sweet longing . . . him**: Odysseus can now greet his whole household with the same feelings that he has already shared with Telemachos (16.213–20) and Eumaios and Philoitios (21.222–6). Cf. 13.353–5, and Argos (17.305).

Book twenty-three

Introduction

A. The centrepiece of this book, and (many would argue) the climax of the
Odyssey, comes with the reunion of Odysseus and Penelope. The episode
(especially 115–172) has been heavily criticised by Page. It does indeed seem
odd that, (a) with Penelope having decided to test Odysseus by secret signs
(109–10), Odysseus should say it is his filthy looks which are preventing her
acceptance (115–6); (b) Penelope should be entirely ignored while Telemachos and Odysseus discuss their plans; and even odder that (c) when
Odysseus has had a bath, it has no effect (163–72). Page (*HO* 114–5) argues
that the whole scene is inserted to prepare the audience for Book 24 (which
117–40 do very well). But Fenik shows that interruptions like (b) are
commonplace in Homer (*SO* 64–104, 7C). Moreover, it is not Penelope's
fault if Odysseus thinks his looks impede her recognition of him. She makes it
quite clear that she fears deception, and that *signs* are all that she trusts
(109–10, 213–7 and see on 99). Odysseus' bath is, for her, irrelevant,
though it is wholly natural that Odysseus should think his appearance has
a bearing (see also 22.401–6, 486–9). On top of this, the technique of
delaying the climax is thoroughly Homeric (see 7B,C).

B. Whatever the problems about his scene, the build-up to the climax is
beautifully handled (1–110). Penelope veers from absolute disbelief (11–
24), to half-belief (35–8), back to disbelief again (62); she cannot bring
herself even to address the beggar at first (93); she talks to the beggar
through Telemachos to start with (105–10), but excludes Telemachos from
the process by which she will know whether the beggar is Odysseus or not
(108–10). All the time, it must be remembered that she has excellent reasons
for thinking the beggar to be someone else (see on 99). It is a fine irony that
when recognition does come, it comes through a trick which Penelope plays
upon the great trickster himself (177–230), and which he does not appear to
see through (183).

C. Once the recognition is complete and the two have gone to bed, made love
and recounted their stories to each other, the poet turns his attention to the
problem of the relatives' revenge for the deaths of the suitors, and prepares the
way for a reunion between Odysseus and his father Laertes. A famous
Homeric problem here obtrudes: did the *Odyssey* end at 23.296? See note
there. It seems to me that a lot of very odd, and some extremely feeble, things
happen in Book 24 at any rate, especially in the closing scene. While the
conception of Book 24 is surely authentic, it may well be that the poet of the

211

rest of the *Odyssey* was not responsible for some of it (cf. *11B,E,F*).

3.   **tottering**: the meaning of this word in Greek is disputed, but the ancient commentator Aristarchos is surely right to argue that the poet means that Eurykleia is trying to run fast but cannot.

5.   **Wake, Penelope**: she had been dismissed from the hall back to her bed by Telemachos at 21.350–8.

16–17.   **happy/sleep**: for the sleeping Penelope, see *4.625–847B*. This is the first time that sleep has brought her happiness (though Athene sends a dream to comfort her at 4.795–801, 838–41, and cf. 18.200–5).

30.   **did not betray the plans of his father**: an important accolade for Telemachos. See *16C* for the demands which Odysseus makes of his son.

32.   **in her joy**: Penelope's emotions fluctuate wildly during this conversation with Eurykleia. Cf. 62, 83–4. Penelope's refusal to believe any sort of evidence and Eurykleia's desperate efforts to convince her (e.g. 79) recall the conversations between Odysseus and Eumaios (e.g. 14.361–405).

38.   **they were always lying in wait, in a body**: wrong emphasis. The suitors were not lying in wait for Odysseus to return. They were convinced he was dead (e.g. 20.328–33). Read 'and there were crowds of them always hanging around inside the palace'.

41.   **hidden away**: see 21.380–7, and on 21.236. For 'storerooms' read 'bedrooms'.

43–4.   **until . . . do it**: see 22.393–7.

45–7.   **There I . . . around him**: see 22.389.

47–8.   **You would . . . a lion**: see 22.401–6.

cheered to see him,/spattered all over: for the same sort of sentiment, see *Iliad* 6.480–1.

59.   **in triumph**: see on 22.412. Penelope refuses to allow Eurykleia to boast over what has been done because it cannot have been done by Odysseus, who is dead (67–8). It must have been done by the gods (62–6). *Human* triumphing is therefore inappropriate.

64–7.   **wicked deeds . . . recklessness**: see *22C*.

74.   **that scar**: see 19.467–72.

76.   **he stopped my mouth**: see 19.479–81.

81.   **baffle**: wrong translation. Though the meaning of the word is disputed, it probably means 'uncover, understand'.

82.   **clever**: see 2.346 and note on 2.349–76.

85.   **pondering**: see on 17.235 for the usual pattern to such scenes. Here Penelope shows the extent of her indecision by abandoning both alternatives (86–7) and opting for a third (89, 94–5).

94.   **would look at him**: the text is disputed here. Some prefer an emendation meaning 'would notice a likeness in him'.

99.   **and ask him questions**: these are irrelevant to Penelope's needs. She has already been deceived enough by imposters' tales (14.122–32). Moreover, she has been deceived by Odysseus himself when, disguised as a

beggar, he convinced her that he was brother of Idomeneus (19.165–307). Even the 'infallible' signs that she demanded at that time could not prevent the deception (19.215–9, 249–50). The issue facing her now is not 'Is this Odysseus?', but 'How can I be absolutely certain that this man will not deceive me?'. For Telemachos' attacks on Penelope, see *1.325–444A*; on 1.249–51, *16D*, 17.108–49 (where Telemachos moderates his hostility, cf. on 18.215). Penelope now replies to these attacks for the *first* time (105–10).

109–10.   **signs . . . secret from others**: see on 99. Penelope has finally decided on the means of ascertaining the truth about this man—signs known *only to her and Odysseus* (and therefore different from the sign she demanded at 19.215–9).

115.   **I am dirty**: Odysseus' reasoning, that Penelope does not recognise him because of his filthy appearance, is proved faulty at 215–7.

118–22.   **For when one . . . consider**: cf. 20.42–3 and Theoklymenos' story at 15.272–7. This concern of Odysseus' motivates the action for the rest of the epic.

124–8.   **You must . . . with us**: Telemachos continues to look up to his father. Cf. 16.235–320.

131.   **wash, and put your tunics upon you**: the hoax 'marriage ceremony' (149–51) is a delaying tactic till Zeus shows them a plan (139–40). But he never does; and in fact, Odysseus goes to his estates to be reunited with his father Laertes (359–60).

153.   **bathed**: see on 19.320.

156–62.   **and over . . . shoulders**: this simile is the same as that used by Homer when Odysseus is glorified after his bath in the river at 6.224–37 (see note there).

168.   **No other woman**: Odysseus reiterates the complaint of Telemachos at 97–103.

177.   **bed**: see on 16.34–5. For the bed as symbol of harmonious marriage, see *Iliad* 14.205–10.

183–4.   **What man/. . . another place?**: Camps *IH* 85 (note 26) argues that if Odysseus thinks the bed has already been moved, it cannot still be in his bedroom. Therefore, the text should be emended to read 'inside' (178 and 179). But 202–4 make it clear that Odysseus does not know whether it has been moved *or not*. This casts light on Odysseus' answer at 184ff. Penelope has told Eurykleia to move the bed. Odysseus' answer is that it would be quite impossible for Eurykleia to do that unless it had been done already. So—either it is still in place (203), and someone is playing a trick, or it has *already* been moved out, so that Eurykleia *could* handle it. In other words, Odysseus' question at 183–4 really means 'Is my bed now a moveable one?' Finally, although Penelope no longer sleeps in 'her' bedroom (16.34–5), could she be seen even to *offer* a stranger its sanctuary, in her own house?

188.   **one particular feature**: this is used to translate the Greek *sēma*, 'sign'. This is the word used at 109 ('signs'), 202 ('character') and 206, 225 ('proofs'). In other words, the Greek word *sēma* means a 'mark' of some

kind, which may turn out to have conclusive defining power. Cf. 19.250, and the episode of the scar, especially 19.390–1.

192. **laid down my chamber**: note that Odysseus builds the chamber round the olive-tree before he builds the bed. In this way, the construction of the bed is kept secret.

198. **bed-post**: presumably Odysseus then added three more posts, boring into them the holes (198) into which the wooden sides and ends of the bed could be fitted. Across this frame he tied the thongs (201) which supported the bedding.

204. **moved it**: the Greek says 'already moved it'.

207–8. **but then she . . . head**: as she had thought of doing, but held back from, at 87.

211. **in jealousy**: at 5.116–20, Kalypso accused the gods of being jealous that she, a goddess, should have a mortal lover. Here, Penelope argues that the gods brought trouble on herself and Odysseus because they were jealous that two humans should be together for so long. Kalypso's selfishness contrasts well with the value Penelope places on a long-term relationship valued by both partners.

218–224. **Helen . . . also**: Penelope's argument seems to be (i) the jealous gods have kept us apart for a long time (210–12) (ii) but I was determined not to be tricked into accepting an impostor in your place (i.e. despite the length of your absence) (215–7) (iii) because Helen was so tricked into sleeping with Paris (= 'outlander' 219), which she would not have done had she realised the tragic consequences (220–1), but the god drove her on (222–4) (iv) but now that I have secure evidence that you are Odysseus (225–9), I can entrust myself to you (i.e. without fear of the unhappy consequences that ensued for Helen). Observe how Penelope clears Helen (her relation: see on 1.276) of blame for the Trojan war by imputing responsibility to the gods. Cf. 4.259–64. The fifth century sophist Gorgias devoted a whole essay (*In praise of Helen*) to arguing that Helen was not responsible for her actions. Cf. Euripides' *Trojan Women* 895–1032.

228. **Aktor's daughter**: the Greek says 'Aktoris'. Those who translate it as Lattimore does take it to be the patronymic for Eurynome, the keeper of the chamber (293). But in that case, how can Penelope be sure the beggar has not learnt the secret of the bed from *her*? It is better to read 'Aktoris' and regard her as an old servant long since dead.

233–9. **as when . . . upon him**: as usual, a simile accompanies a moment of high emotion and significance. The simile itself is typical in that it reflects the subject-matter of the *Odyssey* (cf. e.g. 5.313–26, 451–7), but odd in that subject and object become reversed. We would expect that the land appearing welcome to shipwrecked men (233–8) would = Penelope appearing welcome to Odysseus. But at 239 it is Odysseus who is welcome to Penelope. Homer suggests that Penelope's ordeals have been quite the equal of Odysseus', and that she, just as much as Odysseus, has 'come home' as a result of their reunion. Cf. 5.392–9.

243. **She held the long night back**: one would normally expect the night to

be extended so that the couple could make extended love throughout it after their long separation. This seems to be what Athene had planned for at 344–8, but for Odysseus and Penelope the recounting of past trials is equally pleasurable (300–1). Cf. 14.192–8, 15.390–401.

244. **by the Ocean**: early writers seemed to envisage the earth as a round dish, surrounded by Ocean. Some writers describe how the sun tracks in a chariot (cf. 245, unique in Homer) across the sky and at dusk in the west gets into a bowl, on which it floats round Ocean to the East, ready to start off again at dawn (cf. 347–8). (Cf. 10.86).

251. **Teiresias prophesied**: see 11.119–37, which = 267–84. The Phaiakians also have to appease Poseidon at 13.159–87.

296. **and their old ritual**: or 'place, location'. One of the most famous of Homeric problems, because the two great ancient critics Aristarchos and Aristophanes (see *GI G*) say that this is the 'end' of the *Odyssey*. We do not know what their evidence was, but they have to be taken seriously on the matter. The modern case *against* Homeric authorship of the rest of the *Odyssey* rests on (i) the claim that there are many more and very violent non-Homeric linguistic usages in what remains than anywhere else, especially in the Laertes episode (ii) there are inexplicable cultural oddities (iii) much of the composition is extremely feeble. The case *for* Homeric authorship denies (i) and (ii), arguing that the whole of Homer is full of linguistic and cultural oddities (true to an extent: it is the *extent* which is the central point at issue) and points out that the poem could hardly end without any reaction to the killing of the suitors (an issue prepared for already at e.g. 20.42–3, 23.118–22) and without a meeting between Odysseus and his father Laertes (a standard feature of return stories). One way out of the problem is to argue that Aristarchos' and Aristophanes' words for 'end' (*telos, peras*) mean either 'climax' or 'logical conclusion'. That interpretation seems forced and unnatural.

310–41. **He began . . . clothing**: an interesting summary of Odysseus' adventures, covering Books 5–13. 310–11 = 9.39–61; 312–13 = 9.166–555; 314–17 = 10.1–79; 318–20 = 10.80–132; 321 = 10.133–574, 12.1–150; 322–5 = Book 11, especially 150–224; 326–8 = 12.165–259; 329–32 = 12.260–446; 333–7 = 12.447–9, 5.55–268 (especially 209); 338–41 = 5.269–13.185. Note that the adventure with the Lotus Eaters is omitted (9.82–104). Since the summary is so cursory (e.g. the whole Circe episode in one line (321)), and deficient, it is unlikely to be an oral poet's mnemonic. Aristotle (*Rhetoric* 1417a) says the summary is 60 lines long. He may be including 264–84 as well.

344. **what to do next**: cf. 241–6.

359. **I shall go to our estate**: prepared for without motivation at 138–40.

Book twenty-four

Introduction

A. There are considerable problems about the authenticity of this final book. The issue is briefly discussed at 23.296, and in detail by Page, who finds against authenticity with his usual *brio* (*HO* 101–36). It is extremely difficult to judge arguments based on cultural and linguistic considerations (see *11B,E,F*). But the literary arguments are more persuasive, which I discuss in reverse order. The last episode (412–548) in particular is so absurdly constructed (see on 476) that one hesitates to assign it to Homer. But the epic must have ended somehow and a divinely engineered reconciliation seems thoroughly Homeric (cf. the end of the *Iliad*). At the same time, the challenge of Odysseus to Telemachos to live up to his family's reputation reiterates and brings to a climax an important theme of the *Odyssey* (see on 506–15) and the restoration of Laertes to his former heroic splendour (375–82, 513–25) creates a persuasive picture of a household fully restored to what it used to be by the return of its true master, Odysseus.

B. The reunification of Odysseus with Laertes (205–411), whatever the linguistic and logical oddities of the episode (see Page and notes on 324 and 386–411), is an essential episode in an epic in which a son returns to his homeland and his father. Laertes features so strongly in earlier episodes (e.g. 1.187–93, 2.99–102, 4.734–41, 16.138–4) that he can hardly be left 'in the air' when his son returns; and a meeting between father and son seems an obligatory feature of such oral epic (Lord *SoT* 177ff). But did *Homer* compose the episode? Fenik (*SO* 47–53) agrees that the narrative conventions so loved by Homer in the *Odyssey*—disguise, delay, suspense, despair etc. (see *7B,C,D*)—are here rather badly used, but this (as Fenik points out) is not unknown elsewhere in Homer. If the episode is not Homeric, it is not anti-Homeric either, and the description of Laertes and the technique of recognition itself are thoroughly typical (see notes on 206, 21.188–227; see also above on the significance of the restoration of Laertes).

C. The episode in the Underworld (or *Second Nekyia* as it is often called to contrast it with the first in Book 11) (1–204) has its peculiar cultural difficulties (see on 13, but also on 99), but it is coherent with a number of important Odyssean themes. First, it completes the story of Achilleus with its account of his death and burial (cf. on 26, 39, 77 and 8.493); second, it raises the question of the nature of Homeric heroism again, especially the relationship between heroic life and death (see on 15–17, 83 and 94); and third, Agamemnon uses the death of the suitors to offer a handsome tribute

216

to Penelope (which completes a complex series of parallels and contrasts between the houses of Odysseus and Agamemnon (see on 194)). It is important to observe that the souls' conversation on heroism takes place before the souls of the suitors, punished for their wicked behaviour by the heroic Odysseus (the slaughter of the suitors continues to be justified in Book 24 on moral grounds—see 282, 325–6, 351–2, 458–60 and *22C*). These young men had deprived themselves of a share in the glory that heroes like Achilleus, Odysseus and now Penelope (196–8) will enjoy for ever. It is noticeable that Agamemnon makes no response whatever to Amphimedon's appeal for sympathy at 186–90.

D. This episode is also particularly interesting for another reason. The *Iliad* and *Odyssey* are the only epics to come down to us in full, but ancient writers make constant reference to other epics about Troy almost certainly constructed *after* Homer. Homer often seems to be alluding to other material of this sort (see notes on e.g. 3.106–12, 135, 184, Book 11 *passim*) and the burial of Achilleus looks to come into this category. An outline of these other epics (known as the Epic Cycle) was made by the 2ndC AD writer Proclus, and this outline was summarised by Photius the 9thC Byzantine scholar, who published it in his *Bibliotheca* (along with outlines of 279 other works, many otherwise lost to us). Photius' outline of Proclus' summary survives and is most readily available in *Hesiod, Homeric Hymns and Homerica* (with translation), by H.G. Evelyn-White, Loeb 1936. The summary chart of what survives of it (from Lattimore's *Iliad*) appears on p. 218.
See further J. Griffin 'The Epic Cycle and the uniqueness of Homer', JHS *97* 1977. Aristotle *Poetics* 1459b contrasts the episodic Cyclic epics, containing material out of which many epics could be constructed, with the thematically more coherent and concentrated Homeric epics. Cf. *GI I*.

Book 24 is, on the whole, thematically consonant with what goes before. Much of the composition is Homeric in style and quality. But there is a number of genuine oddities and weaknesses which give one pause for thought. One can only guess how it reached the state it did (see Clarke *AO* 83–5).

1. **Hermes of Kyllene**: Hermes here acts in the role of 'escorter of souls' (*psychopompos*). For his general function as the god of boundaries and his staff (3), see on 5.47. Kyllene is a mountain in Arcadia where his mother, Maia, bore him.

2. **to come forth**: from the courtyard, where they had been stacked (22.448–50). Cf. 20.356.

9. **gibbering**: for the noises the dead make, cf. 11.605–6, where they are likened to birds.

10. **the kindly healer**: an epithet restricted to Hermes. Its precise meaning is uncertain. It could derive from a stem meaning 'heal' or one meaning 'innocent, guileless'.

The Epic Cycle

Part of Story Covered	Name of Work	Name of Author	Traditional Date[1]	No. of Books
From the decision of the gods to cause the Trojan War to the quarrel between Achilleus and Agamemnon	Cypria	Stasinos of Cyprus (or Hegesias or Homer)	Not given	11
From the anger of Achilleus to the burial of Hektor	Iliad	Homer	In question	24
From the coming of the Amazons to the suicide of Aias	Aithiopis	Arktinos of Miletos	776	5
From the death of Achilleus to the fall of Troy and the departure of the Achaians	Little Iliad	Lesches of Lesbos (or Thestorides or Kinaithon or Diodoros or Homer)	Evidence obscure, conflicting	4
From the building of the wooden horse to the fall of Ilion and the departure of the Achaians	Sack of Ilion	Arktinos of Miletos	776	2
The returns of the various heroes	The Returns	Agias of Troizen (or an unnamed Kolophonian or Homer)		5
The return of Odysseus	Odyssey	Homer	In question	24
From the return of Odysseus to his death	Telegony	Eugammon of Kyrene (or Kinaithos of Lakedaimon)	568	2

[1] Dates (traditional) are, as usual, absolutely unreliable, but may be relatively sound.

11. **White Rock**: a landmark otherwise unmentioned in Homer.

12. **the gates of Helios**: i.e. the far west, where the sun dipped below the earth before travelling back east to rise again (see on 23.244).

12–13. **country/of dreams**: see 19.560–7.

13. **asphodel**: across which Achilleus strode (11.539). It is strange that unburied souls should enter such regions (see *Iliad* 23.72–4 for the prohibition against the unburied crossing the Styx).

15–17. **Achilleus . . . Patroklos . . . Antilochos . . . Aias**: for these heroes, cf. 11.467–9 and see on 3.106–12. For the meetings of Odysseus with Achilleus, see 11.466–540; with Aias, 11.543–64.

20. **Agamemnon**: for his death, see the versions of 3.254–75, 4.512–37, 11.405–26.

23. **First . . . to speak**: if this whole conversation down to 97 seems rather forced—haven't they had it before?—it is no more forced than when the Trojan King Priam, in the tenth year of the Trojan war, asks Helen who the Greek heroes are (see *Iliad* 3.161–244). Some consider the conversation irrelevant to the concerns of the *Odyssey*. But it is very relevant if one of the concerns of the poet is to reflect on the nature of male and female heroism and the connection between fame and death. Cf. Odysseus' meeting with the heroes in Book 11, and Teiresias' prophecy concerning his death (23.264–84 and note).

26. **because you were lord over numerous people**: the argument between Achilleus and Agamemnon in the *Iliad*, which led to Achilleus' withdrawal and tragic consequences for himself, Patroklos and Hektor, hung on the issue of valuation: is the king, who rules many, more to be valued than the warrior who kills many? See *Iliad* 1.274–84 (Nestor's wise summary of the issue). It is tempting to look for irony in this exchange between Agamemnon and Achilleus, but both appear to speak with great politeness towards each other.

31. **met death . . . in the land of the Trojans**: Odysseus wishes for such a death at 5.306–12. Cf. Telemachos' wish at 1.236–43.

39. **as they fought over you**: the death of Achillleus, foreshadowed in the *Iliad* (18.80–99, 22.355–66), was described in *Aithiopis* (see *24D*). See 5.308–10 for Odysseus' part in the battle over Achilleus' body.

47. **your mother**: Thetis, a goddess of the sea (see *Iliad* 18.34–69, where she and the Nereids lament the death of Patroklos).

59. **with . . . them**: wrong translation. Read 'and clothed him in immortal clothes' (cf. *Iliad* 16.670).

60. **nine Muses**: the earliest mention in literature of the specific number. Homer is not so explicit elsewhere (cf. e.g. 1.1 with *Iliad* 1.604).

64–92. **we wailed . . . gods**: for burial ritual involving hair-cutting (46), lamentation, burning, burial, construction of a grave and funeral games, cf. *Iliad* 23.43–53, 161–73, 216–25, 249–57, and 258ff. (the burial of Patroklos), and the shortened version at 24.782–801 (the burial of Hektor).

75. **Dionysos**: this otherwise important god (see e.g. Euripides' *Bacchae*) receives brief mention four times in Homer and is little noticed elsewhere in other epic literature (what little we have of it). The reason cannot be that

Dionysos has come 'late' into the Greek pantheon, because his name appears on a Myceneaen Linear B tablet from Pylos and there is a sanctuary to him on the island of Keos, datable to the 15thC. Perhaps there is something unepic about his particular concerns. As god of transformation he is associated with e.g. drink and drunkenness, sexuality, mystery cults etc.. See on *9B*, and the final observation on 3.430–63.

77.   **mixed with the bones of . . . Patroklos**: as Achilleus and Patroklos had wished (*Iliad* 23.91–2, 243–4).

83.   **it can be seen afar**: a hero is glorified by a monument which all can see (on the importance of public acclaim, see on 21.323 and cf. *Iliad* 7.86–91). Classical Greeks glorified their gods by building temples to them on the tops of hills, conspicuous to all.

87.   **I in my time**: the Greek text Lattimore is using says 'you in your time', though most manuscripts read 'I'.

94.   **your fame shall be great**: the consolation that Agamemnon offers Achilleus here seems to be more persuasive than that offered by Odysseus to Achilleus at 11.478–91. Odysseus talked of Achilleus' 'glory' among the dead: Agamemnon concentrates on his glory among the living.

95.   **what pleasure was there for me . . .?**: if an implication of Agamemnon's complaint here is that there is no monument to celebrate his fame, at least Menelaos set one up for him at 4.584–5.

99.   **there came approaching**: but had not the suitors already 'found' the heroes at 15? Page uses this argument to 'prove' that the conversation between the dead heroes has been inserted later on. But in fact, the sequence (i) A finds B (ii) B is described at length (iii) A goes up to B, is typical. See e.g. 24.226 and 24.241. Cf. on ring-composition at 1.10.

103.   **Amphimedon**: killed at 22.284. The *xenos* relationship between him and Agamemnon (106, 114–9) is not mentioned elsewhere and may well be an invention of the poet.

109–113.   **Was it with . . . women**: = 11.399–403.

118.   **a whole month**: presumably Agamemnon refers to the passage of time that elapsed between leaving Mycenae, sailing to Ithaka, persuading Odysseus and sailing to Troy (or perhaps to Aulis, whence the expedition set off). In other circumstances it took three days to sail from Troy to Argos (3.180–2).

119.   **having hardly persuaded Odysseus**: traditions later than Homer tell us that Odysseus feigned madness in order to avoid going to Troy, but that his bluff was called by Palamedes and eventually he consented. Agamemnon's unexplained observation about Odysseus' conduct does not fit very well with the *Odyssey's* account of Odysseus' whole-heartedly heroic behaviour at Troy.

128–46.   **stratagem . . . finish it**: almost identical to Antinoos' account at 2.93–110 and Penelope's at 19.139–56.

148.   **At that time**: it is not obvious from the rest of our *Odyssey* that Odysseus returns at the very moment when the shroud-trick has been discovered.

150. **where his swineherd was living**: see 13.404–11, 14.1ff.

152. **from sandy Pylos**: see 15.1ff.

153. **after compacting their plot**: see 16.233–320.

155. **Telemachos led the way**: see 17.1–30.

155–6. **the swineherd/brought in Odysseus**: see 17.182–325.

161. **we treated him rudely**: see *16C*.

165. **took away the . . . armour**: see on 16.281–98.

167–9. **urged . . . slaughter**: see *19D* for the problem here.

170. **Not one of us was able**: see 21.144–269.

172–5. **when the great bow . . . give it**: see 21.275–379.

176–9. **Then much-enduring . . . Antinoos**: see 21.404–22. 21.

180–5. **Then he shot . . . were broken**: 22.81–309.

187–90. **our bodies . . . perished**: this is the only time that the burial of the suitors is made an *issue* in the *Odyssey* and it gets no sympathetic comment whatsoever from the other ghosts. See on 417–9.

194. **How good was proved the heart**: Agamemnon had praised Penelope's virtue at 11.444–6, but still warned Odysseus to take care when he returned home (11.455–6). Agamemnon's unstinted praise of Penelope here brings to a climax the contrasts and parallels of the house of Odysseus and Agamemnon, which run like a thread through the *Odyssey*: Agamemnon/Odysseus, Klytaimestra/Penelope, Orestes/Telemachos, Aigisthos/suitors. See *1.22–95A*.

198. **the song for prudent Penelope**: women in Homer can gain immortal fame, for good or ill, in the same way that men can, and the bards are responsible for ensuring that fame is handed down the generations. Cf. Klytaimestra at 199–202 and 11.432–4, Helen at *Iliad* 6.354–8.

199. **daughter of Tyndareos**: i.e. Agamemnon's wife Klytaimestra.

204. **gates**: the Greek says 'house, halls', but 'gates' does appear in some manuscripts.

205. **The others**: i.e. Odysseus, Telemachos, Eumaios and Philoitios mentioned at 23.366–72.

206. **Laertes**: for his place, and life-style, cf. 1.189–93, 11.187–96, 16.139–40.

211. **an old Sicilian woman**: Laertes' wife Antikleia was dead (11.152–224). For Sicily and the slave trade, see on 20.383.

219. **their**: wrong translation. Read 'his'.

222. **Dolios**: see on 4.735.

224. **wall retaining**: we are on a terraced hill-slope. Cf. 1.193.

227. **spading out a plant**: this is presumably the same activity as 242 'digging round a plant'. Plant is wrong: we are in an orchard (226, cf. 244–5). Read 'tree' here and at 246. The words 'spading out' and 'digging round' are unique in Homer and there is some doubt about their meaning, but surely 'hoeing around' makes the best sense. Laertes is either preparing the ground for planting—it was common in the ancient mediterranean (as in the modern) to plant crops around trees in orchards—or removing the weeds round a tree. On the connection between fertility and good kingship, see 19.106–14.

240.   **to make trial of him**: for Odysseus' propensity for testing people and stirring them up, cf. on 19.45–6, *24B*. Odysseus' words are not 'mocking'. The Greek word is based on the *kertom-* stem and means 'cutting to the quick' (see on 8.153). Odysseus chooses to test Laertes in such a way as to provoke a fierce emotional response in the broken old man.

246–7.   **plant . . . leek**: where fertility is poor and the weather unreliable, it is important to hedge one's bets against disaster by concentrating on variety.

253.   **You look like a man who is royal**: for appearance vs. reality, see *17A*. There is a sense in which Laertes' foul condition makes him like Odysseus-as-beggar—he is a 'stranger', an outcast, in his own land. The return of Odysseus will revivify the old man—see Athene's restoration at 365–82 and his heroic feat at 520–5.

266.   **Once I entertained**: compare Odysseus' version of meeting 'Odysseus' at 19.185–202, and its effect upon Penelope at 203ff.

273.   **presents**: see on 1.309–18.

276.   **mantles**: woven goods (made by women) are of high honorific value. See 2.117 and note.

289.   **did he ever live**: Laertes' imaginative vision of Odysseus' death (289–92) parallels Eumaios' (14.132–6, cf. 1.160–2), but his wish for what might have been (292–6), as one would expect of an old man living out his last years separated from his family, concentrates on the intimate, not the heroic (cf. Telemachos' wish at 1.234–43 and Odysseus' at 5.306–12).

304–6.   **Alybas . . . Eperitos**: significant names. Alybas seems connected with the *al-* stem in Greek, meaning 'wander'; Apheidas means 'generous' (a nice compliment to Laertes), while Polypemon means 'full of grief', again an apt description of Laertes' present plight. Eperitos means 'selected' or (less likely) 'fought over, man of strife'.

307.   **Sikania**: see on 20.383.

315–7.   **He spoke . . . incessantly**: why should Laertes react like this? Odysseus has not told him 'Odysseus' is dead (cf. Achilleus on the news of the death of Patroklos at *Iliad* 18.22–4). Laertes' reaction is surely due to overwhelming disappointment: for a moment his hopes have been raised (266–79), only to be dashed (cf. his question at 288–9 with Odysseus' answer at 309–10). Five years is long enough; but if the omens were good when Odysseus left the stranger's house (311), the time-lapse becomes even more ominous.

319.   **there was a shock of bitter force**: the Greek is indeed odd and striking, lit. 'up through his nostrils a keen pang/force pressed forward'. This feeling is more likely to be the precursor of tears than of anger.

324.   **the need for haste**: despite the fact that Odysseus has been 'testing' his father since 232!

329.   **give me some . . . sign**: see on 21.188–227 for recognition scenes.

331.   **scar**: see 19.392–466.

355.   **Kephallenian cities**: according to the Catalogue of Ships (*Iliad* 2.631–5), the term 'Kephallenian' seems to take in the inhabitants of all the

local islands and some of the mainland. Most of the suitors came from outside Ithaka (16.247–53).

365.   **Sicilian serving maid**: see 211.

371.   **looking like one of the . . . gods**: compare the description of Laertes here with that at 227–31 and see 22.185 and note.

377.   **as I was when**: another glimpse of the life of the palace in the distant past when, presumably, Odysseus was a young boy. See on 17.293–4.

378.   **Nerikos**: possibly the town on Leukas mentioned in Thucydides (3.7.4).

386–411.   **and now . . . Dolios**: at a time when there seems to be so much urgency (324), the concern with food and the extended (and rather pointless) introduction to Dolios become rather tedious.

387.   **Dolios**: see 222–5.

404.   **Does . . . Penelope know**: Dolios was a faithful servant of hers (4.735–7).

413.   **Rumor**: foreseen at 23.362.

415.   **the people**: misleading. The 'people' of Ithaka are not involved. The poet means 'the suitors' relatives'. Note that justice in Homer remains in private hands. It is only later that the Greeks develop the notion of public as opposed to private responsibility for punishing crime (cf. Finley *WO* 77).

417–9.   **They carried . . . ships**: the issue of the burial of the suitors is raised once, in Hades, by Amphimedon (see 187–9 and note). The revenge of the suitors' relatives, is a far more important issue—and this is the subject of this final episode (see 20.42–3, 23.118–22).

420.   **gathered in assembly**: the ensuing ordering of the forces of Odysseus' men and the suitors' relatives is typical of the *Iliad*. There are assemblies (420ff., 489ff.(?)), armings (466–7, 496), parades (468, 497–9—even a brief catalogue), an advance (501) and a harangue (505–19). See e.g. *Iliad* 16.1–283 (J.B. Hainsworth *GR* 1966).

424.   **first to be killed**: see 22.1–21.

427–8.   **First he took . . . people**: this is the accusation from which the poet is at pains to exculpate Odysseus in the proemium to the whole poem (see *1.1–21A*).

432.   **shamed**: for Homeric values, see on 21.323 and cf. 21.253–5.

439.   **Medon . . . singer**: Medon and the bard Phemios had both been saved by Odysseus, although they appeared to be working for the suitors (22.330–80). Hence the people's surprise at seeing them (441).

445–6.   **I myself say . . . Mentor**: see 22.205–309. Medon rather exaggerates his understanding of events, presumably to appear the more persuasive.

451.   **Halitherses**: he spoke to equally little effect on behalf of Telemachos at 2.157–76.

456.   **You would not listen**: Halitherses refers to the assembly at 2.157–256.

472.   **Now Athene spoke**: the change to the scene in heaven is abrupt, but not unparalleled. See e.g., *Iliad* 18.355–6.

476.   **will you establish friendship**: since Zeus proposes this alternative (482–6) and Athene is keen to implement it (487), it seems odd that fighting should be allowed to break out, and at Athene's instigation too (516–9). Things become even odder when Athene then intervenes to *stop* the fighting (529–32), Odysseus ignores her advice (537–8) and Zeus throws a thunderbolt not at him, but the goddess! (539–40 cf. *Iliad* 8.401–6 for a similar *threat*). This is lame stuff: Page is right to argue that it can hardly be Homeric (*HO* 112–4).

489.   **feasting**: see 412.

503.   **likening herself . . . to Mentor**: see on 22.206.

506–15.   **Telemachos . . . courage**: amid the oddities of this final scene (see on 476), here at least is an exchange which is integral to the *Odyssey*— the development of Telemachos into a fighter worthy of his father's blood (see *16C*).

521.   **strength**: compare this Laertes with that of 226–31, and cf. his shield, mouldy with disuse, at 22.183–5.

532.   **without blood**: an absurd command from Athene, who was herself responsible for the blood that has already been shed (516–27).

544.   **Zeus . . . may be angry**: a ripe hypocrisy from the goddess who herself started the fighting (see on 476).

546.   **pledges**: observe how the settlement, divinely ordained by Zeus (482–6), is now divinely ratified by Athene (547). The gods, Zeus and Athene, who began the action of the *Odyssey* (1.28–95), have brought it to a close.

Bibliography and key to the abbreviations

Austin *ADM*, Norman Austin *Archery at the Dark of the Moon* (California 1975)

Bowra *HP*, CM Bowra *Heroic Poetry* (Macmillan 1952)

Burkert *GR*, Walter Burkert *Greek Religion* (tr. J. Raffan) (Blackwell 1985)

Camps *IH*, WA Camps *An Introduction to Homer* (Oxford 1980)

CH, *A Companion to Homer* ed. Wace and Stubbings (Macmillan 1952)

CHCL I, *The Cambridge History of Classical Literature* vol. 1 ed. Easterling and Knox (Cambridge 1985)

Clarke *AO*, Howard Clarke *The Art of the Odyssey* (Prentice Hall 1967, republished by Bristol Classical Press 1989)

Clarke *HR*, Howard Clarke *Homer's Readers* (Associated University Presses 1981)

Clay *WA*, Jenny Strauss Clay *The Wrath of Athena* (Princeton 1983)

Fenik *SO*, Bernard Fenik *Studies in the Odyssey*, Hermes *Einzelschriften* 30 1974

Finley *WO*, MI Finley *The World of Odysseus* (second edition, Pelican 1979)

GR, *Greece and Rome*

GRBS, *Greek, Roman and Byzantine Studies*

Griffin *HLD*, Jasper Griffin *Homer on Life and Death* (Oxford 1980)

Grimal *DCM*, Pierre Grimal *The Dictionary of Classical Mythology* (Blackwell 1986)

Hesiod *WD*, Hesiod *Works and Days* (*Hesiod: Theogony and Works and Days* tr. ML West Oxford (World's Classics 1988))

Huxley *GE*, G Huxley *Greek Epic Poetry* (Faber 1969)

JHS, *The Journal of Hellenic Studies*

Kirk *NGM*, GS Kirk *The Nature of Greek Myths* (Penguin 1974)

Kirk *SoH*, GS Kirk *The Songs of Homer* (Cambridge 1962)

Lloyd-Jones *JZ*, H Lloyd-Jones *The Justice of Zeus* (second edition, California 1983)

Lord *SoT*, Albert B Lord *The Singer of Tales* (Harvard 1960)

LV, Fondazione Lorenzo Valla *Omero Odissea* (six volumes) 1981–6 (to be translated and published by Oxford (forthcoming))

Meijer *HSCW*, Fik Meijer *A History of Seafaring in the Classical World* (Croom Helm 1986)

Morrison *AT*, Morrison and Coates *The Athenian Trireme* (Cambridge 1986)

Murray *EG*, Oswyn Murray *Early Greece* (Fontana 1980)

Page *FHO*, DL Page *Folktales in Homer's Odyssey* (Harvard 1973)

Page *HO*, DL Page *The Homeric Odyssey* (Oxford 1955)

Stanford, WB Stanford *The Odyssey of Homer* (two volumes) (second edition, Macmillan 1959)

Stanford *UT*, WB Stanford *The Ulysses Theme* (Blackwell 1968)
Trypanis *HE*, CA Trypanis *The Homeric Epics* (Aris and Phillips 1977)
Willcock *CQ*, MM Willcock 'Mythological *paradeigma* in the *Iliad*', *Classical Quarterly* 14 1964
WoA, *The World of Athens*, Joint Association of Classical Teachers, Cambridge 1984

Further Reading

The books marked * are particularly recommended.

* S Halliwell, *The Poetics of Aristotle* (translation and commentary) (Duckworth 1987)
  CR Beye, *The Iliad, the Odyssey and the Epic tradition* (Macmillan 1966)
  CM Bowra, *Homer* (Scribners 1972)
* HW Clarke (ed.), *Twentieth Century Interpretations of the Odyssey* (Prentice 1983)
  DM Gaunt, *Surge and Thunder: Critical readings in Homer's Odyssey* (Oxford 1971)
* J Griffin, *Homer: The Odyssey* (Landmarks of world literature) (Cambridge 1987)
  JP Holoka, 'Homeric Studies 1971–1977', *Classical World* 73 1979
* C Nelson (ed.), *Homer's Odyssey: a critical handbook* (Belmont: Wadsworth 1969)
  Adam Parry (ed.), *The Making of Homeric Verse: the collected papers of Milman Parry* (pbk., Oxford 1987)
  WB Stanford and JV Luce, *The Quest for Ulysses* (Phaidon 1974)
  G Steiner and R Fagles, *Homer: a collection of critical essays* (Prentice 1962)
  CH Taylor (ed.), *Essays on the Odyssey* (Indiana 1963)
* A Thornton, *People and Themes in Homer's Odyssey* (Methuen 1970)
  WJ Woodhouse, *The Composition of Homer's Odyssey* (Oxford 1930)

The Iliad: Translations
R Lattimore, *The Iliad of Homer* (Chicago 1951)
M Hammond, *The Iliad* (Penguin 1987)

Commentary
* MM Willcock, *A Companion to the Iliad* (= Lattimore's translation) (Chicago 1976)

Index

This refers by book and line-number to the Introductions and notes in the commentary.

I THE HOMERIC WORLD

Names in brackets do not occur in Homer

ADRIATIC SEA

Samoth

PIERIA

Mt Olympos

Lemnos

THESPROTIA

Peneios

Mt Ossa

Mt Pelion

AEGEAN

Corfu

Dodona

Skyr

Doulichion?
(Leukas)

Acheloos

EUBOEA

AITOLIA

Ithaka

Thebes

Samos
(Kephallenia)

Mycenae

Argos

Cape
Geraistos

Zakynthos

Alpheios

Pylos

Sparta

Cape
Malea

Kythera

CRE

KYDONIANS

Knos

R. Iardanos

Phaistos

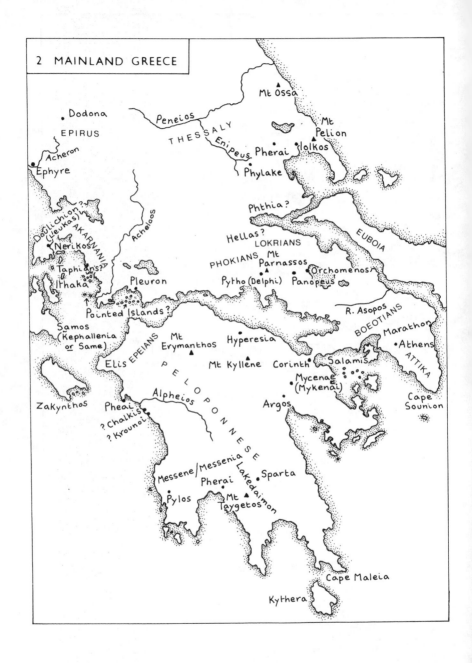

2 MAINLAND GREECE

Mt Ossa

Dodona

EPIRUS

Peneios

Acheron

Ephyre

THESSALY

Enipeus

Pherai

Mt Pelion

Iolkos

Phylake

Doulichion? (Leukas)

AKARNANIA

Nerikos

Acheloos

Phthia?

Hellas?

LOKRIANS

EUBOIA

Taphians?

Ithaka

Pleuron

PHOKIANS

Mt Parnassos

Pytho (Delphi)

Panopeus

Orchomenos

Pointed Islands?

R. Asopos

BOEOTIANS

Samos (Kephallenia or Same)

ELIS

EPEIANS

Mt Erymanthos

Hyperesia

Marathon

Athens

Elis

P E L O P O N N E S E

Mt Kyllene

Corinth

Salamis

ATTIKA

Zakynthos

Pheai

? Chalkis

? Krounoi

Alpheios

Mycenae (Mykenai)

Argos

Cape Sounion

Messene/Messenia

Pherai

Lakedaimon

Sparta

Pylos

Mt Taygetos

Cape Maleia

Kythera

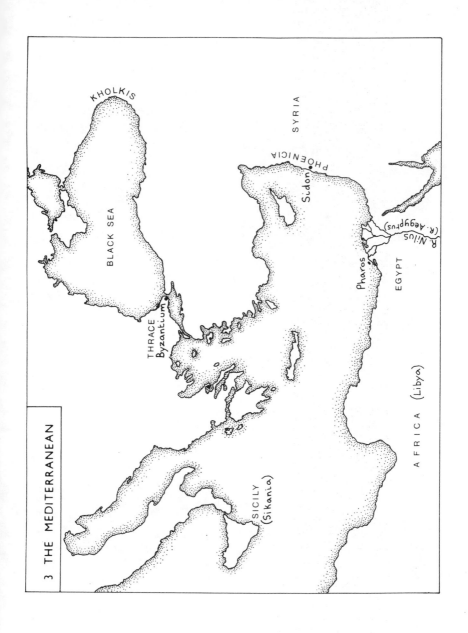

3 THE MEDITERRANEAN

KHOLKIS

BLACK SEA

THRACE
Byzantium

SICILY
(Sikania)

SYRIA

PHOENICIA
Sidon

Pharos

EGYPT

R. Nilus
(R. Aegyptus)

AFRICA (Libya)